by Auberon Waugh

THE FOXGLOVE SAGA

PATH
OF
DALLIANCE

Auberon Waugh

SIMON AND SCHUSTER

NEW YORK · 1964

Library of Congress Catalog Card Number: 64-17498
Manufactured in the United States of America
By H. Wolff, New York

For Teresa

PART ONE

Chapter 1

The great bell of Cleeve Abbey boomed out over the dank, cold fields. Godless cottagers in gray flint cottages looked sourly into their plates, far removed from the exuberance inside the church, where the organist was fiddling around with stops in the tantalizing seconds before he burst into the great anthem "Heavenly Queen."

This hymn was traditionally sung on the evening before the school broke up, and it was a great favorite. Brother Theodosius, who combined the functions of school organist with the composition of ascetic, tuneless pieces of music that were well thought of in the proper circles, regarded this ritual as his termly penance. But with some generosity of heart, and with teeth clenched and face set, he opened one final stop before laying all ten fingers on different parts of the intricate keyboard.

A great roar of five hundred young voices at various stages of evolution answered the cue. Once the singing had started, nobody listened to the organ, and Brother Theodosius could wander off into his own driveling inventions with a happy smile. For the boys, it was the supreme moment. Even MacLaughlin, famous for his idiosyncratic rendering of the Psalms, agreed that this was not a moment to spoil, and his coarse unevolved voice followed the words and music in a submissive drone.

> Heavenly Queen, all Creation beguiling,
> Star of the morning, our morning star bless'd,
> Lady sublime, gentle, chaste, clement, smiling,
> Take us anon to thy heavenly breast.

Beyond MacLaughlin, and on an even higher plane of esthetic and spiritual bliss, Jamey Sligger and Frazer-Robinson avoided each other's eyes as they sang the finishing lines, the last time they would be able to sing together at the top of their voices, for as long as either could envisage. They did not wish the moment to be spoiled by any embarrassing reflections. Everything had its place. This was no time for cynicism, or any except the noblest private emotions, as each personality, for whatever it was worth, was merged into a raucous body of sound which held them together as a mighty army. It was a glorious moment.

(Neither Jamey nor Frazer-Robinson had actually ever seen a woman's breast, nor could they claim that they had with any likelihood of being believed, although Jamey had heard it described at an art lecture as the most beautiful thing in the world, which gave him a certain insight. But both agreed that they were an obstacle and could be done away with.)

The school filed out of church to fluting noises from Brother Theodosius, momentarily cowed by the intensity of its emotions.

"It is not only that I like to keep up with my friends—" Brother Rapey Rawley turned full-face to young Sligger, who squirmed under the hot, wet eyes burning, as they always did on these occasions, with a passionate insincerity—"but I like to know what is happening to everybody."

Sligger was mesmerized by the pink hand which, with the slightest tremble, managed to indicate a whole world outside the privileged circle of Brother Richard's friendship. He had been dragged much against his will into that circle as the result of some information that had come into Brother Richard's hands two years ago. The Rapists, as the circle was known, had to feed Brother Richard's insatiable appetite for intelligence on the moral welfare of boys in the school.

"I am not interested in the school rules," he used to say indulgently, "and you can be sure that nothing you tell me will go any further. But I think it is wrong that anything should go

12

on without my knowing." His Friends were not supposed to know of one another, so that they should bring him news of the other Friends as well as of the rest of the school. Sligger had only brought him one tale, about MacLaughlin, with the result that in the next few days MacLaughlin was seen to become a Friend.

"If you can write me a fortnightly letter while you are at Oxford, I shall know you are all right." Rapey's manner seemed to suggest that there were positive advantages to be gained from his knowing Sligger was all right. "Tell me anything that's going on. What MacLaughlin's up to with his troubles, what you yourself are up to, how your brother's getting on." Jamey's brother was another pact between them, adding weight to the intimacy which already existed. Sligger put on a bright smile and tried to look frank and disarming.

"I'll do my best, sir," he said boyishly.

"I know I can trust you, Jamey," said Brother Rapey, trying to stare into his eyes in the unfortunate manner he had.

As Sligger left the room with a conscious feeling of relief, he noticed MacLaughlin sitting outside the door to wait his turn.

Brother Athanasius looked into his coffee while thinking of something to say. He never knew what advice to give boys who were leaving, as his own experience of life in the world outside Cleeve was not so very much greater than their own. He wished them all well, and was always sad to say goodbye after sharing with each new generation of Alexandrians the miseries and uncertainties of adolescence. When they came back after a few years, he was often shy.

"When I see you again, MacLaughlin, I expect you will have some pretty girl on your arm," he said. MacLaughlin could think of nothing more likely, but thought it in rather bad taste of the monk to say so. He guffawed uncertainly. Girls were an unexplored and wicked pleasure to come, not something to share with the grown-up world where he must try to present a respectable front.

13

"Have a good time at Oxford, Jamey."

"Thank you, sir."

"I hope you get on well with your accountancy, Mullen." Everybody seemed to be becoming an accountant nowadays. Perhaps it was because nobody had any money of his own to look after. "Oxford, you know, is quite different from what it was in my day. You get every sort of person there now. It must be fascinating."

Sligger and the other Oxfordians had already been given a lecture on what to expect at university. These people were there in order to broaden the outlook of people like themselves who came to Oxford the normal way, from a public school. It was their duty to encourage people from humble homes, and above all to take an interest in them. They must treat them as complete equals and encourage friendships. This would show that the people above them were quite decent after all, and it would discourage them from becoming socialist. The working classes were some of the nicest people in the world, said Mr. Snippet, the English master who also gave lectures on current affairs. In addition to this, it was up to them to show that the public schools still had something to offer by seeing to it that they did better than the grammar-school types in exams. The humbler students would probably work very hard, as they had their way to make in the world. Some of them were quite intelligent, and it would be a great shame if they showed up better at the end of the course than people who had received a proper education at Cleeve.

Brother Athanasius was not sure that he understood what it was all about, but he was sure it was a good thing. Oxford life was such a pleasant thing, he thought everyone would enjoy it, and it was an excellent idea to give it as a sort of present to people who otherwise would have no chance of knowing what it was all about. He thought of the gardener at Cleeve, a man of immeasurable wisdom and charm, with whom anyone would be happy to spend a few years at Oxford. The stoker, it is true, was a bit more difficult to get on with, but perhaps a sojourn

14

at Oxford would have mellowed some of his harsh judgments. Some of the electricians who came to Cleeve would have been written off by a less kindly person than Brother Athanasius as plain nasty, but he supposed they felt ill at ease, and then it was this kind of feeling that was being conquered by the new idea in university education.

"Don't drink too much beer, Jamey," said the old monk in a bantering way, but Sligger thought he was referring to his brother and blushed. "Or you, Frazer-Robinson, or you, Woronzot," added Brother Athanasius, until it became a general indictment of the whole room.

"I am looking forward to meeting these people, and I know that some of them are first-class chaps, but what shall we talk about, sir? They probably won't be interested in the same things as us."

"I should not worry too much about that. Just take them as they come, you know," said the monk, feeling he was being quite wise. He really did not know what advice to give, but he was very fond of everyone he knew, and well disposed to everyone he didn't. "I expect they will come and talk to you."

Chapter 2

In the Porter's Lodge at Godolphin Hall, Mr. Tradiscant, the Head Porter, was scanning the list of new arrivals with evident disapproval.

"Not much we can do with this lot, Mr. March. Never seen such a drab collection as this lot here. Saunders, three Smiths, one Smithson, whatever that may be, Thorpe, Tracy—well, I ask you."

"There's the Honourable Guy Frazer-Robinson."

"Never heard of them."

"Son of Lord Robinson, a life peer I understand."

"I knew they'd be coming sooner or later," said Mr. Tradiscant grimly. "I expect that'll be the malt."

"And the banking and the nylon pipes and the textiles."

"Very well, Mr. March." Mr. Tradiscant felt that his deputy had exceeded the bounds of decency. One could not be too choosy these days, and Mr. Frazer-Robinson would have to go in the Beaufort Quad, but there was no need to gloat. He sometimes felt that Mr. March did not really know what was what.

"I see there's a Mr. James Sligger wants to share with the Honourable Guy Frazer-Robinson," said Mr. March, who really did not know what was what at all, but had settled down, after a long and undistinguished career in the Kenya Police, to be as helpful as he could.

"I wonder if that would be any relation to young Mr. Sligger as came here three years ago," mused Tradiscant, with a worried frown. "From Cleeve, I see. Must be his brother or worse. Him in the Beaufort Quad I will not have—not at any price. Nothing but trouble comes that way, and it wouldn't be safe. Better put him somewhere quiet and out of the way. It is not even as if he has much to shout about."

"We could put him in Digs, down at the station."

"A very sensible idea, Mr. March. However, if you perceive, the rooms are already allocated by a superior power, and Mr. Sligger and Mr. Frazer-Robinson are down for Beaufort Nine Two, one of the finest sets of rooms the College or the University as a whole has to offer. I shall have a word with the Procurer's secretary about this matter." He strode purposefully over the ancient lawn, his bowler hat pressed down over his bulging, red neck, like a trapper advancing on a wired rabbit to kill it who knows how.

"Some things I will not have"—he was rehearsing to himself —"and that's this. It's neither reasonable nor right to make extra work when it's not reasonable. If the Sliggers had more to say for themselves than to make trouble, then that would be one thing. Just rowdy hooligans with no breeding and nothing else either." Social progress and all that he had to put up with, but this was another matter altogether.

Unfortunately for Mr. Tradiscant, things had changed even less than he supposed. Godolphin had just issued an appeal for nearly a million pounds, to build accommodation of a standard more suitable to the new sort of undergraduate, who did not take readily to a life without baths or central heating, or any of the other things which made life worth while. Lord Robinson had not himself been at Godolphin, but with a son safely installed in one of the better sets of rooms, there was every hope that he might take an interest in the appeal. Nothing must be allowed to stand in the way of that. It was not so much Lord Robinson's money they were after as his kindly interest, which would obscurely be more valuable. If his son wished to share with young Sligger, then share he must.

"That young puppy had better watch out, or he'll find himself in even more trouble than he is already," said Tradiscant darkly.

"That's right," said Mr. March.

Lunch at Farnham Green was always a melancholy affair. Mrs. Sligger was not a good cook, preferring intellectual pursuits of an undemanding kind, like reading Evelyn Home in *Woman's Own* (just for the laughs), doing the *Daily Telegraph* crossword puzzle and discussing controversial topics like television with friends. She occasionally announced that she was going to vote Liberal at the next election, as if the Liberal Party were her own discovery, a rare and sophisticated taste which few could be expected to appreciate.

Perhaps many of her interests were affected to prove her superiority over her husband, a man slow to pass judgment, but unshakable in his conviction when judgment was passed. One of his early judgments had been that his son Jamey was a sickly child, needing careful attention. Nobody knew how the idea had been born, but as the child grew to magnificent youth, and as youth began to give way to sturdy manhood, Mr. Sligger's solicitude remained constant. On his return from school, Jamey was never asked what sort of a term he had had but how his health had been, whether the journey had been tiring and, most embarrassing of all, whether his bowels had been operating regularly.

It was this last question which occupied Mr. Sligger's undivided attention. Every day before lunch, to Jamey's mortification, he would ask the same question, the only concession being when there was a guest, as now, when Mr. Sligger merely raised his eyebrows and Jamey nodded. It sometimes seemed to Jamey that this was the limit of his father's interest in him. Whenever they were alone together conversation was difficult and always returned to the subject of his health. They had no interests in common. Indeed, it would be difficult to say what Mr. Sligger's interests were. He evinced a determined lack of interest in anything his wife produced. Much of his time was occupied in preventing something from happening.

If Mrs. Sligger wished to put up a clothesline, buy an electric iron, rearrange some furniture, or alter her newspaper order, he would give all his energies to dissuading her. If his son wished to ask a friend to stay, go away himself to stay with a friend, read a book or go to the cinema, Mr. Sligger would momentarily give him his attention, pointing out how dangerous any of these activities might be for his health, how unwise it was to follow one's impulses in whatever direction they led.

Frazer-Robinson, who had stayed with the family several times before, had been invested by Mr. Sligger with some of his son's infirmity but inquiries never progressed from the general to the particular, as Mr. Sligger considered, quite rightly, that it was really no concern of his, if this young fellow chose to expose himself to a certain amount of risk. On other occasions, Jamey's brother Philip had been there, adding a touch of the unpredictable to an otherwise monotonous board. Sometimes Philip would burst into impassioned abuse of his father,

18

or the Government, or some inanimate object which had attracted his attention. Philip's visits had been rather less frequent of late, as Mr. Sligger dryly remarked to Frazer-Robinson on his arrival.

This had caused a certain amount of confusion, as Frazer-Robinson knew that Philip still had six months to serve in the Scrubs, but he did not know whether he was supposed to be acquainted with the fact. Jamey knew his friend knew, because he had told him, but he did not know if it was right to have told him. Only Mrs. Sligger smiled indulgently. She enjoyed discussing her son's prison sentence with her women friends in an intelligent way, and they greatly admired her for the sensible view she took of it all. Mr. Sligger could, of course, have redeemed the bad checks which had turned up from every corner of the country, but then there was no guarantee that the same thing would not happen again. Philip had been too old to learn lessons the easy way. She had no doubt that after serving twelve months of an eighteen-month sentence he would come out a steadier, more reliable person. It was not as if prison carried a stigma any more. Several members of the Labour Cabinet had been to prison in their time. As far as she was concerned, the whole thing would be forgotten as soon as Philip was released.

After lunch was over, Jamey and Frazer-Robinson took their guns and went off to a nearby farm where the farmer had a soft spot for young Mr. Sligger. More than anything else, they wanted to get away from the bright chatter of Mrs. Sligger and the general obstructiveness of her husband into the loneliness of wet, green fields. There was seldom much to shoot on Farmer Arckwright's land, but he, being a stockbroker who commuted daily to Waterloo Station, was unlikely to be there.

Frazer-Robinson said he saw a squirrel at one moment, but that was probably nothing more than the politeness of a guest. After a time they started shooting into the air or at bottles floating on the pond in recognition of the fact that half the pleasure of shooting consists in letting off guns. When Jamey thought

19

they had let off as many cartridges as he could afford, they sat down by the pond and threw stones, which was quite fun.

"I heard from the Procurer at Godolphin," said Frazer-Robinson. "We've got a set of rooms in the Beaufort Quad. He says he hopes we find them comfortable." He showed the letter, which started "Dear Guy" and ended "Yours very sincerely, Alec Scroton-Wise, Chief Procurer." Sligger, too, had received a note, which had started "Dear" in Roneoed typescript, with "Sligger" written in by an obviously menial hand. It assured him that his request to share rooms was being investigated, and was unsigned, but under where a signature should have been was the legend "p.p. Arthur Grace, Procurer's Secretary."

Jamey mused about this, but did not tell his friend. At Cleeve nobody had questioned the system whereby Sligger was called Jamey by teaching staff, groundsmen and fellow pupils alike, and even, behind his back, by lower boys. Nobody had thought of calling Frazer-Robinson by his Christian name. If one was being formal, one called him Robinson, if friendly, Frazer. Jamey's success was a tribute to his general amiability, which was remarkable, and to his looks, which were clean, lively, likable and, if one is to admit it, startlingly handsome. Frazer-Robinson, too, was quite good-looking, but in a swarthier way, suggesting the possibility of some foreign blood, an uncertain temperament and untrustworthiness with money. Perhaps they liked them foreign at Oxford, Sligger caught himself thinking, a trifle uneasily.

"How are we going to decorate our rooms?" said Sligger, thinking of his travel poster from Spain, his empty Chianti bottles, his cricket cap with a gold tassel.

"Your brother," Frazer-Robinson coughed, "kept a kangaroo in his rooms I believe."

"It was a young wallaby, and it died," said Sligger shortly.

"Anyway I agree. We may get that sort of thing later, but not to start with. My father says he will have the rooms done for us by a fellow called Potinue. He is meant to be quite good, and he is a cousin of the chaplain's."

20

"Yes, I think that is quite a good idea," said Sligger, as if he had been considering it all along.

"What's your father doing about money?"

"He said six hundred a year. Nearly twelve pounds a week." It sounded enormous. The Robinsons were well known to be rich, but Jamey felt for once his father had not let him down, and that he could compete with anything his friend was likely to produce. Frazer-Robinson, who had been promised well over twice that sum, with an assurance that if he needed more he had only to ask, said kindly, "I expect that is all one needs."

That evening, Mrs. Sligger had chosen love as her talking point. "You see, you boys have never really loved," she said. "If you had, you might know what I was talking about. I don't know about you, Guy, but Jamey here only really loves himself." It was half humorous, half malicious, intended to discomfort and put at a disadvantage.

"I don't think so," said Jamey, trying to sound open-minded, as if he was only interested in the truth, but not quite succeeding.

Mrs. Sligger pounced. "There you are. But can you really tell me what love means? Have you ever felt that you want to give yourself, complete and entire, utterly, to someone? That you live for them, breathe them in with every breath? That you want to throw yourself before them, washing their feet with your tears?" Jamey glanced at his father's feet, encased in a very dirty pair of brown felt slippers, and wondered. Mrs. Sligger gave a hard little laugh that was supposed to be bitter and realistic, but sounded tearful. "When you've done that, my lad, then you can come to me and start talking about love." Jamey had not started the discussion. He had merely remarked that an old lady had been found battered to death in Aldershot. Mrs. Sligger had said that sort of thing would not happen so often if people loved each other more. No doubt she was right.

"You young people think of nothing but sex," said Mrs. Sligger, "but you never give a thought to the love that must go with it if it is to mean anything. You probably think of love as something sentimental, found in women's magazines."

"No we don't," said Jamey indignantly.

"Not at all," said Frazer-Robinson.

"Just let me tell you this," said Mrs. Sligger, getting angry. "Again I'm not speaking for you, Guy, but if it wasn't for this so-called love which you young people sneer at, young Jamey wouldn't be here. He simply wouldn't exist." Again Sligger glanced at his father, buried in gloomy reflection of his own, and felt acutely embarrassed. Frazer-Robinson thought that there hadn't been much love in that particular marriage, nor much of the other thing, either, but he was quite interested to see if Mrs. Sligger would say anything revealing.

"Wouldn't he?" he said, anxious to learn.

"No he would not," said Mrs. Sligger emphatically. But she was not going to follow that particular line. "Do you ever think what it is makes us feed you, clothe you, put ourselves to all this trouble to get you educated properly? What do you suppose it is if it isn't love?"

Mr. Sligger said he had some work to do, and shambled out to his study. Work consisted in signing some papers and sending them back to his man of affairs. If Mr. Sligger had signed and returned all the papers sent to him he would have been quite a rich man. His agent was extremely clever and had made several decent fortunes for his clients in the boom years after the war, when most shares had trebled in value and some had gone even higher. But just as Mr. Sligger felt his only justification in life was to prevent people from doing things, so his obstructiveness could not allow him to agree to any action without long argument and often last-minute cancellation. As a result, his income had risen to keep pace with the falling pound, but no more. It was to prosecute this task that he left the three together.

"Without love, nothing I do, nothing anybody does, has any meaning at all. You may not know it, but you would be a drifting hopeless way, not knowing where to turn, probably a crimi-

22

nal. Look at Philip. I fastened all my love on that boy, and so did your father." Whatever her argument was, it was plain she was going to win it. "He doesn't care. Of course not. Why should he? We might have thrown him into the gutter at birth, for all he cares." This was Mrs. Sligger's second approach to the problem of her elder son, one of abject self-pity. "I treat you as one of the family, Guy, because I know you're intelligent. But what would you do with a son like that?" Frazer-Robinson looked at Sligger, and Sligger looked at his shoes.

"I don't really know, Mother," said Sligger.

"Of course not," said his mother triumphantly. "It's no good asking you boys about love. You only think of women as things to have a good time with, roll in the hay, do what you like." Mrs. Sligger felt she might be going too far and gave one of her laughs. Sligger felt miserable. He had given very little thought to women at all, and even if his thoughts had been marked more by a shy wonder than by the conscious shouldering of a heavy responsibility, he did not feel that he was entirely to blame for his brother's delinquency. But it was no use arguing with Mother.

"Oh well," he said. Mrs. Sligger saw that she was getting nowhere.

"Perhaps I was wrong. Perhaps you're both too young to know even what I am talking about. Anyway, I expect I can look after things quite well, thank you both very much." With that final thrust she began to make choking noises which might have meant she had something stuck in her throat, might have been tears. It was the way most of these conversations, half on an intellectual, half on an emotional plane, ended. The two boys, leaving her, went up to bed. Before they had shut the drawing-room door, the noise became unmistakably that of sobbing.

Chapter 3

"Can I come in?" said a small voice at the door. The room which Anne Etherington, secretary of the Inter-University Students Union and Food Officer of the St. Rachel's Junior Common Room, entered was nothing if not tasteful. Taste, for Humphrey Potinue, the little-known Pont Street interior decorator, was Truth; Truth, Taste. Either one had it, or one had not.

Frazer-Robinson was standing in his shirt when Anne arrived, fiddling with an ash tray which stood on a fluted column in the centre of the room. If you pressed a button above the ash tray, its bottom spun like a top, discharging its contents into the body of the column. He was changing into a dinner jacket to dine with Father Angus Potinue, the university chaplain and cousin of the decorator. So absorbed was he that he had not time to feel embarrassed without his trousers before Anne had smiled indulgently and said, "Don't mind me. I am used to it."

In fact, Anne was not used to it at all; it was the first time she had seen a man without trousers at such close quarters. What she meant was that she had seen it on films, and even on the stage, and was in any case unlikely to be shocked. The experience, long expected whenever she barged into men's rooms, left her feeling slightly sick and a little bit afraid.

There was nothing indecent about Frazer-Robinson's condition, but he felt at a disadvantage, and with a mumbled "Excuse me" he went to put on some trousers. In his confusion, he accidentally opened the door of Sligger's bedroom. It was their first day at Oxford, and Sligger was still unpacking.

"Oh, sorry," said Frazer-Robinson. "Can you lend me a pair of trousers? There's a girl in our room." He did not deign to go out again and admit his mistake. Sligger handed him a rather worn pair of the regulation black trousers they used to wear at Cleeve.

"What does she want?"

"Goodness knows. I suppose she wants to see one of us." The thought appealed to both of them. They had never doubted that when the time came round, women would find them irresistibly attractive. Everyone else had. Although the details had not been worked out, it seemed certain that Oxford would hold, among other things, a series of love affairs, passionate and yet beautiful, with a series of similarly minded girls. The girls might be diffident, or their silence might indicate consent, but when they were jumped, they would enjoy it. That was the pattern of these things. Male impetuosity conquering feminine bashfulness. All that was needed was the courage to jump. Sligger grinned wolfishly.

"Shall we date her?" he asked. Dating was something his mother talked about. Sligger imagined it was a euphemism for sexual intercourse. Whatever it was, Frazer-Robinson could probably help.

"You can if you like," said Frazer-Robinson airily. "She isn't very pretty. I have got to have dinner with the chaplain at Bede House."

"Of course you have," said Sligger, put off. On their arrival, they had found a little embossed card with the invitation, and a few words scribbled below in a handwriting so elegant it might have been Green Cursive—"do so hope you can come, A.P."

"Is she attractive?" asked Sligger, as dispassionately as he could.

It had not occurred to Frazer-Robinson to consider whether she was attractive or not.

"Yes, very attractive," he said, "not at all pretty, though, and not much shelf-kit."

"That's all right. I like them like that." The two were already getting quite expert. Sligger wondered where his friend had got that splendid expression. From MacLaughlin? Or from some of his other, little-known friends at Virginia Water?

Anne Etherington was saying, "It's just a survey we are conducting. Of course, as soon as you've signed your name on the bottom, everything is in the strictest confidence. The results will be published and printed by the end of the term. Whatever they are, they should make the Government sit up."

Sligger and Frazer-Robinson accepted three sheets of paper each looking like an application for a driver's license. After name, age, date of birth, sex, college and subject studied, the forms began to ask more tricky questions: carreer (spelled wrong); religion; public school or Government-educated; estimated parents' income; own income from all sources; are you married? Do you belong to a political party? Have you come to Oxford (1) to make friends who might be useful later; (2) to get a better job; (3) to have a good time; (4) to meet girls, or, if you are the latter, to find a husband?

The next paper was even more embarrassing. It was headed "Personal Questions." Do you think that intercourse outside marriage is all right? If not, is this because 1) it is immoral; 2) you might have a baby; 3) you have other, more important things to do at the moment? In either case, do you practice what you preach?

The final page was headed "Moral Questions." Do you condone Dr. Verwoerd's deliberate and calculated policy of murder, espionage and fascism in South Africa? Do you consider there is any justification for the Government continuing to resolutely disregard the recommendation of both its own advisers and the Students Council (a national, interparty body) for an immediate and incisive increase in students grant allocations? (N.B. This is now an emergency issue.) Do you believe that civil disobedience is justified in the face of the nuclear threat,

26

or do you hope to make the Government see sanity by more outdated means?

"You may not want to fill them all in now. In fact, you probably want to think a bit and work out just where you do stand," said Anne with a brilliant smile. "Perhaps one of you would be so kind as to pop round to my room in St. Rachel's with them. It is quite easy to find." Sligger gazed at her in wonder at such brazenness. He had never dreamed it would be as easy as that. "If I am not in, just leave them on my desk." She was anxious that she should not appear too anxious. Sligger felt he understood. He might decide to rebuff her.

"How shall we find it?" That was lame.

"Oh, just ask for Anne Etherington's room. Most people know where it is." A shade too casual. Poor girl, felt Sligger, she had obviously suffered a lot, been through a lot with men. It added to her attraction. "There are some other things," said Anne—a shade too briskly? She was anxious not to be drawn into any imbroglio. No doubt she had suffered too much already. For the first time, Sligger began to feel inadequate. Could he make her suffer any more? No, he would show her that theirs would be a lighthearted affair, with no complication.

"Would you like to have dinner with us?" he asked, forgetting in his hurry to put in the sinister undertones, and that he was only one person. He had not been heard.

"I don't know if either of you are interested in banning goods from South Africa."

Frazer-Robinson did not seem to be, but Sligger said, "Yes, I think so."

"Good. That will be five shillings. You will get your membership card if the Committee accept your application next week. That is just a formality. Now, I don't know if either of you are interested in joining Friendship and International Peace."

"What would that be for?"

"It's a small committee we've started, to try and bring pressure to bear on the University Labour Club."

27

"What sort of pressure?" Frazer-Robinson's political creed was rudimentary, but anything that seemed to torment the Socialists was worthy enough.

"Just to try and get a tiny glimmering of sense into their heads," said Anne lightly. "That will be half a crown each," when it was apparent that both were interested. Sligger produced a ten-shilling note.

"Would you like to have some dinner?" he said.

Anne Etherington was not often asked out to dinner. She had an extremely busy evening, with a social at nine and a committee meeting at nine-thirty, before she even began to sift through the reports and count her contribution money, awarding something to the South Africa Prisoners Defense Fund here, something to Friendship and Peace there. If, at the end, there was a surplus, it went to the General Purposes Emergency Fund, scrupulously entered, for such emergencies as Sharpeville, the fire in St. Rachel's Junior Common Room kitchen, the Chinese invasion of India and the Women for Peace outing to Wycombe Abbey. She hesitated.

She was not the sort of girl to be impressed by the social or financial prestige of being taken out by an undergraduate from Godolphin. Others waited in vain all those years of their university life for an invitation to tea there. Anne went roaming the corridors like a tank, armed with subscription forms and manifestoes, crashing her way into undergraduates' rooms. She had never actually been asked to dinner by one before. Invitations from John Whale at Magdalen, or the other fellows inside her various movements, were not quite the same thing, involving as they did a shared plate of spaghetti at the Fantastacherie in Cornmarket, with expenses, likewise, shared. And there was no question that for some reason a sensible, Leftish, progressive intellectual at Godolphin somehow had twice the standing of one somewhere else.

"Thank you very much," she said awkwardly. Sligger felt dizzy.

"Where shall we go? Is there anywhere good to eat round

here?" He did not wish to feel anything other than a man of the world, but it was unreasonable to expect him to know everything on his first day at Oxford.

Anne hesitated. She did not wish to seem grasping, but he must be very rich or he would not be at Godolphin. There was the Mitre, the Randolph, the Elizabeth. Outside Oxford there were the East Arms and the Bell at Hurley, the Old Bell at Woodstock, the Bell at Aston Clinton. A chime of bells rang through her head. She lost her nerve.

"There is a little place called the Fantastacherie in Cornmarket," she said.

"Good, let's go." Sligger wanted nothing to stand in the way of his new resolve. Nor did he want to meet Frazer-Robinson's eye, but he remembered that he had just given his last ten shillings to Love and Friendship or something. It was all part of the exciting, emancipated world in which he had arrived. He led Frazer-Robinson aside. "I say, Guy, you don't think you could lend me a little money until the banks open tomorrow, do you? I expect two pounds will do the trick."

At Cleeve, school had been back nearly a month. Brother Richard Rawley had every reason to be pleased with the way the term was shaping. For the first time in four years, a Friend was head of the school. The Rapists were now the most powerful body in Cleeve and had infiltrated even Brother Augustine's Poetry Circle, over which an enormous moral question mark had always shimmered. The reports which came in from these meetings were most illuminating.

He drew out the batch of reports from Sandhurst. Cleeve was, after all, only a very small part of the whole picture, but it was the breeding ground where small, grubby things were collected, to be sent out into the world as beautiful butterflies under Brother Richard's fond eye. Soon reports would begin coming in again from Oxford and Cambridge, to join those from the Slade, the Halberdiers, stationed in Germany, from the R.A.F. officers' mess outside Nicosia, from both Houses of

Parliament and from countless foreign embassies and legations. There could be no doubt. The movement was gaining strength.

"It is the ignorance which we are trying to combat." Anne Etherington was speaking in an excited, high voice above the din of young voices at the Fantastacherie. She was halfway through her second plate of spaghetti and had nearly finished a glass of Chianti. Soon she would suggest *scampi* to follow.

"Last year we did sex. The survey revealed that sixty-five per cent of women undergraduates coming up to Oxford had slept with a man during their first year. Forty per cent had slept with more than one man. After their second year twenty-five per cent had been given abortions or terminated pregnancies."

"What had happened by the end of their third year?" asked Jamey.

"I am in my third year," said Anne shortly. She knew that she was not in this respect a typical undergraduate, and found the conversation rather boring. It was the function of herself and her friends to conduct surveys, just as it was the function of the other undergraduates to sleep with each other, have abortions or terminated pregnancies, and have their ignorance combated by Anne Etherington. Hers was the gilded circle of super-students who studied and advised on student trends. Even if they felt the inclination to behave as other students, they were far too busy to do so. Also, as a result of their superior position, they were constrained from behaving like other people. Not that they disapproved; they were only interested in the facts.

"If these children"—Anne, from her exalted height, could regard them all as children—"had received instruction in the proper techniques at school, none of this need happen." Sligger was flattered to be included in the circle of those who, even if they had not had instruction in the proper techniques at school, had somehow acquired knowledge of them afterward. It did not occur to him to doubt that Anne was an adept at the proper techniques.

"Why, there's John," shrieked Anne. The Chianti and unnaturally large quantity of spaghetti were having effect, and she sounded louder than she intended. She knocked her way over to the table where John Whale was discussing how to interest the indifferent mass of undergraduate opinion in the need for comprehensive schools. Left alone to himself for a while, Sligger reflected.

Father Potinue was always embarrassed by the commercial side of his cousin's business. "How do you find your rooms? I do hope they are not too frightful. Of course, I do not always agree with everything Humphrey does myself, but everybody always says how pleased they are."

Frazer-Robinson said how pleased he was. Father Potinue listened attentively, trying to spot a reservation. There was none. "I expect you like the curtains in *toile de Jouy*. They came from a small village just south of Carcassonne, actually. Practically Spanish."

Frazer-Robinson said he liked the *toile de Jouy* curtains. Father Potinue listened attentively, then turned to carry on an animated discussion on French monasticism with his neighbor on the other side, a young history don from St. Anthony's. Guy turned to his neighbor, an unnaturally stout young man, whose name—Peter Garlick—was written on the small card placed in front of each place. Father Potinue's handwriting would have made the merest White or Brown look distinguished. The Honourable Guy Frazer-Robinson, written in Greek with a profusion of full stops in black ink, came from some Admiralty document of the eighteenth century. Peter Garlick Esquire came from the menu of a gay dinner in some city tavern, attended by Garrick, Goldsmith, Reynolds, Ben Jonson, Nell Gwynne, the Prince of Wales, Lord Curzon, Sir Somebody Dashwood, Geoffrey Chaucer and Bernard Shaw. Unfortunately, the food at Bede House was disgusting, and the wine, though good, was not plentiful.

"Actually, I come from Stockton," said Garlick, in a voice which suggested that among company from equally distinguished schools, there was no need to be embarrassed at having been to such a good one. Father Potinue beamed encouragingly. Stockton was the smallest of the reputable schools, but it was too little known to be taken seriously as a rival by any of the large religious foundations.

"I was at Cleeve, actually," said Frazer-Robinson, feeling sorry for him.

"Then you must know Frank Pratt-Bingham. I gather he's coming up this term." Pratt-Bingham had been two years Guy's senior. A lot of water had flowed under that bridge, Guy felt. It was too embarrassing that they should be contemporaries at Oxford because Pratt-Bingham had been caught in the last call-up for National Service and Guy hadn't. Pratt-Bingham would learn that he, Frazer-Robinson, had changed a lot, and was not going to put up with any more sentimental nonsense. It did not occur to him that Pratt-Bingham too might have changed.

"I think," Father Potinue was saying to the company at large, "that if the Church is going to keep its hold on the younger generation, we are going to have to change a lot of our ideas. The old way of just mucking along is no longer good enough. It is a worry, of course, but also it is a challenge. I myself have arranged that this term services shall be conducted facing the congregation, as if I personally were speaking to them, rather than as if I were just some sort of intermediary between the congregation and Someone Up There." He pointed an elegantly manicured finger to the plaster cornice. An inaudible surge of applause went round the room.

"Exactly, exactly," said the young history don. "This is the sort of idea we must try to get over to people, however much they may dislike it."

"Do you think that is enough, Father?" asked Garlick. An awkward silence followed. "I mean, are you sure that the younger generation do not want more?"

"I am open to ideas. You, Garlick, must tell us what you think the younger generation want."

Garlick missed the ponderous sarcasm, and prepared to be the spokesman for the younger generation.

"Well, I think the great thing is that they don't want to think of the Church as outdated. It must be up to the mark, sympathizing and encouraging the latest trends."

"And what are these latest trends?" To anyone less sublimely egotistical, the hostility would have been obvious.

"Well I read that in Caerphilly or somewhere, the Methodist parson bought an electric guitar and led his congregation in singing Negro spirituals. He sometimes blacked his face, and never had sermons—which were outdated—but friendly talks."

"Yes, I think there is an idea there." Father Potinue was too careful a man to be scornful of anything which might be called progressive. "Particularly in the idea of friendly talks having an advantage over the more formal sermon nowadays. I always have an open house at teatime on Tuesdays, as you may know, and encourage frank discussion of any present-day problems which may have turned up. I don't know how much good they do." Father Potinue was modest. Everybody present knew that they did an enormous amount of good. Garlick, who had never attended one of those tea parties, was meant to keep quiet. He said:

"Yes, but I still feel that there is a gap. They feel it, I mean. If we could make services less formal and Victorian, I am sure people would come to them more. If we were all less stiff and rigid in our approach."

"Exactly, exactly," said the young history don. "This is the sort of thing I mean. People won't like it, of course." Garlick thought he had made a point and was carrying the meeting with him.

"If we had soft lights in church, and pastel shades, and soft music in the background from a concealed relay system. That is what people nowadays understand. And I could bring my transistor radio." Garlick was only trying to be helpful. He would be quite prepared to lend his transistor wireless for Sunday mornings. It was a machine which he had only recently acquired, and he was inordinately proud of it. It seemed to combine all the qualities of sophistication, wealth and elegance with being a permanent source of pure animal pleasure. He could think of nothing more suitable than for him to conduct religious services around his little box, the congregation sprawling in glossy leather armchairs like a superior air-terminal waiting room, in each chair a girl sitting carelessly over a boy, his arm round her waist, all waiting reverently for Garlick to manipulate the knobs and make the music louder or softer, clearer or less clear.

To the others, however, it was apparent that Garlick had gone too far, and the conversation became general.

It had been a lively, controversial evening with no punches pulled. Many things had been said which cleared the air, and Sligger felt that his mind had been clarified on many points as the bill arrived and Anne's two friends who had joined them stood up to go. The bill was £2.10.0d. A ghastly feeling of insecurity overcame Sligger as he reflected that he had only £2.

"Anne, I am most terribly sorry, but could you lend me ten bob? I seem to have come without enough. You'll get it back tomorrow morning."

Anne was well used to this sort of treatment, but she was a bit shocked that Jamey had got into these habits so young. Her own bill could not be much more than ten shillings, but then Whale and his friend had joined them for a glass of Chianti each. She should have thought before she asked them.

As she handed over a crumpled ten-shilling note, Sligger recognized with a pang the one he had handed over earlier in the evening toward International Free Love and Happiness or something. When the change came back, Sligger realized he had made a mistake, and the bill had only been £1.10.0d. Nobody seemed to notice, as he pocketed his old friend the ten-shilling note and some silver, but he was always happier with a little money in his pocket.

34

"We've got to go to Philip Fringe's social in Magdalen," said Anne, "I would like to ask you, but I don't think we can."

"There's a guest fee of seven and sixpence a head," said John Whale.

"That'll be all right," said Jamey. He sensed the general approval, and proffered his ten-shilling note as the talisman which seemed to open every door at Oxford.

Whale and his friend, Brian Greaves, put on their duffel coats and long woolen scarves. Anne disappeared for a minute. She was not a pretty girl. Her eyes were protuberant and she blinked too much. Her face had an unnatural flush and her voice was too high. But he had Frazer-Robinson's word for it that she was attractive, and attractiveness, he felt, was all that he needed.

Whale said, "Have you left your duffel behind?" Jamey supposed that he had.

"Here, you can borrow my scarf." Jamey's heart warmed to this unexpected pill of kindness. It stuck in his memory for a long time, as proof that Whale was basically a kind person as well as a leader of thought. The scarf was long and slightly damp and smelled of fried eggs. Wearing it, Jamey felt that he had taken a great step, he had associated himself with all that was bravest and most progressive in the world, he would fight to the death for all the new ideas, whatever they were, which were going to be explained to him. He was now one of them, the John Whales, the Brian Greaveses, the vivacious Anne Etheringtons, the exciting Philip Fringes.

Anne Etherington was explaining that socials were always rather a bore, but people expected it of one, and she personally believed it was right that there should be a social field of activity in university life. "So much good can be done if we show the world that we have our gay side, as well as the important things. Besides, I think it is part of human nature to want to let off steam occasionally." She sounded as if she was not quite sure. Perhaps Jamey would be shocked by the scenes of frivolity which awaited him.

35

In the Magdalen J.C.R., Bill English was dancing with a chair over which he had draped his duffel coat while everybody watched and smiled indulgently or laughed. Brian Greaves took hold of the chair and started dancing with it, but as he had just arrived his dancing lacked spontaneity and people looked away. Jamey wondered whether to seize Anne and start dancing with her, but judged that the moment was not ripe. He was quite correct in this. Among the Oxford intelligentsia, as this group presumed itself to be, one did not dance with members of the opposite sex. At socials, men played the fool, women watched them and laughed. Perhaps they laughed a little louder for handsome, decent people like Bill English, than they did for awkward, chippy creatures like Brian Greaves, but that was as far as the processes of sexual selection were allowed to go. They often discussed sex seriously and frankly among themselves. They all approved of it in theory, and thought it a scandal that women were not allowed to spend the night in men's colleges and vice versa.

"If they treat us like children, they cannot expect us to behave any better than children." But in fact none of them seemed ever to get round to behaving like children in this way. The men noticed it occasionally, the women never seemed to. Sligger met Angela Hammock, who laughed when she was introduced and said, "You're from St. Godolphin's. You must know Stephen Goyle." Sligger said he had just arrived. Angela had been up two years and laughed. Sligger thought she must know a lot about sex, and wondered how to get her into a frank discussion. "I expect you must know a lot about sex" was too blunt, and "How is life in the women's colleges these days?" sounded wrong. Angela said, "Shsh," and looked toward where Bill English was sitting apart, plucking at a guitar on his lap. Unlike Anne, Angela was definitely quite pretty, and she laughed in a very open way. Sligger wondered if she was attractive and looking at her turquoise knitted jersey decided she probably was.

Bill English looked very serious about something, and continued to look thoughtful until there was absolute silence. Then he plucked his guitar.

"Go on," everybody said, nobody louder than Angela.

"Yes, go on," said Sligger in the silence that followed. Everybody looked at him.

"What do you want me to play?" asked Bill English sarcastically. Sligger said:

"Do you know 'You Are My Sunshine'?" He had heard of it somewhere. It had been very popular two years before in the shower rooms at Cleeve.

"No, I don't know that one."

"Old Smoky," everyone shouted.

"Your eyes will be steaming," said Bill English.

"Your eyes will be STEAMING," everyone shouted.

"But not tears of grief."

"But not tears of grief."

> Your eyes will be steaming
> But not tears of grief
> If you vote Tory
> You're worse than a thief.
> Your face will be FLESHLESS
> Your loved ones deformed
> Your home fire is burning
> But your home has been bombed.
> They'll hug you and KISS you
> And tell you more lies
> On top of Old Smoky
> Where everyone fries.

Sligger sang as loud as he could. It was a glorious moment. The melody and the concentration made Angela's face positively beautiful as she nodded her head to the time of the music. Even Anne's face seemed to take on a certain gentleness. Sligger was part of this glorious army. "Again, again," everybody shouted. "Your face will be FLESHLESS."

·   ·   ·

37

On the way home, Sligger met Guy outside the great gate of Godolphin. They went in together.

"Good night, Mr. Frazer-Robinson," said the porter from the lodge.

"Good night," they both said.

Chapter 4

"Really, the state of morals in this university are appalling," said Garlick, waving the cigarette holder which he affected. He always said it was to prevent his getting lung cancer, in a sentimental voice, as if anybody cared whether he got lung cancer or not. He was sprawled in Frazer-Robinson's armchair, smoking one of Frazer-Robinson's cigarettes, sipping Frazer-Robinson's drink and talking to Stephen Goyle, as both had discovered that Frazer-Robinson was out. In contrast to Garlick, Stephen Goyle was unnaturally thin and pale as milk.

"Morals," said Stephen, who had rather a hobbyhorse on the subject. Morals were a sign of immaturity, whether in a nation or in an individual. They were part of the primitive voodoo which had held society together when men were little better than apes. Now that mankind had reached the final consummation of its evolution in the person of Stephen Goyle, there was no further need for morals. He had written a piece along this sort of line in *Isis*, which everyone had read.

"Look what has happened to our friend Jamey Sligger," said Garlick.

"That's not morals," said Goyle angrily, not to be put off. Nobody could approve of what had happened to Sligger. Garlick sensed the approach of boredom, and turned up his transistor wireless which had been mumbling in the background. A man was giving a talk in *Schools' Hour* on rock climbing in the Andes. Garlick listened intently.

"Young Sligger does nothing immoral. That's the trouble with him. If only he could get out of himself a bit, he would have no need to wear such extraordinary clothes and have such unsuitable friends." Goyle always spoke in a soft voice. It emphasized the maturity of what he had to say. "There is nothing wrong with him as a person. I feel he just hasn't developed completely yet. I wonder if we could do anything to help him on a bit. I think he needs a steady relationship with a girl."

Garlick nodded his head and stared at the wireless as if he had not been listening to a word that Stephen had said. Perhaps, thought Stephen, Garlick too needs a steady relationship with a member of the opposite sex.

"I wonder," said Garlick, "what Guy sees in Sligger."

"He is quite good-looking."

"You don't think . . . ?"

"What I mean is that he has looks of a certain kind which might appeal to somebody who had not, as it were, found his feet in terms of human relations."

"You mean slept with a woman."

"Dear Peter, I do so admire your euphemisms. I am sure it shows sweetness of character rather than an inhibited, immature outlook. I mean coition, sexual intercourse, copulation, you know. The act by which a man—"

"Yes, I know." It was a convention of such conversations that both must assume the other's experience, whether it was of life in a Portuguese prison or of coition, sexual intercourse, copulation. "You don't think he ever has?" It was something that nobody dared call to question in the presence of the person concerned. Each member of the Godolphin set had had it questioned behind his back, and in each case the decision was that he never had, with the solitary exception of Goyle, about whom nobody was sure.

39

"I am absolutely sure he hasn't," said Stephen complacently. "And you think that he and this revolting Sligger . . . ?"

"I think it more than likely." Garlick was definitely shocked, which Stephen wrote down as another sign of immaturity. He frequently remarked that some of his best friends were homosexuals, which made his friends, all of whom were well known to each other, wonder whom he meant. Jack Piccione came in.

"Oh Jack, Stephen here says there's something for your father to look into." Jack, whose father was Home Secretary, looked serious. He had a very rough time of it at Oxford, what with petitions from undergraduates on political prisoners in the colonies, South Africa, Portugal and Spain, or capital punishment whenever a hanging was planned, or homosexual law reform and on increasing the grants of state scholars. He had given up writing reasoned replies, and tried to avoid deputations. He had not expected to find one in Guy's room.

"Oh yes?" he said suspiciously.

"He says that Sligger and Guy are living in sin."

"Oh yes?" said Jack. "I was looking for Guy."

"Well, he's not here. Have some crème de menthe or some brandy."

"A little brandy, perhaps." If only Goyle had not been so mature, Jack would have told him to stop spreading venomous gossip about his friend while he was swilling his crème de menthe. But Goyle probably thought he was paying Guy a compliment, and Jack rather liked the idea of a glass of brandy just at the moment. They were united in one thing, at any rate, which was contempt for Jamey Sligger, to which, in Garlick's case, there was added a certain amount of jealousy and in Goyle's a conscious desire to educate and ruin him. Piccione's antipathy dated from that moment, in a disinclination to be compromised with somebody of Jamey's moral coloring. But the antipathy did not, for some reason, extend to Guy.

Jamey was feeling ebullient as he led Bill English past the Porter's Lodge, into Godolphin. He knew Frazer-Robinson was

40

out, and judged it a good moment to show Bill the advantage of having a friend in Godolphin. There was a wide variety of drink and cigarettes for Bill to choose from, and he could admire the Attic ash tray and deep armchairs unembarrassed by their owner's presence. Bill's tipple was neat gin, to which he added a drop of water if he wished to appear respectable, but at least Sligger would be able to show him all the other possibilities.

Bill was secretly rather pleased to be asked to Godolphin, although his cautious, slightly suspicious "All right" in answer to Jamey's invitation scarcely suggested it. He told himself that it would be interesting to see how the other half—the enemy—lived, but in fact he thought it was a compliment to his intellect to be chosen from all the others. In this he was quite right. He was easily the most respectable of his set.

"Quite a party here already, I see," said Jamey when he opened the door and walked into a haze of cigarette smoke.

"We're waiting for Guy," said Garlick coldly, obviously thinking that he had much more right than Jamey to be there.

"I am just going, anyway," said Jack Piccione, as if that explained his presence.

"Ah, Jamey," said Goyle, "I am so glad you've come. We were just talking about you, as a matter of fact."

"I don't think any of you know Bill English. Peter Garlick, Stephen Goyle, Jack Piccione."

Jack knew him slightly. He had presented a petition, signed by twenty friends, protesting about the refusal to grant a pay increase to miners in South Wales. Jack had read it and put it in the wastepaper basket.

"I was most interested in some of the points you made in your preface," he said, "but, of course, my father is not responsible for coal."

Bill English looked modest.

Goyle too had obviously met him. "Hullo, Bill, I didn't expect to see you here," he said, suggesting that he would be rather out of place. Stephen liked to keep his worlds separate. To his expensive friends, he dispensed a kind of general, unpolitical

41

maturity, giving advice on modern art and premarital problems. To the other, less elegant world in which he moved, he was the crucible for all its amorphous, ill-considered political ideas which under his patient direction were diverted into some mold which he had already prepared in the soft, rounded recesses of his brain.

Only Garlick had obviously never met Bill English, and found it slightly amusing that he ever should. "What college would you be at?" he asked.

"Magdalen, in my second year, at P.P.E."

"Ah, Magdalen." To the real Godolphin man, he might as well have been at Cambridge or Keele.

"Now that Jamey has come, perhaps I can offer you something to drink," with insidious old-world politeness. Goyle was up to something.

"Have you got any gin?"

"I fancy that's on the cards. What would you like with it? There's this stuff, Carpano, or some Angostura, or tonic, or some dry Martini but I can't see any ice, or there's something in this bottle, yes, Campari."

"Just some plain gin, please." Goyle knew perfectly well what Bill's tipple was.

"Just gin?" Goyle raised his eyebrows.

"With some water, please."

"Water appears to be the one thing we positively have not. There is soda water, but that is not the same thing at all. No doubt the problem is surmountable. If you walk across the Quad to Staircase Seven, then turn left, you will find the baths, where any quantity of water is readily available. It is not a thing which Jamey or Guy have seen fit to supply." Garlick sniggered openly, but Goyle was being quite serious.

Normally Bill would have told them not to bother, but as he was being sent to fetch the water for himself, he got to his feet. In doing so, he knocked over the Attic ash tray. It was bound to happen, thought Jamey, unhappily.

"Never mind," said Bill, as nobody else had said anything. "I will go and get some water." He gathered his duffel coat about him.

"Mind the grandfather clock," Garlick called after him.

After he had gone, Jamey busied himself clearing up the mess on the carpet. Before he had got far, the door opened and Guy came in with a pretty girl behind him.

"Hullo, Jamey, giving a party?" he asked. "Do you know Sally Pratt-Bingham? She's Frank Pratt-Bingham's sister."

"How do you do," said Jamey, scrambling to his feet.

"Been throwing the furniture about I see," said Guy good-humoredly, but with a hint of rebuke in his voice.

"That was one of Jamey's other friends," said Garlick, "called Bill English." He pronounced the name as if it was the most extraordinary thing he had ever heard. Jack Piccione looked uneasy. "I am just going, Guy," he said.

"Don't go. Do you know Sally? Sally, Jack Piccione."

"Piccione," said Sally, "no, but the name sounds familiar."

"That's probably his father," said Guy.

"What does he do?"

"He's Home Secretary."

"Oh yes. I thought I'd heard the name. That must be fascinating." Her tone suggested that nothing fascinated her less, but one must be polite.

"I must really go," said Jack, "I've got an essay to hand in, and Mr. English will be coming back soon."

"English? Who's he? What a beautiful name," said Sally.

"He's a friend of Jamey's," said Garlick, as if he were saying something rather clever.

"Goodbye, Jack," said Sally. After he had gone she said, "How fascinating to think I've met Mr. Valentino's son."

"Piccione's," said Guy.

"That's right. I am always so hopeless about names. Guy was telling me he knew somebody called Mr. Snigger, who always wears a duffel coat and is trying to grow a beard. I would like to meet him. He must be fascinating." Jamey went on clearing up the mess left by the upset ash tray. "Where is Mr. English? I

43

can't wait." She watched with satisfaction the room settle down to be fascinated by Sally.

Bill was halfway across the Quad before he realized that he had forgotten his glass. He did not want to go back to the room, so he walked uncertainly to the baths, hoping to find some receptacle. There was none. He stared for a time at the taps, then turned one on, and bending his mouth to it, drank deeply.

DEAR BROTHER RICHARD,

The Oxford term seems to have settled down now. Frank Pratt-Bingham is up from the Halberdiers in Germany. He seems a steadier sort of person, although I have not got round to seeing him yet. He has made no attempt to see either Frazer-Robinson or myself, which is probably all to the wiser. I did not see him in Church last Sunday, nor MacLaughlin, but Frazer-Robinson and I were there. No doubt there are lots of other places at Oxford besides the Chaplaincy, but we are told it is better to use it if we can. Frazer-Robinson seems to be taking an interest in Pratt-Bingham's sister, called Sarah, who comes down from London at the week-ends. She says it is to see her brother, who is always out, but I expect it is alright. She takes an interest in lots of other men, too. Frazer-Robinson keeps up the good name of the school and has many friends. One of them is the son of the Home Secretary. We might be able to use quite a lot of influence there.

Unfortunately, there is someone called Stephen Goyle, who is trying to influence everybody the other way. I don't think Frazer-Robinson is very impressed with him, but he gets everywhere, and Piccione must have listened to him. I will keep my eye on that, of course. The harm which Goyle has done among the less well-known people must be incalculable. Unfortunately, there are quite a lot of people like him around, but he seems to do the most harm. I read in "The Times" that Cleeve had a strong XV this term. Everybody must be pleased, but as you know, I preferred cricket.

Yours sincerely,
JAMES SLIGGER

Jamey put down his Biro and read it through. He had not gone to the Fantastacherie that evening, which meant he could catch up on things. He supposed he might even write to his mother, although the thought filled him with dejection. He had also received another letter from his brother. He always read them in the lavatory, fearful that anyone should guess where they came from. He asked for a wireless set. How on earth could Jamey send a wireless set to Wormwood Scrubs, even if he had one? He would have liked a wireless set very much himself, and saw no reason why Philip should have one just because he was in prison. It was most improper that they should be allowed wireless sets in prison, anyway. Philip said it was a privilege.

Jamey thought longingly of the other Philip, from whose company he was debarred tonight. Fringe and Greaves and English and Whale, as well as a sprinkling of girls, the delectable Hammock and his own Anne Etherington, all would be at the Fantastacherie tucking into spaghetti. When Bill had not returned after going to fetch some water for his gin, Jamey had at first been relieved and then desperately ashamed. He should have known that Bill would not have liked the silly, shallow people of Godolphin. Jamey's place was with Whale and Hammock, shoulder to shoulder in the fight against nuclear warfare, the South Africans, the Americans, the French, Fascists and Reactionaries, the fight for increased grants for state scholars and the fight against censorship by the proctors. He had no place among the Garlicks and Picciones. Also, he owed Guy a total of thirty-two pounds, and felt a bit uneasy with him now, although he was much more aware of it than Guy.

He read through his letter again. It seemed all right. It did not occur to him that his friends at the Fantastacherie would think it rather odd. Like Goyle, he liked to keep his lives separate, so that in either he could feel he had reservations. He would have made a good spy, he felt.

There was another job to do. "DEAR MUMMY," he began.

.   .   .

The Fantastacherie was abuzz. Jamey had had a row with Bill English, that much was certain. What was it about? English sat alone, playing moodily with his plate of spaghetti. Greaves was of the opinion that Jamey had gone too far over the disarmament question. English was notorious for his moderation. Fringe and Greaves and almost anybody who really thought about the matter regarded the disarmament campaign as nothing more than a means to an end. When all the radical fury which the prospect of being blown up excites had been channeled into overthrowing the government, and a panel of intellectuals had been set up to run the country, then they could turn on the other European countries and threaten to exterminate them unless they accepted a similar social revolution. The Americans would not dare intervene, of course. Russia would be behind them. Only English thought they really should abandon nuclear weapons. It was this sort of sloppy thinking that stood in the way of any truly radical change, as Fringe and Greaves pointed out. They would not have stood it from English if he had not been such a charming fellow. He had no idealism in him, he was too soundly practical. It would be insane to renounce the only weapon they had just when it might be put to some radical purpose. It would reduce England to the status of an off-shore island, and the power of the intellectuals who governed it to nothing at all. Of course they could destroy their nuclear weapons without telling anyone they had done so, or, even better, they could claim to have destroyed them without actually having done it. That might be sensible. But English was too simple-minded to understand that sort of thing. When the whole world was governed by Students' Councils, then they might be able to dispense with the nuclear threat as something outgrown and childish. Until then, it was no good living in a pipe dream. For their part, Fringe and Greaves were definitely on the side of Sligger.

"What do you think, Anne? He is practically your lover." Anne blushed, and Angela Hammock laughed. It was true that Anne had been seeing a great deal of Jamey, but there was

46

nothing like that between them yet. They had discussed a multitude of things very seriously. Perhaps that was love. Perhaps it would ripen in the natural course of things to a more personal relationship. Anne was not sure how it would come about, but she expected that Jamey knew.

"I think Jamey has a very good point about the ultimate aim of the movement," she said. It was curious how they all seemed to know what the quarrel was about. Bill would probably accept their diagnosis in the end. He did not like to think it was crippling shyness and anger at his own helplessness which had caused him to leave Godolphin rather than return to Jamey's rooms after the drink of water. No doubt there was an intellectual explanation.

"But we must all work for what we think it stands for. If Bill thinks it stands for one thing, he is quite right to put everything he's got into it, even if it stands for something quite different. We must all try to remember that the movement is everything, we are nothing."

Everybody agreed heartily. None of them really thought they were nothing, but they thought it was a good thing to say, and a good principle to instill into the rank and file of the movement. English was pretending not to listen, staring intently into his plate of spaghetti, with its many obtuse riddles and insoluble problems.

Chapter 5

Mrs. Sligger saw no reason why she should send Philip a wireless set. It was the sort of thing which had landed him where he was. She prided herself, quite rightly, that she had not been an overindulgent mother. No part of the blame for his moral delinquency could rest on her shoulders, as she confided to Mrs. Arckwright, the wife of a neighbor, although there were others who might have cause for self-searching. As Mr. Sligger was never present on these occasions the innuendo was lost, but both she and Mrs. Arckwright knew quite well to whom she was referring. Mr. Sligger had not been a particularly overindulgent parent either. His bad influence took other forms, like a lack of interest in new trends, a general indolence and an unbearable habit of leaving his slippers in the sitting room. But it was constant listening to the wireless and suchlike things which made the younger generation what it was. Instead of going out for themselves and discovering things as she had done, they sat cooped up all day listening to other people's ideas, predigested and tasteless, before their minds were properly formed.

Besides, it would be absurd to expect her to give up her own wireless set, which was indispensable and the only one she had, and she could hardly buy another just for the remaining five months which Philip had to serve. It was no good approaching his father; of that she was certain. If Mr. Sligger was indifferent to his son James and pointedly obstructive to his wife, he actively detested his elder son, Philip. Mrs. Sligger had established that fact soon after Philip's birth, and as Mr. Sligger was too idle to bother to remove the fixation, it had remained. She would write to Jamey, much as she detested writing letters, which nearly always were unnecessary, as one could put over one's ideas so much better face to face. But Jamey was safe from the telephone at Godolphin, and a letter was the only thing which would serve her purpose.

Jamey's letter had caused the amount of pleasure that his letters always did, a reassurance that he still depended on her. He gave the scores of a rugger match between Godolphin and Hertford College, a thing in which he knew she was interested, or tried to be, for his sake. He complained about the weather, but humorously, in case she worried whether he was happy or not.

He mentioned that he had been to the Pitt-River's anthropological collection with "a girl called Anne Etherington." Mrs. Sligger sighed. How bored she was with it all, she thought, as her mind raced eagerly ahead with prurient curiosity.

DEAR JAMEY,

I was pleased to have your letter and know that you are having such a good time. Nothing much to tell you from here to cheer you up, I am afraid. Life is much as usual. The boiler looks as if it will not last much longer, which means we are going to have to find £250 from somewhere, or do without hot water. Sometimes I almost think it would be as well to give up the idea of hot water, and let the house go to the dogs. When it rained last Friday, damp patches appeared again in your Father's study, as usual. Mrs. Arckwright's niece is in hospital with a fractured spine after falling between the train and the platform at Farnham Station, but I am sure it will cheer them all up to know that someone, at least, is having a good time. It does not look as if she will ever be able to walk again, without crutches. The worst part of it is that she had been staying with Mrs. Arckwright, so she feels she is part to blame. Poor Mrs. Arckwright. I keep telling her it's none of her fault if the silly girl couldn't look where she was going. It's her own fault and she deserves it. But Mrs. Arckwright is in a terrible state. However, I doubt if you've got time to worry about my small problems.

I expect you will want to bring someone home with you in the vac—some girl or something. Well, as I've told you often, I don't want this house turned into a brothel, but if she's sensible I'll try and talk your Father round. But for Heaven's sake see that she's tidy.

Your Father and I think it would be a good idea if you sent Philip a wireless set. It would not be suitable, coming from us, and as you have an independent income now it seems the least you can do. Philip is allowed one now as a privilege for having behaved so well in the past six months, and I feel we should do nothing to discourage it. You have our permission to send him one and I think you should.

I was very pleased to hear your College had done so well against

Hertford. It looks as if you have gone straight from the best school to the best college—at sport, anyway.

Bless you then, and think of me sometimes.

Love from
MUMMY.

"Sligger, Beaufort Nine Two," said a small man in the Quad. "Letter for you and for your mate." Guy's letter was in a dark-blue envelope, addressed in an enormous childish sprawl to "Guy Frazer-Robertson Esq." in light-green ink. It was obviously from Miss Pratt-Bingham. Jamey never seemed to get any letters from girls. He recognized his mother's familiar pointed hand with a sinking heart. She very seldom wrote, and it always portended either an emotional crisis or a demand of some sort. Often it was both, as the two seemed to go hand in hand.

Guy read his letter with a superior smile and threw it into the wastepaper basket.

"Her mother's organizing a cinema premiere in aid of Freedom from Hunger, and would I like to buy a ticket for twenty-five guineas," he said.

Sligger smiled, too. His set disagreed with Freedom from Hunger, Famine Relief and all that sort of thing, although he could not for the moment remember why. He suspected it might be because they were escapist, but he was not sure. If he could have remembered, it was because Fringe had pointed out that anything which relieved the lot of the underdeveloped peasant also lulled his political and social consciousness, and for that reason was dangerous.

Guy said, "Everybody seems to think that just because my father's so stinking rich, I must be made of money, too." He had already asked for and received an additional two hundred pounds.

"Is he mean, then?" Sligger thought Guy must be talking about the thirty-two pounds he was owed, and felt awkward.

"No, he's not mean, just insensitive. He expects me to write to him every time I want some money. It doesn't seem to occur to him that I may not like writing to him."

50

"Goodness, hard luck." For practically the first time in their acquaintance, Sligger was guilty of conscious hypocrisy.

Guy sensed it. "Well, it's better than just not getting any," he said.

"I didn't mean that," said Jamey hastily. His mother's letter had caused some worry, amounting as it did to two firm orders, the first to bring a girl home in the vacation, the second to buy a wireless set for his wretched, undeserving brother.

It would be easy to ask Anne Etherington, although a trifle embarrassing, as it would bring a personal streak into their relationship conducted hitherto on a purely theoretical plane. He dared not guess what she would think of the Farnham Green ménage, and would have asked Guy for advice if he did not think it would be an act of disloyalty. Guy may have been to Farnham Green, but Anne was his greater friend. It was over the second order that Jamey despaired. He could not possibly ask Frazer-Robinson for a loan of fifteen pounds on top of everything else he owed him, and even if he could it was by no means certain that he would get it. Jamey would merely have jeopardized his only remaining source of income. He already had only fifteen pounds in the bank to pay his battels at the end of term, which, he had been told, amounted to some 120 pounds. He might be able to pay them out of next term's allowance, but how could he live in the meantime? It was true that, theoretically, he could eat in Hall, that all the cigarettes and drink he required were supplied by Guy, and he only had his fare home at the end of term to worry about, but that showed, as Greaves would have said, the wide discrepancy between theory and practice. Somebody might have lent him a wireless for five months, but Jamey did not want to have to explain why he wanted one. There was no question of gainsaying his mother. A wireless must be sent, he thought, and within a week.

Anne Etherington lay on the bed in her tiny room and blew bubbles. She was always worried about something, often about many things, but this afternoon she was happy, or experiencing those sensations which passed for happiness in her ill-favored life. That evening there was to be a party in Jamey's rooms, as Guy was spending the night in London at a debutante dance. She would practically be the hostess. It would be the first time she had been to a reception at the Godolphin's, as she persisted in calling the College, despite Jamey's hints, but she could see that she was well suited to the job of being hostess. Perhaps, after the party, Jamey would take her in his arms, and . . . her mind went a blank. Propose to her? Hardly. Take her into another room, where they would fondle and dally? That would be perfect, she decided. Philip Fringe had said that he disapproved of deep petting as it was neither one thing or the other. Well, she knew enough about one thing, whatever that was, and as for the other, she felt it could wait. Not like Deirdre, the bad girl of St. Rachel's, who went with men. Deirdre was held in awe, but they all went out of their way to be friendly to her to show how broad-minded they were. Anne had no reason to suppose that Philip Fringe knew anything about it at all, even deep petting, which was a very unattractive word, she agreed, but one had to be realistic. She and Jamey would indulge in deep petting. The only thing was, could she be sure that Jamey knew the rules, knew how to set about things? That was her worry of the moment, as she blew a particularly optimistic bubble and composed herself for sleep. The gas fire hissed away in the corner, and in her dreams she heard the babble of a brook and the contented cries of lovers.

Dear Brother Richard,

The term seems to have settled in now, and I am sorry not to have written earlier. The Cleeve contingent is rather dispersed and it is difficult to keep my eye on all of them, but I think you should know of rumors which are going round about Sligger and Frazer-Robinson. There may be nothing in them, but it doesn't do the school any good. I particularly noticed how close they used to be at Cleeve. I heard about them from someone called

Stephen Goyle, not one of us, but highly intelligent, and I am sure you would like him.

As you may know, there are lots of girls here. Frank Pratt-Bingham has a sister who is said to lead a very immoral life, and I am trying to get an introduction so that I can keep my eye on her. In St. Rachel's College there is a girl who actually goes with men for immoral purposes called Deirdre Black, but there is nothing I can do about it as I have not met her yet. They say she is very difficult to get to know.

I hope you are well.

Yours sincerely,
J. MacLaughlin.

P.S. I did not see either Sligger or Frazer-Robinson in church last week.

Chapter 6

"Bill, don't you want anything to drink?" Jamey was finding it hard work to coax his friends into the high life.

"Oh, all right."

As the party was being given with Guy's knowledge and consent—Jamey said he would supply some Spanish white wine—it was to be a respectable affair, and Jamey had asked all Guy's friends as well as his tutor and Father Potinue, the chaplain. Father Potinue had declined, but in such a charming way and in such elegant handwriting that Jamey was not sure whether he was coming or no. Mr. Price-Williams had accepted, and shyly asked if he could bring his wife, who was Principal of St. Rachel's and not a great partygoer. Jamey had kept the knowledge a secret, thinking it grander to introduce the lion as if she had just dropped in.

Philip Fringe said, "I admire your taste very much, Jamey, particularly the curtains."

"Oh yes?" said Jamey. "They come from a small village just south of Carcassonne, actually. Practically in Spain."

"I wish we all had the money to decorate our rooms as we liked."

"It was my roommate who did most of it. His father's terribly rich."

"I know. Lord Robinson, the man who refused danger-money to his synthetic fiber workers last year, although it was shown that many of them had a rash, because he wanted to increase the dividend for the third year running. Very interesting."

Jamey began to feel awkward. "I don't expect Guy knows much about that," he said.

"I don't suppose he does," said Fringe, sipping his Pimm's in a suggestive way. "I wanted the workers to come out on strike, and wrote a piece about it. Most of them were redundant anyway, and the management would have had to lock them out. Being reduced from twenty-six pounds a week to six pounds National Assistance might have opened some of their eyes to the need for industrial action."

"I expect you're right," said Jamey tactfully, feeling the burden of hypocrisy rather heavier than usual. The trouble with Jamey's hypocrisy was that everyone saw through it immediately.

"Of course he's bloody well right," said Bill English, with an angry gulp at his neat gin. It went much against the grain to agree with Fringe about anything, but there were some propositions which could not be challenged.

Jamey wished the other guests would arrive and turn the evening into something more like a party and less like a court-martial. Anne Etherington jumped to Jamey's defense. She had not been listening to the conversation, but had been concentrating on breaking up some ice for Greaves's whisky. This was her evening. In honor of the occasion, she had put on some rouge and lipstick and a little toilet water behind her ears, but the general effect was much the same. Her plan was clear. She would stay behind after the other guests had gone, to help clear up. Nobody would think there was anything in the least odd about that. Then she and Jamey would discover that it was beyond the hours during which women were permitted in the college. Desperate with worry, she would sink into his arms . . .

"What on earth do you mean?" she demanded fiercely. "You none of you know what you're talking about. You didn't even understand Jamey's point."

Angela Hammock laughed. Fringe looked ironically polite. Greaves said, "Of course Anne's quite right. What Jamey was trying to say was that by refusing the workers' pay claim, Lord Robinson was in point of fact helping what he set out to hinder. He sharpened the workers' discontent and made them more aware of the need for a radical change in our society, which is what we must work for."

"But if he had granted the wage claim, sooner or later it would have made the factory uneconomical and put thousands of people out of work," explained Philip, as if he were speaking to an extremely stupid person. "Industrial discontent is all very well, but it is not an end in itself. What we want is a great mass of unemployed on whom we can rely for support in whatever measures we propose."

"But what would happen if it did not make the factory uneconomic, but just made the workers richer and more contented? Then you are back where you started."

"Then we would have to wait a little longer," admitted Fringe, "for the next wage claim."

"I still think Jamey had a good point," said Anne stoutly, looking appealingly at him.

"Anyway, what are you going to do when you do get into power?" said Jamey.

"Don't you know?" asked Philip sarcastically.

55

"We discussed that at the last meeting," said Anne in an embarrassed aside. The first, immediate thing was to increase grants for students. The other things—setting up Student Councils for Regional Government, abolition of the Monarchy and the Establishment everywhere, declaration of war on South Africa—followed later. Jamey had missed the meeting, because he had to take Guy and Sally Pratt-Bingham to Blenheim for the day.

Bill English felt he was out of his depth. "Of course you bloody well can't refuse workers their wage claims," he said. Angela Hammock laughed.

"Bill's right," she said. Fringe let the matter rest there.

When Peter Garlick arrived, it was evident he felt out of place.

"Jack Piccione's coming, and Stephen Goyle, and Father Potinue said he might look in," said Sligger. "Would you like some crème de menthe?"

"Good old Jack, and Stephen," said Garlick. "Is there some crème de menthe? I think I would prefer some of Guy's Cointreau, actually, if there is any left." He took it to a corner, where he turned his back on the others and listened to his wireless, jigging up and down to its music.

"Does he want to dance?" asked Greaves kindly.

"What's that?" said Fringe to the suede-covered back which extended down to a shuddering bottom and some short legs which were performing a dance step which was so modern that none of them recognized it.

"It's an Omega Beam Ergomatic, actually," said Garlick, referring to the wireless, as one might drop the name of a Grand Duchess.

"I believe they are making them smaller, now," said Fringe spitefully.

"Not with a calibrated tuner you just switch on," said Garlick, who knew all the answers. Fringe could think of nothing to say.

"I expect that's one of the Japanese ones," he said.

"Swiss," said Garlick.

"That's what it says," said Fringe. Garlick treated the remark with the contempt it deserved and concentrated on keeping time with the music. It was exhausting work.

When Piccione arrived Garlick said, "Jack, thank God you've come." Piccione looked round.

"Thought I'd just look round," he said. "I can't stay long. I have an essay to hand in."

"Jack, do you know the Gangly? I think I've just discovered a good tune for it."

"The Gangly?"

"You know, the dance."

"I am afraid I am not an expert."

"Yes, you know." Garlick's feet started wobbling again.

"No, I am afraid I don't know."

Garlick obviously felt Jack had let him down. "Oh well, I just thought you might be interested that this tune fits it rather well."

"Well, we've made one important discovery," said Fringe nastily. Piccione smiled at him. He obviously regarded Jamey's set as future constituents, with whom he might have to get on well. Equally obviously, he did not regard Garlick as an elector, or perhaps he felt he could rely on his vote anyway.

"We were talking about Associated Nylon's refusal to grant its workers a pay rise," said Jamey, who felt that Jack should be drawn.

"Oh yes. It was an awkward business that. We were trying to keep the wage restraint going."

"Wage restraint," said Bill English. "Bloody rubbish." Angela Hammock laughed.

"No it bloody well isn't," said Garlick, who wasn't quite sure what it meant, but wanted to meet these people on their own ground. "You can't just pay people more and more."

"Why not?" said English.

"Of course you can't," said Garlick argumentatively.

"Why not?" said English.

"It encourages them to be bloody idle," said Garlick. He wished he had not joined in the conversation, or come to the party at all. He was much happier lying on his own bed, listening to the wireless, gazing at the life-size photographs of Anita Ekberg pasted on his bookshelf.

A meaningful silence followed. Greaves, Fringe, English, and even Sligger, stared accusingly at Piccione. He was acutely embarrassed by Garlick's support. "Well, there are many points of view," he said.

"Points of view," said English. Angela Hammock got ready to laugh.

By the time Stephen Goyle arrived, Piccione had extricated himself and left. The Price-Williamses had not yet arrived, and Sligger felt it a pity they had not met Piccione. It would have impressed on his tutor that even if Sligger was not particularly good at the absurd things which Mr. Price-Williams seemed to feel important, he was an important fellow in college life.

Goyle said, "Quite a collection here," and asked for some brandy in a way which suggested that only he was capable of appreciating all the nuances of the situation.

"I am not sure which is the brandy," said Anne in a likably vague way. If only she knew it, she was taking a few blundering steps on the path which Sally Pratt-Bingham trod to perfection.

"In the bottle shaped like a pineapple, I should think," said Garlick, anxious to show himself acquainted.

"No, that's the Marsala," said Jamey.

"Marsala? Is somebody going to do some cooking?"

It had been Guy's first mistake, confusing it with Madeira, which he felt to be an undergraduate drink. Nobody had yet asked for either.

"The brandy is in the flat bottle marked X.O." said Jamey.

"There we are," said Anne, pouring it into the glass which Garlick was holding. "Ice?" Goyle and Garlick grimaced. Sligger, too, felt uncomfortable, but made a decision. His loyalties were with Anne.

"Yes, give him some ice," he said firmly.

"Water?"

"No, no water," said Goyle hastily. He took the balloon

glass, clinking merrily, to a chair, and looked at Garlick significantly, as if there was a conspiracy between them.

Everybody was walking about when Garlick suddenly said in a high, unnatural voice, "All right, joke over, everyone. Where is it?" A surprised silence followed. "All right, joke over. Can I have my wireless back please?"

Nobody moved for a moment. Then Angela Hammock laughed, and everybody decided it was a capital rag.

"Shall we give him his wireless back, then, Bill?" asked Greaves.

"We could make him swim for it," said English with a roguish twinkle. Goyle obviously thought it childish, but quite amusing.

"Did you have it here, Peter? I never saw it."

"Of course I did," said Garlick impatiently, "you don't expect me to leave it in my room where anybody could go in and play it. It cost twenty-five pounds, free of purchase tax, so it's getting beyond a joke. Say you just give it back to me, whoever's got it, huh?"

"I didn't see any wireless set, did you, Greaves?"

"No, I didn't see anything. There's something in the corner which may be one." He pointed to Guy's radiogram, which had needed three men to move.

"I think we should give it back to him," said Anne, who saw how unhappy Garlick was becoming, and was a kind girl at heart.

"Well I haven't got it," said English.

"Neither have I," said Greaves.

"Neither have I," said Sligger.

"Neither have I," said Fringe. They all looked at each other, not sure which was joking.

"All right. It's a very good joke, but I am afraid that unless I get it back soon I will have to report it to the college authorities and the police. It will save a lot of trouble if you just give it back to me now. Have you got it, Stephen?"

Goyle obviously thought it a very childish question. Even

59

more infuriating, he seemed to consider it a sign of immaturity to have one's wireless stolen. "Even if I had, Peter, I would be unlikely to tell you, as that would defeat the purpose of my taking it in the first place." Everybody accepted that.

Sligger suffered from an innate sense of guilt whenever theft was mentioned, and always thought people suspected him. The result was that when he was perfectly innocent, he behaved like a caricature of a guilty man. On this occasion, he reflected, it should be easier. "Peter, you don't think I'm the sort of chap to pinch a fellow's wireless, even if he wasn't my friend." Everybody glanced at Sligger oddly, but Garlick was too distraught to notice anything.

"Of course not, Jamey," he said, grateful that anyone was taking him seriously, "but I wish I could say the same of these filthy louts, who shouldn't be allowed in the Beaufort Quad. Your place is in the gutter," he shouted at John Whale, who had just come in. "All right, keep my wireless set. By God, you'll be sorry for it in the morning. I'll move heaven and earth, if necessary, to have you all thrown back in the gutter where you belong." Garlick stood with his back to the fireplace, like Horatius before the bridge, facing the Tuscan hordes. He was near to tears.

Goyle took command.

"All right," he said, "I don't know who has got your wireless, or even if anyone has. I dare say you left it in your room. But if I had it, I know I should hold on to it after that. If you get it back in a few days, that will be more than you deserve. Honestly, Peter, your lack of self-control disgusts me. If you can't put up with a little bit of ragging without crying, you don't deserve to have a wireless set at all."

"I'm not crying," said Garlick, "it's you who's crying, or will be when I get started on you. You might as well enjoy your little joke now. Goodbye, Jamey. I'm sorry you can't control your friends better." Sligger was the only friend he had left in the room. "If you find out which of them has got my wireless set, just tell him from me that if it isn't back in my rooms within an hour, he had better take it back to the police, as it will be out of my hands by then." He walked out of the room, a pathetic, defeated figure which would have wrung their hearts if he had not forfeited all claim to sympathy. He lifted his head in a miserable effort to appear dignified, as if dignity was possible where there was no transistor wireless set. Unaccommodated man, he felt, was no more than such a poor, bare, forked animal as he was. He hesitated before going to Piccione's room to lay his grievance before the Home Secretary. Would Jack receive him, without his wireless set? But the matter was too urgent for consideration of the social niceties.

"Your father is meant to be Home Secretary, Jack," he began, and poured out his tale. He believed the Home Secretary had plenary powers to imprison anyone who was known to have committed an offense while proof against him was collected. Jack told him the Home Secretary had no such powers.

"They even say I never had my wireless in the room. You saw it there, didn't you, Jack?" Jack was not going to be drawn into either side of the argument. He could not for the moment recollect whether he had or had not seen the wireless set in Jamey's room.

"If I were you, I should go and see the Procurer in the morning," he said.

"I'm bloody well going to do that. Don't worry," said Garlick threateningly, as if Piccione might conceivably have worried in either case. "And if he doesn't do anything I am going to the police."

"I shouldn't do that," said Piccione. "Now, if you don't mind, Peter, I've got an essay to finish by tomorrow morning."

"I don't care who's got his silly old wireless set," said Greaves after Garlick had left. Goyle obviously thought the whole matter boring, but further discussion was prevented by the arrival of the Price-Williamses, who had been delayed because Mrs.

Price-Williams had forgotten to buy any dinner for her husband, and then had burned three lots of omelets running. They were in quite a jolly mood as a result.

Anne gave a little cry of horror when she saw her Principal arrive, and Miss Hammock jumped up from the sofa and re-arranged her skirt. It made her look as if she had been embracing someone on the sofa, which she hadn't.

"Hello, Anne and Angela. Not the first people I should have expected to see here. A little lemonade, please, if you have any." They had none. "Well then, whatever you have got, please." Anne gave her some whisky and soda.

Mr. Price-Williams asked for some wine, and got a sharp glance from his wife. Anne, after a moment's thought, gave him a glass of the Marsala.

Garlick wandered round the cold, cruel confines of the Beaufort Quad, every door barred to him, every back turned. He was terrified of meeting anyone he knew. Seeing him without his Omega Beam Ergomatic, they would be sure to ask, "Hello, Peter, where's your wireless set?" When told he had been robbed, that by a stroke of bitter misfortune he was now dispossessed, their faces would freeze, and they would say, "Oh really? Well, I have an essay to finish by tomorrow morning. I doubt if I shall be able to see you for some time actually, as I am dreadfully busy. Good night." There was no question of getting another. Omega Beams with the calibrated tuner you just switch on were unprocurable in England as everyone knew. By some unthinkable, outrageous stroke of fate, Garlick was now to be counted among the despised mass of undergraduates who had nothing to distinguish themselves from the rest. Garlick could no longer lift his head in the salons of Beaufort, in the elegant halls of Godolphin. He retired with a heavy heart to his room, knowing that it would have lost its soul. It had. He switched on all the lights and put on the gramophone as loud as he could. It was no good, something was missing.

In a frenzy, Garlick walked round the room, switching on and plugging in every gadget he had. The electric fire glowed in the hearth, the electric kettle steamed. Nearby, a fan whirred, and his tape recorder recorded the sound. A small electric egg poacher he had never used was soon connected and started poaching imaginary eggs with a kind of imbecile animation of its own. His American electric razor—it had never had much to contend with—gave a well-bred buzz, and Garlick moved to switch on his pride, the cocktail mixer which would also clean by vacuum, heat and scent the air, remove a stone from a horse's hoof and dry one's hair. When everything buzzed and hummed around him, Garlick lay on his bed and a great tear of self-pity welled up in his eye. He knew he was overloading the current, but there were some moments in one's emotional history when even overloading the current was justified. Not all the overloaded currents in the world would compensate for the loss of one, small wireless set. He looked at his cigarette holder with distaste. It was a pity that no one had invented an electric cigarette holder. Without it, he might get lung cancer. Nobody would notice much if he did, now that he had lost everything.

Surrounded by the consoling noise of his battalions, Garlick dropped into a dreamless sleep.

"I think this is the point you are trying to make," said Mr. Price-Williams, speaking in his jocular, social manner to Fringe, "that where there isn't a bottle of whisky on that table, the consequences of there being one, if one did happen to be there, are irrelevant, or immaterial, or what you will."

"Yes," said Fringe doubtfully. He had meant something quite different.

"Whereas what I would say is this: There is a bottle of whisky on that table. The consequences are such and such. Alternatively, there is not a bottle of whisky on that table. The consequences are such and such. Both my statements are made irrespective of whether there is or is not a bottle on that table, and irrespective even of whether the table exists or whether there is such a thing as a bottle of whisky."

"All I meant was that I'm afraid the whisky is finished, and would Mrs. Price-Williams like to go on to the brandy," said Anne, who felt that politeness was more important. On the whole, she thought the party was going well.

Sligger had had exactly the same conversation with Mr. Price-Williams about a tree in a field, and thought he knew the answer.

"But how are you ever to know whether there is a bottle of whisky on the table or not?"

"By studying the consequences."

"Oh, I see." Sligger felt that the party had gone on long enough. Mr. Price-Williams had only one topic of conversation, only one point to make, and nobody ever understood it anyway. In tutorials he talked of trees in fields, at parties about bottles of whisky on the table, but it was all the same. Sligger wanted to get away and explore his new acquisition, at present a small bump under the cushion on which Mrs. Price-Williams was sitting. She saved the situation by looking at her watch and saying in a half-jocular way: "St. Rachel's girls have ten minutes to be back or they will be locked out."

"Can't I stay behind and help clear up?" asked Anne desperately.

"No, Anne, I expect Mr. Sligger can manage quite well," said Mrs. Price-Williams.

Only after Anne had left and was trudging toward St. Rachel's did the full realization of the evening's failure break upon her, and she let out a long wail. Angela Hammock, who was walking beside her, laughed and then said "Sh." In the shadow of the gates of St. Rachel's, a couple were locked in a close embrace. As they walked past, Anne recognized the shape of Deirdre Black. "How disgusting," she said, with less of her liberal condescension than usual.

"She's a nice girl, Anne, and I like her very much, but I sometimes wonder . . . I mean, do you think . . . ?" Goyle had left the party some time before, but now returned rather breathless, and paused. He was not usually a slave to other people's notions of good taste, but there were a few subjects at Oxford which one had to approach with caution.

"You mean she has not a first-rate brain?"

Sligger had gone too fast.

"I did not say that," said Goyle. "I mean she may have a very good brain indeed. It is difficult to say. But if so, it is difficult to say whether she uses it or not. Of course, she may just have an extremely good second-class brain. I think that may be it. What do you think?"

"I think you may be right," said Sligger, pleased with the discovery. The conversation tacitly accepted that he and Goyle were first-class brains, or they would not be qualified to judge.

After the Price-Williamses had left, everybody who did not belong to Godolphin had to go. Nobody mentioned the stolen wireless, but the English set seemed to agree that Goyle had taken it, and Goyle's mind was impenetrable. As Garlick had shown himself in such an ugly light, nobody minded whether he got it back or no.

"Tell me," said Goyle, "do you find Anne attractive as a woman?"

One by one, he unpicked all the scales from Jamey's eyes which had prevented him seeing Anne as she was. Of course, Goyle was right. She was a mediocre person, who desired some vicarious glamour from the importance of the matters she discussed so incompetently. Other than this, she had no sexual allure, was inexperienced, and probably felt a revulsion from the male sex. She was immature and hysterical. It would have been true to say she was a virgin if there was validity in any discussion of Anne Etherington's sexual potential, it being a non-existent quantity.

Jamey felt that a great weight was lifted. It explained his failure to achieve what Goyle described as "intermittent physical contact," which was so essential to the emotional make-up of the artistic man. It explained why everybody seemed to be getting ahead of him in the race—for the moment Sligger no longer doubted all the hints dropped, the allusions made. Goyle's last remark seemed the most damning thing that could ever be said of a woman. There could be no doubt, he was wasting his time with Anne Etherington.

"I will introduce you to a girl called Deirdre Black, if you like," said Goyle.

Jamey felt sick with apprehension. "Yes, do," he said, "I feel I could do with a change."

Just then a great noise broke out in the Quad, of shouting and running feet. Jamey looked at Goyle, and decided the mature thing to do was to ignore it. Goyle agreed, and said, "You are right, Jamey. A man must always be on the move, never tied down to one place, or one woman, or one set of ideas. That is why I find it so useful at Oxford to have many different circles of friends, each on its own level, as it were."

The noise outside was getting too loud to ignore. Glass was being broken and people were shouting "Fire" and other ribald remarks.

"It must be somebody's birthday, or perhaps it is a rugger celebration," said Goyle.

"Bloody hooligans," said Jamey.

Chapter 7

So it was that they missed the greater part of the evening's drama. A scholar in biology who lived on the humble attic floor above Garlick's rooms gave the alarm. By then, choking black smoke was pouring up the staircase, and his eyes were smarting. Having given the alarm by shouting "Fire" at the top of his voice, he returned to his room to rescue his week's essay on the

66

invertebrate limbless worm. This and various other treasures—the fetus of a rat preserved in spirits, which belonged to the college library, his General Certificate of Education in biology, mathematics, chemistry and chemical biology, his duffel coat and his second pair of spectacles—he threw upon the soft, damp grass in the center of Beaufort Quad.

As an ambulance and three fire engines arrived, so did Mr. Scroton-Wise, the Chief Procurer, a terrible sight in azure pajamas with his academic gown thrown around them. He watched with kindly interest as Garlick's blackened form was carried coughing from his room, piggyback on the shoulders of a sturdy fireman.

"Is there anybody left in the staircase?" he asked, wrinkling his nose against the smell of hot rubber and plastic which came out of Garlick's room.

"There is John Gentle on the top floor," an undergraduate volunteered.

"Who is John Gentle?" asked the Chief Procurer.

"He is in his third year studying biology."

"That is immaterial. Has he not come down?"

"Nobody could come down now, sir. The staircase is gone."

Four fireman ran a ladder up to the topmost window and one climbed it. He could see nothing in the smoke that filled what used to be Gentle's bedroom. He came down again, slowly and regretfully.

"Nobody could be alive in that," he said. "It is an inferno."

"Can't you try again?" asked Mr. Scroton-Wise desperately.

"No," said the Chief Fireman. "It wouldn't be safe."

"Oh my God," said Mr. Scroton-Wise. "Has anybody seen Gentle?" He went to a knot of six undergraduates who were watching the fire, asking them one by one.

All denied seeing him, except the last, who said, "You mean John Gentle, sir? That's me."

"Gentle, thank God you're safe," said Mr. Scroton-Wise, holding him fiercely by the arm. "How did you make it?"

"I came down the stairs before the smoke got too bad."

"Well done, well done. Brave lad. I can't tell you how worried we've all been."

The knot of undergraduates glanced curiously at their fellow who had suddenly come into prominence and who was busily collecting his possessions strewn about the lawn. Nobody knew John Gentle. People who lived on his staircase saw a dark, hunched figure from time to time. The real Gentle was contained in his Certificates of Education, now neatly rolled on the grass, and in his essay on the invertebrate, limbless worm, being collected from a puddle in the corner.

"You had a pretty close shave," one of them suggested.

"Yes," said Gentle, with a grateful smile. "Phew!"

After the catastrophe, he was housed in the college annex near the railway station. He seemed quite happy there, and was occasionally to be seen, a dark, hunched figure in a duffel coat with an enormous pair of black-rimmed spectacles.

"What has happened to Garlick?" demanded the Chief Procurer.

"You mean the student we took out?"

"I mean the young gentleman on the first floor."

"He didn't look too good to me," said the Chief Fireman.

"You mean he's in some danger?" The thought was absurd.

"I mean he looked like he'd got some inflammated lung there. I expect they'll have him at the infirmary and they'll tell you. Is it all right if we damp down the rooms on either side?"

"Do whatever you consider best. Within reason, of course." The Procury was only a few doors away. "I must find out what's wrong with Garlick." The Procurer spoke in a bluff way, as if he was dealing with a malingerer in the Royal Air Force, a branch of the services in which he had taken an interest during the war. But there was panic in his heart.

"What is it, Alec? What has happened?"

"Nothing, my dear. There has been a small fire, that is all. Go to sleep again. Everything is being dealt with." The Procurer turned his back on the recumbent form of his wife to slip off his azure pajama bottoms.

68

"What are you doing, Alec? Why are you naked?"

"I am not naked, my dear, as I still have my pajama top. I am merely dressing to go to the hospital." He was struggling into a pair of hair-striped trousers.

"Why are you going to the hospital, if nothing is the matter? Are you unwell?"

"No, my dear," a slightly harder note had come into the Procurer's voice, "I am merely doing my duty and looking after the people entrusted to me. That is all. Good night."

"Have you heard there was a terrible fire at St. Godolphin's last night. At least one of the students was burned to death."

"How awful. Who was it?" With slight variations in the degree of horror and curiosity in each case, the same question was flying round the refectory of St. Rachel's College at breakfast. When Anne heard it, she turned white and pushed away her plate.

"Who was it, who was it?" Nobody seemed to know.

One of them, better informed than the rest, said, "I think there was more than one. There had been a party."

Anne left the room, stumbling for the solitude of her own quarters. She knew she had been wrong to leave Jamey to do the clearing-up after the party for himself. She could still scarcely bring herself to believe that he was dead.

Behind her, in the refectory, the chatter went on.

"A whole gang of them were trying to roast a stag they had caught in the Magdalen deer park, I should think."

"Yes, then the stove overturned and they were all burned instead."

"Poor creature, how did they kill it?"

"Ropes. Then slit its throat. That's the usual way."

"How many undergraduates did you say lost their lives? Seven? Still, it's a good thing it happened, in a way. It draws attention to some of the things that go on in men's colleges. It's no good living in ignorance about that side of things."

For once, Angela Hammock was not laughing. "To think that

I was in Godolphin only last night. It all must have been going on within a few yards of me. How disgusting." Everybody sympathized with Angela, as if she had been the sacrificial victim at some particularly disgusting primitive rite.

"What did it feel like, Angela?"

"I didn't actually see anything."

"They tried to get Angela to help them. She refused, of course. She didn't even see the point in some of the things they expected her to do, but they blindfolded her, so she couldn't see all the disgusting things that went on."

"What about the others she could see?"

"Oh, the usual sort of thing, you know."

"I'm glad you're all right, sir." The policeman at the end of Garlick's bed was deferential but wary.

"All right? You think I'm all right. I'm going to sue that lousy College for twenty thousand pounds. You think I'm all right." Garlick's voice was hoarse, and he felt nervous. He did not know what the policeman wanted.

"Now just suppose you give me your account of events leading up to the fire, in your own words. Then, if you agree, I can make up a statement for you to sign."

"Events? Statement? There weren't any events. I was just lying in my bed fast asleep when I woke up to find the room full of smoke and a filthy din going on outside."

"I see. There wasn't anything about a party you was giving in your room."

"No, I was completely alone."

"I see. There wasn't a party in your room the whole evening."

"No, not to the best of my knowledge. I mean of course there wasn't."

"I see. You mean there wasn't a party in the room to the best of your knowledge." It was impossible to tell whether the policeman was being sarcastic or not.

"And there wasn't nothing about a bonfire being lit for some purpose—shall we say roasting a stag? And there wasn't nothing about a young lady in a state of partial or otherwise undress? I leave it to you, sir. You can tell me what you like."

"I don't know what you are talking about, constable, honestly." Nothing could have sounded balder than the last word. "I was out most of the evening, anyway."

The policeman, who was an inspector, said, "And where would that be?"

"With a friend called Jamey Sligger, in Godolphin. You ask him. He's a great friend of mine. He'll tell you where I was."

"I see. Well, I'll go and see this Mr. Sligger, described as a great friend, and see what he has to tell me. No doubt I shall be coming back to see you later, when you've had time to think about it. While I'm gone, perhaps you'd be interested to take a look at this newspaper." He gave Garlick an evening paper, and left.

On its front page was a large picture of Angela Hammock. It was captioned: "I saw nothing." The story was quite simple. An undergraduate, nameless, who had been holding an orgy in the normal course of the Oxford social round, tried to throw a struggling deer on a bonfire in his rooms, with the result that the whole of Godolphin Hall, one of Oxford's oldest prestige colleges, had been burned to the ground. Girls who had been attending the party in a state of undress ran through the streets of Oxford back to their colleges. Fun-loving Angela Hammock, of St. Rachel's, who was there earlier, says she saw nothing of what happened later. It was not known how many people were injured, and reports that three undergraduates had been burned to death were still unconfirmed at the time of going to press. Mr. Alec Scroton-Wise, the Chief Procurer (Principal) of Godolphin, said last night: "Of course anything which tends to disrupt the smooth running of the academic curriculum is to be regretted." He had nothing to add. A small photograph, inset, showed the Procurer in academic cap and gown, with the caption "Regrets . . ."

Garlick's reaction was one of blind fury. He, the only person concerned in the tragedy, and the only person injured, was not even mentioned. Miss Hammock and the Chief Procurer had between them robbed him of his deserts. It should have been Garlick's face which stared from the front page, with the caption: "Hero of fire says: 'My first thought was for the other students.'" Or more soberly: "'It is my considered opinion that until the college authorities wake up in the twentieth century, and adjust the electrical facilities to suit the requirements of the modern student, these tragedies will recur and recur.'"

The cock-and-bull story about an orgy and a deer-roasting was the wrong angle altogether, he felt. He could have managed the story much better if he was not kept in bed. The thought began to germinate in his mind that perhaps there was nothing wrong with him at all, and he was kept in bed only through the machinations of the Chief Procurer and Miss Hammock, who wanted to hog all press coverage of the story for their own filthy ends. Once it had taken root, nothing would supplant it. Garlick put away the earphones through which he had been following a tinny parody of "Listen with Mother" and devoted himself to serious thought.

Sligger had never been very good at tying parcels, but a transistor wireless did not present a great problem. When Anne Etherington burst into the room unannounced, Jamey jumped guiltily and put it under the cushion on the sofa.

"Hello, Anne," he said politely.

"Oh Jamey, I've been worried to death. Everybody said you had been lost in the fire."

"I didn't even know it was going on until afterward. Garlick's in hospital, the silly fool. What on earth happened to Angela?"

"She came home with me. They got all that part of the story wrong. Deirdre Black was the only person we saw, being disgusting with someone." Anne wondered whether this was the moment to fall into his arms, and decided it wasn't. There seemed to be something cold about his manner. No doubt it was shock from the narrow escape he had had.

"Deirdre Black? I've heard about her."

"She's not good enough for you, Jamey. We try to be broad-minded about that sort of thing, but really she does go too far."

Everything that Goyle had said about Anne was being confirmed.

"Well, if you don't mind, Anne, I've got an essay to finish." Anne stared aghast. It was well known that Jamey never wrote essays, that Mr. Price-Williams did not expect them, and probably would not know what to do with them.

"What about?"

"Oh, the positive identification of trees in fields or something." Jamey's understanding of the things he was supposed to study was extremely vague.

"Perhaps I can help you," said Anne in desperation. "I can tell most trees by sight."

Her naïveté was astounding. How absurd of Jamey ever to have thought she was intelligent.

"Not that sort of thing, I am afraid," said Jamey kindly, "I mean how you can tell whether there is a tree in the field, and whether, if there isn't, there is such a thing as a tree which ever could be in a field."

"Of course you can tell. That's easy."

In another frame of mind, Sligger would have agreed with her. Now, she seemed infinitely superficial. He had no essay to write, of course, but he imagined he had, and Anne was getting in the way.

"Well, you go and tell Mr. Price-Williams that," he said. "But I am afraid I am rather busy."

"When can I see you?"

"Whenever you like. I am going to be rather busy for the next few days, and I don't know how much I will be in."

"All right, Jamey," Anne smiled bravely, "I'll try and keep away for a time. Remember I'm always there. I'll look in tomorrow morning and see how you are."

"I'll be out tomorrow morning."

"Tomorrow afternoon, then."

"I still may not be back."

73

"I'll try just the same. Goodbye, Jamey."

"Goodbye." It was incredible how these women clung. Goyle was quite right. One never wanted to get tied down.

Sligger had just finished addressing the parcel to its ignominious destination when there was a discreet knock on the door. He hid the parcel under the cushion on the sofa, and was almost sick with fright when a policeman came in.

"Oh it's you," he said, as if he had been expecting him. "Come in." He sat down on the cushion, where he could feel the reassuring bump of Garlick's wireless set.

"Mr. Sligger?" said the policeman. "I was making inquiries about events leading up to the fire on Staircase Four last night. Mr. Garlick, the young gentleman concerned, tells me he spent the evening in your rooms here."

"He was here for a bit," said Jamey, "but he left quite early on, about half past nine. A long time before the fire."

"I see," said the policeman. "Did he give any reason for leaving so early? He wasn't expecting people in his rooms?"

Jamey felt this was not a topic to dwell on. "He may have," he said, "but I don't think he gave any particular reason for leaving."

"He just walked out of the room?"

"Well, there was a party on, and I didn't really notice."

"I see, a party. Who would have been there, for instance?"

Jamey gave the names, with particular emphasis on Mr. and Mrs. Price-Williams.

"This Miss Hammock," said the policeman, "would she be seen to be behaving perfectly normally toward the end of the evening?"

"Yes, perfectly normally. But Mr. and Mrs. Price-Williams are extremely respected senior members of the University."

"I agree," said the policeman. "The less said about that side of things the better."

When Guy came into the room, he said: "Goodness, Jamey, are you in trouble?" Only Jamey smiled.

74

When he had introduced himself, Guy said, "Now then, Inspector, what will you have to drink?"

"Nothing just for the moment, sir. Not on duty."

"Come on then, what will it be? Jamey, will you get the inspector some whisky?" Jamey was unwilling to leave his seat, but he could think of no excuse. Sure enough, the inspector sat down where he had left, right on top of Garlick's wireless. He looked uncomfortable and moved his position.

"I was just saying to Mr. Sligger, the less about Mr. Price-Williams's presence at this—ahum—party the better. No good ever comes of dragging people like him into it. I shall not be mentioning it in my report, and I don't expect he'll want to bring it up again."

"Quite right," said Guy, who had not the faintest idea what he was talking about. "Have your inquiries got you anywhere?"

"Well," said the inspector, winking at Jamey, "it seems the official reason for the fire is an electric short circuit. The insurance is accepting that, and there doesn't seem to be a good reason for inquiring further. I know Mr. Scroton-Wise doesn't want us to ask too many questions. I asked him about all these stories of naked people running around, and he said there was no such thing. But I noticed his wife give a funny look, and that made me think there was something in it. Or shall I put it this way: She may have seen things he didn't see."

"How fascinating," said Guy.

"I didn't see any naked people," said Jamey regretfully.

"Very well then. That's your story and you stick to it," said the inspector, who felt snubbed. "I'll send in my report just the same."

As he left the Porter's Lodge, he was called over by Mr. Tradiscant, whose first wife had been a sister-in-law of his.

"Who have you been seeing?"

"Mr. Sligger, in the Beaufort Quad."

"Him! I should watch out very careful with that sort. What did he tell you? Not one word of it has any bearing, I bet. He's so careful, you can't catch him at anything. But watch him very careful, and one day we'll get him."

When Jamey hurried through the gate with his parcel for the post, the two were still in deep discussion. Tradiscant gave him a suspicious look, and Anne was outside the gates. He ran past without a word. Anne looked after him and sighed. She had nowhere to go, no one she wanted to see.

"Yes, young lady?" said the porter truculently.

"Nothing," said Anne, and wandered alone into the street.

Jamey posted the parcel. It cost four shillings, but he felt it was worth it to get the burden off his chest. The Post Office clerk gave him an odd glance, but Jamey did not mind. He felt he had done something really kind, and he pictured Philip's joy when he opened the parcel and found not *any* wireless, but an Omega Beam Ergomatic of a pattern unprocurable in England.

Unfortunately, a careless porter in Swindon dropped the parcel and broke the wireless before it reached its destination.

Chapter 8

Garlick's return to Godolphin caused less of a sensation than he might have hoped. Limping among the ruins of his room, he found his electric shaver was the only possession which had not been destroyed by the fire. Cradling it lovingly in his arms, he took it to Frazer-Robinson's room and connected it to a light-plug. When it buzzed, he rubbed it against his face, more in the way of affectionate reassurance than because there was any work for it to do.

"Wonderful things these," he said. "American, of course."

Nobody seemed impressed that he had walked out of the hospital without permission. When he said he was going to sue the Chief Procurer for the return of his wireless set, Jamey told him he could get it back from the insurance, as if it had been burned in the fire. When he said that he was going to sue all the newspapers for defamation of character, Piccione pointed out that not only was he unnamed, but no newspaper had even hinted at his existence. Nobody understood why he should feel aggrieved. Angela Hammock had a far stronger case, but she was a minor.

"I should not have minded if I had been mentioned. It is the innuendo," said Garlick. His eyelashes and hair had been burned, and he was less beautiful than ever, but people agreed that a dinner should be given to celebrate his escape, and Garlick was consoled.

"Who shall we ask?" said Guy. Sally Pratt-Bingham was an obvious candidate. Angela Hammock could come, as she seemed to have had some vicarious share in the adventure.

"But you must make it plain that the party is for me, and Angela is just a guest," said Garlick. Jack Piccione said he didn't want a girl, as he was tired of them, and everybody looked at Sligger.

"Do you want to ask your Anne Etherington?" they asked.

"Goodness, no," said Jamey. "She was all right while she lasted, but one does want a change sometimes. Who else is there?"

"I thought you'd grow out of her," said Garlick. "Weren't you getting anywhere?"

"Of course I was," said Jamey, "but there's no life in her. She's as cold as a fish."

"They're often like that," said Garlick, "when they have got freckles." Anne Etherington, although plain, had no freckles, but Jamey decided then and there that she had.

"There's Phyllis Chinney, if you like them small, Antoinette Ogilvy if you like them large and buxom, Hetty Goyle if you like them dark, Mary Quitch, if you are not choosy." Garlick

77

was showing off. He used to keep a list of girls' names in his room, scored with secret signs.

"Who's Mary Quitch?" asked Jamey. Piccione said he couldn't come if Quitch was going to be there. She gave him the creeps.

"Quitch is just a perfectly ordinary nice, well-adjusted nymphomaniac," said Garlick.

"What about Hetty Goyle?"

"She's all right if you don't mind Negresses. In fact, of course, they're very good in bed."

"You never have, Peter." It was Guy, braver than the rest.

"I never said I had, but how do you know I haven't? Anyway, I was telling Sligger about them. What do you suppose I did for women in Bermuda last year?" They all had a pretty good idea, but there were conventions to be observed.

"Fat, white American millionairesses, I should think," said Piccione with a note of contempt.

"There were those, too," said Garlick generously, "but they were work, not play. One had to let one's hair down sometimes." Everybody was almost certain that Garlick had never kissed anyone, let alone been to bed with a Negress in Bermuda, but conversation had to be made, and unless one made concessions, there would be absolutely nothing to talk about.

"Is Hetty any relation to Stephen Goyle?" asked Jamey.

"First cousin. Nobody can explain why Stephen is so white. Doctors think he must be an albino Negro. In Africa, of course, he would be thought to have magical powers, and they would worship him."

"Not at all," said Piccione, who had been nurtured in the liberal tradition, "a lot of Negroes are just as white as we are."

"Well, Nini certainly wasn't. I'll tell you about her, then, if you don't believe me. She was on the beach at Bermuda, eating a yam." There was a knock on the door. "Damn," said Garlick and opened it. It was very seldom that Anne Etherington knocked. "Well, what do you want?"

"Is Jamey in?" said Anne timidly.

78

"Jamey who?" said Garlick, who did not like to be interrupted.

"Sligger."

"Miss Etherington wishes to know if Mr. Sligger is in," said Garlick from the door.

"No, he isn't," said Jamey.

"You heard," said Garlick.

"Can I go in and see him, please?" said Anne, frightened but firm.

"No you can't," said Garlick. "If he's not in, you obviously can't see him."

"Well, can I come in please, just the same?" said Anne.

"No she bloody well can't," shouted Jamey. "I'm out."

"Very well," said Anne, with quiet dignity.

"I think he may have gone to the Bodleian to do some work," said Garlick, trying to be kind. He did not want to seem too brutal.

"I'll go and have a look," said Anne gratefully.

"What did you want to tell her I had gone to the Bodleian for?" demanded Jamey, when Garlick had shut the door.

"Just to put her off the scent," said Garlick. "She knew perfectly well where you were." He proceeded with his story. Nini had been fascinated by his portable transistor wireless. She had obviously never seen one before. Garlick showed her it and, without actually saying anything, had given her to understand that if she complied with a perfectly simple request he might feel well disposed toward considering the idea of making her a gift of it. Their passion had been consummated under a spreading coconut tree in the afternoon to the scraping of crickets and the distant hum of a deep-sea motor launch.

"Did you give her the wireless?"

"Of course not. I had never promised anything. And afterward, she was so happy and contented that she seemed to forget about it. I don't think she had ever been made love to by a white man before."

79

"Rubbish, it's well known that black men do it far better."
One could dispute details, but never the nub of Garlick's tales.

"That is a popular fallacy. It's just that black women expect more. I ought to know." A short silence followed this statement.

Then Jack Piccione said, "I think that's all wrong."

"What do you mean, wrong?" said Garlick. "I never said I would give her the wireless. In fact I never even mentioned it. She would not have known what to do with it. It was an Omega Pi Omicron, I'll have you know."

"I mean making love to people you do not love. I could not do it."

"Couldn't?" said Garlick, interested.

"Well, I wouldn't. It would be wrong. I dare say I couldn't, either. It would seem so unnatural."

"There's nothing unnatural about it. It's the most natural thing in the world, when you've done it." Garlick did not seem sure of his ground. Sligger and Frazer-Robinson exchanged glances. They knew the rights and wrongs of it all quite well, and so should Garlick, if he were not so advanced. They weren't going to have a moral lecture from Piccione, who was not even a Christian. It would be Sligger's painful duty to inform Brother Richard that Piccione, in whom they had so much hope, believed in free love. That was what the country was coming to.

"I don't think it's any wronger, just because you don't love. I don't see what love has to do with it. If you decide to sleep with a girl you're not married to, it's probably better if you don't love her."

"Exactly," said Jamey. "You don't want to get tied down, unless you're going to marry her anyway. Of course it's wrong, whichever way you look at it. But you must do something sometimes."

"I can't accept that," said Jack. "If it's wrong, you shouldn't do it. But it can't be wrong if you love her, because that's what it's for." Jamey and Guy agreed that this was absolute rubbish, but they did not want to get tied down in a religious argument,

80

which would have been out of place. It was typical of Piccione's hypocrisy to try and justify his self-indulgence, idealize his normal appetites.

"Anyway," said Garlick earnestly, "in Nini's case I really did love her when she was in my arms. Of course I did, or I wouldn't have done what I did." The progressive churchman seemed to get the best of every world. Sligger would have paused to admire it, but the two nauseating images, of Garlick in love and of Garlick holding someone in his arms, usurped further thought. The Negress, he thought, must have been most undiscriminating. Garlick was sure that although he might not be considered handsome, he was attractive to women. Sligger accepted that, and tried to fit himself into the same mold. He knew that he was handsome; he had often been assured so in the past, even if there had not been ugly episodes to confirm it. But was he attractive to women? He knew that he did not fit into the Garlick mold, but he rather fancied he was. Time would tell.

Anne Etherington left Jamey's room in a daze of misery. She knew it was his voice which had shouted out, and she could not think why she was being treated like this. Quite suddenly, she seemed to have lost her attraction for him. It might have been her clothes, but she had chosen them with the greatest care. Perhaps he did not like green as a color. But in her heart of hearts she knew that it was something more fundamental. It was herself. She would gladly have changed to anything, if she had known for sure what Jamey would like. In the meantime, he had cast her off and done her an injustice.

With the cold air of the Beaufort Quad, common sense returned. She would go to the Bodleian and make sure he was not there, so that he would not have a leg to stand on when confronted with his bad behavior. She did not know what revenge she would take when he was made to admit his wickedness. She thought she might forgive him. In fact she knew she would. In her mind's eye, she could see his relieved face, when she gave his hand an understanding squeeze. All lovers had quarrels. She just wished she did not feel so miserable.

The Bodleian was almost full. People sprawled over the tables. There was an overwhelming smell of fried eggs. She went to the librarian and asked if Mr. James Sligger, of Godolphin, had been in. He said that no such person was a member of the library. That settled it. She took out a book on sex from the biology section, and strode purposefully with it under her arm back to her cozy little nook in St. Rachel's. In the room next door, which was Deirdre Black's, she thought she heard the bed creak.

"How absolutely disgusting and filthy," she thought, and threw the window open. Later it got cold, and she closed it again, and sitting by the gas fire she tried to make sense of her book, which was called *Sexual Cycles*, but it might have been Greek for all the help it offered.

"Unaccustomed as I am to public speaking," said Garlick; and Piccione laughed. The idea that any friend of his should be unaccustomed to public speaking struck him as infinitely droll. "No, I really am," said Garlick, getting sincere, "and all I should like to say is thank you all for coming to celebrate my release from the terrible clutches of the National Health, coupled with the name of absent friends and Miss Angela Hammock—" loud and prolonged applause—"who although not absent herself has decided to grace our presence with her company in this noble gathering from all over the civilized world and many savage tribes. Miss Hetty Goyle, who has lost neither her beauty nor her charm in the ravages of Oxford life, nor her virtue, as we hope Miss Hammock hasn't, despite what the newspapers would have us believe to the contrary, without mentioning any names, of which Mr. Jamey Sligger is an excellent example. Without his presence I may say we ourselves would be the sufferers. It is also extremely nice to see Mr. Guy Frazer-Robinson"—getting sincere again—"our host this evening.

Among the other names I should mention, Miss Sarah Pratt-Bingham, whose beauty is only exceeded by her wit, and Mr. Jack Piccione, the well-known undergraduate, with whose father's political opinions some of us may disagree and others find themselves in complete agreement."

Sligger's port was beginning to cloy, and he felt he could quite well have done without the last course, which was called a Scotch woodcock and turned out to be a great disappointment. He called for brandy and said:

"Ladies and Gentlemen, I should like to propose the toast of Love. It is love which inspires us to rejoice tonight in the recovery of Peter Garlick from his unfortunate affliction. ["Steady on," shouted someone.] It is love which is the most important thing in the world. We have come to Oxford to learn about life, and love is the most important lesson we have to learn in life, as Miss Hetty Goyle has just been explaining to me. As I can't remember any of the other rubbish she talked, I shall now sit down, with this important quotation in mind, 'Love is the quintessence of Experience,' by Hetty Goyle."

Sally Pratt-Bingham rocked back in her chair with laughter, and started singing "I Love a Lassie" in a most engaging way. She had a soft, sweet little voice, and when her face was concentrating it looked quite beautiful. Nobody in that party seemed to have a care, except Miss Goyle, who sat with her mouth open, thinking. Sligger rather regretted asking her, but he supposed he needed a change. She would certainly not do for a guest in the vacations. It looked as if he would have to ask Anne Etherington, which he did not really mind, as he knew, in his present charitable state, that he liked her a lot.

Hetty was still working out the implications of the speech. It really did not matter whether she took it in good part or not, as she was the most ponderous, humorless person he had met, and had only her sex to recommend her. He had really been much better off with Anne Etherington, and he felt a twinge of remorse. But he did not suppose it would be very difficult to make friends with her again, even after his cruel treatment.

"Ladies and Gentlemen." Jack Piccione was not even going to pretend to be unaccustomed to public speaking. He paused to collect a napkin as if it contained his notes. There was a respectful hush. "I wish to propose the toast of innocence. Although, I fear, innocence has little application to the assembled company, we should none of us forget the days of our innocence. If we can truly say that we are happier people having lost it, I can only say that our standards must be wrong. What makes a kitten so infinitely more endearing than a cat?"

"Hear, hear," said Garlick, who thought there was a dirty reference somewhere.

"What makes the sparkle in the eye of a child so much prettier than the avaricious gleam in the eye of an actress?"

"Steady on, now, easy there."

"Before we lose it, we should consider what we are losing. Having lost it, we should not think of it as a discreditable episode in our past, but as something precious to be savored. Above all, it is a quality to be admired in others, not despised. I should like to propose the toast of everyone in Oxford who preserves his innocence."

They all drank dutifully. In the chatter afterward Sally Pratt-Bingham said to Guy, "What was all that about?" And Garlick was heard to remark: "I think Jack went a bit far that time. I expect he has had too much to drink."

Anne Etherington sat at her desk and knew she must be sensible. She had hundreds of things to do and no time to waste on self-pity, but even as she started sorting survey returns and correcting the spelling mistakes in the typescript of one of her notices to go on the J.C.R. notice board her eyes filled with tears and she knew she was not concentrating. Philip's new statistics from South Africa, of over a million people imprisoned, five hundred being tortured to death every week, ought to take her mind off her own small troubles, but she found that even the figures from South Africa had lost their terrible fascination. They were not much up on last week's anyway.

She lay on her bed, and, by force of habit, started to blow bubbles. Everybody knew that Anne Etherington was sensible. Some hideous inner compulsion always drove her to be sensible against her natural feelings. How could she explain to Jamey about her softer side, her tender yearnings, when they only talked about South Africa and allied subjects? If only he was as sensible, she could have explained her inclination sensibly, and they could have set about having an affair in the most sensible way possible. But things did not work like that. Why could not he charge into her room and take her as she lay on her bed blowing bubbles? She stopped blowing them.

The gas fire, hissing away in the corner, no longer suggested a babbling brook where lovers haunt, but its conspiratorial whisper had all the odious intimacy of the Serpent in the Garden of Eden. Anne Etherington was alone with her soul. Soon she would have to attend a meeting, organize the junior cell of the St. Rachel's J.C.R. nuclear committee into some vestige of discipline, make representations, attend demonstrations, sign petitions, call the world to order. There was no comfort in that, when her softer side lay bleeding. Nobody would recognize in this wild, romantic thing that lay alone the intelligent, bustling girl they thought was Anne Etherington. The nuclear committee would manage without her. All that really mattered in the world was that Anne should love and be loved.

"She bloody well can't come in. I'm out," Jamey had said, but it was Anne who was out, alone in the world outside Jamey's room, with nobody to know that her heart was broken, that it had even been touched. Through the daze of her misery she heard the gas fire whisper, and crept with infinite slowness on her hands and knees over the cocoa-stained rug in front of the fire.

PART TWO

Chapter 9

"You might have told me you weren't going to bring your so-called girl friend here," said Mrs. Sligger. "The battles I had with your father persuading him to allow it! I suppose you didn't think we were good enough for your Oxford friends. Well, you must tell that to your father, and try to get him to understand." Mrs. Sligger was seriously piqued. First Jamey expected her to turn the house into a brothel to suit his convenience, next she wasn't even allowed to know what was going on. The fact that Jamey had never mentioned bringing a friend home did not impinge. She had told him he could.

Jamey, too, was piqued. The fact that Anne Etherington had tragically taken her own life the day before he intended to ask her home was not his fault. Guy and he had decided in private conversation that none of the blame for her death rested with him. It was her own fault if she had misinterpreted his customary affability. But he had still not quite got over the shock of the news.

"I suppose you had a quarrel," said Mrs. Sligger. "That's always the way it is. Well, I don't care whether you make it up or not. It's just puppy love, you know. One day you'll realize it. You're not old enough for the real thing, even if you ever will be. But I don't think you younger generation understand about love, or ever will. You just associate it with sex, with getting your greens. That's all you ever think of."

"Not at all," said Jamey.

"All right, then," said Mrs. Sligger triumphantly. She had

89

obviously been thinking this one up during the term. "You just tell me what love is. In three plain words."

"Love," said Jamey, "is the quintessence of experience."

"What?"

"The quintessence of experience."

Mrs. Sligger was angry and puzzled. Jamey reflected it was the sort of rubbish she might have talked herself if she had known what quintessence meant. "Experience, exactly, there you are. Experience and experiments is all you young people, you famous younger generation we're all supposed to know such a lot about, ever think of. One of these days your experiments will land you in trouble, my boy. Then don't you come running to me as if I hadn't warned you. Experiments indeed! Well, you go away and experiment with someone else for a change, not with me, if that's all you're after. Poor girl, I'm not surprised she wouldn't come and stay with us."

As Jamey walked away, he wondered how his mother would measure up to the standards of intellectual conversation at Oxford. Nobody, not even Philip Fringe, he felt sure, could beat her in an argument. She had a unique quality of unreason coupled with a robust pugnacity which made any argument seem to be the irrefutable, conclusive proof of her own point of view. But he had every reason to be grateful to her, as she was not slow to remind him, for having conceived him, nourished him and kept him on for so many years. She could easily not have conceived him, have exposed him at birth, or turned him out at some tender age. He supposed she would go to heaven when she died, but it was an academic point, as she had many years to live. In any case, he saw no reason to approve of someone the more because he, or she, was going to heaven, although Mrs. Sligger had assured him that if anyone deserved a reward after all she had been through, she did. It was a pity, really, that non-Christians like his mother were allowed in heaven, as it would certainly detract from the joy of it if ever he succeeded in getting there. In any case, she would look rather silly, having resolutely declared all her life that it did not exist, and there was nothing more important in the world or outside it than her own love, which she took so seriously, although it was hard to see where it was directed. Perhaps he was the target of it all, as she sometimes implied. Jamey squirmed with embarrassment, and secretly hoped that his mother would go to hell. He was glad that poor Anne Etherington had not been exposed to her withering scorn.

Anne's passing had merited a brief announcement in most of the national newspapers, which Mrs. Sligger obviously had not noticed or, if she had, did not connect with her son's "so-called girl friend." In Oxford, as always on these occasions, it had caused a greater stir. The front page of *Cherwell*, the university newspaper, carried a large picture of Brian Greaves, who was described as the man in Anne's life. He attributed her death to worry about the Government's delay in raising students' grants and recognizing married students. "The reason so many students have to live together out of wedlock is because they simply cannot afford to get married," said Brian, although that of course did not apply to Anne, who had lived a chaste and celibate life in St. Rachel's. "But it was worry for the future that got her down. The guilt for her death rests squarely on the shoulders of the Minister for Education, Sir Edgar Piccione, the Home Secretary, the Government as a whole, and Mrs. Agnus Price-Williams, Principal of St. Rachel's, for her persistent refusal to allow men visitors in the college after 10:30."

A small picture of Mrs. Price-Williams hanging out the washing in her Cumnor home was accompanied by the information that she intended to hold an inquiry into the causes of Anne's death. An even smaller picture on an inside page was unrecognizable, but it was captioned "Philip Fringe." His explanation of the tragedy was that Anne wished to draw attention to present conditions in South Africa. The editorial, entitled "Another St. Rachel's Tragedy," blamed Sir Edgar Piccione for doing nothing about South Africa, the local M.P. for not looking into Anne's case before the tragedy, the city authorities for not inspecting conditions inside St. Rachel's and laying down minimum standards, Mrs. Price-Williams for discouraging sex, "as if it was something Victorian the modern student should be afraid of," and the university proctors for their censorship, which might have prevented Anne from saying something important. It called for a Government inquiry to look into the matter, at which the Students' Council could be represented.

Jamey could not help feeling it was all as Anne would have wished.

Mrs. Price-Williams was tired. "We have discovered the girl had not been tampered with. It just shows what rubbish these people talk. Sex had nothing to do with it. She owed the Junior Common Room seven and sixpence, but her bank account had forty pounds, so it does not look as if it was money. Her work was not going well at all. She seemed to take no interest in it— I am afraid that is the root of the trouble. I don't see how she could have had time for work, being surrounded all the time by these young men. Who on earth is Brian Greaves? I have never heard of him."

"I think he was at the party we went to in Godolphin, given by one of my young men, Sligger."

"I remember. When you were so amusing about a bottle of whisky on the table, although I don't think half of them understood what on earth you were talking about. You were in very good form that evening. I wish Anne had seen more of your Godolphin friends. They are much more Anne's class of people."

"To talk of Anne's class of people," said Mr. Price-Williams, mournfully, "presupposes the existence of Anne. Without Anne, talk of any class of people peculiar to her is meaningless. Whatever *did* hold them together in that class can do so no longer, although they may have other qualities in common. But those would be irrelevant to their grouping as 'Anne's class.'"

"You're right, of course, Agnus. Now I must see about collecting her things."

"That, too, would be a useful occupation only if any of the

things you collected could still be said to belong to her. Whatever assortment of objects could formerly be grouped together under the collective heading of 'Anne's things' must now be assembled under some other name, if at all."

"You mean you don't want me to go?" Their eyes met, and Mrs. Price-Williams melted. "Goo, goo," she said, "who's my pet pony?"

Mr. Price-Williams whinnied, and pawed the ground. "I'se a small baby," he said.

"You're my little baby gee-gee."

"I'se a great fierce wuff-wuff." Mr. Price-Williams got on his hands and knees and said, "Wuff."

"Look, wuff-wuff has had kittens." Mrs. Price-Williams fetched a small Teddy bear from the drawer where it was kept for these occasions, and placed it under her husband. "Kitten has been naughty," said Mr. Price-Williams. "Papa's not pleased. Wuff."

"Say you're sorry, kitten."

"Kitten not sorry. Kitten just 'tending to be sorry."

"What's the kitten done?"

"Kitten has wet the floor in the drawing room."

"Naughty kitten, say you're sorry to Papa."

"I'se a great, big, fierce wuff-wuff."

DEAR BROTHER RICHARD,

I am sorry not to have written for so long, but I have been very busy with the end of term and everything. Oxford is quite interesting, but I am afraid the sense of moral awareness is not high, as must be expected nowadays. Foul talk is pretty widespread, and people have been committing, among other things, suicide, as you may have read. One point about this last one, which was not mentioned, is that the girl concerned is thought to have done it to draw attention to the present situation in South Africa. We know that one may not do evil that good may come of it, but she was not a Christian and probably didn't. I think that probably makes it less bad.

On the first count, I heard MacLaughlin and a friend talking in a pub, and although I could not catch the words, I was pretty sure they were indulging in foul talk. I pretended not to see him. I did not see Pratt-Bingham in church for the last two weeks, but MacLaughlin was there, although he did not seem to be paying much attention. Many other people go in for foul talk, and seem to think it is the normal thing.

Do you remember the boy who was expelled from Cleeve for being vile? I don't think there is much of that sort of thing, but quite a lot of the other, which some people seem to take for granted. Father Potinue sets a good example by refusing to have any dirty books in his Christian library, although Peter Garlick, whom I mentioned who comes from Stockton and seems to be well up in the latest ideas, said we should know what we are combating. What do you think?

I am afraid I did something of which you may not approve. Philip, my brother, is nearly finishing his time and is now allowed a wireless set, so I sent him one. Do you think this was wrong? I know he should be punished for what he did, and I have no business to interfere, but as he is allowed one, and as we are encouraged to visit the imprisoned, if not give them wirelesses, I thought there was no harm in it. I hope I have not done wrong.

With a bit of luck, the moral climate at Oxford may improve next term.

Yours sincerely,
J. SLIGGER.

DEAR BROTHER RICHARD,

Life goes on much as usual here. The general moral tone at the moment is surprisingly high. One of the men, a "trusty" on fifteen years, said the recent intake was of as high a quality as he could remember.

I wonder if by the way you have any spare wireless sets at Cleeve? I am allowed one now, as they can think of nothing against me, to prevent it. Even one of the warders, called Joe Kraczitsky, said I was coming on.

I hope all goes well at Cleeve.

Yours sincerely,
PHILIP (SLIGGER)

94

P.S. The wireless really is most important, as they say without it I may go to the bad again. Of course I would try not to, but every helping hand from outside helps a little.

DEAR JAMEY,

Your wireless set was no good as it arrived bust, but still I appreciate the thought. Where did you get it from? It looked quite good.

When I come out I want my pyjamas put ready, a bottle of whisky on the table and a nice long rest. They work you quite hard here, keeping on at you the whole time. A chap here says it's perfectly legal signing someone else's name on a check provided there isn't a twopenny stamp. If I'd known that I could have saved myself a lot of trouble. Another chap told me how to use a phone box without putting any money in, but I can't entrust it to paper, as they can get you for knowing it, even if you never do a thing. Keep cheerful, and remember the bottle of whisky.

Yours, etc.,
PHIL.

The Oxford term opened without any noticeable improvement in the moral climate. Sligger fancied that he and his friends in the Godolphin set had lost something since Anne's death. Perhaps it was their innocence. The soul seemed to have left their endless conversations about Garlick's amorous adventures in Bermuda, Piccione's theories on love, Sligger's own small fiction, meticulously invented during the vacation, of a love affair with Miss Arckwright, the daughter of a neighboring farmer. He had to let Guy in on his secret, as he knew the Arckwrights, and it removed much of the fun of invention when Guy knew that it was all untrue. "I jumped her, of course. But she was expecting it, was not in the least surprised, and responded."

"What did she say afterwards?" demanded Garlick.

"I can't really remember much. We just talked about this and that. Then she fell into a deep sleep."

"Yes, they often do. Funny you should have noticed that."

Yet there was no thrill in it. Something had been lost. Perhaps their invention was poorer, perhaps there was no longer the expectancy of a new revelation round the corner, perhaps they had exhausted all the variations. All that had happened was the death of a girl one of them knew, but it had taken all the fun out of conversation. Guy felt Jamey was holding something back, Garlick seemed jealous of Jamey, as if Anne's death was in some way a feather in his cap. Piccione disapproved of the whole incident and did not like to hear it discussed. Goyle was rather a mysterious figure these days. He seemed more deeply involved with Fringe and the intellectuals than before, and only occasionally came to Guy's rooms. He seemed to regard them all as more immature than ever and spent long hours bustling round the colleges. Garlick said he was soliciting for his cousin, Hetty, but most of them accepted that he was trying to arrange some revolution in thought, or possibly a circle of friends who would listen to recitations of his prose poems, which had been a source of great embarrassment to them all when they used to see him more often.

Only Garlick had pretended to take them seriously and used to maintain that Goyle had, if not the seeds of genius, at least a formidable ability which, unless discouraged, might present a challenge to their own work, when produced, at a later date. Few people at Oxford in those days supposed that they were going to be anything but writers when they left.

"Goyle certainly has a mastery of words which, if facile, is still effective occasionally," he used to say. "Of course, I don't think he'll ever get very far, as he hasn't the ability for sustained effort."

One of Goyle's prose poems had gone something like this: "You enter Oxford as one might enter a dark crystal, pale and refracted. Until the pristine flash of greater, inner perception comes, all is as in a mist or fog. How can I get out of this dark crystal, one thinks. Then, corkscrew-like, come the sensations, falling on one's inner ear. As one settles in, so does the dust settle, the sea subside. Things take a new perspective. You kick your feet, you are free. Only when the evening sun goes down, when you have traveled a long way round the plain, do you realize that Oxford is empty of men, that you are in a great void."

"I think that's jolly good," said Sligger warmly.

"I like the bit about the corkscrew," said Garlick, "but I can't see what you mean about Oxford being empty of men. I always think there are a sight too many of them, and we could do with a few more women."

"No," said Goyle, "I think Jamey's right. I think it is trying to sum up the essential loneliness of the artist in Oxford. I think it is trying to say something—this is only what I think—that we may all have missed, except possibly Jamey. What do you think, Jamey?" Goyle was admirably detached about his own works. As he pointed out, it was not his task to interpret them. That was a job best left to critics.

"I think you're quite right," said Sligger. "Of course the loneliness of the artist is quintessential, wherever he is, but I think at Oxford it may be something to do with the absence of women. The great thing for the artist is that he must never let himself get tied down."

"Exactly," said Goyle. "I think Jamey has the best idea of what it is like to be an artist."

In Goyle's absence, the Godolphin set talked about sex in a desultory way. Sligger had the feeling that they were all waiting for something to happen, as if last term's fire and the suicide of Anne Etherington had opened new vistas.

"It's not so much that I mind the idea, but one must keep up appearances, and many of the more forward-looking undergraduates would be terribly shocked if they knew we had not taken precautions. They seem so elementary, but just that afternoon the shops happened to be shut. If Deirdre had a baby, it wouldn't do her name or mine any good at all. I don't think she would mind so much, but it would make the whole of Oxford look silly if people thought we did not know how to handle these things." Goyle was speaking more urgently than usual, and his urgency created a certain sales resistance.

"I know we have the good name of Oxford to consider," said Fringe, "and certainly I always approve of terminated pregnancies wherever possible, except, of course, where the girl is not pregnant, which might seem the best solution. But eighty pounds seems an exorbitant sum for what is, after all, a trifling service. There is really no excuse nowadays for not putting them on the Health Service. I think that might be the best line. Let things take their course, and let people see that the blame for this unwanted child rests fair and square on the Government. On the Ministers of Health and Education, on Sir Edgar Piccione, the Home Secretary, for persistently ignoring representations from the Students' Council, on Mrs. Price-Williams . . ."

Goyle cut short the familiar litany. "But by publicizing the fact, we should do irreparable harm to the good name of Oxford. People already think we are a backward-looking, reactionary mass no longer having any relevance in the twentieth century. How could we show our faces in the Students' Council, among all those chaps from Nottingham and Keele, if they knew we did not even have the resources to arrange a simple termination of pregnancy?"

"Or that we did not even have the resources to make it unnecessary," said Fringe spitefully. Goyle hung his head. He had sinned.

Fringe relented. "Well, there is five pounds ten in the Nuclear Fighting Fund, then Universal Peace and South Africa Defense could make that up to ten pounds. Anne Etherington had about fifteen pounds for general emergencies, but I don't know how we will get that out of her bank account. I think we will have to approach Mrs. Price-Williams. We have no time to lose."

"Good, you see to Mrs. Price-Williams, and I'll see to the other end of things."

"No, I think you had better see Mrs. Price-Williams. She likes people from Godolphin, and I have crossed swords with her once this term over that thing I wrote about Anne, saying she was trying to draw attention to conditions in South Africa. She sent for me and gave me an hour's lecture about irresponsible and callous behavior. I didn't say it was she who was being irresponsible and callous wearing blinkers so that she cannot see what is happening in the world outside St. Rachel's and her cozy little nest in Cumnor."

"No, of course not," said Goyle hastily. "Poor Anne, I am sure she would have approved of this. Let us call it the Anne Etherington Memorial Fund."

Deirdre Black sat knitting in her tiny, ill-favored cubbyhole in St. Rachel's. She was knitting a pair of mittens for a baby, and if anyone asked her, she would say it was for her cousin who was happily married and expecting her third baby at home in Surrey. She even told Stephen that, who had promised to look after her and see that everything was painless and swift, but if Stephen bungled it, or could not raise the money in time, or even decided he was too busy with other things, then she might as well be prepared.

On the shelf was Dr. Benjamin Spock's book on baby care. She would have a lot of things to buy if Stephen did not manage to do anything about it. Her mind could comprehend the idea of Stephen doing something about it, but then went no further. But she was a brave girl, and could probably bear up to whatever it was that had to be done.

She would need a layette, whatever that was, some zinc-oxide ointment, to prevent sores on the baby's bottom, a kidney-shaped bowl, a nursing chair, baby's powder, soap and hairbrush, a dozen nappies and two strong safety pins of a certain pattern, and a baby's bath. Where on earth could she get a baby's bath? Deirdre, having no younger sisters or brothers, had never seen one and was not sure that they had existed in her day. No doubt Stephen would know about them. He would provide.

One baby's mitten, almost finished, struck her as the sweetest thing she had ever seen. She held it to her cheek, but there was no time to be sentimental. She wished Stephen would come and reassure her, hold her in his skinny arms and say she was safe, nothing mattered, he would look after her. But there was no time to be sentimental, and she resumed her knitting with a frown of concentration. When Stephen did come, he would have some news, but she was not sure what she wanted to hear. If only Stephen would tell her he loved her and felt for her, she would knit him the wooliest and cuddliest romper suit in the world.

Goyle was finding that the obligations of parenthood placed an unbearable strain on his time. "I want you to meet Deirdre, Jamey, because I think you and she will get on well together. You have both of you seen a lot of the world, and have much in common. I dare even say she can show you a few things you don't know already."

Jamey felt that was more than likely. He was eager to meet the notorious Deirdre Black, although a bit frightened. Perhaps she would not take to him, would guess at his inexperience, would make a fool of him. Perhaps there were certain rituals to be observed of which Jamey was ignorant. "I should very much like to meet her," he said, "and I dare say she knows a lot of things I don't." He spoke as a connoisseur.

"You may find she's a bit preoccupied with other things at the moment, so you mustn't try and rush things. Quite frankly, I would be grateful if you could take her off my hands for a bit. You, of all people, know how women can get. It is for her own good as much as for mine, as there isn't much point in her seeing too much of me, even if I didn't have this thing about not being tied down."

Jamey felt he was prepared to risk being tied down with Deirdre Black. There would be a great deal more point to it than being tied down with Anne Etherington. He liked the idea of having someone he could visit at any time, whenever the inclination arose, but he admired Goyle tremendously for the way in which he seemed to have outgrown even this stage. "You can trust me," he said.

Mrs. Price-Williams thought the idea of an Anne Etherington Memorial Fund most unsuitable. "It will do nothing but harm," she said, "and encourage other girls to behave in this silly sort of way. As for the money in her bank account, that is nothing to do with me. You will have to write to her parents if your society has any claim on it, although I must say you have not made it plain which society this is. I can only give you her parents' address. I am glad, of course, you are taking an interest in her, and only wish she had more to do with your sort of people before it was too late."

Goyle had been particularly convincing, and Mrs. Price-Williams did not want to lose her reputation for good sense among the privileged undergraduates of Godolphin.

"Although, officially, I can make no recognition of your fund, I should not like you to think I was completely stony-hearted." Mrs. Price-Williams felt a greater degree of guilt for Anne's death than she would ever acknowledge. Perhaps, if only she had been more *understanding* about Anne's failure to turn in an essay . . . "Therefore, I intend to make a strictly unofficial gesture, on condition that you tell absolutely nobody." She opened her purse and took out five shillings. "I don't wish to know anything more about the Fund. This is not given by the Principal of St. Rachel's, but just by an anonymous friend of Anne's."

Goyle pocketed the two half crowns. "Thank you very much indeed," he said. "Anne would have been deeply touched, if she could have been here. As you do not wish to hear how the money will be spent, I shall not tell you, but I can only say it will be in a manner of which Anne would have approved."

Mrs. Price-Williams beamed. Goyle smirked. As he left the college, he reflected that she was really quite a good sport. As he walked down the Turl on his way back to Godolphin, he reflected that he had no cigarettes, and went into a shop to buy some. As he smoked the first, the gift of an anonymous friend of Anne Etherington, he reflected that he had much to thank Mrs. Price-Williams for. Her name, discreetly placed, on the subscription list would make a lot of difference.

Fringe had outlined the situation. "Well, there we are," he said. "I think Goyle deserves everything he would get in the normal course of things, and I can't say that Miss Black has ever used her influence in Oxford to a single good purpose. But I still think we should help them. Even if we did not know either of them and the University's good name was not at stake, I do not feel that ordinary termination of pregnancy is a thing we can afford to discourage nowadays. People like Goyle who blithely set about taking risks might never have heard of the population explosion. We have, and we must act."

"I agree," said Greaves. "Eighty pounds is an awful lot of money, but we'll get it somehow."

Miss Hammock looked distressed. "But are we sure that Deirdre wants a termination of pregnancy?" she asked.

Fringe gave her a scornful look. "Even if she doesn't, that is no business of hers. She has let the matter get out of her hands now, by her own carelessness and ignorance, and we must look after it. She may be so utterly worthless she does not care for the good name of Oxford, or of her so-called lover. She might be content to have all the fun of having a baby, which is after all the only thing that women want, and she might not care about the consequences for Stephen Goyle, but we can't let her get away with that. She has done us all enough harm as it is. Wherever we go, we would be pointed out as the people who don't know about the ordinary precautions, or as people who don't dare take the necessary steps. And for Stephen, life would be unendurable."

"He's right," said Greaves. "We can't let Deirdre be as selfish as that."

"You can't do these things against their will," said English. "Anyway, who says she doesn't want a termination in the normal way?"

102

"Exactly," said Fringe. "Now we must decide how to raise funds."

"Goyle could give a recitation of prose poems, and I could accompany him on my guitar," said English.

"Yes," said Fringe.

"We could have a C.N.D. Demonstration and whip-round," said Greaves.

"Yes," said Fringe.

"I suppose I could mobilize the women for a sale of work like Anne used to," said Angela.

"Yes," said Fringe. The others realized that something was missing.

"We could have the usual round of socials," said Angela.

"Yes," said Fringe. "But I feel that this calls for something more. After all, we are not only collecting for a good cause, but it is also a memorial to Anne Etherington. I think we should give a full-scale party and invite everybody. After all, it is as much their concern as ours. We will ask the heads of all the colleges, distinguished people in politics, the arts, business. The only way to get things done is to aim at the sky. Anne Etherington, after all, was not just anyone. She was the first undergraduate to lay down her life in the cause of justice in South Africa. Nobody will dare refuse." There was a respectful hush.

"They won't come," said Bill English.

Chapter 10

Mrs. Sligger had taken a bold step. So bold, in fact, that she could not help being a bit frightened by its possible consequences. In submitting her name as Liberal candidate for a

Welsh constituency notorious for the virulence of its Labour sympathies she had merely been making a gesture in support of the sincerity of an argument she had been holding at the Arckwrights' and expected to hear no more of it. But a respectful letter had arrived that morning to say she had been accepted. It was signed Joy Biskett, and informed her that as she was the first Liberal candidate to stand in Llanwtyth for over twenty years, she would be expected to supply most of the funds of the newly formed Liberal executive for Llanwtyth of which Miss Biskett was the acting chairman and secretary. They hoped to hold a Liberal ball later in the winter, and would much appreciate Mrs. Sligger's support. She enclosed a banker's order, a blank check form and some nomination papers left over from the last election, in which Mrs. Sligger could see she was supported by Miss Biskett, Miss Ogilvy-Jones and two Misses Price.

It seemed that in addition to the official Labour candidate, two independent Labour candidates and a Communist one were standing. Miss Biskett hoped that the electorate would be so confused that many would vote Liberal in error. "In any case you can be assured of the votes of myself and the other members of the Liberal executive for Llanwtyth. We think it is right that we should be allowed to exercise our democratic right of voting for the party of our choice. Nobody here understands that, of course, and it is no good pretending that your interference will not present problems. But we shall support you wherever the need arises."

Mrs. Sligger's immediate problem was to tell her husband. Then she must learn Welsh. Miss Biskett said very few people in Llanwtyth spoke or understood Welsh, but they had the greatest respect for anyone who did. If she sent her election address, Miss Biskett would have it translated for her at the British Travel and Holidays Association office in Regent Street, where there was a poet who translated things in his spare time. Few of the other candidates could say more than "Good morning" in Welsh. People in Llanwtyth had the greatest respect for babies. Did Mrs. Sligger have a baby available? If not, perhaps she could arrange to have one before the campaign started. It would be the greatest help. Otherwise, Miss Biskett would have considered standing herself.

Liberalism obviously involved more than she had reckoned for, but Mrs. Sligger was game for anything except the last demand. It seemed she would have to teach the backward people of Llanwtyth the facts of life, a duty she did not find at all uncongenial, and one that was inextricably bound up with the Liberal cause. Jamey would help her and Philip, who would be coming out of prison during the next vacation and would need something to keep him busy. She looked forward to the battle with her husband. Perhaps it would give him a glimpse of all she had suffered being married to him. First, she must write some letters.

The film, for some reason, was in Swedish. Deirdre let Sligger hold her hand, as if it was the normal way to watch a film in Swedish. Her hand was dry and cool, Jamey's hot and clammy. Occasionally he wiped it on his shirt. Goyle had said he must not try to hurry things, but he thought he was making excellent progress. If only she would stop talking about Goyle. They had come to the film because Goyle had said it should be seen.

"Apparently it's not a good film, but one should have seen it," said Deirdre. Jamey knew perfectly well that when they told Goyle they had seen it, he would take it as a sign of immaturity that they had been to such a bad film, which he had evaluated some time ago.

"Stephen said he'd take me to it," said Deirdre, "but of course he's seen it already, and he has lots of other things to do." She glanced at Sligger, trying to decide whether he knew about what was keeping Stephen busy.

"He's probably quite wrong about the film," said Jamey. "I don't think he has much judgment."

Deirdre smiled. It was a sweet, sad smile. "He says it is full of dramatic flaws, but if one has not seen it, one is in no position to see what is happening in the cinema that needs correcting. It is a serious attempt, he says, but it just doesn't quite come off."

Much as it went against the grain, Sligger felt he agreed wholeheartedly with Goyle's assessment. He did not know what they were saying, but if their conversation bore any relation to the subtitles it was of an inconceivable banality. "Of course, it's much better if you understand the original Swedish," Goyle had said, hinting that he could. "These things never come out properly in translation."

It was not about any of the things Sligger was prepared to recognize as high-brow: nuclear disarmament, the crimes of the Church in Sicily, the working classes, misunderstood youth, South Africa. It seemed to be about the soul, which was not a proper subject for a film. He felt he was gaining nothing of value, as it had already been dismissed as intellectually unsound, and Sligger did not feel he had anything to add to that.

"Shall we go?" he whispered to Deirdre.

"If you want. I think it is quite interesting." Jamey thought "interesting" was the last adjective to apply to it; "compelling," perhaps; "stark," "uncompromising," "bold," "realistic"—there was a whole set of epithets which were applied to this sort of rubbish, but nobody had ever pretended it was interesting before.

"What do you think it is all about?" he whispered.

"The girl can't make up her mind."

"What about? Whether to put the soup on the stove or not?"

"Whether to obey the man, or strike out on her own."

"Oh I see. I didn't realize that. That's jolly interesting."

"Do you mind?" said an angry, loud, aggressive voice behind his back. Jamey looked behind him at a bearded, duffel-coated figure which was leaning forward threateningly.

"Hello, MacLaughlin," he said. "I didn't know you came to films much."

106

"When I do, I expect to see them," said MacLaughlin at the top of his voice so that everyone could hear. "I don't mind you two making love in front of me, provided you don't start shouting about it."

"Sh," said everybody.

Jamey thought MacLaughlin was being intolerably offensive. "The day you get anyone to make love to you, that will be something to shout about," he said, no less loudly.

"Sh," said everybody.

"I don't happen to believe in making love in public," shouted MacLaughlin, "and when I do it, I don't choose the chief prostitute of Oxford to do it with."

"All right," said the commissionaire, "out."

"Who, me?" said Jamey.

"Out," said the commissionaire.

"All right," said Jamey, "I wasn't going to stay anyway. Filthy bloody film, and there are too many homosexuals in the cinema for my liking."

"That'll do," said the commissionaire. "And the young lady." When they were outside, leaving MacLaughlin very smug and looking round for praise, the man said, "Now just suppose you come to my office and give me your name."

"John MacLaughlin," said Sligger, "and if you want to know the girl's name it is Hetty Goyle."

"We're not interested in her," said the man. "What college are you from?"

"I don't know," said Sligger. "How on earth do you expect me to know a thing like that? I think it's called St. Bede's or something."

"Teddy Hall," said Deirdre. "He comes from St. Edmund's Hall."

"That's it," said Jamey, "St. Edmund's Hall. Bloody silly name for a silly, common little college."

"That'll do," said the man. "Now just suppose you leave this cinema quietly, and don't make any fuss, and don't try coming back here never again."

107

"You can't keep me out. I'm a member of the public."

"You'd be surprised what we can do, young man. If you want to come back, you must apply in writing to the manager, after a period of time has elapsed. Then he may allow you, or he may not, as he sees fit, depending on circumstances. But don't try creeping in. I shall be watching for you, and then you'll be in serious trouble."

After they had left, Jamey said, "I never knew you knew MacLaughlin."

"I don't really," said Deirdre.

"How did you know he was in Teddy Hall, of all bloody ridiculous places?"

"He tried to pick me up. I think he thought I was good for a quick lay, or something." Jamey wondered what she supposed he thought she was good for. MacLaughlin had obviously been unsubtle in his approach, as one might expect.

"Dirty brute," he said.

"I rather agree," said Deirdre. "I object to people thinking I am just something to be used."

Sligger wondered if she was getting at him. "I don't think that," he said. Deirdre smiled. She had a sweet, sad smile. Jamey thought how much she must have been used, and felt protective. Their adventure with the apelike commissionaire had created a bond. He was now on her side against the people who wanted to use her.

"Stephen said he might call in at St. Rachel's and leave a message," she said. They went to St. Rachel's, but there was no message.

"I think Stephen may just be trying to use you," said Jamey, getting bold. Deirdre's smile was even sadder.

"Don't say that, please. I think Stephen and I know each other just a little too well for that. Tell him I looked for a message. I don't think I'll come out to dinner, as I'm not feeling very hungry. In fact I feel slightly sick. I expect it was the cinema. Tell Stephen if he cares to call before locking-up time I shall be in all evening."

Really, thought Sligger, her preoccupation with Goyle was morbid. It was one of the very few things he did not like about her. He could tell her a few things about Goyle which would soon make her see through him, but some remnant of a schoolboy feeling for male solidarity prevented him. After all, he was as much in Goyle's confidence as in Deirdre's, and he'd told Goyle some things which would be most embarrassing if repeated. The girl would realize in time that her precious Stephen did not want to be tied down, then she would come to him for use afterward. But he could not help feeling that she was being extremely unintelligent.

"Well, what do you expect me to do about it?" demanded Guy. "I am not going to help you procure an abortion."

"It is not an abortion," said Goyle patiently. "It is a termination of pregnancy. Abortions were abolished in the nineteenth century. Anyway, they are illegal. I am merely asking you as a friend to help me out of a jam." This approach to Frazer-Robinson was noticeably different from his approach to his other circle of friends. "The poor girl's life will be ruined if she is allowed to go through with it. I am not saying it is right that people should hold it against her, but one has simply got to accept the fact that they do. Nobody will give her a responsible job, and nobody will want to marry her or have an affair with her if she has a child. They will not want to get tied down."

"Why can't you marry her yourself?"

"My dear chap, that is not what I am asking you. I am merely asking you to help a friend by lending him some money. You'll get it back, with interest if you like." Goyle spoke bitterly. He had forgotten the great principle of usury which all the rich held sacred.

"Why can't you marry her, then?"

"Because I do not want to marry her. I do not love her, and I don't want to be tied down." Goyle was getting angry. He had degraded himself enough. Many people would have felt privileged to be asked to contribute, but he should have known that Guy was still immature enough to be influenced by primitive tribal taboo. "Can't you see it would be fatal for me at my age to tie an enormous millstone round my neck and throw myself into a pond? One has got to have freedom. Freedom to develop and expand on whatever lines one chooses. You want me to be arrested where I am, shackled to a whining wife and squawling brats, going into the office every morning at nine and coming out at five." It was a moving speech, he felt. He must work as if he was an advertising man trying to sell his product to an unwilling public. There was nobody who could fail to be moved by the image of Stephen Goyle going into the office at nine o'clock every morning, a prisoner in all but name, an automaton who jerked obediently at instructions from a faceless overseer.

Nobody except Guy Frazer-Robinson. His father went into the office most mornings at eleven, but he could not see that the other fate was so frightful. He seemed to have no understanding of Goyle's special case. If, after three months' acquaintance, he had not grasped the fact that Goyle was somebody different, an artist, a genius, an outsider, a man who walked alone, then there was nothing that Goyle could do for him. He was sorry, that was all.

"There is another thing I wanted to talk about," he said. "We are thinking of starting a fund to be called the Anne Etherington Memorial Fund. Mrs. Price-Williams has already contributed. It will be spent on some cause with which she would like to be associated, and we're trying to get all her friends to join in." Frazer-Robinson felt he had been a bit mean on Goyle, who could not be expected, after all, to share his own knowledge of good and evil, and listened with a receptive ear.

DEAR JAMEY,

I have decided to take a decision of which I know you will approve and join the next Parliament as Liberal candidate for

Llanwtyth. I have not yet told your father, but I want you to help by mobilizing Oxford opinion in my favor. I know there are a lot of Liberals in Oxford, and I think it would be a good idea if you arranged a party for some of them to meet me and I could tell them what is going on and what we Liberals must do. So I am coming up to Oxford on Saturday to do this. Philip will be out of prison soon. He, I know, was always a good Liberal and will not let me down. I found one of your vests returned by the laundry a week late, but you must come and collect it as I cannot possibly bring it up to you.

Love from
MUMMY

Damn, thought Jamey when he read it, I haven't written to Rapey Rawley for nearly a month. He sat down to do so.

DEAR BROTHER RICHARD,

I feel you should be acquainted with an incident that occurred in the cinema here. I and a very nice friend of mine called Miss Deirdre Black were compelled to go to a most unsavory film—she had been told she must see it—and there saw MacLaughlin, who had obviously gone just to see the film and gloat. On seeing Miss Black, he tried to molest her, shouting out foul language at the top of his voice. Eventually, he had to be removed by the commissionaire. Later, she told me that she had suffered in the past from MacLaughlin, who wanted to use her for his own foul purposes. I know that I am in part to blame, taking Miss Black to a cinema where she was likely to meet bad company, but I cannot help feeling that MacLaughlin is no credit to everything we have been taught about the use of our bodies, etc. She is a good girl, but slightly simple, and very sensitive to vile influences. Nor have I seen MacLaughlin in Church throughout the whole term.

Yours sincerely,
J. SLIGGER

DEAR BROTHER RICHARD,

Our fears for young Sligger are all too well founded, I fear. Seeing him in the cinema with Deirdre Black, the most immoral woman in Oxford whom I mentioned recently as going with men

111

for immoral purposes, I thought I should keep my eye on them. Sure enough, our worst fears were confirmed. I had to call the commissionaire and have them removed, still together. I did not want to tell you, but thought you ought to know.

Yours sincerely,
JOHN MACLAUGHLIN

P.S. I think this is pretty disgusting.

The invitations arrived on Wednesday. There had been no time to have them engraved, but they were impressive enough by any standards.

Lord Robinson of Grindley and Mrs. Aidan Sligger, Liberal Parliamentary Candidate for Llanwtyth, under the auspices of Mrs. Agnus Price-Williams, D.Phil., M.A., request the pleasure of your Company at a Celebration in honor of the Anne Etherington Memorial Fund (Organizer: Stephen Goyle Esq., Godolphin) in the Procury Gardens, Godolphin, by kind permission of Mr. and Mrs. Alec Scroton-Wise. Please bring this card with you. Admittance £1. 1s. -d. proceeds to Anne Etherington Memorial Fund.

On certain of the cards, the admittance fee was changed to a shilling. It would have been most unsuitable, as well as unwise, to have excluded the intellectual set. Lord Robinson was not coming, but he had given his blessing and a check for five guineas, with instructions to his son not to emphasize the South African part, as one of his subsidiaries had interests in Johannesburg. Goyle agreed that Anne had been a martyr to repressive college controls and inadequate Government grants as much as to the South African business. Mrs. Price-Williams, surprisingly enough, accepted. So did Mr. Cyril Jesmin, the grandest and most aloof of all dons, who occupied a chair which nobody had ever heard of and studied things which few people knew existed. Some people said he was a philosopher, others a mathematician, a chemist, a Hebrew scholar, an economo-sociologist, a nuclear physicist, a physio-therapist, but nobody really knew. He was very ugly.

Mr. Price-Williams, the day before the party, said, "I was so glad you were able to ask my wife to the party. I would have liked to make a contribution myself, I thought it was such a pity about that poor girl. My wife, of course, was very upset."

"Haven't you been asked?" said Jamey. "I will get you sent an invitation immediately. I hope you will accept it."

"As the invitation has no existence at the moment, my immediate acceptance or refusal would be equally irrelevant," said Mr. Price-Williams primly, but Jamey suspected that he wanted to come very much. He had not known that his tutor was such a stickler for formality.

"I will have one delivered this afternoon," he said. But of course he forgot.

"Of course I'd like to come," said Deirdre, "but Stephen says I can't. I must keep out of sight, he says, until it's all over."

"It's got nothing to do with him," said Jamey. "He's just the organizer. My mother's giving the party."

"But I don't know her."

"That's easily solved. I must go to the station and meet her. Would you like to come too?" Jamey was always diffident about invitations to Deirdre. She seemed so infinitely more grown-up than he, and she nearly always had to refuse them for one reason or another. But she agreed to come to the station with him.

"I hope Stephen doesn't call while I'm out." Jamey longed to tell her that Stephen did not care a penny for her, that he hated being tied down and had practically hired someone to rid him of her. Goyle had paid for two dinners which Jamey had given her, and Jamey had pocketed the money thinking he was a master of intrigue, little realizing that he was selling his soul. He bitterly regretted taking the money now, but he could not afford to give it back, even as a gesture.

"Hello, Jamey," cried his mother, giving him a loud wet kiss on the cheek, "this is a nice surprise, I must say." Her tone suggested that he might have met her in the railway carriage, instead of on the platform.

"Mummy, I want you to meet Miss Deirdre Black." Mrs. Sligger turned suspicious, hostile eyes on her for the first time.

"Pleased to meet you, I'm sure. You must be the young lady who said she would come and stay with us in the vac, and then decided she couldn't be bothered after all."

"No, Mummy, that was someone else."

"Well, please yourself, that's what I say. We older people are only here to make arrangements for you. Say you're coming one minute, you're not coming the next. We can't make up your mind for you. We're probably pleased you can't come, with all the trouble we've been to."

"I think you're mistaken, Mrs. Sligger," said Deirdre in her sweetest, most submissive voice. "Jamey never asked me to stay last vacation, or I should certainly have come."

"That's very kind of you. So it's me you were deceiving, Jamey, not her. I've got a good mind to step straight back on that train and go home." The train was beginning to move. It would have taken her to Reading and then goodness knew where. Jamey stared at it wistfully.

"I was going to ask somebody to stay, Mummy, but it was not Deirdre. It was someone else who was later unable to come."

"For reasons out of her control, I suppose."

"Not exactly."

"I know, you had a quarrel. Now you've got a new girl friend whom I'm expected to welcome with open arms. No fault of yours, dear." She bared her teeth at Deirdre. "It is just the normal process of male evolution. We have all got to put up with it. They just use you, then cast you off like a wet rag. Personally, I am not sure that I would lay myself open to being used like that."

"Neither would I," said Jamey warmly, and got a suspicious glance from his mother.

"Excuse me," said Roper, the scout on Staircase Two, who was helping, "there is a man at the door who hasn't got a card. Says he's a friend of Mr. Sligger's. Shall I let him in?"

"Friend of Mr. Sligger's indeed," said Mr. Tradiscant, who had appointed himself the major-domo. "I should say you do not let him in. I have never heard such rubbish in my life. Friend of Mr. Sligger's!"

"Right you are." So it was that Mr. Agnus Price-Williams, Senior Tutor of Godolphin, was turned away from his own college. As he left for Cumnor, a sad, small figure on a bicycle, he saw Mr. Cyril Jesmin arrive, and looked the other way. In everything that Mr. Jesmin was accounted grand, Mr. Price-Williams was accounted dim. Perhaps they would never meet socially.

"Where's Chris Robinson?" shouted Mr. Jesmin when he arrived. "I was told to expect my old friend Chris Robinson here."

"I don't think he's come yet, sir," said Mr. Tradiscant.

"That's too bad," shouted Mr. Jesmin. "I wanted to tell him what the Prime Minister was telling me the other day about Natal Concessions."

"What was that?" said Mr. Scroton-Wise timidly.

"Yes, he did," shouted Mr. Jesmin, "and Transvaal Consolidated."

"I am not sure Lord Robinson is coming."

"Well, I shall wait here until he does. Can't wait any longer."

"I am Joan Sligger, and I am giving the party with Lord Robinson. I hope you've got everything you want."

"What was that? Who is she?"

"She's called Mrs. Sligger. I believe she's the mother of one of my people."

"Pleased to meet you, Mrs. Sligger." Mr. Jesmin paid no more

115

attention to her. "Chris may find there is some good news coming to him," he said.

"I hope he will remember the Godolphin appeal," said Mr. Scroton-Wise. "We place a lot of hope in him."

"You must be the Principal of Godolphin," said Mrs. Sligger brightly.

"I am the Chief Procurer."

"How fascinating. I want to have a long talk about our education program. Of course, all this will be done away with." Her wave embraced the Procury Gardens, Mr. Jesmin, the knot of undergraduates. It was meant to include the whole of Oxford. "We believe that all the old concepts must be swept away."

"I see," said the Procurer coldly.

"Like cobwebs, you know. We think that everyone who cannot go to a comprehensive school should go to a primary school then a high school. For boys and girls who are brighter than the rest, there is a slightly higher school. Then for those who are going to influence world affairs, there is an extremely high school. Of course, not many people would go to that. But we Liberals happen to believe that education should not depend on the color of your old school tie, or class." She spoke the last word as if it was a bizarre oath. "We will get rid of all the universities as they now are to make way for some really high schools where people can learn citizenship and love and all the things that really matter."

"This is the Liberal Party program?" Mr. Jesmin was interested again.

"It may not be the official program yet," said Mrs. Sligger, "but it is the way we are all thinking. You see we happen to believe in certain basic human rights." Her tone suggested that her listeners, of course, would wish to disagree with her on this point. If they accepted it, they would have to accept everything she said, but Mr. Jesmin had lost interest. She turned to the Chief Procurer. "We happen to believe that even if men are not born equal, they all have an equal right to fair treatment and not to be treated as scum or the *hoi polloi*, as you would wish to call them."

"My dear Mrs. Sligger."

"That is why the universities have lost their appeal to young people nowadays. Especially young working people. They no longer have any interest in what happens at Oxford or Cambridge or any of the conventional places of so-called learning. They will have to be abolished, for their own good, to make way for something really dynamic which will appeal to young working people and prevent them from voting Socialist." Mr. Scroton-Wise, like most of his generation in Oxford, was a convinced Socialist. "Now I've said something that interests you," said Mrs. Sligger triumphantly, "now you see the point in what I'm saying. If we are not to be overrun by these hordes of common working-class people, we must lead them. It is our duty. *Pour preserver, il faut changer*. I'm trying to get as much support at Oxford for my plans as I can."

"I thought I told you not to come. There is no admittance without an invitation card."

"Jamey said I could come and gave me a card."

"Jamey is a silly little fool. If you realized all the trouble I'd been to, and the risk I'm taking for you this afternoon, you might have listened to me instead of that fatuous, half-baked, little puppy. If you're seen here, people will realize what the party's in aid of. I should have thought you would have had more sense."

"I'm sorry, Stephen, but I had not seen you for so long, and it is very lonely."

"What's Sligger doing? He's supposed to be keeping you company."

"Jamey's sweet, but I wish you would come and see me sometimes."

"Good heavens, woman, don't you realize I have been working for you night and day since the beginning of the term? Just because you were so silly and immature as to go and conceive a child."

"Sh."

"Don't tell me to shut up."

"I'm sorry, Stephen, but you don't want the whole world to know."

"But you do, coming here and flaunting yourself around like a prostitute. That's all you are. A great fat prostitute on the make."

"Stephen." Deirdre's voice was pleading and distressed. If Sligger had been within earshot he would have died for her.

"Well get out of here and don't come back. I'm doing the honorable thing by you and all you try and do is get into my hair. Your gratitude overwhelms me."

"I'm sorry, Stephen."

"I wonder what you think I am. After all this is over, I don't want to hear or see you again. What on earth is Sligger doing? He's been hired to take you off my hands."

"What do you mean?"

"You ask young Sligger. He knows what I mean. Now get out of here and don't come back. The less I have to do with your sort of person, the better I will feel."

Deirdre felt numbed. She walked back to St. Rachel's in a daze. She knew she should not have disobeyed Stephen in the first place. In her room, she took her temperature and felt her pulse. The books all said that she should avoid sudden shocks. Both were normal. With a sigh, she took up her knitting. She had finished two mittens and a pair of socks. Now she was engaged on a pink woolen matinee coat.

Sligger said "How do you do?" to the dark stranger whom Fringe had introduced.

"I knew your brother quite well when he was up at Oxford, and I think you may know my brother at Cleeve. He is a minister there."

"I'm sorry, I did not catch your name."

"Christian Rawley. My brother is now known as Brother Richard, although, of course, I always remember him as Dave. He used to be quite a talented singer in his time, you know. Hullo, Cyril." Mr. Jesmin acknowledged him with a nod. "Good old Cyril, he is not one to waste a kind word. Do you know the story about Cyril on his first arrival at a Palace garden party?" Rawley told it to them. When he had finished, he said, "Well, I must go and talk to some of my friends. I am very glad to have met you, James, and I expect we shall see more of each other in the future. Goodbye, Philip—I feel quite strange talking to another Philip in front of you—remember me to your aunt. I expect I shall see you at the Jesmins? No? Well, I am often around."

Rawley's friends included Mrs. Price-Williams, who was looking lost in a corner, the Chief Procurer, Stephen Goyle, Jack Piccione, an earnest young don from St. Catherine's and even Angela Hammock.

"Who on earth is he?" asked Sligger.

"Don't you know Creepy Crawley? I thought everyone knew him. He is one of the institutions of Oxford. He's something to do with the press, I'm not sure which. I think he acts in an advisory capacity to all of them, or at any rate most—the *Daily Cenotaph*, the *Reverser, Sunday Mimes*."

"What does he advise on?"

"Art and contemporary trends generally. He is quite interested in politics, and wanted to know if you were a member of our Inner Cell. He helps us quite a lot."

The revelation that Rapey Rawley had a brother was equaled only by the revelation that Fringe had an aunt. Both seemed equally ridiculous.

"Who is your aunt, Philip?"

"Don't you know? You must have heard of Tilly Eukallipagos, the Spanish War heroine?"

"I think so. What did she do?"

"She was called the Bloody Hag of Barcelona. After the war

she was tortured, of course, by the Fascists, but escaped and singlehanded she hanged the whole village of Vjodriz on the border."

"Why did she do that? They must have been very simple-minded villagers to let her."

"It was war, and in war you can't always behave as if you were at a tea party. Of course they were simple-minded. They had been ground down for generations by the Fascists. Now she lives in Tangier and does what she can to make life unpleasant for the Fascists."

"How does Creepy Crawley know her?"

"Oh, he knows most of us."

Earlier, Jamey would have been delighted to be included in whatever class of people it was of whom Creepy Crawley knew most. Now, he was not sure. He had seen less of the intellectual set this term, more of the Godolphin people, and his loyalties were about evenly divided. Apart from anything else, their life was so squalid, and nothing ever seemed to get done.

He was not enjoying the party. Always aware of his mother at the other end of the room telling people about the Liberals, he longed to explain to everyone how his father had married beneath his station. Guy had understood perfectly, when Sligger explained that she had been the secretary at the Agricultural College where Mr. Sligger went as a very young man. But Fringe would not understand, and it was difficult to lead the conversation round with people like Mr. Scroton-Wise, who had obviously received the full treatment. Jamey detected a disapproving look in the Procurer's eye when he spoke, and knew what had happened. He wished Deirdre was present to comfort him and hold his hand. He was never very happy out of her company nowadays, and could not understand where she was.

"Hullo, Johnny," shrieked Sally Pratt-Bingham, who had found herself momentarily left alone.

"Hullo," said Jamey. "Do you know Philip Fringe?"

"No, I don't," said Sally. "Hullo, there's Guy. Come here,

Guy, I want to talk to you. Do you know Johnny Nigger?" She giggled nervously, fearing she had gone too far. "I mean Snigger, of course. I'm so sorry, but I'm hopelessly vague about names. Do you know Guy?"

Frazer-Robinson and Sligger bowed formally to each other. "We have met," said Sligger ponderously.

"How silly of me. Of course you have. In fact you introduced me to each other. I want Guy to introduce me to Mr. Jesmin. He looks fascinating."

"Well, I won't," said Guy. Sally pouted.

"Well, take me away from here, anyway. I'm bored stiff. There's nobody I know except the usual people, and I've seen enough of Garlick to last me a month. He wanted me to contribute to a fund to buy him another wireless set. I said I'd already paid a guinea to get in, and that was quite enough."

Mr. Tradiscant said the takings were fifty-six pounds, and obviously expected a large tip. Goyle gave him ten shillings, which which was not generous, but as Tradiscant had already pocketed three pounds of the takings he had no cause to complain. The party was all but over. Mrs. Price-Williams was still there, infinitely vulnerable without her husband, listening to a harangue from Mrs. Sligger. Jamey looked disconsolate in a corner. Mr. Scroton-Wise was watching from an upstairs window of the Procury.

"Where's Deirdre?" said Jamey.

"I told her to go away as she had no business here."

"What do you mean? She was my guest."

"I don't know why you weren't looking after her properly then. She told me she was often lonely, so I said I didn't know what you were up to, as you were meant to look after her and had been paid to take her off my hands."

"You didn't."

"I said I didn't want anything more to do with her, and that if she could not even get on with someone who is paid to be nice to her, she could not expect me to give her my time free."

121

"You didn't." A sickening rush of apprehension reminded Sligger of the times when he was called to the Prefect of Discipline's study at Cleeve for a beating. He knew that Goyle had told her, and thought of another episode in the recent past when he had sent a girl back to St. Rachel's. Deirdre, too, had a gas fire in her room.

"You are a filthy, callous bear," he said, "and if you lay your stinking hands on that girl again, I am going to kick you into a jelly." Sligger was in a panic. He must get to St. Rachel's immediately at all costs, make sure that Deirdre was all right, assure her that he loved her, that Goyle was a liar and a thief.

"Steady on there, Mr. Sligger," said Tradiscant. "We don't want no ugly scenes in the Procury Gardens, and it would be a pity if I had to throw you out." His manner suggested that it would not be a pity at all. Jamey looked at him with undisguised hatred, but had no time for him. The important thing was to get to St. Rachel's.

"Jamey," called his mother, "I must collect my little one. It has been extremely nice meeting you, Mrs. Price-Williams. It is most interesting that your husband's family come from Llanwtyth. I was beginning to think nobody lived there. I am sure you will want to come and vote for me, if you are both Liberals, as you say, even if you feel you can't agree with my policy for education. Remember, we are nothing, the party is everything. Jamey, help me with my coat and say goodbye to Mrs. Price-Williams. We must go." Mrs. Sligger felt she may have lost some votes, and was not happy with the way things had gone. People at Oxford made no allowances for the individual approach, she decided. "Hurry up, Jamey, we don't want to be kept waiting. What are you doing? Do you want me to freeze to death?"

Jamey realized in desperation that nothing in the world was more important than that his mother should have her coat. Not the life or death of the girl he loved, not the anguish of uncertainty, the inexpressible happiness of love returned, the coming and going of the four seasons, the great expanses of the ocean

122

and the rolling tides of history could hope to divert such an issue.

"Coming, Mummy," he said.

"I can always tell when they've had too much to drink," said Tradiscant after he had gone.

Chapter 11

Goyle took Creepy Crawley to lunch in a small Spanish restaurant he recommended in Curzon Street. A lot of people there seemed to know his guest and gave Goyle odd, appraising glances, but none of them spoke to him.

"My appointment with Dr. Pimento is not until two-thirty," said Goyle. "Are you absolutely sure he's the right man?"

"I have never had to use his services myself, but everybody says he is the best." Rawley named a well-known duchess, and they both looked at their plates.

"I would not like the girl to come to any harm," said Goyle. "There would be the hell of a stink."

"If there is any danger of that, the man will refuse to do anything."

"What do you mean? He can't refuse. I would report him to the police."

"It is not quite as simple as that. He is a highly respected man in his profession."

"Is he one of us?"

"I don't think so, although a lot of our people go to him. But you must lower your voice when talking here. There are a lot of people from the press, and a lot of people who hang around trying to pick up stories to sell to the press. I am pretty well protected, of course, but you know how they like Oxford stories."

Goyle went on eating his soup. "There is a very good new young artist I want you to see," said Creepy Crawley in an unnaturally high voice. "At the Eukallipagos Gallery, actually. I think he should prove a very good investment indeed if you have any money to spare. He's called Sturgeon, and this is the first London exhibition he's had, although, of course, he's very well known in Brazil." Goyle had eighty-seven pounds in his pocket, of which sixty would go as Dr. Pimento's fee. He had intended to allow himself a margin of twenty pounds for what he called to himself freedom of action, but the success of the Anne Etherington Memorial party had given him another seven.

On their way to the gallery, which was in Knightsbridge, Rawley said: "I am sorry I had to be so unpleasant in the restaurant, Stephen, but you simply can't be too careful in London. It's not like Oxford. I wanted to tell you about this painter Sturgeon. He's a new idea which the Eukallipagos Gallery have had. All the money goes to their Spanish fund, and I think it'll prove a great money-spinner. A Sturgeon bought now will have trebled in value within months. There's going to be a great thing about him in the *Reverser*, and the *Sunday Mimes* Encyclopaedia Section is devoting a whole number to him. We have even got the *Daily Cenotaph* to play along. He is non-representational, of course, and there may be a bit of resistance at first from the populars, but there is nothing like an outcry to boost the sales."

They were met at the gallery by a pale girl with long dark hair which came over her shoulders and ended on her bosom.

"Good morning, Mr. Rawley," she said, "the exhibition is not open yet, but most of the stuff seems to have been sold."

"Good morning, Phyllis. What a shame you are sold out already. My friend Mr. Goyle wanted to buy something."

"I expect we can find something for him. What does he like?"

Goyle contemplated the first picture. It was a thing of greens and browns, with here and there a hint of orange. He put his head close to it, as if inspecting some minutiae of the brush-work. Goyle was not a person to form rash judgments, but he could see that this painting was quite exceptional. As he later said, it was one of the most exciting moments of his life. There was a pulsing harmony, a kind of inner activity to which no words could do justice. It was as if the artist was living inside the picture, occasionally pushing out and jabbing one in the eye with the end of his paintbrush. He moved to the next one. It was decorative, pleasant, excellent of its sort, but no more. It was the work of an accomplished artist who had said, "Let us now rest and produce not a potboiler but some light enter-tainment, something to divert and titillate. This is my 'Mid-summer Night's Dream.' The last was my 'King Lear.'" The next painting was somber in the extreme. Occasionally it jarred. Perhaps the artist had not yet found his legs, perhaps he had been crossed in love. It was of historical interest, but no es-thetic moment. The next, more ambitious, was magnificent, but did it achieve an integral tonality? Goyle would not have liked to rely on his judgment on that point, particularly when so much money was involved. His own money, too. The others were all excellent. If he had seen them independently, each would have excited a certain amount of rapture. But none quite achieved the tour de force of the first.

"How much is that one?" said Goyle, pointing.

"Funny thing, everyone asks that question," said Phyllis. "I'm afraid it's sold. I dare say we can find something similar in the basement."

"Who has bought it?" said Rawley.

"That was Mr. Frickberg. He bought eighteen for his new hotel."

"Couldn't you give him another?" said Rawley. "He prob-ably only bought it because it was the first."

"You may be right," said Phyllis. "That one is seventy-five guineas. Let's see if we can find another similar."

Downstairs was a treasure trove of Sturgeons, stacked one against the other in rows. Goyle felt that he must be surfeited, as none seemed to make the impact on him which the first had achieved. They found one that was similar to the chef d'oeuvre, and substituted it. Goyle felt there was no comparison. Undoubtedly he had the masterpiece. "Well, are you going to buy it?" the girl asked. Goyle felt it was not a moment to hesitate. He had just come through a supreme experience. If art meant anything at all, now was the moment to show it. He had begun to have doubts about Dr. Pimento when Rawley had said he might not do the job. Now his duty was clear.

"Yes," he said.

"Make the check out to International Peace and Friendship between Nations," said Phyllis. When she saw his money, she said, "Ooh. We don't often collect as much as that at one time." Goyle asked if he could take the picture away.

"I'll have it wrapped up," said Phyllis. She went to the bottom of the stairs and shouted, "Fred."

"Tell me about Sturgeon," said Goyle.

"I don't think much is known," said Rawley. "He may have died of consumption in Brazil, or he may have drunk himself to death. He was quite a young man. Or he may be in a Portuguese prison in Angola. His story is much what you make of it. I don't think anyone has seen him in England, not recently, anyway."

"Fred," shouted Phyllis.

"He was born of working-class parents, of course, and largely self-taught." Goyle marveled that anyone should be able to achieve so much without even the rudiments of training. "He had them, of course, at the Wolverhampton Art School, but then he passed on."

A disheveled young man came down the stairs. He was covered with paint. "The wheel is not turning properly," he said. "We need some grease. It's bloody hard work up there."

"Is he the artist?" said Goyle in a breathless whisper.

"He's just an assistant here," said Phyllis. "You've been cleaning some pictures, haven't you, Fred?"

"That's right," said Fred, "me and the others."

126

"Will you wrap up this picture for the gentleman?"

Fred looked at the picture proudly. "Yes, I liked that one. I think it came out very nicely," he said. "I think you've got a very good buy there."

"Thank you, my man." Goyle rather resented the young man's interest. "Will you wrap it up particularly well, as I have to take it back to Oxford this evening."

"You must be at the University," said Fred. "I have just come down from Brasenose, actually. Where are you?"

"I am at Godolphin," said Goyle shortly.

"I had a great friend at Godolphin. You wouldn't know Philip Sligger? I don't expect he can still be up."

"No. I know his brother."

"It's a small world. There goes the telephone, excuse me." He spoke into the receiver. "Eukallipagos Galleries. Women's page of what? Oh, the *Daily Cenotaph*. What does Mr. Sturgeon fancy in interior decoration? . . . Let me see. . . . Scandinavian. . . . Yes, he told me. . . . No, he won't be making any New Year resolutions this year. . . . He was born in April. . . . I don't know whether that makes him mercurial or not. . . . What does he like for a birthday present? Drink, I should think. Marijuana, you know, that sort of thing. . . . Yes, I expect he'd like a pair of bedroom slippers at Simpson's for four guineas with his initials, if they were offered to him. . . . I couldn't say if he's the sort of husband who likes to be welcomed home from the office by his wife in something frilly, because he isn't exactly married. You can say he thinks he would be that sort of husband, if he were married. . . . No, of course he doesn't smoke in bed. He very seldom goes to bed, as a matter of fact. Works throughout the night, as a general rule. . . . No, that wouldn't be much fun for his wife. . . . I mean, I'm sorry, I didn't hear what you were saying. . . . Is he *looking* for a wife? Oh yes, in a very general sort of way, you know. He'd prefer an English wife because they're cleaner, but he would put up with a foreign one if necessary. . . . No, we haven't got a photograph yet. We're trying to get one. . . ."

"No, we never give receipts," said Phyllis with a dazzling smile when Goyle had paid the money. Creepy Crawley felt it was time for him to go.

"The press are such a nuisance," he said. "I must get back to Fleet Street and see if they need any advice on this story. You don't mind if I refer to you as an Oxford Charitable Trust? Remember the seventy-five guineas, Phyllis. Goodbye, Stephen; thank you for a delicious and memorable luncheon."

"You wouldn't mind doing me a tremendous favor," said Fred. "You see we haven't got a photograph of this fellow Sturgeon, and all the papers are crying for one. You couldn't possibly come downstairs for a moment, just while I take a snap. It doesn't matter who's on the photo, really, so long as they have someone."

"Certainly not," said Goyle. "Anyway, I'm much too well known already."

"Sorry then. Only you've got an interest in it now, and I thought you might oblige." Fred was expertly wrapping up the picture. For a dismal moment it seemed to Goyle that his purchase was no different from the other pictures in the room, but the mood passed. Everybody—Creepy Crawley, Phyllis, Fred—agreed that his was the best.

"I may be writing something about this when I get back to Oxford. Have you got any definite material on Sturgeon?" he asked.

"What sort of thing would you be writing? We've got this handout for the quality's art critics, this one for their news desks, another for populars and women's papers, an educational one for children's magazines, and we're thinking up one with a religious angle, but that won't be ready until tomorrow."

"I'll take them all. I don't think I'll need the religious one. Thank you very much." As Phyllis had the door open, something about the way she wore her jersey made her look appealing, but Goyle resolutely turned his back and walked into the bitter, gray air of Knightsbridge. Women had got him into enough trouble already.

Sligger was appalled. "You mean he's gone to London to see this filthy doctor?"

Deirdre nodded. "You see, he must care for me, or he would not put himself to so much trouble."

"Goyle doesn't care for anyone in the world except himself."

"I know he cared for me last term. I think he loved me."

"How do you know? When did it happen?"

"It was the evening Anne Etherington died, which makes it so awful. But I know he loved me then. He told me so, and a girl can usually tell." Jamey remembered that two evenings before Anne Etherington died, Goyle had offered to introduce him to Deirdre in order to further his education. Perhaps that was the way Goyle demonstrated his love. It was his own way of flaunting the loved one, soliciting admiration from his friends. Perhaps Goyle already had been getting a little tired of her. But the enormity of it all took Sligger's breath away. He had never really believed that anyone went to bed with anyone else at Oxford; it had been a pious article of faith to which one had to defer in conversation, and the idea had been full of interesting possibilities, but now that he was face to face with the real thing, Jamey was disgusted. He thought of the revolting white body of Goyle, all skin and bones and wrong-headed theories, clambering over the plump gray form of Deirdre, too lazy to do anything but lie inertly on her back like a dead whale. For the first time he felt the stirrings of genuine moral indignation and just anger.

"But you can't just have the baby removed."

"What else can I do? Nobody will want to employ a young girl with an illegitimate baby, let alone marry her. It would not be fair to expect Stephen to marry me and tie himself down when he is so young."

Under normal circumstances, Jamey considered, he would not have hesitated to say, "Don't be so silly, Deirdre, I'll marry you." Then they would have fallen into each other's arms in happy, tearful laughter and lived happily together for the rest of their lives, Deirdre filling an important gap in his life whenever required to do so. But he was deterred by the thought of Goyle, creeping like a snail, leaving a long, glutinous trail wherever he had been.

"What nonsense," he said. "Everybody is looking for cooks these days, and all you can ever get is an unmarried mother. Often they have several children, too."

"I can't cook."

"Nor can any of them. The Robinsons had an unmarried mother to cook for them, with one child which she swore was by virgin birth. She couldn't even boil an egg, and then she suddenly announced she was going to have twins, also by virgin birth."

"But I'm not sure I want to be a cook."

"You can't be choosy, I'm afraid. You are absolutely sure that your baby is not by virgin birth, and you dreamed up this whole Goyle episode?"

"Absolutely sure." Formerly, Sligger would have thought her smile sweet and sad. Now it merely seemed lascivious and sick. "Jamey, what do you advise me to do?"

"Well, you certainly can't have an abortion."

"It isn't an abortion."

"It sounds like one to me."

"Even if it is, why shouldn't I have one? It is entirely my own affair. If Stephen wants me to have one, of course I must."

Jamey was at a loss to explain to her why she should not have an abortion in terms she would understand. It was no good explaining to her that it was just wrong. Murder was too strong a word to introduce into intellectual conversation, and anyway it would be extremely rude. He must be mature. "These things always create more problems than they solve," he said.

"What do you mean?"

"If everybody had abortions, no babies would ever get born and the human race would die a lingering death."

"Don't be so silly. I am not everybody, and there is a world population problem anyway. It is just one more mouth to feed in a hungry world. Forty Afro-Asian peasants could live off what that baby is going to eat."

"They couldn't, and even if they could they won't. They've got no business taking food from the mouth of an innocent baby."

"If you'd seen all those poor black men dying on their feet, you wouldn't be so anxious to go on starving them."

"I am not anxious to go on starving them. You have never seen them either."

"I never said I had." The conversation was deteriorating, but Jamey had the feeling that he was not winning the argument. He had tried his mother's tactics, but they never seemed to work with him.

"If you want an abortion so much, why do you spend all your time knitting those ridiculous garments for a baby? It sounds very psychological to me."

"I don't want a termination, but if Stephen says I must have one, he is quite right. I don't want to have the baby either. I've got to do something with my time, and there must be people who would be very grateful for some baby's clothes. I daresay I shall give them to Famine Relief. They're not at all ridiculous. All the books say that babies must have a woolen stomacher to go underneath their vest, or they have no sense of security and get diarrhea."

Jamey saw in his mind's eye the scene that was going on in London at that moment. Goyle would be handing over the money in pound notes to a wheezing, avaricious sawbones whose breath smelled of whisky, and they would be discussing the most convenient way of destroying an unborn baby, the most painless, noiseless, unnoticeable way in which a living thing could be turned into something disgusting to be thrown away. Deirdre sat knitting, like an idiot, complacent cow.

"Goyle won't mind if it does get diarrhea," he said.

"John Sturgeon was born in 1927 of working-class parents whom he never saw. Educated at Wolverhampton Church of England Foundation, he ran away at the age of nine to join the International Brigade in Spain, where he met Tilly Eukallipagos and other heroes of the fight against Fascism. The outbreak of war found him in Tangier with Mrs. Eukallipagos. Being judged 'too young' to join the fighting, he stayed with his protectress. Later, their friendship may have ripened into something deeper, as it was this association between the gaunt, fifty-year-old warrior of Barcelona and the impetuous, freedom-loving youth which is believed to have inspired Rejvic, the well-known Yugoslav poet and Resistance leader, to his epic poem 'Cvic Street.' Later, Sturgeon decided that his path to self-realization lay not in the taking of life but in painting, the creation of life. This led to a quarrel with his protectress, which was only made up after many years, when she saw that what freedom had lost in the field of battle, it had gained in the field of art. She wrote to him: 'I see now that you were right to paint in the face of all opposition, as you are probably the greatest painter who has ever lived. For that reason, you have my blessing.'

"Sturgeon's later life is shrouded in mystery. He is known to have been imprisoned in Brazil, and he was last heard of taking an exhibition of his paintings to the Angolan Africans who live in the bush behind St. Paul de Luanda in undesirable conditions, in the hope that appreciation of fine art would do something to relieve their suffering."

Goyle read it all with interest. He felt he could have improved upon it in places, but it was a good job of work. The mystery of who Sturgeon actually was remained. He would have to solve that question in his own article for whichever Oxford publication he chose. The train carrying him and his painting away from the cruel, mercenary world of London back to the homely circles of Oxford rushed and swayed on its mission. The Anne Etherington Memorial Fund couldn't have been better spent, couldn't have been better spent, the wheels seemed to say. He had never heard of such a ridiculous waste of money as the idea of spending eighty pounds on making a silly, immoral girl more comfortable. He had washed his hands of her. Sligger could look after her now. The Anne Etherington Memorial Fund couldn't have been better spent. He turned to the next piece of paper. It was headed "Artist with a Difference."

"John Sturgeon is not at all everybody's idea of an artist. Although his work is now commanding record prices at the Eukallipagos Galleries, Knightsbridge, and his brush has been hailed by Europe's foremost critics, he does not believe that, to be artistic, you must necessarily be untidy or dirty. Not a bit of it. He paints in a dark suit, immaculately pressed, and never gets a drop of paint on it. Sometimes he reads *The Times*, neatly folded, while he is painting, because he finds that if he concentrates too hard on the canvas his work becomes too studied. His hobbies are life and numismatics (numismatics—coin collecting to you). He enjoys painting, but does not like it to be thought of as a dirty profession. 'I do not like it to be thought of as a dirty profession,' he said, showing me his spotless hands. 'See, it is quite easy to keep clean if you take trouble.' It was true. His hands were spotless." Underneath was written: "Sorry no photos. Sturgeon will not let himself be photographed, as he says photography is the enemy of art. A snap of his girl friend, lovely art student Miss Phyllis Plimsoll, is available on request."

There was not much material in that one, Goyle reflected. It might be interesting if he could show that the tactile appeal of coin collecting was reflected in his painting, but he doubted if that was quite the right angle. The thing about shunning a camera might make a tailpiece, but Goyle rather felt it had been done before, by Hemingway or Picasso or someone. Whoever or whatever Sturgeon was, Goyle possessed his finest work.

133

Perhaps he would ask for a snap of Miss Phyllis Plimsoll. The Anne Etherington Memorial Fund couldn't have been better spent, couldn't have been better spent.

Chapter 12

Meetings of the Inner Cell had never been quite the same since Anne Etherington died. She had kept the agenda and taken notes in a neat hand, somehow elevating the most petty squabbles to the level of an intellectual argument in the course of her account. Angela Hammock, with all the good will in the world, did not have her gifts, and Fringe, in the reports he sent after each meeting to Christian Rawley in London, often had to invent what had happened. At the first session after Anne's death they had passed a motion regretting the event, with only one abstention, from Fringe, who pointed out that if anything worthwhile was to come of it they had no time to waste in morbid and sentimental reflection.

Sligger had missed the second meeting, where Deirdre Black was voted adequate funds to pay for an abortion. Even if he had been present, it would have made no difference, as members did not vote against each other's proposals. The only way to mark disapproval was to abstain, with the result that every motion proposed was automatically passed, even if there was only one vote in its favor. Then the quarrels would begin. People would propose contradictory motions and amendments and recommendations that no action be taken on the last motion. Very little action was ever taken in any case, as most discussions referred to ideological matters, like what attitude the

Cell was to take toward the Berlin Wall, the earthquake in Persia, the Potato and Egg Marketing Boards, Mrs. Price-Williams's secretary, the Albanian prime minister and President Tito.

At the term's third meeting, which had Greaves, by rotation, in the chair, there was an air of expectancy. Condemnation of the American warmongers' action in appointing a new Secretary of Defense was perfunctory; the English were condemned for whatever action they proposed to take over the current crisis in the Middle East, without a murmur. It was the third item on the agenda, the Anne Etherington Memorial Fund, for which they were all waiting.

"I would like to propose that this meeting approve of the action of Mr. Stephen Goyle in directing the money in the Fund from its original purpose, the termination of Miss Deirdre Black's pregnancy, to the greater and more important cause of art and international understanding," said Fringe. In an icy silence the motion was passed by two votes against three abstentions. Angela Hammock always voted for everything, unless someone had told her not to. Greaves, English and Sligger all began talking together, until Greaves banged the table with a tire pressure gauge he had been sucking.

"Mr. English," he said.

"This motion thinks it's bloody disgusting what has happened, and a committee of inquiry should be set up to look into Goyle's behavior and if necessary bring it to the notice of the proctors," said Mr. English.

"Exactly," said Greaves. "Art is for the people not for Stephen bloody Goyle when we've paid for it. That money was devoted to a specific purpose."

"And Deirdre doesn't want an abortion, anyway," said Jamey. "It was just a cock-and-bull story by Goyle to get the money." This shocked them. After a short silence, it began again.

"Then it should be devoted to a general Termination of Pregnancy Fund."

135

"Who is this filthy girl anyway? What right has she got to interfere?"

"Some tart of Goyle's. She was probably in on it." Eventually, the meeting observed with regret the misapplication of the Anne Etherington Memorial Fund (three votes); condemned the immoral behavior of Miss Deirdre Black and recommended that this be brought to the notice of the authorities (two votes); and remarked that there was something very wrong with the outlook of contemporary students on moral matters (five votes). Then the meeting adjourned to the Fantastacherie for lunch. Goyle was eating in a corner with a swarthy stranger he had discovered.

"Hullo, Goyle, how's the art collection?" they called derisively.

"Very well, thank you," said Goyle wolfishly. "Sturgeon gets two pages in the *Reverser*. Have you seen this?" He showed them the newspaper he was reading. Nearly half a page was taken up by a photograph captioned, "Sturgeon: Man in Search of a Motive." Nothing would have been remarkable about that, if the photograph had not been unmistakably a portrait of Philip Fringe.

"Jolly nice," said Greaves sarcastically. "I did not know you could paint Philip."

"They just asked me for a photograph. I have nothing to do with the production side," said Goyle modestly. "The gallery is rather a family affair, and it all goes to the Cause."

"I'm surprised they use Philip's ugly face to advertise it," said English rudely. "What's so wrong with Sturgeon's?"

"He may have got leprosy in Equatorial Africa," said Goyle. "I've got a much better photograph for my article in Oxford *Prism*. By the way, do you know Secretti, the editor?" Secretti showed them a large studio portrait of Miss Phyllis Plimsoll, the girl in the Eukallipagos Gallery.

"Is Sturgeon a transvestite, then?" asked English. He was very simple.

136

"That's his girl friend, or mistress, or what have you," said Goyle.

"I think she's absolutely lovely," said Sligger.

"Well, she seems to satisfy him for the moment, but I dare say he does not want to be tied down." Goyle seemed to be imparting some secret message to Sligger, but for the life of him Jamey could not think what it was. "Secretti and I are thinking of holding a Sturgeon exhibition in Oxford. Of course, we'll only have my painting to show, but I think it should create a stir. It will show that Oxford is ahead of the times in art."

"That is the best idea I've heard for a long time," said Fringe, although his companions seemed lukewarm in their enthusiasm. "I'll get the gallery to send down a couple of dozen, if you like."

Goyle did not seem to think that was a very good idea. "I was thinking more in terms of a single picture exhibition. We could call it the Anne Etherington Memorial Exhibition, and ask all the people who came to the party."

"No, we don't want to get art mixed up in politics. What on earth would be the point of it when we can have any number of paintings down? We might even be able to get the gallery to sell them at cut rates, in the interests of education." That was obviously not at all Goyle's idea of how the exhibition should be run.

But Secretti said, "It could be sponsored by the Oxford *Prism*. You might even arrange for the gallery to give *Prism* a small share of the takings."

"Of course," said Fringe, "and Goyle, as the originator of the idea, would certainly get a share."

"Tell me more about Sturgeon," said Secretti. "We're going to devote a whole number to him."

"Sturgeons come in three sizes," said Fringe, "the smallest, eighteen inches by thirty-six inches, sell at about fifteen guineas in Knightsbridge, but here we might make them as little as two pounds. The next size, thirty inches by forty-eight inches, sell at forty guineas—say five or six pounds here. The biggest, of which Goyle has a good example, are more in the nature of an investment. We might ask fifteen pounds here. Of course, if we have a large order, we can produce them rather cheaper, which leaves a good margin for *Prism* and Stephen and even myself to collect a little pocket money."

"My picture must have pride of place, as the finest thing he has ever painted," said Goyle.

"That can be arranged. I think it is a very good thing for students to patronize the arts. If a small proportion of all the vast sums wasted on education was invested in art, people like ourselves would never have to worry about money. You have started something very big, Stephen, when you wisely decided to invest all the Anne Etherington money in a Sturgeon."

"The Anne Etherington Memorial Fund couldn't have been better spent."

DEAR BROTHER RICHARD,

I think you should know of a new development at Oxford around the person of John Sturgeon, an artist of whom very little is known. It seems that he was a highly immoral person who lived in sin with a woman some years older than himself. Everybody at Oxford is very excited about his paintings, but they look no good to me, and I don't see how they can be anything but worthless if the man's moral position is wrong. Peter Garlick, whom I told you about, says he is going to buy one when the exhibition opens, and he wants the chaplain, Father Potinue, to decorate his church with them. Everybody agrees that they would be a very good investment, but I do not see how one can ever morally justify supporting an immoral cause. MacLaughlin is not, so far as I know, involved in this, but he is the general sort of person who might be. Me and Frazer-Robinson, of course, are keeping ourselves quite apart. I don't know if this information will be of any use to you.

As Sligger licked down the envelope, it occurred to him that Brother Richard was not really being treated to a very full picture of Oxford life, but he felt sure that he was right not to tell him about such things as Goyle's immoral behavior with Deirdre and the Anne Etherington Memorial Fund. They were really none of his business, in any case.

"Who are you writing to, Jamey?" asked Guy.

"A friend."

"A girl friend?" said Garlick suggestively, as if the sexual act could somehow be done by post. He took the envelope out of Jamey's hand. " 'Brother Richard Rawley.' What extraordinary friends you have. I did not know your taste lay that way."

"Why are you writing to Rapey Rawley?" asked Guy.

"I just thought I'd drop him a line on the spur of the moment," said Jamey, although he felt his tone did not carry conviction.

"What on earth about?" Guy knew perfectly well the terrible hold which Rapey had over Sligger. He was being malicious.

"Oh, nothing in particular."

"I often write to my housemaster at Stockton," said Garlick surprisingly. "He was more of a father to me than anything else."

"What's happened to your real father, then?" said Guy. Nobody had ever bothered to inquire before.

"He's dead," said Garlick, in a sentimental voice.

"Gosh, hard luck." Dead parents were one of the few things which were absolutely sacred.

Garlick thought he could press his advantage further. "My mother's far from well," he said.

"Neither's mine," said Guy. "She's got phlebitis. What's wrong with yours?"

"Nobody seems to know. We think it may be cancer."

"Gosh, hard luck," said Jamey.

"What makes you think that?" said Guy.

"She has terrible recurring pains down her back, where the spine runs. At other times, they completely vanish, and she is as active as you or me."

"It sounds like phlebitis to me," said Guy. "Has she tried blue pills?"

139

"We've tried everything there is," said Garlick mournfully. "It is only a matter of time. If they can invent a cure for cancer before it gets any worse, there is still hope. I sometimes think I may have cancer myself." Nobody was going to say "Gosh, hard luck" this time. He said, "I get frightful pains in my chest."

"Well, go to a doctor then."

"Doctors!" Garlick obviously held the profession in the greatest contempt. "They just give you an injection of penicillin and send you away."

"Probably do you the world of good."

"How can it do me any good, you fool, when I've got cancer?"

"Try an aspirin, then."

"I'm glad you think it's funny."

There was a knock on the door, and Deirdre came in. "Keep away from me in your condition," said Garlick. "I am not feeling at all well."

"German measles?" said Deirdre, starting back.

"No, cancer."

"Gosh, hard luck." Deirdre was visibly relieved.

"Can I help you?" said Guy to Deirdre with a touch of coldness. He felt that she had caused enough trouble already.

"Do you know each other?" said Jamey.

"We met at the Anne Etherington Memorial party in aid of art," said Guy austerely.

"I just wanted a word with Jamey," said Deirdre.

"Go ahead," said Garlick. "Don't mind us, if all you want to do is talk. If you want to do anything else, I suppose we should leave the room."

"Oh, shut up, Peter," said Jamey. Garlick was a boorish lout and had no delicacy at all, but he wished Deirdre would not come calling on him now that everyone knew she was Goyle's castoff.

"I suppose you want us to watch you both performing some ghastly and inexpert rite on the sofa," said Garlick nastily. "I'm afraid you must recruit your audience from somewhere else. I have an essay to write. And quite honestly, I do not believe in performing my immoralities in front of the public eye." Nobody prevented him from leaving, so he got up and limped to the door. When he was there, he gave a heart-rending little cough and left.

"Do you want me to leave? Not because of anything Peter said, but because you want to talk in private."

"That's all right, Guy. What do you want, Deirdre? Guy knows everything, of course."

"Of course," said Deirdre. "So does the whole world."

"That's not my fault," said Sligger. "If you must choose Stephen Goyle as your—uhum—well, as the father of your child, you must expect the whole world to know."

Deirdre looked worried about something. She said, "I've just come to tell you that I've decided to have the baby, as you said."

"Well done," said Guy and Jamey warmly. After Goyle had absconded with the memorial fund, it had not occurred to them that there was any other course of action open to her.

"What are you worried about, then? Don't you know what to call it?"

"If it's a boy, I shouldn't call it Stephen. That sort of thing only causes trouble. I think Barnabas is rather a nice name for a boy."

"Or Bucephalus, after Alexander the Great's horse."

"If it's a girl, you could call it Lavinia. Very few people seem to call their daughters Lavinia nowadays."

"Or Anne, after poor Anne Etherington. I think that would be a very nice idea, particularly as the two are so closely connected."

"Yes, I think all those are quite nice names, except Anne," said Deirdre. "I wouldn't always like to be reminded of poor Anne and the night she died. And she already has a memorial in that hideous picture of Stephen's. But it wasn't really that which was worrying me."

"What was it then?"

"Oh, everything." She looked as if she was going to cry.

Guy, who was a kindly person at heart, said, "Have some brandy."

"No, thank you."

"Go on, it's quite good. Hennessy Extra."

"No, thank you. It would make me sick." If she refused the most expensive brandy procurable, there must be something wrong with her.

"Are you unwell?" Perhaps she had a touch of cancer, like Garlick, or perhaps the pregnancy was not going smoothly. Jamey had a theory that he had read somewhere that intercourse outside marriage often brought venereal disease. Nothing would surprise him about Goyle, but he reflected that he had had a narrow escape.

"No, I think everything's all right. The books say I must avoid shocks and untoward exertion. I am drinking two pints of milk a day."

"That can't be healthy. You'll get phlebitis, or something."

"What's that?"

"My mother gets it. Nobody knows the cause, but some people say it's milk. She's given up milk now."

"Perhaps I'd better lay off the milk. I think I will have some brandy then. I can't tell you how nice it is to be able to talk. In St. Rachel's everybody seems scared stiff, and avoids me like the plague, as if they could catch babies like mumps or chicken pox."

"Well, I would avoid milk, then."

"But what shall I do after I have told Mrs. Price-Williams? She will have to send me down, and I can't just live at home for the rest of my life."

"You must go to the local welfare adviser, or I can give you the name of an agency in London which supplies jobs for unmarried mothers and mothers-to-be. My father happens to be on the board—I don't know why—and we always get our staff from there. It would be funny if you turned up as our cook. Can you cook?"

"No."

"Neither can any of them. It seems to be the only way you can be sure of not ending up an unmarried mother, if you learn to cook. One might suggest that to the underdeveloped nations as a cure to their population problems."

"Not at all," said Sligger, who was regarded as the population expert in the Inner Cell counsels. "It is extremely good for the underdeveloped nations to breed. It is their only chance of survival. And the reason that no unmarried mothers can cook is because if they could, someone would marry them."

"I can't see Goyle marrying Mrs. Beeton herself."

"Please don't make a joke of it. I'm sure Stephen isn't as bad as any of you think."

"None of us said he was bad at all. It's just that he's not the marrying sort, as you probably know," said Guy.

Jamey wished he could remember the reasons Fringe had given for encouraging the underdeveloped nations to breed. It had gone something like this: the more undernourished people there are in the world, the more we in England will have to feed them. To that extent, we shall become less affluent and less contented, and so the chance of a socialist awakening will become greater. English had said, "Of course we've bloody well got to feed the underdeveloped, but the rich should do it, not us." Everybody admitted that the more you feed them, the more they breed, the more mouths there are to be fed. Sligger felt that breeding was a good thing in itself, Fringe that anything which made Europeans poorer was a good thing in itself, English that anything which inconvenienced the rich was a good thing. To talk of discouraging babies by teaching cooking was clearly absurd, particularly as they had nothing to cook. Sligger had a mental image of rows of Negresses standing over empty cooking pots, stewing, frying, boiling, baking, sieving and marinading their imaginary contents. Perhaps the activity would

143

take their minds off the nasty urges to which women were prone, but Guy missed the whole point, which was that they should be encouraged to breed.

"I can't tell you how nice it is to have somebody to talk to," said Deirdre.

"Hullo, Agnus. I didn't see you at Lord Robinson's party." There were very few dons whom the Chief Procurer of Godolphin called by their Christian name, but Price-Williams could scarcely be called by anything else.

"I didn't want to encourage young Sligger, whose mother was giving the party with him," said Mr. Price-Williams. His being turned away at the gate still rankled. "My wife was there, of course, as we do not want to offend Lord Robinson. But I am none too satisfied with young Sligger at the moment."

"Who is he?"

"You know, the one who shares with Guy Frazer-Robinson."

"Tradiscant was complaining about him. His mother was the most ghastly woman I had ever met. She said if I had any intellectual integrity, or some such rubbish, I would turn Godolphin into a coeducational school to teach teen-agers the facts of life. I said I thought they already knew them, and she replied not properly. I don't know what she knows and we don't." Both men were childless, so they laughed heartily. Most teen-agers could certainly teach them a thing or two.

"I really feel Sligger is wasting his time here. He has not handed in a single essay this term, and the questions he asks are unbelievable."

"I don't care for him much myself. I will never really feel safe from that ghastly mother of his until he has left. There was a brother, who never came to much good. He kept some sort of animal in his rooms, which frightened the life out of Tradiscant when he went in there once. But we can't really get rid of him without something more concrete to go on. We don't want to offend the Robinsons." Scroton-Wise knew quite well that the senior tutors never expected essays. It was very rarely that Mr.

Price-Williams complained about a pupil, and then it was nearly always because he had been rude. There was no excuse for being rude to anyone as gentle as he, but one did not want to offend the Frazer-Robinsons.

Mr. Price-Williams sighed. He really felt something should be done about Sligger, who was idle and mischievous as well as rude. Most undergraduates would be delighted to have the Senior Tutor of Godolphin at their parties. It must have been because Sligger did not think him a suitable person to meet Lord Robinson, who had not turned up in any case. But there was no excuse for hinting that he might be getting an invitation, then giving instructions that he was not to be admitted. He would write a memorandum to the Chief Procurer, mentioning that Sligger was idle and uninterested in his studies, and suggesting that he was wasting his time unless he could be moved to another school.

When he told his wife this at luncheon, she said, "Oh but Agnus, I thought he was such a well-mannered boy. We went to a party of his in Godolphin the night before the fire there. If only there were more of his sort around, my girls would not get into so much trouble."

"I am not at all sure you are right about what sort of person he is. His mother, I believe, is ghastly."

"I did not have time to speak to her, but she looked a very intelligent sort of woman. She seemed to know Mr. Jesmin very well, and I saw Alec talking to her at some length."

"I wouldn't be at all surprised if he was the sort of person to get one of your girls in serious trouble. I have discovered he is not to be trusted."

"Really, Agnus, I don't know why you say that. If there was any trouble of that sort, of course you would be right to get rid of him at once. But I don't know who you think you are, saying things like that."

"I am a cuddly bear," said Mr. Price-Williams, pouting.

"Oh are you?" said Mrs. Price-Williams. "Well I think you are nothing but a naughty bow-wow."

"Bow-wow," said Mr. Price-Williams. The Principal of St. Rachel's went to the cupboard to fetch his Teddy bear out of the drawer.

A regular mechanical noise came out of the library, like simulated thunder in a poor repertory production of *King Lear*. Mr. Sligger was asleep. His wife sat in the drawing room alone and wondered what to think about. "I am terribly worried about Jamey," she began, but found that the reflection led nowhere. Somehow she did not feel as emotionally committed in the fortunes of her two children as she had been during the years of their adolescence. Then she had been able to wound them mortally with a few well-chosen words, shape them like Plasticine into whatever mold seemed attractive at the time. She had given them enough rope to hang themselves with, and now the only consolation left was to watch them hang, reflecting that she had told them it would happen, but she could not expect them to listen to a garrulous old woman who was too busy already.

It is not much fun for a woman of intelligence and sensibility to be known as the mother of a jailbird, she thought. But she had used that one up, and instead of the flood of self-pity she found herself rather pleased with the idea. It gave her stature as a mother, like the Spartan women who were so pleased to see their sons carried home dead on a shield. To have a son in prison showed that she was in touch with youth, understood their doubts and troubles, had firsthand experience of the sort of thing which made them go wrong. Everybody had to listen respectfully while she gave her views on the juvenile crime wave, the teen-age movement, youth clubs and related matters. It would no doubt come in very useful when she was in Parliament.

Philip's last letter said he had a friend in prison called Lofty Parker, also a public-school chap, who was thinking of getting adopted as Liberal candidate for the next election when he came out. Did she think she could use her influence to help him find a constituency? He was a very respectable chap and had been a trusty for over three months. He was also very clever financially, and could probably help the party a lot in that way. If Philip had met him earlier, there would have been no need for him to be where he was now. He had also told Philip how to save money on local telephone calls, which his mother would appreciate very much when he came home.

If Mrs. Sligger could get Lofty Parker into Parliament as well as herself—and Mrs. Arckwright said she knew of several constituencies which were looking for a Liberal candidate—she would already have the nucleus of her own sphere of influence in Parliament. If Parker was not amenable to friendly discipline, Mrs. Sligger could threaten to announce that he was a jailbird of known bad character. Already Mrs. Sligger felt some of the elation of power. The country would be carried off its feet, just as Cuba had been by that tiresome working-class tyrant, but Mrs. Sligger would be at the helm, her opinion would prevail. In her mind's eye she saw a great sea of faces, tense, listening. Mrs. Sligger stood alone on a great platform, wearing blue jeans, giving her opinions into a concealed microphone. Her voice would boom out over the plain, speaking on education, youth problems, sex, preaching the doctrine of love, Mrs. Sligger's love for the whole world, especially young people of the working class, the whole world's love for Mrs. Sligger. When she had finished speaking, a great sigh would go over the assembly— hundreds of thousands of people, from all walks of life, all dressed in blue jeans—then there would be tumultuous cheering. To restore order a brass band would strike up, and the assembly would sing as one man, all singing of their readiness to die in the cause of Mrs. Sligger and her opinion. She was not sure what the tune would be. Possibly "The Dam Buster's March" or "The Eton Boating Song." Probably the latter. It would be more symbolic. The people would be showing their realization of the fact that they could only be governed by a member of the upper classes. Equality was an excellent thing, but it had to be taught by such a one as Mrs. Sligger, who could lead the masses to a greater knowledge of themselves, scarcely noticing that they still held her in respect for what she was.

It was a beautiful thought, and a most pleasant way to spend the afternoon. The grinding noise from the library had stopped, and Mr. Sligger appeared looking disheveled and cross. "It's past teatime," he said. "You let me work late. I wasn't watching the time."

Mrs. Sligger said icily, "It doesn't seem to occur to you that other people beside yourself might be busy. I have a lot of things to attend to nowadays, and cannot always be thinking of tea." Then she went to fetch it.

Jamey sat on the bench outside the Principal's study in St. Rachel's and wished he had not come. Girls walking past glanced at him, some covetously, some appraisingly, many pretending to be looking at the wall behind him. They suddenly noticed that the wall had something in front of it and looked away quickly. He could hear nothing from the study, and he wanted to go to the lavatory, as he primly worded it to himself. In a women's college nothing was more unfortunate, no desire less likely of fulfillment. Angela Hammock walked past with a friend when things were reaching a crisis.

"Hullo, Jamey. What are you doing here?"

"Waiting for Deirdre. She's in with Mrs. Price-Williams. Angela, I wonder if I could have a word with you."

"Of course." Angela Hammock laughed. "Do you know Willie Rogers?"

"How do you do?" The girl with Hammock smiled, and Jamey saw that she had very good teeth, but there was something more important on his mind. When Angela heard, she laughed and told him where to go.

"But don't let anyone see you," she said. "I'll wait here, in case Deirdre comes out, and tell her where you've gone."

After five years as Principal, Mrs. Price-Williams was well prepared for Deirdre's sort of emergency. Nowadays, she tried to be kindly and tolerant in her attitude toward girls who came to her with this story. The first time it had happened, she refused to believe it and sent for a doctor on the spot, who told her he could not tell her until he had taken the most revolting test and seen whether it was positive or negative. Nowadays, she tended to expect the girl to have arranged about this sort of thing.

"You're absolutely sure, Deirdre? I mean there's no possibility of a mistake?" Deirdre shook her head, and Mrs. Price-Williams felt relieved. She had done her duty in that respect. "Well, my dear, I'm very sorry for you, but we both know you have done something awfully silly, and there's only one course of action left open to me. You say it's three months. You can stay until the end of term, and I don't want you to talk to anyone about it. The most dreadful things get around." The last time a girl had been sent down for this reason—not, she was glad to remember, from St. Rachel's—somebody had written an article in one of the university magazines saying it was a scandal that women's colleges did not provide abortion for their girls who got into trouble. The argument was that far more money had been wasted on the girls' education to date than would be justified unless, with a little extra outlay, the state was prepared to see it through. It was another example of reckless waste by the Government. Personally, she felt the Government was right to be just a little extravagant sometimes. "Well, Deirdre, I shall be sorry to see you go. Have you told your parents? If you want to have the child adopted, there is a very good adoption society run by someone called Charles Potinue. He also runs a domestic employment agency, and does most of the university girls."

"Thank you very much, Mrs. Price-Williams," said Deirdre.

"Now there's just one thing more. I'm afraid I must ask you to tell me who the father of this child is, if you know." Mrs. Price-Williams was very vague about these things. "Nothing much will happen to him, as the men's colleges don't seem to care what happens to my girls, but I think it right I should know, in order to stop him messing about with other of my girls."

149

"I'm afraid I can't tell you that."

"Why not? He will only get fined a pound, or at worst gated for a week. If you propose to marry him I shall find out who he is in due course, and take steps to prevent him coming into the College again to get my girls into trouble."

"We are not getting married."

"I should think not. I expect he's one of those untidy young men at Keble." Deirdre was stung by this. She knew no one at Keble.

"He is at Godolphin, actually."

"It doesn't make any difference. If he's that sort of person, I can't have him around my girls. It's extraordinary how you don't seem to be able to trust anyone nowadays. Well, Deirdre, if you don't tell me, I shall just have to wait until he strikes again. It's no good pretending the fault will be anyone's but yours. I am only sorry you are not more sensible about the matter." So very few of her girls seemed to be sensible. Anne Etherington had been sensible, and then she had to go and do that silly thing. She had been mixed up in Godolphin, too. Perhaps they were breeding a bad sort of person now for Godolphin, but Mrs. Price-Williams preferred to think that there was only one bad apple in the fruit basket. If only she could discover which one it was.

She led Deirdre to the door. "I expect you will have a lot of things to do, so you needn't worry about handing in your essay until next week. But try and make it more tidy, this time. There is no excuse for untidiness."

Angela Hammock was standing outside. "Yes, Angela?" said Mrs. Price-Williams sternly.

"We're waiting for Deirdre. That is to say, I'm not," said Angela, but at that moment Jamey came out of a nearby door. Behind him there was the unmistakable sound of a flushing lavatory. Mrs. Price-Williams stood still and stared.

"Are you waiting for Deirdre Black?"

"Who me?" said Jamey. "I don't think so." He caught Deirdre's eye. Judas Iscariot must have felt the same. "I mean of course I am. I just thought I'd go to the lavatory."

"So I observe," said Mrs. Price-Williams, to whom everything had become clear. "Now you've seen Miss Black, you must leave the College, and I do not want to see you here again. If anybody tells me they have seen you hanging around, I shall report the whole matter to the Chief Procurer of Godolphin."

"Why, what have I done?"

"I do not propose to talk about the other thing, although both of us know perfectly well what I mean, but apart from anything else gentlemen undergraduates are not encouraged to hang around my young ladies' lavatory. You are not a credit to your college, and I do not know what my husband would think if he knew."

"No, Mrs. Price-Williams," said Jamey, subdued. This was quite a different person from the one who had accepted a glass of sherry in his rooms the term before.

"As for you, Deirdre, I am disappointed at your choice. I do not expect my girls to associate with young men who spend their time defiling other people's lavatories."

"No, Mrs. Price-Williams."

"Now, the two of you show him out to the main gates, and see that he does not come back." Mrs. Price-Williams watched them go. Her husband had been quite right. How silly of her to have misjudged Sligger so much. Agnus was a sweet man, but he was also a good judge of character.

On their way out, Sligger said to Angela, "I'm sorry I was so long. Who was that girl you introduced me to?"

"That was Willie Rogers. Did you like her? We all think she's absolutely lovely. Some of the girls call her Ginger."

"I thought she was beautiful. She has such a nice smile. What does she do?"

"It's rather sweet. She's a history don, although she's only twenty-two. At her tutorials girls talk about their boy friends mostly, and in summer she takes them out of doors and they drink Pimms under the yew tree in St. Rachel's gardens. I once made a daisy chain for her to wear, and she didn't mind at all, but wore it for the rest of the afternoon."

"What's her love life?"

"Nobody knows really. She spends most of the time in St. Rachel's, so people think it may be very sad." Sligger was infatuated. Miss Rogers became a remote, godlike figure, untouchable, utterly grown up, living in an aura of her own beauty.

"I think she's probably extremely nice," he said. "By the way, Deirdre, what did Mrs. Price-Williams say to you?"

Chapter 13

The Inner Cell was kept busy for the remaining week of the term by the problems of organizing the John Sturgeon Exhibition. Fringe had to report that he had been unable to get the artist himself to be present, but he would be represented by his girl friend—some said mistress—Miss Phyllis Plimsoll, who was traveling down with the pictures from the gallery. They had arranged to send half a dozen of the large, or investment, size, two dozen medium and four dozen small size Sturgeons from their stocks in Knightsbridge. The collection, it was to be announced, was insured on the journey for £340,000.

Creepy Crawley had promised to get a mention of it in the national press, provided he could have a list of people attending the opening, and people buying pictures. Goyle's picture was to take the place of honor, with a plaque explaining that it had been purchased by the Anne Etherington Memorial Fund in the interests of art and international understanding. A smaller plaque, on the frame, said: "From the Collection of Stephen

Goyle, Esqre." The catalogue emphasized that it appeared by kind permission of Stephen Goyle, Esqre, Godolphin, Trustee of the Anne Etherington Memorial Fund. The arrangement of the exhibition allowed about a dozen pictures to be shown at a time, the rest being kept in reserve.

"Like an iceberg, four fifths under water," Fringe explained.

"Yes, Anne Etherington would have liked that," said English, irrelevantly.

When Jamey told them that Deirdre Black had been sent down, there was only time to register conventional indignation.

"It is typical of the Oxford mentality. If you do not like something, you must hide it away and pretend it does not exist," said Fringe.

"If they treat us like children, they must expect us to behave like children," said Greaves stoutly, as he drew an artist's impression of John Sturgeon, for use on posters and publicity handouts.

"I don't think Sturgeon has a mustache," said Angela Hammock, looking over his shoulder. "That's not my idea of him at all."

"We must ask Phyllis Plimsoll."

"She probably wouldn't admit it if he had," said Greaves. "Girls don't like to be seen with men with mustaches."

"I wouldn't mind that," said Angela, "but your mustache makes him look like a South American dictator."

"All right, draw him yourself," said Greaves, the artist, in disgust.

"Aren't we going to do anything to help Deirdre?" asked Sligger.

"The time for that is past. By her actions she has put herself outside the pale of civilized behavior," said Fringe.

"Like the South Africans," said English.

"Exactly," said Greaves; "has anyone seen a tire pressure gauge?"

"But it isn't her fault," said Jamey. "Besides, we all know the college authorities are being tyrannical."

153

"Last time it happened, I wrote an article in either *Prism* or *20th Century Student* pointing out the need for a state abortion system, particularly for young people. It caused quite a stir at the time, but when one has said that, there does not seem to be anything more to say."

English was examining one of the small, two-pound Sturgeons. "It doesn't look as if the genius was feeling quite on form that day," he said. "Look, he's painted it on the wrong side of the canvas, as well as on the right side, and he's got paint all over the edges and on the wooden frame."

"An important work. Three pounds extra," said Fringe.

"Are you sure? It looks like a faulty one to me, an export reject," said English doubtfully, holding the important work by his fingertips to avoid getting dirty.

"Perhaps you're right," said Fringe. It seemed a waste. Then he had a bright idea. "Let us present it as a leaving present to Miss Black. It would show our defiance of the college authorities. Mrs. Price-Williams would look an awful fool. In a few years' time, the picture may be worth thousands of pounds. Think what people pay for a postage stamp which has been printed upside down, or on the wrong side."

"Do you think she'd like it?" said English. It certainly was not an object which could be to everyone's taste. The right side of the canvas was a deep brown, practically in monochrome, with some signs which looked like fingermarks in one corner, possibly intended by the artist, possibly where someone had held it when it was wet. A splash in the center of slightly lighter brown still was wet, and a few pieces of wood shaving stuck to it. The picture smelled pleasantly.

"It may not be one of his more important works artistically, but I think its historic importance overlays that. The signature is there, which is, after all, the most important thing. I think the brown is a very pleasant color; it has a warmth about it which is sometimes lacking in his more conventional works."

"Anyway, who said we wanted to be conventional?" said Greaves aggressively.

154

"Exactly. Even if Miss Black is not sufficiently developed in her tastes to appreciate it, she must have the humility to realize that it is good art, and people who do understand these things can tell her how good it is. Her children will treat it as an heirloom, and her grandchildren will preserve it as an old master. Nobody thought El Greco was any good until a hundred years later, but people who bought El Grecos at the time are laughing now."

"I don't think I've seen an El Greco, but I don't like most of those old paintings," said English.

"Exactly. They have no relevance to present-day problems or trends. We think they are passé, and we may be right, but we are ahead of our time. Now this picture has relevance. You agree about that?"

"I suppose so."

"In a thousand years people may think it is passé, although I doubt it. Where, after all, can art go from here? But that still gives it a thousand years of upward trends in value, as people begin to realize its merit more and more. Its value in a short time will be incalculable."

"Why should we give it to Deirdre Black then? She has done nothing but make trouble."

"It is just a gesture. We've got to get rid of this picture as no one will buy it, because, as you say, it is defective, and we've got to give Miss Black something to show our defiance of authority, so we might as well give her a completely worthless object she won't like."

"Now you're talking sense. I thought you wanted us to give her the *Mona Lisa* or something."

Fringe sighed. If he did not have to waste so much time putting his ideas across, he would have twice as much time for ideas.

"So you see, Alec, even my wife now agrees with everything I say about Sligger." To Mr. Price-Williams this was final proof of the injustice of his cause. "Not only does she suspect him of interfering with one of her girls, but also he is always prowling around the lavatories in St. Rachel's, using them on occasion."

"I wonder why that is. I have heard no complaints of the facilities on Beaufort Staircase Two. We must look into it, as it would not do if Lord Robinson were to hear of anything wrong."

"Of course there is nothing wrong with the lavatory on his staircase. It is just that he is a generally unsatisfactory person; never content with what he has got, he must use the facilities of others."

"I see. Agnus, I assure you that nothing would give me greater pleasure than to get rid of young Sligger, but one cannot do it without a just cause. Until he has failed his Prelims twice, or committed some other outrage, we must simply regard him and his mother as a cross we must bear for Godolphin." The Procurer had received a letter from Mrs. Sligger soon after their meeting, suggesting she should give a talk to his students on education and contemporary affairs. He had replied that she would have to get in touch with some university club, as it was not normal for the Procurer to arrange extracurricular lectures. Then she had written to his wife, suggesting they should work as women together to bring some twentieth-century educational theories into the syllabus at Godolphin. The Procurer's wife was an invalid, and Mr. Scroton-Wise had answered the letter for her, saying his wife regretted it was not normal for the Procurer's wife to arrange the syllabus of gentlemen undergraduates, so he doubted if she could be of much help. He did not know where she would strike next. There could be no doubt about it, Mrs. Sligger was a menace. The next thing he had was a bundle of letters forwarded by Lord Robinson's secretary, in which Mrs. Sligger proposed Lord Robinson bring his influence to bear and turn Godolphin into a coeducational super-high school for young people, especially young people of the working class, where they could learn the proper use of sex instead of the false ideas of its use then current. Mrs. Sligger hinted that, armed with this knowledge, young people of the working class

156

would no longer be tempted toward socialism, a point she felt sure Lord Robinson woudl appreciate. Lord Robinson passed them on without comment.

"He arrived late for his last tutorial, wearing his academic gown inside out."

"Alas, Agnus, we need more than that."

Creepy Crawley studied the latest report from Oxford with something approaching despondency. He felt about Fringe rather as a Curé d'Ars must have felt about the good woman in his parish who pestered him to do something about the Christain Mothers' Guild of Home Knitting. One could not afford to despise fellow members of the movement whose enthusiasm carried them to absurd lengths, but it was no good pretending that they were more of a help than an embarrassment. Creepy had other facets to his identity, which sometimes reflected a gleam from Fringe's information. Although he described himself as a general consultant to several well-known newspapers, advising on matters of taste and art, and lending his attainments as a rounded, cultivated man to their raw judgments, his position also carried more specific responsibilities. He sat down to his typewriter and produced his own version of Fringe's intelligence, using two fingers with immense speed to produce a rounded, cultivated account in triplicate.

"Mr. Jack Piccione, the popular undergraduate son of Sir Edgar Piccione, the Home Secretary, has accepted an invitation to be present at this week's opening ceremony in Oxford of the John Sturgeon Exhibition. Mr. Philip Fringe, the undergraduate organizer, who is at Magdalen, may well be surprised, as the proceeds are going to Peace and International Friendship, the charitable organization devoted, among other things, to combating Apartheid and neocolonialism throughout the world. Sir Edgar had no comment to make last night on his son's choice, but even at Oxford, where Piccione is known as the bulwark of the Young Conservatives, people are saying this may reflect a liberalizing trend in Conservative thought.

157

"Perhaps young Piccione feels that art is more important than ephemeral political squabbles. In this case, he is to be congratulated. Sturgeon's work has already raised several thousands of pounds towards the liberation of Southern Rhodesia and the overthrow of fascism in Spain, Portugal and South Africa."

Creepy Crawley read through his composition with a satisfied smile. He could not see it getting past the *Daily Cenotaph*, but both the *Reverser* and the *Sunday Mimes* were terribly keen on antifascism at the moment. Even the *Cenotaph* might be tempted by a juicy piece about the home life of Sir Edgar Piccione. But he had other duties to attend to. On one piece of paper he wrote, "Piccione, Jack, a known risk?" On another, "Jack Piccione, the son of the Home Secretary, is a sympathizer. Given time, he might join us. Await Goyle report."

He studied Fringe's letter even more closely. On the debit side of the Sturgeon account was the entry: "To unmarried mother —one Sturgeon size one (defective) Gratis." In the ledger, Crawley wrote in his tiny, rounded hand: "Was this justified?" He then forwarded it to the appropriate person.

Deirdre was more touched than she could say when Fringe and Jamey arrived with the Sturgeon awkwardly tucked under Jamey's arm. Although neither of them mentioned it, she knew that it must have been Stephen Goyle's idea to give it her. It was so sweet, so utterly male to make this gesture, when she thought he must have abandoned her in disgust. She knew it was her own fault, it was morally wrong to be having a baby, but she could not bear the thought of being despised by the man she loved. By this charming little gift, he showed that he forgave her. She cuddled the picture as if it was a woolly animal.

"Do tell him how much I loved it. It makes all the difference to have something to take away as a reminder." She could think of nothing more hideous or cumbersome than the sticky, smelly piece of canvas, but that was what made it so sweet, as she knew how much store Goyle set by art. For him, it was probably a sacrifice. She packed it tenderly with pieces of tissue paper in her suitcase between her clean petticoat and her pink, frilly nightie.

As they left, Fringe said, "I think she imagined we were bringing it from Goyle."

Sligger said, "If I'd thought that, I'd have taken it away again. I wonder which is the quickest way out. If I'm seen here, I'm for it, as Mrs. Price-Williams said I was not to set foot in St. Rachel's again after using their lavatory once."

"Typical," said Fringe.

As they approached a corner, Jamey heard footsteps which he was sure could only be those of Mrs. Price-Williams. He panicked, and dived into the nearest door. Fringe walked on, and said "Hullo" to the bursar's secretary, who was having difficulty with an enormous wicker basket of dirty hockey shirts.

Jamey found himself in a large room facing the unspeakably lovely Willie Rogers.

"Hullo," she said, not a bit surprised.

"I'm afraid I have the wrong room. I thought you were Mrs. Price-Williams," he said in confusion.

"Her room is on the second floor," said Miss Rogers. "Aren't you Angela Hammock's friend, Jamey Sligger?"

"That's right," said Jamey, dazed by her beauty.

"You have only to go up the stairs. I will show you the way, if you like."

"That's all right. I wondered if I could leave by the window. It sounds a bit unusual, but I don't particularly want to be seen."

"If you want to, do be careful." Miss Rogers's smile sent a dagger of guilt through Jamey's body. How could he be so puerile as to want to climb out of the window? How could he do it with dignity?

"It is extremely kind of you, Miss Rogers. I do not make a point of climbing out of windows, but I happen to be in rather a hurry. I hope it is not too much of an inconvenience."

"Not at all. Please call me Willie, if you are going to make a habit of it. Shall I give you a hand?" She advanced toward

159

Jamey, holding out a hand. Jamey felt the warmth of her approaching, and shrank from the touch of her tiny hand, from the unimaginable delights concealed underneath her thin, woolen jersey.

"No, thank you, I'll manage." He climbed over the window-sill, trying not to grunt or make any other undignified noise. With a reckless, carefree wave, he swung down, missed his footing, and fell heavily from the first-floor window.

"Are you all right?" said Willie from above.

"Of course I am," said Sligger ungraciously. His ankle was dislocated, if not broken, and he would have found it hard to believe that such pain could exist. Tears streamed down his face, but they were more in anger at himself than in pain. The earth smelled damp and fresh and homely, reminding him in some obscure way of his childhood. He would have liked to stay there, watering it with his tears and whispering the secret of his pain and his love to the earthworms, but his pride was too great. He limped agonizingly away, past some lilacs which were already showing leaf in the early spring. No passion inside his breast could ever alter the sweetness of the lilac's fragrance, no evil humor ever arrest the miraculous beauty of St. Rachel's gardens in the early spring, made even more beautiful and wonderful by the realization which had come to Sligger, that for the first time since a balmy, sweet-smelling summer term at Cleeve he was in love.

Deirdre picked up her treasures one by one, unwilling to put them into her suitcase and acknowledge that they were now part of the past. There was a highly polished walnut-wood pipe with a split mouthpiece, which Stephen had once left in her room, telling her to throw it away, as he intended to give up a pipe and concentrate on cigarettes. There was a photograph of herself, taken during a summer holiday in Cornwall, which she always found particularly winning. Three knitted matinee coats, one pink and two blue—Deirdre made no secret of the fact that she would prefer a boy—and a giant-size tin of Johnson's baby powder reminded her of her new station in life. Mrs. Price-Williams had said that she could stay to the end of the term, but the place in Hastings where she was going said they could not wait. Even if she was not an unmarried mother yet, she soon would be, and that placed her in the same category, and the unmarried mother who had worked for them up to now had proved unsatisfactory.

Mr. Potinue was vague about what the home was. He said it was for training girls who wanted to become "qualified infant superintendents," which he rather supposed meant "nannies." They particularly liked unmarried mothers, as it gave the girls a chance to practice on the baby while the mother was busy with the cooking. In any case, it was very kind of them to take her, and four pounds ten a week was a very good wage considering how few people wanted other people to cook for them nowadays.

When Deirdre arrived, she was introduced as Mrs. Black to the departing cook, called O'Gravy. Mrs. O'Gravy said, "Your little one isn't born yet. All I can say is heaven help him when he is. They painted my daughter's bottom blue, said they were curing her of recurrent habits. And she's only three years old."

"Is that your daughter?" said Deirdre. "What is she called?"

"She's called Winifred," said Mrs. O'Gravy, "but that's not what she's known by normally. Tell the young lady what your mother calls you sometimes." Mrs. O'Gravy was obviously proud of her daughter's ability to talk. She seemed such a respectable woman, Deirdre could not think how she ever got round to becoming an unmarried mother.

"She calls me a ripe little bugger," said Winifred in an attractive lisp.

"No she bloody well does not. She calls you Winnie the Whiffler after as how you're always whiffling, you ungrateful little thing. I can't think how I ever bring myself to call you anything nice if that's the way you behave. Don't know where she gets such words from. As you can see, Mrs. Black, she is not a respectable young girl yet."

161

Deirdre soon settled in. The girls who paid large fees to qualify as "infant superintendents" had only one thing in common, extreme ugliness. They used to boast about their love affairs to each other in hysterical, high voices, but none of them ever asked Deirdre for her experiences. She was considered at least one class beneath them—in the case of Judith de Green, an ophthalmic surgeon's daughter, probably two classes—and anyway, they found it disgusting. Few of them spoke to her at all, unless to say, "Did you remove the *Woman's Own* from my room when you were cleaning it this morning, Mrs. Black? If so, you might be kind enough to return it, as there are rules against stealing, you know."

She hung her presentation picture by John Sturgeon in her bedroom until told to remove it by the matron, as it was unsanitary and probably contained germs. After that, she defiantly kept it under her bed where it gathered dust, taking it out occasionally during sentimental moments. In the fullness of time, she gave birth to a fine young son, whom she called Robin. She brought him back to the home, where twelve eager young "infant superintendents" to be were waiting in clean white aprons. Robin had his nappy changed on the average thirty-six times a morning, and was given six baths each afternoon. He was treated several times for every known ailment, and never produced a symptom of any disease. Later, he grew up into a typical, healthy English boy with typical, healthy English interests and merged effortlessly, unnoticeably into the English scene.

The Grand Opening of the John Sturgeon Exhibition in Oxford was hampered from the start by not having Lord Robinson as its patron. None of the grand dons accepted their invitation, and even Miss Willie Rogers, to Jamey's despair, declined in a pretty little note on blue paper. He kept it in his pocket book for a long time, until it got too worn to open, then relegated it to his private museum in an envelope of its own marked

"Highly Personal. To be destroyed after death." He would not like the irreverent eye of his biographer to gloat over his selfless passion.

Piccione did not come to the party, but sent a message through Guy that he had been detained by an essay. In all his time at Oxford, Jamey never actually saw anyone writing an essay, or any evidence that an essay had been written. They were a useful convention, to be used in a wide variety of social predicaments—when asked to a party by one's inferiors, who had no business to ask one, when registering one's disapproval at the way conversation was turning, when avoiding the friend of a friend whom one disliked, when demonstrating that the company was not up to one's own standard of social or intellectual brilliance. Jamey had only written one essay at Oxford —in his first week—which Mr. Price-Williams had set in a moment of absent-mindedness. It was on the subject of "The Hook," which Sligger had heard him talking about as some logical device to floor one's opponents. None of the works of reference had mentioned it, so Jamey had to improvise as best he could:

"Just as no angler is complete unless, in addition to rod, line and bait, he has also a hook with which, as it were, actually to catch the fish, so must the logician equip himself in each case of logical argument with a hook. The necessity of the hook is in no way better illustrated than in a simile with that very different, yet parallel image of boxing. There the opponents measure each other's defenses with the left port lead, the undercut, but it is the hook which finally knocks out the opponent, as all boxers know. Logicians in the past have tended to ignore this obvious fact, with the result that their opponents often tended to beat them in argument, or argumentation as it then was."

Jamey had handed it in, but Mr. Price-Williams never referred to it, and presumably did not read it, which Jamey thought rather a pity as it had made some good points and in places shown considerable erudition. But having experienced

163

an essay, he felt he had exhausted that side of Oxford life.

The party was a bit constrained to begin with. Guy bought two of the small Sturgeons and said he would hang them on either side of Mr. Potinue's baroque mirror. Garlick said he was going to buy one of the investment-size Sturgeons, but he made no move to do so. Miss Plimsoll served a kind of punch with an unpronounceable Spanish name, which tasted of salt and sugar. She served a Spanish delicacy which was dried dog-fish carcasses cut into strips.

"Delicious," said Garlick, and started talking to her in Spanish.

"*Je ne comprends pas*," said Miss Plimsoll with a mysterious smile. Garlick continued talking volubly in Spanish until everyone told him to shut up, but the ice had been broken.

"Can't any of you sing or anything?" said Miss Plimsoll, swinging her hips. The exhibition was held in a hut about half a mile out on the Woodstock Road, so English was sent back to his college to collect a guitar.

Goyle obviously thought it a bad idea, but everyone else was very pleased with it. Art appreciation was all very well in its way, but one couldn't keep it up for very long. Goyle said:

"The great point about Sturgeon, in my opinion, is his unexpectedness, which one can't exactly put one's finger on. What is it that makes this picture incomparably his greatest work?" He was standing by the Anne Etherington Memorial, and paused courteously as if he were paying them the compliment of supposing that somebody in his audience might be prepared to try and answer that question.

"Do you know 'Chichita Senorita'?" asked Garlick.

"Who's she?"

"It's a song."

"No we bloody well do not," said Greaves. Garlick, undeterred, started singing it to himself, making no noise but wagging his head up and down and shuffling his feet.

"The answer," said Goyle, "lies, I think, in our very inability to comprehend it. Art is not something which can be reduced to

164

mathematical formulae. Art is something which is inside every man, and yet outside him. It is a projection, as Freud would have it, of the superego."

"Do you know 'You Are My Sunshine'?" said Guy, anxious to appear with it. "You Are My Sunshine" had been very popular in the showers at Cleeve, and was often sung by the few savants who knew the words, on school buses.

"No, they don't know that," said Sligger.

"Thus, to appreciate this as his greatest work, as it undoubtedly is, involves acquiring a higher degree of sensibility, of involvement with the artist and what makes the artist tick. One must identify oneself with the personality of John Sturgeon. That is the crux. If one is unable to do that, one has no right to be here."

"Have some more drink, Stephen," said Phyllis, who thought he was being left out.

"Thank you, Phyllis. I am sure you understand. You are in a tremendously privileged position, you know, being able to live with these works of art. They must mold your character tremendously."

"Oh, I don't know." Phyllis was being coy.

"But they *must*. Of course they must. I should think you are the only person present who is qualified to judge which one really is the best."

"I'm not sure. They all seem much the same to me. I think I prefer the small ones."

"She's right," said Garlick. "Your picture isn't as good as the one I'm going to buy."

"Which is that?" Goyle prepared a damning appraisal.

"I'm not sure yet. It is going to be one of the big, investment-size ones."

"You're quite right," said Fringe, "they're much the best investments."

Phyllis came round to Jamey. "Aren't you Philip Sligger's brother?" she asked.

"Yes."

165

"I used to know Philip so well. You are just like him, only if anything more handsome." Sligger was overcome with confusion. Phyllis's face was wreathed in smiles, and her quick brown eyes were trying to catch his as if they had some secret message to impart. Plucking up courage, Jamey allowed their eyes to meet. The message was unmistakable. She said, "Stay behind and help me clear up afterward, and we can have a talk."

Jamey could scarcely believe his luck. As usual, on these occasions, he felt slightly sick with anticipation, but the certainty and the drink combined to turn it into a feeling of elation. All thoughts of the lovely Miss Rogers were driven from his head. This was something quite different in any case.

By the time English got back with his guitar, the hut was full of cigarette smoke and the drinks had circulated freely. Guy said, "We'll have to be back in half an hour unless we want to climb in."

"Of course you'll have to climb in. You're not frightened, are you?"

"Of course I'm not. It's just that I thought I might try and get an essay written, but I can easily leave it till tomorrow."

Garlick had just been about to say that he had an essay to write, but Frazer-Robinson took the wind out of his sails. He would have to stay. In any case, if there was going to be singing, they would probably need him. He had a very pleasant baritone voice, knew all the latest songs, and could sing in a most amusing falsetto when called upon to do so.

"It's a pity none of you know 'Chichita Senorita,' " he said.

Bill English looked serious for a long time, but it was obvious that no one was going to be silent; so he said, "What shall we have?"

" 'Old Smoky,' of course," said everyone. Bill stared at his guitar, deep in thought. Eventually, everyone was quiet and he pulled a few wires.

"Your eyes will be steaming," he said.

"Your eyes will be STEAMING," everyone yelled.

166

But not tears of grief
If you vote Tory
You're worse than a thief.
Your face will be FLESHLESS
Your loved ones deformed
Your home fire is burning
But your home has been bombed.
They'll hug you and KISS you
And tell you more lies
On top of Old Smoky
Where everyone fries.

It was a glorious moment, and a lovely noise to make. Glancing up at the Anne Etherington Memorial picture framed above the gathering, Jamey felt that she would have approved. "Again, again," everyone shouted.

"Your eyes will be STEAMING."

When it was over for the second time, Garlick stood up a bit unsteadily and said, "I am now going to sing 'Chichita Senorita.'" Everyone groaned. Garlick stood on a chair and began intoning the words "Chichita Senorita" in a soft, suggestive monotone. It was obviously not the words or the tune that mattered, but the gestures which accompanied them. John Whale discovered a disused lavatory in the corner of the hut, and came back with a roll of lavatory paper which he threw at Garlick. It described an elegant parabola, leaving a trail of paper behind it. Everyone cheered, and someone threw it back. Then came pandemonium. Sometimes Inner Cell socials ended like this, and it was the greatest fun. English threw a chair at Greaves, who took it in good part and answered with his glass of drink, which contained every sort of vegetable matter.

"Mind the pictures," screamed Phyllis.

"That's all right. There's plenty more where they came from," shouted Fringe. "We can turn them out at the rate of twenty-five an hour if necessary." Greaves broke a medium, or fifteen-pound, Sturgeon over his head, and everyone saw they were on a good thing.

167

"Don't be such utter fools," said Goyle, when he saw English, too, decorated with a medium Sturgeon round his neck and a small one as a bracelet.

"A bate, a bate," everyone shouted, and all attention was turned on Goyle.

"It must be very bad canvas to break like that," said Sligger, who was standing apart.

"Sh, it isn't canvas at all. We had to cut down on our overhead," said Fringe.

Guy, surprisingly, entered into the fun of it with unrivaled glee. Jamey saw him chasing Goyle round the room, carrying the Anne Etherington Memorial picture aloft. Then Goyle was cornered, there was a sickly tearing noise and a bump, and his head appeared through what was unquestionably John Sturgeon's greatest work.

When the tumult had subsided, there was an uneasy hush. Goyle's face, appearing through the picture, was more pallid and unhealthy even than usual. He did not try to get up from the kneeling position in which circumstances found him, and there was a glazed look in his eye.

"What's the matter with Stephen? Is he having a fit?"

"I think Guy must have accidentally hit him with the picture."

"That's what it looks like. Come on, Stephen, it was only an accident." Goyle did not move.

"What does he think he's doing? Come on, Stephen, can't you take a joke?" Goyle did not move, and his eyes remained fixed on something in front of him.

"He's only play-acting. Somebody give him a kick in the arse." The target was obvious and tempting. Greaves obliged, with a force which he might not have used if he had been more sober. Goyle swayed, but did not fall over, and remained staring ahead of him.

"Gosh, sorry, Stephen. I did not mean it to be quite as hard as that."

"I think we ought to get the picture off his head," said Guy. They did. It stuck on his ears, but with a bit of maneuvering became free. Goyle swayed on his knees. Suddenly, he was violently, atrociously sick on the floor in front of him.

"How disgusting," said Garlick. "I'm sorry, but I can't bear other people being sick in my presence."

"It looks as if he's had too much to drink. Come on, Jamey, we must get him back to Godolphin."

"I can't come. I've got to help clear up. You and Peter take him." Slowly, the word got round.

"Goyle's drunk!"

"How disgusting. Serve him right. People should learn how much they can take. Fortunately, I have a very strong head, but Goyle obviously didn't know that he hadn't."

"Come on, Stephen old man. We're going home."

"You take his other arm. One, two, three, whoops. Steady, put him down again. I'm dropping him. There."

"Come one, Stephen old man. We'll soon get you to bed."

When everyone had gone, Jamey and Phyllis were alone, and Phyllis smiled. Jamey said:

"First, I think we should put Anne Etherington's picture straight, back up where it belongs." They did so. Jamey was now utterly committed, ready for whatever Phyllis Plimsoll proposed.

"Whoops. Steady there. Peter, you're going too fast."

"It might help if Goyle could make a tiny effort. How are we going to get him in? I can't carry this dead weight over the Procury Garden wall."

"Neither can I. We'll have to knock up old Tradiscant. He's quite a friend of mine."

"So long as he knows that." They passed several people in the street. A policeman paid no attention to the inert figure between them, which occasionally made whimpering, wordless noises; he just said "Good night" to them as they passed. A

169

woman crossed to the other side of the street. When they reached Tradiscant's small cottage, set in the Godolphin wall, they hammered on the door until a light appeared.

"Who is it?"

"Mr. Frazer-Robinson. We want to get in."

"Why, bless my soul, Mr. Frazer-Robinson, I didn't expect to see you here. Young Mr. Goyle's in trouble, is he? I expect he'll regret it in the morning." Tradiscant wore not a nightshirt as they might have expected but a bright azure pair of pajamas, just as the Procurer had worn on the night of the fire. His only eccentricity was a pair of knee-length stockings in thick gray wool. "The less said about this the better, I expect, Mr. Frazer-Robinson," he said. "Just go out through my front door and walk straight on. You'll find yourself in Beaufort in no time. Don't thank me, it's a real pleasure to see young gentlemen enjoying themselves occasionally."

"I have lost my wallet," said Guy. There was a recognized fee for these things.

"Don't mention it. There's no hurry. I expect young Mr. Sligger has borrowed it. I shouldn't be surprised. You want to be a bit careful with young Mr. Sligger, sir. I ought to know."

"Oh, he's all right," said Guy. "He'll be coming in later this evening, but will probably be climbing in the usual way, and won't disturb you."

"Now Mr. Frazer-Robinson, sir, you should not have told me that. You know I have my duty to do, same as anyone else. You have put me in a very difficult situation."

"Your duty," laughed Guy, who assumed he was joking. "Well, good night, Tradiscant. And remember, mum's the word."

"You can trust me, sir. But you should not have told me about Mr. Sligger."

Sligger walked back alone, dispirited and slightly unwell. The evening had taught him something. Now he knew what was meant by deep petting. It seemed the most fatuous and frustrat-

170

ing activity it was possible to imagine. Why were teen-agers so keen on it? The whole world smelled of fish paste, and Jamey was disgusted with himself. The gray light of early morning was just beginning to appear as he climbed the wall of the Procury Gardens. Normally, he would be met by the smell of damp earth, flowers breathing their sweetness into the night, soft, springy turf. Now, it was Tradiscant.

"Mr. Sligger, you young 'ooligan. I've been waiting three hours for you, and now you've condescended to come home. It will all be in my report to the Chief Procurer tomorrow morning first thing. Good night to you, and see if you can stay in your bed for the rest of the night!"

Jamey did not care. There might be serious trouble. He could have stayed on in the hut if he had not been so bored. He had learned something under the mutilated canvas of Anne Etherington's Memorial, but it had not really been worth learning, and now he was alone to himself he could admit what it was, that the whole world smelled of fish paste and nothing else mattered.

PART THREE

Chapter 14

Mrs. Sligger removed the electric fire from Philip's bedroom. She had never approved of his having it and thought it might well have been responsible for his criminal tendencies. It was certainly no time to indulge him, when he returned home from prison. He must be set on the right path without delay. Mrs. Sligger had been in touch with two ex-convict welfare societies, one of which had offered her five pounds toward Philip's lodging expenses until he could find a job. The money had gone on a sort of tape measure which had caught her eye in a shop, which by measuring certain parts of an animal could give its weight. She felt it was a small recompense for all the inconvenience she was being put to. She tried it on herself, but as it only gave the dead weight, disemboweled, in kilos, she was not sure how accurate it was. Still, it was a useful thing to have. One deserved some reward for having two totally useless children, whose only purpose in life was to distress their mother.

Jamey made himself rather scarce these days, after the dramatic moment when he announced that he had been sent down. He had moved out after three days, to stay with Guy at Virginia Water for a fortnight, then he had gone to Lowndes Square to stay with the Picciones and had remained for a week after he had outstayed his welcome, sleeping on the sofa. After that he met a friend from Cleeve, who had taken him to a Chinese restaurant in the East End where his wallet had been stolen and he had come down with food poisoning, so he had stayed at the friend's house for a few days, borrowed some money and come home to welcome Philip. His behavior, in short, could scarcely have been more unsatisfactory, and he had done absolutely nothing to help his mother. Now, when he could have been making himself useful about the house and getting things ready for his brother, he had disappeared again. Mrs. Sligger was in despair as she measured the window seat busily. Disemboweled and skinned, it would have weighed twenty-two kilos. That was most interesting. She converted it incorrectly into avoirdupois and wrote the figure on a piece of paper, thinking she had too much on her hands to be able to waste time worrying about her sons.

The lanes around Farnham Green had never seemed so countrified, and as Jamey wandered among them he felt a selfish serenity of heart which can only come to people when they are totally adrift and alone. Lilac drooped over the path, seeking to embroil him in its affairs, but Jamey walked past, sturdily independent. Slowly, however, the gentle scents of spring began to work their influence, and he found himself reflecting what a lucky man he was. Lucky to be such a delightful person, lucky to be able to appreciate the joys of the country, lucky to be alone with himself. Love was quite unnecessary when there were so many other charms to feed the errant soul. An intoxicating breath of warm air suggested the fresh grass where one day he would lie with his loved one when all the problems had sorted themselves out. On reflection, he decided there were no problems. It was true that he had no money, no clear idea of what he was going to do for the rest of his life, no plans of any sort for the future, but these were quite unimportant compared with the pleasures of wandering by himself on a spring day. All he lacked was a loved one. He still thought of the sublime Miss Rogers with a pang, but he decided she must think him a complete oaf. How little did she know this gentle side of his character, the Sligger whose heart was made radiant by a spring flower. She thought of him as a figure of fun, who spent his whole life climbing out of other people's windows on cold, damp evenings, although he thought her smile had been specially friendly on that last, humiliating encounter. Perhaps she would be amused by him if he fell down on the green, springy turf and kicked his legs in the air. He practiced comic falls, until, in one of them, he landed on a stone, then resumed his walk, feeling humiliated again.

He turned into the lane which led to the Arckwrights' farm, reflecting that perhaps he would meet Miss Rogers, and lead her, without a word being said, to a soft and grassy bank, where they would be together. It seemed unlikely, but one could never be sure, and Sligger rearranged his tie. Perhaps he would meet a nymph, a shepherdess, who would invite him to chase her through the mossy copse behind the Arckwrights' home, finally collapsing in tresses of long black hair and musical laughter beneath the enormous trunk of an ancient chestnut, which must have witnessed many such scenes in its day.

He met the elder Miss Arckwright in the lane, Barbara, a plump, red-faced girl with small eyes. She said, "Hullo, Jamey," and walked to the other side of the lane. Perhaps she thought she was going to be raped, Jamey thought bitterly. In fact, it was only that she did not wish to seem to want to be raped. Nor indeed, if she had thought about it, did she want to be, but that was a secondary motive.

"Minny, Minny," she shouted in a shrill, preoccupied voice. A minuscule animal appeared, and they walked on. That idyl was over.

Nature had not really cast Barbara Arckwright for the role which Jamey had in mind. She had an enormous bust, which men were thought to find attractive, but which frightened Jamey to death. It was most unlike Willie Rogers's intoxicating shape. Perhaps nature had cast him for a homosexual, but it did not really matter, as life in Farnham Green was without temptations in either direction.

"Goodbye, then, Sligger. I'll call you Mr. Sligger now. I don't expect we'll be seeing you again, but it was a pleasure having you at Honey Farm." Warder Donaldson was a gentle, kindly man who would have been better employed almost anywhere else than in the prison service. His reluctance to believe ill of anyone had made him hopelessly unsuitable for anywhere except Honey Farm, even at a time when there was an urgent shortage of prison warders, and many tougher, nastier men in other prisons would have sacrificed three years' promotion for a posting to the rehabilitation center in Sussex. Virtue had been rewarded.

Philip said, "Not likely you won't see me again. I'm not going to let them catch me a second time. Still, goodbye, Mr. Donaldson. If all the people in prisons were like you, we shouldn't mind the occasional visit so much. Don't do anything I wouldn't do."

Donaldson looked puzzled, but he recognized a joke when he heard one and chuckled. Philip felt he had not perhaps hit quite the right note. Warders at the Scrubs had only been amused by jokes which assumed the whole world was criminal, as well as sexually perverted. It would take a bit of time for Philip to adjust his humor to the gentler tastes of the outside world. Two strangers were in the prison bus taking them to the station.

"What are you going to do now?" asked Philip.

"What I was doing before I came in."

"What was that?" said Philip, full of admiration.

"Oppose the Government by every means in my power."

"That's right," said Philip. "What did they get you for?"

"Section ten of the Official Secrets Act. I was sitting down in the road, saying nothing, harming nobody, when two bloody great policemen pulled me in."

"It's extraordinary the things they can get you for nowadays. What are you going to do now, sit down again?"

"Not exactly. We're thinking of wrecking the Whitehall telephone exchange. I shouldn't be telling anybody, but I know I can trust you. That's the only way of getting things done—action. It's all they understand."

"Of course it is. But what do you hope to gain by doing that? They'd just repair it again."

"Yes, but for twenty-four hours, or however long it takes, the country would be helpless. If there was an international crisis then, if the Russians decided they had had enough of our aggressive threats and launched a defensive war, there would be absolutely nothing the Government could do."

"But perhaps the Russians won't launch a defensive war just then."

"They might, and even if they don't, it'll make the Government sit up and think. They can't treat us as if we were just political agitators, flies on their back. We are a majority of the people now."

"Are you?"

"Even if we're not, statistics show that we soon will be."

The third member of the party had spoken. "People are just not going to allow themselves to be pushed around any more by a Government which is prepared to let us all be blown up, whether we like it or not, whenever the Americans decide."

Philip felt he had really not just come out of prison to listen to the sort of rubbish he had spent his whole Oxford life avoiding. He had four pounds and five shillings in his pocket. "Well, all I want is a girl and a bottle of whisky and a packet of fags, then you can blow up all the telephone exchanges in England for all I care." He wished his friend Lofty Parker were with him.

Jamey arranged the wild flowers in a jam jar and put them on Philip's dressing table. He returned the cuff links with "P.S." in gold which he had borrowed during Philip's absence, and placed a half bottle of whisky beside the bed. It was not just that he could not afford a full bottle—he simply did not have so much money in the world. He brought the electric fire from his own bedroom and switched it on to air his brother's pajamas. Then he laid out Philip's dinner jacket—a rather caddish one with a roll collar and dressing-gown cord decorations on the sleeves. He had provided bath salts from his mother's bathroom and a bottle of hair oil which Guy had bought in a moment of extravagance at Oxford and then decided he did not like. Jamey did not like it either, but it was a very expensive brand.

It was traditional that whichever came back from school first would prepare the other's room to receive him. Jamey was very clever with his hands and spent the hour before Philip's arrival with some crayons preparing a "Welcome Home" card. He drew a comic prison warder, brandishing a stock whip over a cringing, manacled prisoner, representing Philip. On the other side, Philip, still in leg-irons, had arrived home to a scene of domestic bliss. Mrs. Sligger, represented as a homely, middle-aged figure, sat before a blazing fire with a pussy on her knee and a cup of tea on the arm of her chair. Mr. Sligger was pouring out some whisky, and Philip was smoking an enormous cigarette and reading a copy of *Blighty*. Jamey modestly did not include himself in the picture, but even as he finished it he was uneasily aware that it possessed none of the ruthless realism or social involvement to be seen, for instance, in the works of John Sturgeon, by those who had an eye to see these things. The Sliggers kept no cat, Mrs. Sligger was not a homely woman, they had never had an open fire, relying on electricity, and Mr. Sligger had never offered either of the sons a glass of spirits. But there were conventions to be observed, and Jamey hoped that it would make his brother happy to see his efforts. Besides, he was glad to see Philip back. They were both, as so often before, in the same sort of mess.

The flowers had wilted by the time Philip came home. He spent two days in London first, and had to go straight to bed when he arrived, as he was obviously unwell. When he was not on the train, Mrs. Sligger left Jamey at the station in case he caught a later one, and went home to bed. Jamey waited until the last train came in at twelve-thirty, then took a taxi home, telling the man to send his bill to Mr. Sligger. The next day was spent telephoning the prison and the police. Philip had been given a travel warrant to Farnham Green, and had exchanged it for a ticket at the station, but he was no longer their responsibility.

"Can't they have a nationwide search?" demanded Mrs. Sligger. "After all, he's supposed to be a dangerous criminal, and he's at large." She saw herself, the prospective Liberal candidate for Llanwtyth, appealing on television for the return of her son and advising him to do nothing rash. She thought it an excellent idea, but nobody shared her enthusiasm.

"He probably caught the train to Penzance," said Mr. Sligger.

When Philip arrived, looking very disheveled and carrying a small cardboard suitcase, everybody agreed that least said was soonest mended. He was packed off to bed, and Jamey knocked timidly on the door half an hour later. Philip was lying on his bed in his shirt and trousers.

"It's your turn to do the duties, Lofty. I did them last week," he said.

"It's only me," said Jamey. "I came to see if you liked your room."

"Hullo, boy. Yes, I liked it very much. Now let me see, what have you done? Picture of house and home, very nice indeed. Bottle of whisky, excellent. Pajamas out, fire on. All in order." He seemed ill at ease.

"Did you like the flowers?"

"A trifle primitive, boy, but a kind thought."

"What were you doing for the last two days, Philip? We were all worried to death, at least Mummy was." It seemed an unmasculine thing to be, but Jamey was sure he was the only one who really cared.

"I called on a mutual friend of ours, Miss Phyllis Plimsoll, actually."

"She said she knew you. I don't care for her much."

"Phyllis is no good. You'll never get the greens from her. We used to call her Phyllis the Tickle."

Jamey looked down and blushed. "I thought she was a complete waste of time. Very superficial, if you know what I mean."

"Superficial as hell. She's just a stage men have to go through.

I'll introduce you to Tilly Eukallipagos one day. Now she's something."

"I thought she lived in Tangier."

"Well, maybe she does, but she gets smuggled into England sometimes, I can tell you."

"Do you know John Sturgeon, the painter?"

"Oh, John. I shouldn't have thought he'd be your cup of tea. The only trouble with prison was that there weren't any girls. You got so desperate that you'd have settled for the Plimsoll."

Jamey did not say that that was also the trouble with Farnham Green and the whole world as he knew it. By the way Philip changed the subject, it was obvious that he did not know John Sturgeon. Jamey had forgotten how much his brother lied.

"Tell me about Tilly Eukallipagos. I know her nephew, Philip Fringe."

"Tilly's all right if you've got the energy. When she thinks conversation is flagging, she sings the 'Internationale' in that splendid bass voice of hers. I don't much care for those political people as a rule, particularly the women, but one has got to get one's greens somewhere."

Jamey was not sure whether he was lying. "Did you get your greens in London while you were there?"

"What on earth do you think I was doing, boy? Calling on a maiden aunt?" They had no aunts, maiden or otherwise, so Jamey had to agree that he did not suppose Philip was calling on one. But he disapproved of Philip's new attitude to things. Sex was a thing to be wondered at in private, lied about in public, but never a thing to be taken for granted. He thought he would have to send a report to Brother Richard at Cleeve about this. It was nice to think he still had some secrets he kept from the world. Jamey was beginning to believe he was just a nice, openhearted boy with nothing to hide. But he still had to subscribe to Rapey's moral encyclopaedia, and on leaving Oxford he had taken on another task, that of keeping Philip Fringe informed on all political and sociological matters that could be useful. The modern criminal's dislike of politics was one point, his

lack of any sense of morality another. One must keep one's iden-
tities separate.

Philip's home-coming dinner was put off until his recovery,
but it was held then with all the gruesome ceremonial which had
been observed in other, happier times, when the boys had come
home from school. The men wore dinner jackets, and Mrs. Sligger a printed cotton garment which someone had told her was
worn by African peasant women and was the most attractive
thing in the world. On her it passed for an evening dress. Mr.
Sligger grudgingly opened a bottle of the port which had been
laid down at Philip's birth, but not given to him. After dinner
there were speeches. Mr. Sligger said:

"In proposing the toast of my eldest son, and in welcoming
him home for what we trust will be a longer stay than we have
enjoyed since he first went to school, we must also couple with
it the hope that happier times are ahead of him. It would be a
waste of time to pretend that our eldest son has not, at times,
been a source of sorrow to us all, particularly his dear mother,
but we must have trust that he now has a firm intention of devoting all his time to her, so that he can be a comfort to her in
her present, autumnal state, and a solace in the twilight of her
life."

Jamey thought it rather a moving speech, but Mrs. Sligger did
not seem to agree, and Philip grimaced. The next speech was always from Mrs. Sligger. Although she devoted most of her wak-
ing hours to the composition and delivery of speeches, the icy
formality of these family gatherings worried her and she usually
showed up poorly beside her husband.

"In seconding Aidan's, my husband's, motion of my poor
son Philip, of whom, as you all know, I have always been fond,
this is the point, that whereas we are all very glad to see him
back, and I shall continue to say that, we all hope he will now
settle down to a settled life. I often think that the trouble with
youth today, and Philip is no exception, is its superficiality and
complete lack of maturity. That is why you get all these cosh

183

thugs and juvenile delinquents like Philip. It is no fault of their own, but if you could replace them by sensible, mature people of a reasonable age, there would be no problem."

The abolition of youth was Mrs. Sligger's new idea in the campaign to catch the teen-age vote in Llanwtyth. Like the working classes, the only way to keep youth in its place was to lead it, take an interest in the things it did and teach it what to think. Mr. Sligger put on a cynical expression and thought about the autumn of his life. Jamey and Philip were too busy preparing their own speeches to listen, but they assumed it was embarrassing, and laughed in a superior way whenever their eyes met.

After dinner was over, Mrs. Sligger said to Philip, "What are you going to do now?"

Philip said, "I thought I'd get a job in London."

"Jobs," said Mr. Sligger. "That's all the young ever seem to think of nowadays. Never a thought to staying at home and looking after their mother. That's where their duty lies."

Mrs. Sligger agreed that she needed looking after. "We've had quite enough jobs from you for a while, young man. You had better stay here and settle down for a bit, to show people you mean to be respectable."

"All right, but there's nothing much to do here, is there?"

That struck Mrs. Sligger as very humorous. She gave a bitter laugh. "Only so much work I never have a second to myself all day long and can't even hear myself think most of the time." Jamey reflected that even if she couldn't hear herself think, everybody else could hear her at it. "I knew I had something to do. Come here, Philip, and take off your jacket. Lift up your arms." Philip had a made-up tie on and did not want to take off his jacket. He was quite able to tie his own tie, but the present fashion was for a very thin, pointed one, which made him look like a musician and was very attractive.

"Phew," said Mrs. Sligger. "Have you had a bath since you came back?" That was unnecessary. Philip grimaced. "Seventy three kilos exactly. Both my sons are quite different. That's most interesting. I wonder what one should make of that. Perhaps

184

Jamey's bowels are much bigger." She wrote the figure down on a piece of paper. When she had collected enough material, she might make it the subject of a lecture to the Women's Institute, which would listen to anything.

The only communication which Jamey ever had from Godolphin after his leaving, apart from endless appeals for money which he received until the end of his life, was a Roneoed scrap of paper from the Procury Office called "Notice to Undergraduates Going Down at the End of the Hilary Term." Rooms should be cleared of all private possessions and other impedimenta other than college property by March 28, as they would be needed for delegates attending a World Population Conference. Anything found in the rooms after that date would be liable to be impounded.

Jamey could not help feeling that his few possessions would not add up to a grave encumbrance to students of World Population. Everything in the room was Frazer-Robinson's. Jamey had hidden away his travel poster from Spain, his empty Chianti bottles and his school cricket caps on the first day in Beaufort. They were now on top of his hanging cupboard, from where he would have to retrieve them. He rather supposed his cricket caps might help him to get a job one day, although he had no idea what sort of job would require them. He had always been brought up to believe that firms hired chaps as much for their ability to play games as for their academic distinctions, and this would make his caps as important as his school certificates for documentary evidence.

He drove up to Oxford in his father's old Riley, borrowing two pounds from his mother for petrol. He had no source of income at all, and found it degrading to have to fill his cigarette case every morning from the box in the dining room, but neither parent had suggested any other arrangement. Mrs. Sligger liked having people around the house she could talk to, and Mr. Sligger hated the idea of anything happening, and would fight against it with such energy as he had. On the way to Oxford, a resolution formed itself which made Jamey a lot happier. Without telling anyone, he would go round to St. Rachel's and pass the time of day with Miss Willie Rogers, the divine, unattainable, lovely creature who constituted another of Jamey's treasured secrets from the world. He sang to himself, as he always did when alone in the car, first "Drink to me only" in a sentimental tenor, but his voice sounded rather thin against the noise of the car. Then he tried "You Are My Sunshine," but found he had forgotten the words. Next he tried the hymn "Heavenly Queen," but it sounded out of place. In the end he settled for the nuclear disarmers' march, "Your eyes will be STEAMING," and the stirring music echoed round the car and out of its windows to be lost in the Oxfordshire countryside. As he drove, he composed his letters to Rapey Rawley and Philip Fringe, his dear friend Philip Fringe, his very dear friend. A duck was wandering across the road, and before Jamey could give his mind to the creature or its petty problems, he found he had run it over. He believed he had read somewhere that one was the legal owner of anything one ran over on the public highway except human beings, of course, which one had to report to the police within five days, so he stopped the car and picked up the duck. It was extremely difficult to tell with ducks which movements were attributable to the vestiges of life, and which were those of death. Sligger decided that ducks were not animals of sufficiently high intelligence to make the distinction an important one, and threw it in the back of his car. He was not a cruel person, but one had to be realistic, and if one spent one's time worrying about all the suffering ducks in the world, and there must be millions of them, one's own life would soon become very miserable.

At the lodge of Godolphin, Tradiscant said, "You can't come in here, young man, without written permission from the Chief Procurer."

"I've come to collect my things," said Sligger.

"That's what they all say. So long as it's only your things you would be wanting to collect, I suppose I can't complain. But

186

Mr. March had better accompany you to make sure you don't take more than your deserts."

When March was walking beside Jamey toward Beaufort, he said: "You mustn't mind old Mr. Tradiscant. He doesn't like change, you see, that's why he always seems a bit crusty. For myself, I don't care where the young gentlemen come from, and if they're from what you might call 'umble 'omes that's all the same to me. But Mr. Tradiscant, he's a real one for things being like they was when 'e was younger. Bit of a character, really, you might say."

March was obviously preparing himself for a long discussion of Tradiscant's failings, but Sligger was not going to be drawn into the conspiracy. He enormously resented the implication that he came from an 'umble 'ome. The Sliggers were an extremely respectable family of some antiquity. His mother, it was true, came from a different walk of life altogether. Her father, if Sligger remembered correctly, had been the son of a local Government officer in Nottingham. But many dukes had married actresses of much humbler origin, and their children were not accused of coming from an 'umble 'ome.

"Oh really?" said Sligger. "Perhaps you'll be kind enough to carry this poster and these Chianti bottles."

"I call that really nice," said March, looking at the poster. "Extremely good taste, as you might say. I think it gives an impression of warmth and vitality. You can really feel the sun hitting you in the face and smell the perspiration on that ferocious bull. I have never been to Spain myself, but I should like to go. I spent fifteen years in Kenya, of course, before it was all abolished."

Jamey did not want to hear the underporter's opinions on art or African emancipation. He said, "I have three cricket caps there. Be careful to lose none of them."

Mr. March put one of them on his head and giggled. Its gold tassel—costing five guineas at the school tailor's—hung over his vacant, stupid face. Even Jamey had only worn that cap on ceremonial occasions, when he walked from the school to the cricket pavilion and back again. Occasionally he had worn it in front of the mirror in his room, but those had been private occasions, and Jamey would not have admitted them to anyone. He turned away from the sight in disgust. Whatever people said about the working classes, and one had to say things oneself sometimes, they were scarcely ever up to one's own standards. He walked round the room which had been his home for two terms, and felt unutterably sad. So much had happened within these walls, so much boisterousness, so much longing, so much friendship and pleasure. He had no idea that it would be such a wrench to leave. Oxford was a beautiful and hallowed spot in a drab world. Outside it there was no shelter from the idiocies of other people, the strictures of middle age, and the miseries of finding a job and observing the conventions of one's class.

"Mr. Garlick is moving in to share with Mr. Frazer-Robinson next term. I hope they will keep up the gay times. I never thought that room in the Procury was a suitable place for a man of Mr. Garlick's temperament, when he was turned out by the fire. I expect he'll be as happy as you were with Mr. Frazer-Robinson. Now that's what I call a really nice young lad. Not that Mr. Garlick isn't quite a gay one, too."

It was all that was needed. Sligger did not trust himself to speak as he led the loping underporter back through the gates of Godolphin to his car. Mr. Tradiscant did not look up from the lodge, but Jamey felt his eyes on his back. In a quixotic gesture of defiance, he tipped March one of Mrs. Sligger's pound notes. The idiot received it wreathed in smiles, and doffed the Cleeve Junior Colts Eleven Cricket Cap as if he were saluting. When he got back to the lodge, Tradiscant said, "I fancy I observed Mr. Sligger behaving like a gentleman rather late in the day."

He whistled when March handed over the pound note and after he had given him seven and sixpence in return he said, "Perhaps I misjudged the young gentleman after all. But you can't be too careful in these times, Mr. March, and he should of let us know sooner."

"That's right," said March. "I never saw any wrong in him, except he was a bit stand-offish."

"There's no offense in being stand-offish to you, Mr. March. It's only when you've been here forty years you expect to be shown a little civility."

Jamey stared at the ugly, mean exterior of St. Rachel's and marveled that it could hold such a deliciously lovely creature within its walls. In the vacation there was nothing to divert the eye from its shoddy asymmetry. No lanky girls with long hair and multicolored stockings strode in and out, no preoccupied young men stood outside reading the notice about bicycles. For the first time that day, Jamey began to feel his own unworthiness. What would he say to Miss Rogers, how explain that he had traveled over a hundred miles to collect his cricket caps and see her, the only justification of his continued existence? He decided to take her the duck as a present. But first, he would go for a walk in the college gardens, and perhaps he would meet her there, or perhaps she would see him from her window, and call to him. He had only his travel poster of Spain in which to wrap the duck, now undoubtedly dead, but he felt it could scarcely serve a nobler purpose.

The porter said she did not know whether Miss Rogers was in and scowled into her bowler hat. It was none of her business to know, just to see that visitors did not walk on the grass and that nothing of which Mrs. Price-Williams would not have approved happened in the quad. Jamey felt relieved that she did not know. A firm answer either way would have ended his happy uncertainty of purpose. The porter stared suspiciously at the bundle under his arm, but Jamey was fortified by the knowledge that even if it had been a bomb, she would not disapprove more strongly of its contents.

St. Rachel's gardens could never have looked so lovely. Rhododendrons and azaleas were in bud, and Jamey had to tread his way on the warm turf to avoid daffodils and clumps of narcissi. The scent of apple blossom flooded around him as he stood beneath the window he had identified as the one from which he jumped one dark, wicked night of the Hilary term. Only the window, dark and unblinking, gave any indication of a harsher world outside the exuberance of his own soul. In fact, he had miscalculated and he was standing beneath the window of the college drying-room, but it did not matter, as Miss Rogers was enjoying a well-deserved holiday in Salcombe. But Jamey sighed, and yearned for the tinkle of laughter coming out of that lovely throat. When he had stood for a while, his neck became sore with looking upward, and he decided to walk round the gardens. Perhaps he would meet her there. Bashfully, her eyes would avoid meeting his—for they knew of their love for each other —and his would dwell on her chest, her maddeningly delightful chest. Then Jamey would take her hand, and they would cry on each other's shoulders with relief that their feelings were known and shared, and neither would any more have to keep the secret locked up. If he did not meet her on the walk, he expected he would leave the duck as a present outside her room, without a word of explanation.

At the farthest end of St. Rachel's garden, in a clearing by the pond is a small, round summer house of unpretentious design, decorated by Snow White and the Seven Dwarfs, done in limestone by an Italian firm. A few waterfowl lived there, fed each evening by the college porter, but the place had such a bad reputation as a trysting spot that no girl ever went to it, for fear of losing her reputation. Jamey was enchanted by it. He and Willie Rogers could live there. He would catch fish in the pond which they could eat. She would keep house for him in the little pavilion, cooking fish and ducks when he caught them. There would be few of the comforts of life in the modern world, but no comfort could match the harmony of two young bodies and souls together, living in peace and understanding and love. Sometimes he would fall into the pond to amuse her, and her laughter would ring through the glade, making the very ducks and fish happy to play their humble parts in the scheme of things. There was laughter coming from somewhere, but it was more of a guilty giggle than the free, open laughter of lovers. Jamey walked up to the summerhouse.

"You're not a doggie at all, you're a little pussy cat," said a voice.

"Miaow, miaow," said another.

"There's a good pussy cat. Now I'm going to give you some cream. Cream for a nice pussy. Say purr."

"Purr."

Mr. Price-Williams was on his hands and knees, rubbing his head against Mrs. Price-Williams's legs, when he saw Jamey standing in the doorway. They both jumped visibly, like a pair of frogs which had been given a prod from behind.

"You," said Mrs. Price-Williams.

"Hullo, Sligger," said Mr. Price-Williams, "I have been reading that essay of yours about the Hook. It's too late to do anything about it now, but I'm afraid you've got hold of the wrong end of the stick completely."

"I thought you had him sent down," said Mrs. Price-Williams accusingly.

"You see the important thing about the Hook is that it is just a conventional sign, without any validity or truth value of its own outside the truth value of the two statements it connects." As Mr. Price-Williams started going over his essay of two terms earlier, Jamey sat beside him on a wooden bench and put down his bundle, staring intently into his tutor's face, trying to register intelligent interest. Mr. Price-Williams spoke very fast:

"You see all the Hook means is this, that of two statements connected by it, it is not the case that the first is true and the second false. It may be that the first is false and the second true, or that both are false, or that both are true, but it can never be the case that the first is true and the second false."

"I see," said Jamey. "It must be very helpful."

"The only case where the Hook can connect two statements of which the first is true and the second false is where the Hook itself has the truth-value of false."

191

"I see. How do you know whether the Hook is a false one or a true one?"

"By whether it is the case or not that the first statement is true and the second false. All other combinations make it true."

"In fact it is practically always safe to use a Hook."

"I think you are missing my point. Take this object." He picked up the bundle. "Now I can equally say that this object is the property of a certain James Sligger, or I can say that it belongs to someone else, but for the purpose of argument we must agree that it could not both belong to James Sligger and to someone else. Are you with me?"

Jamey nodded. At that one side of the travel poster from Spain fell open and Mr. Price-Williams screamed. He dropped it on the floor, where the duck's head appeared and stared reproachfully at an empty world. Jamey did not know what had happened. The duck was clearly dead, and could not have bitten him. Perhaps it had gone bad and a worm had appeared to shake its single gory lock in his face. "Agnus," cried Mrs. Price-Williams, taking him by the hand and staring with disgust at the thing on the floor. "Go and get some water," she said.

Jamey had no receptacle. He remembered his Chianti bottles in the car, and ran to fetch one. On the second time past the porter's lodge, he said, "It's nothing. I think Mr. Price-Williams has been taken ill in the summerhouse."

There was an ominous quiet about Mrs. Price-Williams's manner when Jamey returned. Mr. Price-Williams gratefully seized the Chianti bottle which was filled with pond water, and then seemed uncertain what to do with it. Gingerly, he drank a little.

"I do not wish to know whether you knew that Agnus was allergic to feathers," she said. "That is irrelevant. I wish to know what you think you are doing in my garden, and what you are doing with that duck."

"It's quite all right his coming here," said her husband, who was feeling apologetic after the scene he had caused. "I wanted to talk to him about his essay."

192

"Well you might have told me you were going to give a tutorial here, Agnus." There was an infinity of rebuke in her voice. Their private moments would never be the same again. "And what about the duck? Is that a St. Rachel's duck?"

"No."

"Where does it come from?"

"I just picked it up."

"I suppose you expect me to believe you. Well, I am not going to stand for young men coming in here and slaughtering my ducks. This time, I shall have to speak to the police, as you have already put yourself outside the pale of the college authorities."

Fortunately, Sligger was saved from this fate by the arrival of Miss Gleener, the college porter, carrying a First Aid tin. When she saw that the duck was the only casualty, she said: "I did not expect to be called out to give first aid to a duck." Reluctantly, she admitted that it was not one of St. Rachel's ducks. "I expect it comes from one of the men's colleges," she said, hinting darkly at everything that implied.

Jamey's pilgrimage of love ended with his being led away in the wake of Miss Gleener. He carried the dead duck under his arm with such dignity as he could muster, and threw one last frenzied, passionate glance at the window of the college drying room before following meekly out of the gates and out of St. Rachel's life forever. When he had gone, Mrs. Price-Williams said, "Well, I expect we should be going back to Cumnor now." The chill in her voice would have frozen a much harder heart than that of Agnus, her loved one.

Jamey had an hour or so before leaving Oxford, and a quick calculation reassured him that he could get home on sixteen and sixpence worth of petrol if he spent three and sixpence on a plate of spaghetti. The Fantastacherie was a ghostly place in vacation time. A solitary diner crouched in a corner over a copy of the *Reverser*, marking passages in it with a blue pencil, and writing remarks in the margin. Sligger regarded him closely.

"Hullo, Christian," he said. Creepy Crawley jumped, rather as the Price-Williamses had done, and pushed his newspaper under the paper tablecloth.

"Hullo, Jamey. I was hoping to see you, or at least some of my friends. I just came down to have a word with the warden of All Souls. Do you know him?"

Jamey said he didn't.

"No, I don't suppose you do. I always find something exhilarating about Oxford when the undergraduates are down. What brings you here?"

Jamey told him. Creepy Crawley did not seem at all surprised.

"I heard there was a bit of a rumpus after that Sturgeon party. Of course, Sturgeon is a bit advanced for the Oxford undergraduate nowadays, particularly after they've abolished National Service. It was a mistake of Stephen's to suppose that young, unformed minds could jump so easily. I expect that most of your young friends are just past the Postimpressionists and groping their way toward the Cubists. We were thinking of having a junior Sturgeon exhibition, for people who had not yet got round to accepting the abstract in its totality, but the technical difficulties proved too great. You will find it difficult to believe, but the production department tell me it is easier to produce the more serious works of art on an economic scale than the sort of 'pop' art people want."

Sligger expressed disbelief. It was flattering to be included in the circle of people, far-seeing and more mature than the others, who were qualified to pass judgment and appreciate serious abstract art. "I enjoy Sturgeon's work particularly," he said, and felt he was quite right to say it. Even if it had not occurred to him to look at the paintings as anything but a worthy cause, he was certainly the sort of person who did appreciate them. It was useless to expect such people as March, the underporter at Godolphin, to appreciate serious art. Even if they were not so unfathomably stupid and insensitive, they were the wrong class of people, as it were.

"I'm glad to hear that," said Creepy Crawley. "Of course,

Sturgeon is really only someone to cut your teeth on. You could arrange his works into movements, like a symphony, if you liked. The early works, which set the tone, the second period, sad, and disillusioned after the Spanish tragedy, *maestoso*—you might almost say sentimental—the third, when he had found happiness in Tangier, light and skipping as a gavotte, the last movement, rising to a crescendo then falling away, with somber undertones."

"I think that is a very good idea. I like the third movement most, I am afraid. They are so warm. You can feel the heat of Tangier hitting you from the canvas."

"I know what you mean. I think that's a very good way of putting it. One might make a note of it and use it later. Tell me, Jamey, what are you thinking of doing now? Have you got a job?"

"I am just looking around."

"Quite right. I shouldn't jump into anything."

"How does one set about getting a job like yours?"

Creepy looked thoughtful. "I think that would be aiming a little bit high, just at present, if you don't mind my saying so. But there are openings. I dare say the *Reverser* is looking for someone to help in the library. Not very exciting work, of course; you paste the cuttings and date-stamp them. Somebody else files them. But it might help you get the feel of things. And a few friends in the library are always a great help to the movement—they see that the irrelevant things get lost, and the important things are retained. In the *Sunday Mimes* library, for instance, you won't find a single mention of the affair in Hungary when critical elements threatened to overthrow the democracy. They've just got a card under Hungary, Disturbances, 1956: *see under* Suez, colonialist adventure." But one has to be very careful. It might be better if you tried to get the feel of things in the provinces, first. There's a very good newspaper in Crewe which takes apprentice journalists on a six-year term."

"I think I would prefer to be in London."

"Well, you cannot expect me to help you. I have some influence in Crewe, but I must dissociate myself completely from anything you do in London. It wouldn't be fair to my friends. I respect them, and expect them to respect me."

Jamey had finished his plate of spaghetti and waited for Creepy Crawley to pay for it. He made no move to do so, and Jamey decided to sit it out. Eventually Creepy coughed up, entering the sum of three and sixpence in a tiny hand in his diary. He tapped it and said:

"I have enjoyed my lunch very much. Thank you, Jamey. I expect I shall see you when I can get down to Crewe."

"How perfectly disgusting," cried Mrs. Sligger. "What on earth do you expect me to do with a duck?"

"We could eat it," said Jamey.

"Don't be absolutely ridiculous. You expect me to eat a dirty thing like that? I'm not going to have you bringing your filthy habits into my dining room."

"There's nothing wrong with it. It's just got slightly run over."

"Don't be silly. There's no end of diseases you can get from eating filthy things like that. It hasn't even been plucked or cleaned. It's probably crawling with fleas. Go and put it in the dustbin." Duck were things which arrived plucked and dressed and wrapped in polythene, ready frozen so that one did not have to freeze them oneself. They were headless and hollow, with only the upper leg for decoration, and possibly a bit of decorated paper round where the neck should have been.

"Quack, quack," said Philip, pointing the head at her, and Mrs. Sligger screamed. She was a compassionate woman, and did not like to be reminded that the meat she ate had ever been part of an animal, that the fish had ever swum in the sea or in sparkling rivers. People eating her food might have had the same doubts. Fish arrived in fingers, rectangular shapes covered in silver paper. Sometimes Mrs. Sligger managed to remove all the silver paper, on other occasions she did not. That was all the preparation that food required. In its proper unwrapping lay all the difference between good plain cooking and *haute cuisine*. Meat arrived boned, skinned, frozen and trussed, wrapped always in polythene as a guarantee of hygiene, that it had not touched the horny hands of the meat purveyor or the rude inside of his refrigerator. Mrs. Sligger had very strong opinions about food.

"I like my food fresh, and I like it clean," she explained, as if it was the most extraordinary taste to have. Mrs. Arckwright agreed with her, but said one had to be realistic. They both felt that food was much fresher out of a clean refrigerator, than if it had just walked out of some filthy field. But the decision was not an important one, as they could not have had food prepared in any other way, even if they wanted it.

Philip threw the duck into the dustbin, still saying "Quack, quack." When he got back, Mrs. Sligger said:

"Now I want you boys to help me. The Constituency Association want me to give a present as the first prize in their Tombola competition. They have already sold twelve tickets, but they haven't got a prize. I thought we might make a rug, but it wouldn't give us time. Of course I could buy something, but I do not feel that candidates should be expected to spend money on elections, and I think I am quite right. The difficult part of it is that I simply have not got anything to spare. I could give them my animal bulk-weight measure, but I cannot really do without it here, and I do not think they would understand how to use it. In many ways, the people of Llanwtyth are very backward."

"I have got a bottle of hair oil which is very expensive," said Philip. Jamey felt uncomfortable.

"That is a suggestion, but again I am not sure they would know how to use it." On her one visit to Llanwtyth, Mrs. Sligger had stayed at the Station Hotel and met her three supporters. She had given them a little talk about the Liberal revival and stood them a very expensive tea, then, as there seemed nothing else to do, come home again. But she had a very poor opinion of her voters. "Now, what are *you* prepared to sacrifice?"

Jamey had expected this, and was at a loss.

"Absolutely nothing, I suppose, as usual. Your brother's at least made an effort, but we can't expect young Jamey to move a little finger to help the world situation, can we?"

Jamey really had very few possessions indeed. "I have some Chianti bottles," he suggested.

"I call that really generous," said Mrs. Sligger sarcastically. "You *are* prepared to do a lot for your mother, and to help all the unfortunate people in the world, the people starving in underdeveloped countries and young people at home going off the rails because nobody understands them." All these worthy causes were clearly identified with the success of the Llanwtyth Liberal Party Tombola. "What about your shotgun?"

"That belongs to father."

"No it doesn't. He gave it to you, not being quite as mean as yourself. But I don't suppose you're prepared to make the tiniest sacrifice." The shotgun was one of the very few things in the world that Jamey treasured. He suspected his mother knew this, as it would be a most unsuitable prize for three old ladies to raffle between them. In any case, it was worth nearly two hundred pounds, and he would be most surprised if the Tombola raised more than ten shillings. He thought he could get out of it on a legal point.

"Father never actually said it was mine. He said I could use it."

"That is the same thing. Go and fetch me your shotgun at once."

"No. I won't."

"Nasty, spiteful, disobedient little thing. Your brother offered to do everything he could. I'm going to talk to your father about this."

Mr. Sligger said he had never heard anything so ridiculous as the idea of sending a perfectly good shotgun away. Miners were violent people, and not to be trusted with firearms; there was nothing to shoot at down in the mines; Mrs. Sligger herself would not be safe from assassination, and in any case the gun belonged to him.

Mrs. Sligger retired to her bedroom to cry, while Philip and Jamey, left alone, decided to send the dead duck as a prize for the Tombola. It was retrieved from the rubbish bin, a bottle top sticking to its neck. After a short debate, they decided not to pluck or disembowel it, but measured it and recorded the information that it would weigh less than a kilo in those circumstances. Then they wrapped it up and addressed it rather grandly to Liberal Party Headquarters, Llanwtyth, South Wales, feeling they had done a lot for the Liberal cause.

When the package arrived in Llanwtyth, already emitting a slight odor, it caused a certain amount of confusion, as nobody had heard of a Liberal Party Headquarters. Eventually a sly postal clerk (Grade III) readdressed it to the Labour Party Headquarters, from where it eventually arrived on the plate of Mr. Ephrun Williams, the popular octogenarian Member for Llanwtyth, who had been too poorly to get to Westminster that Parliament and lived in an attic above the party headquarters, where meals were taken up to him on a tray, whenever they remembered.

Chapter 15

Sligger arrived a minute early for his interview in the *Reverser* offices, and was led to a tiny room where there were three plastic chairs of grotesque design and discomfort; he was told to wait until Mr. Delano Kaptain could see him. After he had waited an hour, he began to get restless. The girl who had shown him in was not attractive, he decided, so much as *piquante*. Having decided that, there was little to add. A large photograph on the wall might have been of Mr. Danilo Dolci, Mr. Ben Bella, Dr. Kwame Nkrumah, Mrs. Tilly Eukallipagos, the Secretary General of the United Nations, or almost anybody else. Perhaps it was an abstract generalization, a kind of identikit essence of them all. It could not have been Mr. Jomo Kenyatta or John Sturgeon because it had neither beard nor mustache. Jamey was rectifying this oversight when the door opened, and the *piquante* secretary said, "Mr. Kaptain can spare you two minutes, if you'd be kind enough to step this way."

When he arrived in the office, the mystery of the photograph was solved. It was Mr. Delano Kaptain, who sprawled on a plastic executive's chair, smoking a cheroot, with his feet in an elegant pair of co-respondent shoes on the desk in front of him. Jamey had the greatest difficulty in deciding whether he was a European or—how should he put it?—a non-European. Probably the former, but his sun tan, in that case, was sensational. Of course it did not matter which he was, as biological tests had shown that there was absolutely no difference between the races, and, if anything, blacks were superior and certainly no darker-skinned than anybody else, but Jamey thought it added glamour to this languid young man if he had been born in a mud hut under the name of Marmaduke Ukelele.

"James Sligger?" The voice was like a wireless comedian's imitation of an American accent. Jamey nodded. "You're late." A long silence followed. "Sixty-five minutes late."

"I'm sorry," said Jamey. The tension relaxed.

"That's all right. Now we've got the formalities over. You want a job. I've got several I could give you. Is that right?" Jamey nodded. "Suppose you tell me something about yourself."

Jamey was aghast. Where should he begin? How could he possibly do justice to the infinite diversity of his character in a bald description? Which sides of his fascinating personality, with its many paradoxes and seeming inconsistencies, would be most

200

likely to find favor? "I suppose I'm a pretty normal sort of chap really," he said. "I just happen to be on the side of the under-dog." Jamey produced this as if it was an outrageous, controversial statement which might well shock his listener, but he had calculated well, and his listener was not shocked.

"That's all right. We can manage with a certain amount of that round here. Have you got any particular line?"

Once again Jamey felt he was standing on the edge of a sand dune and the sand was slipping away, inch by inch, from under his feet. He took a step backward. "What do you mean by lines?"

"Good heavens, lines, man. That's what I mean by lines."

"I see." Jamey pondered. At Cleeve, he had been thought a man of parts. He was good-looking, reasonably industrious, good at cricket, not known to be guilty of any flagrant moral turpi-tude, a general favorite. Which of these was his line? "I think I may have a line on education," he said.

"Let's hear it."

Jamey repeated as much as he could remember of his mother's theory of education, how the universities should be turned into co-educational super-high schools for young people, particularly those of the working class, how the students should be in-structed in the proper use of sex, how Mrs. Sligger should be given the over-all control of educational policy.

"I like it. I like it very much. The only trouble is that we had all of that, almost word for word, in the *Reverser* about eighteen months ago. I guess you must have read it subconsciously or something. The only thing that's new is this proposal for an over-all suprema. You call her a woman of your acquaintance. Who is she?"

"My mother, actually."

"I see. Yes, well, that's an idea. How about some other line. Have you got anything on TV, records, drama, teen-agers, books, films, music, sport, psychology of sex, art, or anything else?"

"I know a little about art."

201

"Spill it."

Jamey thought of the art lectures at Cleeve, mostly about Leonardo da Vinci, but latterly moving up to respectable impressionists with French names and Van Gogh. Nothing there, he thought. "I specialize in the postabstractionists," he said.

"Not John Sturgeon?" Mr. Kaptain groaned. "Well, if you've got anything new, I'll hear it."

Jamey told him about the symphony theory, with special emphasis on the heat of Tangier emanating from the canvas in the third movement.

"We've already got it," said Kaptain. "You wouldn't be a friend of Christian Rawley, would you?"

Jamey said he was a great friend, a very close, dear friend, enjoying a particular intimacy which gave him an insight into Christian Rawley perhaps denied to others of his acquaintances. He felt he was on safe ground. Mr. Kaptain showed him a typed message on his desk:

"MEMO: RAWLEY TO KAPTAIN. Add to my Sturgeon-symphony story this insert: Eighth paragraph, after words 'third mvt,' insert 'where the heat of Tangier can be truly said to hit you in the face.'"

"The trouble is," said Mr. Kaptain, "the story falls down because we've already said Sturgeon didn't start painting until a year ago. That is why he is this undiscovered genius. He might have written all his movements in retrospect, but I still don't think it stands up."

Jamey had to agree that it did not stand up. He had never thought a man of parts could seem so worthless. As a last, desperate venture he said, "I used to be quite keen on cricket."

Mr. Kaptain sat up. "Now you've got something. I think we could use a line on cricket, something along these lines." He removed his dark glasses, revealing for the first time a pair of worried, overworked eyes set in the complacent smoothness of his face. He sucked the ends of his spectacles, deep in thought. "I am almost sure it has never been done before. Your line should go something like this. Query: Why is cricket so

202

peculiarly British and what is the explanation for such a pointless activity in the first place? Answer: Cricket sublimates the aggressive urges of class and syphons them into innocuous activity. When a bowler throws the ball at a batsman, he is not just throwing a ball at a batsman. He is trying to kill that batsman, who represents, in his pads and gloves and with his hard, impervious bat, all the entrenched privilege of the upper and upper-middle classes. When the wickets fly, that is a real victory. It is a victory for the worker against his capitalist overlord, for the other-rank sergeant against his weak-chinned young officer. Then, of course, when the game is over, the capitalist overlord and his menial return to their respective positions, and the menial has lost the urge to destroy, overthrow and put aright. Don't you think that is what cricket is about?"

Jamey had never thought about it like that. "You mean so that the working classes will go on working and won't have to vote Socialist?"

"Exactly."

"I think it's an excellent idea. Of course, I always thought cricket was a capital game, and enjoyed it immensely. Now I see why."

"Exactly. And it is the fact that it is enjoyable as a game that makes it so dangerous. Do you see what I mean? It's not cricket, old boy." For the last sentence, Kaptain put on a parody of an English upper-class voice. "It's not cricket, old boy, to question the umpire's decision. And the umpire is always on the side of the batsmen." Kaptain had dropped his upper-class voice, and was speaking urgently in a voice which came from somewhere between Texas and the English Midlands. Sligger was not sure he accepted that analysis of the umpire's position. He could think of several instances when the umpire had seemed to have the opposite sympathies, particularly just before the tea break. But he let it pass. "That is why cricket should not be allowed, nor polo, nor hockey, nor lawn tennis, nor any games which destroy the will to fight by sublimating it into something respectable."

203

"What about the upper classes—the enemy, as it were—shouldn't they be encouraged to sublimate their what-nots? Then the working classes can walk over them."

"Not at all. Aggressiveness among the moneyed classes is just what we want to waken people out of their complacency into a state of awareness."

"Oh, I see." Jamey thought he had heard it all before, but he could not remember where. Perhaps it was at Cleeve, during lectures on contemporary affairs by Mr. Snippet, the English master.

"Well, I think you get the point." Mr. Kaptain was back among the cattle ranches and oil wells of the Deep South. "I don't know if this idea of yours justifies the space, but send it in to me and we'll see. Let me have it typed, not more than two thousand words double-spaced, by Friday morning. I can't promise you I'll have time to have a look at it. All I can say is I'll do my best. Right you are." He nodded.

Jamey was dismissed. He did not feel the interview had been a complete success. There was no offer of a job that he could see, only the vague hope that if he wrote two thousand words about something he imperfectly understood, and with which he did not agree in the least, he would be rewarded by a further few minutes of Mr. Kaptain's attention. Obviously, Mr. Kaptain was a very important person, but Jamey did not feel he was quite important enough to treat people like that. A surge of genuine, pure egalitarian anger overtook him, and he determined to seek out the *piquante* secretary, who at least had not treated him like dirt. Perhaps he would seduce her, make her pregnant until she had to stay away from work, thereby demonstrating to Mr. Delano Kaptain, otherwise known as God Almighty, that Jamey Sligger too was a human being, moved by human passion and deserving to be treated with human respect. Unfortunately, the *piquante* secretary had been replaced by another, much less *piquante*, but with a certain robust charm. In his shock, Sligger abandoned the plan, reflecting that it would not have worked, as they were probably both Mr. Kaptain's mistresses already. The reflection subdued his certainty that he was Kaptain's equal, but replaced it with a healthy hatred of all culture fiends with false American accents.

"Yes, we are looking for a young man. I see you have two passes at Advanced Level and seven at Ordinary Level. Jolly good, but I am not sure it is that sort of thing we are looking for. Have you got any journalistic experience?"

Once again Jamey felt that unaccustomed empty feeling. "Have you done any writing?" Yes, as secretary of the Cleeve Astronomical Society, Jamey had composed the reports.

"Astronomy? Do you know Richard Woolley?" No, Jamey did not know the Astronomer Royal.

"What other interests have you got?"

"I used to be quite good at cricket." The *Cenotaph* personnel officer was not as impressed as they had been in the *Reverser*.

"Everybody here is interested in cricket. It is extremely hard to get them to write about anything else. The ecclesiastical correspondent and the chief ballet critic nearly came to blows with the medical correspondent and African affairs about something one of them had written on it. I should forget the cricket side if I were you." From that moment the attitude of the personnel officer changed to one of gloomy resignation. If the young man was interested in cricket, he would obviously end up on the *Cenotaph* somewhere, whether as book critic, Middle East expert or industrial correspondent.

"Any interest in industrial disputes, pensions, health, overseas affairs, fishery and agriculture, road accidents, music, national insurance or architecture?"

Dolefully, Jamey shook his head.

"Good. We've got people covering them in the newsroom already. Duplication of effort is what we want to avoid. Your interests, I expect, are more in the way of hobbies, life-saving devices, railways, natural history, schools and general?"

"That's right," said Jamey, thinking particularly of the general.

"Good. You'll make a good substitute for MacGhastly."

"Is he leaving?"

"He died." The interviewer spoke in a whisper. Death was the only thing which disturbed the smooth running of the *Cenotaph* offices. In the *Reverser*, it had been known to happen that the chess correspondent had run amok, rushed screaming to the compositing room, where he beat a linotype setter over the head with some rolled galley proofs. The machine room had gone on strike in protest, and refused to return until every man there was promised an extra three pounds a week and another tea break daily.

"That's what comes from employing clergymen on a modern newspaper," the managing director, a nasty young man with bad teeth and an antireligious mania, had explained to the proprietor. "Of course, they'll expect danger money."

But there was no defense against death, no industrial action which could mitigate the cruel suddenness. MacGhastly, it is true, had been dying for many years. He had never been the same since one night in the last war when the chief subeditor had informed him that as their newspaper was reduced to three pages as a result of enemy action, there would be no space for his two-thousand-word story on the threat to the Railway Orphans Foundation from subsidence. The very next day the Foundation had fallen down. Nothing in his forty-five years on the *Cenotaph* had ever resigned him to the fact that life was like that. He died with his socks on, in bed, in his home in Putney.

"The *Cenotaph* will never be the same without old Mac-Ghastly," everyone had said. But of course it was. Perhaps in forty-five years' time Jamey would die, similarly mourned. It was the finest accolade any journalist could have.

"Of course, we are looking for different qualities nowadays," said the personnel officer. "Youth, vigor, all that sort of thing." His cold, gloomy face did not suggest that he conducted the search with any relish. He had not wanted to be personnel officer. He had arrived, bounding with energy and enthusiasm, from the provinces fifteen years ago, eager to realize his ambition of being the chief expert on Chinese affairs and cricket, hoping to put the world aright with a few well-thought-out phrases. After a period in the Commonwealth desk—people felt that even if China was not a member of the Commonwealth it certainly should be, in the light of the mutual ties of sentiment and tradition which unite our two countries—he had graduated to being the secretary of the first cousin once removed of the proprietor, the assistant deputy advertising manager, the letters editor, and now the personnel officer. He felt rather as the holder of a Victoria Cross might feel on being made a soldier servant. Any of the youthful, vigorous candidates he interviewed might eventually become the Far Eastern expert and adviser on Chinese affairs. He had despaired.

"What contacts have you got among people who might help? Do you know Sir Charles Snow?"

Jamey played with the idea, but decided it was too risky. "I know Lord Robinson, the industrialist, and I've stayed with the Picciones in Lowndes Square."

"Not bad. Better than most people we get. I'm afraid it looks as if you've got the job. There's just one more person you've got to see. As far as I'm concerned, you step into Mac-Ghastly's shoes tomorrow. Starting salary three hundred and fifty pounds a year, less deduction for pension contribution, sports facilities, *Cenotaph* widows' benevolence, national insurance, Chapel Festivities, Proprietor's Cup and compositors' drawer. You should get four pounds ten a week cash, not much, but a great deal more than MacGhastly was getting when he started. Subject, of course, to confirmation by the editor and your next interview. By the way, can you spell?"

"Not really. But I know Sir Alwyn Anderson."

"Good for you. Tell the advisory consultant that when you see him. He knows everyone. Now wait here while I fetch him."

The personnel officer was gone twenty minutes, while Jamey congratulated himself on his luck. It was not the job which made him so pleased so much as his own proven ability to be offered a job. Formerly, he had supposed that all the jobs in the world were his for the choosing. Bit by bit, it had occurred to him that he had no qualifications at all, that he and his parents had been taken in by a gigantic confidence trick. Nobody seemed interested that he had been to Cleeve, had an enormous number of School Certificates, had been promoted a full corporal in the Combined Cadet Force with a certificate of competence in signaling, had been Captain of Cricket with three caps. What more could they possibly expect of a chap? It was true that he had left Oxford without a degree, but very few people ever succeeded in getting there, and none of his interviewers had ever inquired as to what he did at Oxford. Now that he had got a job, it was because he was an acquaintance of Lord Robinson and Sir Edgar Piccione and because he had had the sense to invent an acquaintance with Sir Alwyn Anderson, the Minister of Transport.

The personnel officer returned with a sycophantic, well-fed companion, who gave no sign of surprise on recognizing Jamey.

"Hullo, Christian," said Sligger, a trifle truculently.

"Jamey Sligger, is it?" said Creepy Crawley. "I was interested to hear that you wanted to enter journalism. My great friend Delano Kaptain told me you had been to see him. What we always advise young people wanting to make a career of it is to spend a few years in the provinces, on a sound provincial newspaper, learning the ropes."

"I have been offered this job, to replace Mr. MacGhastly on the *Cenotaph*," said Jamey, as carelessly as he could. He savored every minute of his triumph. "I have not really decided yet whether to accept it or not."

"No," said Creepy Crawley, "I certainly shouldn't accept it, if I were you. One must learn the ropes first. I could get you a place on a respectable newspaper in Crewe, where I have a certain amount of influence, but it is no good thinking you would be up to a job on the *Cenotaph* yet. Much as one wants to help one's friends, one has other obligations, too." Jamey

208

thought he understood how Julius Caesar must have felt on seeing Brutus among his assassins.

"But I've got the job, if you back me," he said.

"I'm afraid that is not the point. I warned you this would happen. It is no good trying to short-circuit the natural processes just because you have powerful friends." The powerful friend with influence in Crewe relented a little. "If you come back to the *Cenotaph* in about six years, Jamey, with a good record of service in the provinces, of course I'll be delighted to do everything in my power to help you."

"Do you mean he's no good?" said the personnel officer, immensely cheered by the thought. One more rival for the post of Chinese adviser was removed. "Well, Mr. Sligger, we can't say anything at this stage, but no doubt you'll be hearing from the editor in due course."

Jamey crept away, more miserable than ever before. Once again, he would have to return to Farnham Green with a story of failure. He could not understand what the modern world had against him. Soon he would have to begin thinking of a teaching post at a preparatory school, the last net which caught only the most conspicuously grave casualties of the public-school system.

At an early stage, Jamey had gone to an agency which specialized in finding jobs for university men. The interviewer had asked him many searching questions about his religion, and where the Sliggers came from. On being told they came from Cornwall, the interviewer, who was called Mr. Potinue, had said, "That's what they all say. Only last week we had a man in here, an engineering graduate from Merton, called Iago. He told us his family came from Cornwall. Expected us to believe it, too. No jobs for his sort, of course. We have the agency to consider."

"I was at Cleeve before going up to Godolphin."

"You didn't meet my cousin the chaplain. I don't expect he would move in your sort of world."

"I just met him."

"What sort of a degree did you say you took?"

"I came down before taking my degree, actually."

"Oh well, there is only one sort of job for you in that case, and I don't know if even your sort will care to take it. I can't tell you what it is, as I am not allowed to. All I can say is that if you go to an address I give you and ask for Brigadier Gangradden, he might be interested in your case."

"What would I have to do?"

"That's secret. Here's the address. I don't know if it's any good, but it is all we have got, so it is no good coming back to us. You wouldn't know Jack Waley-Goldston by any chance? No, I didn't suppose you would. He was at Godolphin, too, although I never heard him say he came from Cleeve."

Jamey had taken the address and thought no more of the matter, assuming that the job was something to do with teaching. Now, in his despair, he walked round to the place mentioned, which was in Curzon Street and appeared to be a Spanish restaurant.

A waiter said, "You have come to the wrong door. All the Brigadiers live in the basement."

Downstairs, Jamey was confronted by a man behind a desk with the insignia of a regimental sergeant major strapped round a civilian suit of clothes. "You can't go any further than that without your pass," he said.

"I have come to see Brigadier Gangradden."

"I don't know what you're talking about. There's no such person down here. This is the registered offices of East-West Exports, Ltd., a hengineering concern. Is he expecting you?"

"I don't think so. I come from the Potinue Agency."

"Well, if you want to see the Brigadier, you must say: Can I see Mr. Billingsdale, please? I wish to make some inquiries about steel tubing."

"Can I see Mr. Billingsdale, please? I want to make some inquiries about steel tubing."

210

"That's right. Hold on, and I'll see if he's in." The sergeant major went to an antiquated telephone and said:

"Client for Mr. Billingsdale. Comes from the Potinue Agency. Shall I show him up?" He came back. "Mr. Billingsdale is indisposed, but his assistant, Mr. King, will speak to you. Fill in this form please."

The form asked for Jamey's age, weight, complexion on entering the building, time of leaving the porter's desk, estimated time of arrival at interviewer's office, purpose of interview sought, details of hand baggage left at porter's desk and any peculiarities. The only relevant bit of information it did not seek was Jamey's name.

"I take it you have no cameras or photographic devices, recording equipment, offensive weapons other than pocket knife, explosive or inflammable material?" The sergeant major sounded bored, but Jamey was fascinated by the catalogue, and began searching his pockets scrupulously to see if any cameras or explosive material had slipped in without his noticing.

"Not that you'd tell me if you had, and I have no powers to search you," said the sergeant major indulgently.

"I have got a box of matches," said Jamey, putting them on the desk.

"Are you trying to take the micky out of me, son? Well don't. I'm not interested in whether you've got a box of matches in your pocket or anything else. I just have to caution you that if you've got anything you shouldn't you'd better look out, because they don't like it and I don't like it, and between us we can get quite nasty. Now do we understand each other?" He looked at his watch. "You've now got exactly sixteen seconds to get into Mr. King's office, third corridor on the left last room, and take this bit of paper with you."

Jamey raced down the passage and into the room, panting for breath. It was thick with cigarette smoke. Three men sat in a ring, facing a fourth. He was smoking a thick yellow cigarette, which drooped out of the corner of his mouth, and was talking

211

in a foreign accent. One of the men with him was Mr. Arckwright, their neighbor at Farnham Green. He was looking at the X-ray photograph of a man's chest.

Jamey said, "Mr. King?"

Mr. Arckwright did not look up. "Wait in there," he said, pointing at a door.

Jamey found himself in a tiny cupboard with a strong smell of chemicals. It had a sink, but nothing else. For want of anything else to do, he started washing his hands. The murmur of conversation came through, but Jamey could not make out any words. Eventually, the door opened.

"You have come to the wrong room," said Mr. Arckwright. "Follow me." When they were outside, he said, "Jamey, you must tell no one you saw me here. Do you understand that? Call me Mr. King, and don't let on you have ever seen me before."

When they reached another office, Mr. Arckwright threw himself into a chair, and said, "Phew. I am glad to have got out of that imbroglio. If you want a word of advice in this business, never trust an Armenian. You simply don't know what the beggars'll be up to next. I am very glad you have decided to join us. We need a few young men like you around."

"Was it important, what the Armenian was saying?" Jamey did not like to ask what it was, as he thought he ought to know.

"I dare say, but there's nothing much we can do. When in doubt, initial and pass on. Nobody ever got into trouble for doing that. Now there are just a few questions I must ask you, then you'll have to see my boss; then you'll have to see the head of this department very briefly; then we'll send you on a course; then with a bit of luck you'll come back here. Let me see. Have you ever belonged to a subversive organization; no, you haven't. Are you a homosexual; no, you're not. We don't have any of those rats around here." Was there something too vehement about the way Mr. Arckwright said that? Was there the faintest touch of a wistful look in his eye? Jamey felt he was on home ground.

212

"By the way, who is your current girl friend or mistress?"

"You might say I'm between posts at the moment."

"Foot-loose and fancy-free, are you?" Mr. Arckwright was pleased with the idea. "We'll put Miss Barbara Arckwright— after all, you've known her for years, and Barbara should be pleased. Then I can put 'approved' without any further inquiries."

Jamey thought of that enormous bust, and shrank into his seat.

"I often wish Barbara would bring home a young man one of these days. She should be separated from that filthy little dog of hers. You wouldn't care to come down to the farm for a weekend, and see if you can distract her? No? I thought you probably wouldn't. Never mind. Have you ever had connections with any political organization of any sort?"

Jamey thought of the Inner Cell, of which he was secretary, and of Peace and International Friendship, of which he would have been the Oxford treasurer if he had stayed on. "My mother is standing as Liberal candidate at the next election, and I have been helping her."

"We've got too many bloody Liberals in this office already. Mind you, you're quite right, it's the only thing to be. I'm a Liberal—it's not safe to say anything else here. Not a single person will admit to being anything else. We're not allowed to say what we are, but they like to know, so you have to talk as enthusiastically as possible about Lords Reform and all that sort of rubbish. Now, I've got some papers for you to fill in. Psychological stuff. Then I'll come back with my boss. Pretend to be interested in politics—the Middle East or something. They like chaps to have a hobby."

Jamey was left alone with the psychological stuff. He enjoyed tests of this sort, and fancied he would do quite well, but it was a very silly paper. The first question asked him to describe himself as a friend would describe him, then as an enemy. As Jamey did not have any enemies, the problem scarcely arose. How could he project himself into the mind of a nonexistent class of people and decide what it would think if it did exist? He felt rather as Mr. Price-Williams must have felt about most of his problems. It was easy to think of what nice people would say. Jamey was good at cricket, kind, good-looking, which had better be left out, as it was too obvious and came badly from him, he was intelligent, loyal, likable as a person, a good mixer. There was practically no end to the catalogue. Jamey was aware that he had a few faults, but he was not going to confess them to any psychologist, who was probably a very dim, common little person. He decided instead to write a description of someone who was rather like Garlick, with a lot of Goyle, but most of all like Mr. Delano Kaptain, the quasi-Negro character otherwise known as Marmaduke Ukelele or Almighty God. The enemy's description described someone who was bad at cricket, cruel, ugly, stupid, disloyal, unlikable as a person and quite *insortable*. Clearly, Jamey's enemies were people of extraordinary stupidity, as well as lacking in discrimination. In case the psychologist should not grasp his point, he wrote at the bottom: "Furthermore, he is snobbish and conceited." Since nothing could be further from the truth than that, as anybody could see, even the most stupid psychologist would be able to realize how wrong-headed his enemies were. Jamey was the very opposite of snobbish. He got on with the working classes extremely well. They seemed to trust and like him at first glance, and although their friendliness was usually tinged with a certain amount of respect, which they seemed to be unable to get out of their systems, Jamey always pretended not to notice it. The working classes were the salt of the earth, as anybody who got to know them would testify. It was only the filthy common people from the middle classes who set their backs up, as they did not know how to behave like gentlemen and upset the balance of everything. Jamey detested the middle class.

The next question was quite easy: "Give an account of the incident in your life to which you look back with the greatest pleasure." Although there were many incidents in his life which gave cause for satisfaction, the one he remembered with

214

keenest pleasure was the time he had rescued a small boy at Cleeve from a bully. Although the incident had never actually taken place, it might well have, as there had been a perfectly vile person at Cleeve called Pink-Tweeney, with whom the young Sligger had imagined many such encounters. The next question asked what incident Sligger most regretted. All that Sligger really regretted was the missed opportunity of declaring and consummating his passion for Miss Rogers, the inexpressibly lovely history don. But that would be most unsuitable for the psychologist. He wrote instead a highly colored account of how his indifference had driven "a certain undergraduate named Anne Etherington" to suicide, ending with the justification that he could not have dissembled a love which he did not feel, and, in the long run, it was probably better to behave as he did. The moral was that one could not be too careful with members of the opposite sex—which, he felt, was very mature. "Poor Anne Etherington," he thought; "the uses to which she has been put."

Mr. Arckwright returned with a short, bald man who introduced himself as Mr. Attwood. He surveyed Jamey for a long time through small, gold-rimmed glasses, without saying a word. Jamey preened himself and put on a half-grin to show he did not mind.

"Why do you want to join the service?"

"Well, I'm looking for a job, you see." The answer seemed to give complete satisfaction.

"You don't think you've got a mission in life or a debt to humanity or anything like that?"

"Not particularly." Once again, Jamey was conscious of having scored a bull.

"What's your feeling about Britain's mission to the underdeveloped nations? Is it a good thing?"

"Of course it is."

"Quite right. Not a waste of time?"

"Not at all." Mr. Attwood seemed pleased. It was obviously very rare for candidates to get both answers right.

"King tells me you have a special interest in the Middle East. What do you think about this Jordanian business?"

Sligger had heard of it very vaguely. A lot of people with indistinguishable names were in conflict with each other about something. He tried a shot in the dark. "I think the Government's quite right."

"I am glad to hear you say that. Very few people would agree with you, of course. We haven't done anything yet, but we're studying the matter, as you know. I passed the report to the signals and communications staff to take note. I don't see what more can be done, now."

"Exactly. Who cares about a lot of Arabs anyway?"

For the first time, Jamey had put his foot wrong. Mr. Arckwright, standing behind his chief, put his hands to his ears.

"It is exactly because we care so much for the Arabs that we can do nothing, and should do nothing, and should not ever recommend others to take action. If we did anything to help the present regimes, it might prejudice our popularity with subsequent ones. Arab good will is probably the only thing that really matters in the world today. That is why we should never do anything, anywhere, in case it is endangered. By our past conduct, we have incurred the enmity of the entire Arab race. We must do nothing, now, to make it worse."

"Quite right," said Mr. Arckwright. "That was the point young Sligger was trying to make when we were alone together. Nobody cares about the Arab as much as they should. It is this insensitiveness to Arab opinion which is our weakest point." The fire in Mr. Attwood's eyes died down. It was not often that he encountered opposition.

"All right," he said moodily. "What do you think about the picture at home?"

"House of Lords should be reformed."

"All right. I'll go and see if he's ready to see you."

After he had gone, Mr. Arckwright said, "Not bad, Jamey, but you must remember never to say anything rude about the Arabs. Now you're going to meet the Head of the Department.

Don't say anything until he speaks. You won't be introduced. He may not say anything to you, but he'll be watching you, so don't do anything. If he asks you a question, look him in the face before you answer, and whatever you do, don't call him 'sir,' as you're not supposed to know he's the boss."

The door opened and Mr. Attwood came in, his finger on his lips. He tiptoed to behind the door and nodded to Mr. Arckwright.

"He's coming."

A sudden hush had fallen on the whole corridor. Jamey thought he heard a creak, soft footsteps on the rubber carpeting, then Creepy Crawley came in. Mr. Attwood stood to attention behind the door, and Mr. Arckwright stood up to straighten his tie. Jamey sat numb.

Creepy Crawley walked round the room and stood for a time by the window. "The syringa is not out yet," he said. It was an accusation and a threat.

"Last year it was not even in bud at this time," said Mr. Arckwright. "We had to cut it back in the autumn. But then we had a blooming horrible spring." He laughed unaffectedly at the joke. Jamey half smiled. Mr. Attwood did not relax behind the door, and Creepy Crawley merely nodded.

"Good," he said. He looked round the room without seeming to notice Jamey, nodded again, and walked out the door. Another slight creak, a soft footfall, then silence. Mr. Attwood shut the door and said, "Phew."

Mr. Arckwright was already on the telephone. "Send someone around immediately to attend to the syringa. No, tomorrow's no good. It must be watered, manured, trimmed—whatever you do to put them in order. Yes, this is top priority."

"Do you think I was all right?"

"I don't know. He doesn't give much away."

"I know who he is. He's called Mr. Ch—"

"Sh."

"What's that?"

"Sh."

There was a soft footfall outside the door, then silence.

"Well, Sligger," said Mr. Arckwright in an unnaturally high voice. "Good of you to have called. No doubt you'll be hearing from us in the near future. Just give me the piece of paper you brought in, and I'll sign it for you to let you out."

Jamey found it among his psychological papers. In the corridor, he passed Mr. Rawley. They did not acknowledge each other, but walked on. Jamey had an uneasy feeling that he had failed again.

Miss Barbara Arckwright brought her little dog to tea. Philip said, "Shall I put it outside?"

"She doesn't like to be alone. She likes company, don't you, Minny-winny?" Miss Arckwright cuddled it to her bosom, where it made no more impression than a fly on an elephant. Jamey reflected that this was really not how young people were supposed to get together nowadays. Where was the gramophone, the soft lights, the Pepsi-Cola which flowed?

"Will you have another scone, Barbara?"

"No thank you. I'm trying to slim." This was an extraordinary admission. It seemed to suggest that Barbara saw herself as an ordinary member of her sex, something which needed to be made attractive to men. The idea that Barbara wished to appear attractive to men was patently absurd. She scorned them, regarded her sex merely as something which exempted her from the responsibility of carrying trays or standing up when people came into the room, investing her with an undisputed superiority, but carrying with it no obligations. She was wearing lipstick this afternoon, a hideous cherry-colored gash in her face. Perhaps she, too, wanted to become a typical teen-ager. Jamey felt the stirrings of interest, despite the traditional revulsion, but Barbara's eyes were all for their guest, Lofty Parker, who was taking considerable trouble to show he had a way with animals.

"I just adore Chihuahuas when they flap their ears," he said in an affected voice, leaning over Barbara's chair until his face was nearly touching her jersey.

218

Barbara laughed nervously. "Aren't they just too adorable?" she said. Jamey would never have dared touch a dog which was sitting on Miss Arckwright's chest, but Lofty did. He pretended to be a mouse running over her jersey, and she laughed so much the dog had to be removed and she spilled her cup of tea. When Jamey went to get a wiping-up cloth from the kitchen, Mrs. Sligger, who was sitting in there, said, "I hope you're not having too much fun. What's going on next door? I see I shall have to come in myself soon."

It had been her idea to give a young people's party, and she was acutely conscious of the risks.

When Jamey got back, Barbara was sitting back in her chair looking flushed and a little hysterical. Lofty said to Philip, "I think we can turn the dog out now," and Barbara raised no objection. Minny had served her purpose. Then Lofty turned to Barbara and said, "What shall we do now," in a suggestive voice. She laughed nervously. It was a long time since she had had such a good time, but she did not want to lose face in front of the Sliggers, and she really did not know what this wild young man proposed to do next.

"We could draw the curtains, and Jamey and I could go and help mother in the kitchen," said Philip. Tact was never his strong point.

"Don't be silly. What would Mummy think?" Jamey was genuinely shocked. It was all right to do things oneself, but there was no excuse for helping other people to do them. He thought he would have to send an account of this to Brother Richard. It was a deplorable thing to see how low his brother had sunk since going to prison. One could not expect much of Lofty, who was not even a Christian, but Philip should know better. Although he thought it a good thing that Lofty should get away with Miss Arckwright, and he was most interested to see what would happen, it would be quite wrong to assist them.

There was a deadlock, while nobody knew what to do next. Jamey said, "Shall we play Scrabble?"

Miss Arckwright said, "I've got to go home now, really."

219

Lofty said, "I'll take you home. Jamey and Philip have got to help clean up."

Barbara looked at the two brothers and giggled. "All right," she said, "but we mustn't be long."

After they had gone, Philip said, "Good old Lofty. He's a quick worker."

"What do you suppose they'll do?"

"What do you think?" said Philip, and broke into a song, the refrain of which was "Doing what comes naturally."

Jamey supposed it did come naturally, to people like Lofty and Philip. As he put away the jar of peanut butter it seemed to him most unfair that it did not come as easily to him. He had always blamed his mother and the fact that it was impossible to give teen-age get-togethers in Farnham Green without her coming in and giving them all her views on education, but Lofty had shown them that things could be done even in Farnham Green. All he needed was a little self-confidence.

When Lofty came home, Philip said, "How did it go?"

"We didn't do much. I think she'll need fairly careful handling. They're often like that, at that age. We'll see what we can do next time. She was scared her mother would come out and visit the hay barn. Oh well, the course of true love never did run smooth."

A quotation which they all found quite appropriate.

The two letters arrived simultaneously, both beginning, "We regret . . ." That from East-West Exports came unstamped, pushed under the door during the night. The *Cenotaph* letter added an impertinent footnote, wishing him luck in whatever employment he eventually chose.

Jamey felt bitter as he paced the familiar walks round Farnham Green. If he was looking for adventure and romance and the unknown delights of sin, so highly thought of by those in a position to judge, he would plainly have to find it in the Arckwrights' hay barn. It was not that his neighborhood held no other opportunities. Young men in black plastic jackets were to

220

be seen hanging around outside the cinema with girls of a wildly immoral appearance. All the clergymen in the neighborhood agreed that the general standard of morality was as low as anywhere else in Great Britain, but it seemed to have passed him by. If Jamey had been half a man, he would have invested in a black plastic jacket, taken his place outside the Gaumont with the other local beaux and waited his chance, but something constrained him. Partly, no doubt, because he knew none of them, partly because they spoke in an alien accent and made jokes which were incomprehensible to him, partly through fear of being seen by one of his mother's neighbors, but mostly out of cowardice. His voice and manners seemed to excite an immediate antagonism in people of his own age group but of a different class.

Many of them came from Aldershot on motor bikes, and it was probably because Jamey reminded them of the officers in their squalid, Service Corps barracks that they regarded him with such contempt. Jamey, for his part, felt that it was a pity. They were quite wrong to suppose that because he came from a more opulent background, he despised them. On the contrary, he was most interested in their affairs, and was quite prepared to treat them as equals, but they did not seem to wish ever to be treated as equals. It was most difficult for anyone as resolutely unclass-conscious and unsnobbish as Jamey to put his beliefs into practice. He would have been quite prepared to roll in the hay, or whatever it was they did, with one of those plump, untidy girls in trousers. It was true they were not very attractive, and few were older than sixteen, but neither was Miss Arckwright very attractive, and her greater age had not endowed her with any qualities which were apparent. But the rigors of the English class system constrained him from the natural outlets of his generation. Jamey detested the English class system and wished all classes could come together sensibly.

He sent a withering denunciation of the moral standards around Farnham, particularly those of the working class, to Brother Richard at Cleeve, then began to make plans in a somber mood. They all centered on the Arckwrights' hay barn.

He was saved from this by a letter which arrived two days later. On reconsidering his case, the personnel officer of the *Daily Cenotaph*, in consultation with the advisory consultant, had decided to offer him a post as general trainee on the editorial staff of the *Aldershot Beam*, their subsidiary in Guildford. If he turned up during the course of Thursday afternoon and asked for Mr. Timothy Droppings, he would be put in the picture.

Jamey danced and skipped through the lanes of Farnham. Once again he was in love with himself, with Mr. Droppings, with Guildford, with the whole world. Guildford was renowned for its vice, even in vice-ridden Farnham. Adulterous stockbrokers' wives with immoral daughters abounded. He read the letter again and again. It was his passport to freedom and the modern age, where all classes came together in a delirious and unending sex orgy. London was too complicated, Farnham too staid. The very name of Guildford was music to the ears of a young man in love.

Chapter 16

Brother Richard sat late at night in his study, filing away letters and comparing evidence. The Farnham area was worse than it had been two years before, when Philip Sligger's reports began to arrive. Philip had erred, so had Jamey. That might be important. It was difficult to see how this information might be of use, but one never knew. In the Navy he had Drayton and Griffiths at Malta watching each other. In the *Panther*, off Corfu, he had Sullivan minor, alone. Was that safe? Boyle and Scrim-geour were refueling in Gibraltar. Backwood was on a courtesy visit to Venice in the *Agincourt*. He, too, was alone, but as a lieutenant commander he should be trusted. The nearest person to him was MacThrusty, who was on holiday with three other people in Dubrovnik. Rapey wished that MacThrusty had been more explicit about his traveling companions. Still, the Mediterranean was fairly well covered. Rapey wished he could feel as confident about the North Sea.

Far the most important item, from the news angle, was contained in another report. One of the novices he had found had been given the task of tidying the Abbot's parlor. He had found some silver paper in the wastepaper basket which, when unrolled, revealed that it had formerly contained four tablets of Aspro. There could be no doubt about it. The Abbot was unwell.

Brother Richard had not allowed himself to be thrown into a panic by the news. He had been preparing for this moment for over twenty-four years. A list of the Brothers showed that a larger number were under his influence than were opposed to him. The balance was held by the "Don't knows," but there was no other monk who had such a large body in support. Nobody could seriously contemplate Brother Augustine for the office. Brother Athanasius was too old—so old that Brother Richard had never tried to bring him into the sphere of influence, reckoning that he would be dead before the next abbatial election. Brother Cuthbert had been a recent conversion. Clever, faithful, good little novice had heard him refer to Brother Richard as "Rapey" in the calefactory.

In one of his frank, man-to-man conversations, Rapey pointed out that if there really was an incompatibility, if they were unable to be friends, it was their duty to go and tell the Abbot, in the interests of harmony. Faced with the frightful threat of being sent to a parish in Liverpool, Brother Cuthbert had yielded. One more white bean in the small black box.

It was good news that Jamey Sligger was joining the *Alder-*

shot Beam. With a careful press campaign in his favor, few of the Brothers would dare vote for anyone else. Philip Sligger was organizing the Liberal Party and the criminal classes. John MacLaughlin was doing good work among the second boat crew of St. Edmund's Hall at Oxford. Brother Richard had many friends. Soon—not just yet, but soon—he would let it be known among them, in the most delicate way possible, that, in the interests of world-wide morality and Rapeyism, he would not be justified in accepting anyone else as the next Abbot of Cleeve. A more grasping man might have had higher ambitions. To Rapey, it was the pinnacle of power and dignity, the fruit of all his labors, the proper reward for his ability to hold heart-to-heart conversations.

"Now that Jamey has gone, I feel we can really talk to each other," said Mrs. Sligger cozily, as she busied herself with the knitting she had started seven years before, of a games sweater for Philip. She rather thought it would now be a pair of stockings for Lofty Parker. He was a most engaging young man, frank, intelligent, and not always trying to interrupt like so many of the younger generation.

Philip said, "What about?"

Lofty said, "That's right, Joan. You just tell us what you're thinking."

"I agree with Anthony," said Mrs. Sligger (she had refused to call him Lofty). "I think it's far nicer just to say whatever comes into your head, than to have set subjects. It's often so interesting what people think. I was just thinking this morning that it is thought—the power to think—that distinguishes the intelligent person like me and you from the unintelligent one." Mrs. Sligger plainly included her two sons in the latter class.

Lofty got up and stretched like the splendid young animal he was, then walked over to Mrs. Sligger's chair and sat on the arm. She did not seem to mind.

"I scarcely ever think anything," he said.

224

"What rubbish. Of course you do. It may be bad for your character, but I think you're one of the most intelligent young men I've ever met, and I'm very pleased Philip's met you. You can't be a fool, or you wouldn't be so interested in the Liberal Party. Between the two of us, we can do a lot of things together, which people like Philip and Jamey never even think about. I know you talk sense about education, because I spoke to you this morning. You can be my adviser on penal reform. I dare say there are even a few things you can teach me about conditions in the prisons, which I know to be disgusting."

Philip said, "I could tell you about prison conditions, Mother, if that's all you want to know."

Mrs. Sligger ignored him. "And I hope you will stay on until we have worked out things together. We must have a coherent policy on education and penal reform. I shall tell you what to write, and you can draw it up for my approval. Then we can present it at the next conference, and nobody will be able to do anything about it. It's no good pretending we're not going to be busy."

Lofty leaned over and held the knitting in his hand. "This is the finest piece of knitting I have ever seen," he said.

"Not at all," said Mrs. Sligger, delighted. "It is just a perfectly ordinary piece of knitting. Now we are going to be busy. I do not know how you can help, Philip, but I am sure we can find some work for you to do. It is no good pretending that you have quite got Anthony's touch. I could tell Anthony was going to be good by the intelligent way he talks about things. He realizes that it is of absolutely no use to say, 'Now we're going to talk about this or that.' As soon as you know what you're talking about, everybody loses interest. You've just got to keep going and see what comes out of it all, haven't you, Anthony?"

"It's the only way," said Lofty.

On the way to get ready for dinner, Philip avoided his friend's eye and said nothing. Lofty said, "Well it looks as if I'm going to stay a bit longer than either of us thought, doesn't it, old boy?"

"The subeditors' room is what you might call the nerve center of a newspaper," said Mr. Droppings. "Among the subeditors you have all the brains which go to produce the paper. Old Mr. Tooley, who was chief sub when I arrived, used to say that a subeditor must have the eye of an eagle, the claw of a lion, the nimbleness of a ballerina, the wit of a glass of champagne and the propriety of a bishop."

Another thing Jamey noticed they had in common was that they were all bald. Mr. Droppings sat down on a high stool and began rummaging through some papers. When Jamey got to know him better, he made another list: the eye of a mole, the claw of a Pekingese, the nimbleness of a rhinoceros, the wit of a crocodile. But for the moment he was astounded by the list of qualities expected of him.

"This is where all the raw material of news comes. We process it, cut it down as small as we can, put a top on it, then send it down to the printers. Watch." He rolled up his sleeves like a conjuror demonstrating that he had nothing to conceal. "What have we here? Proposals for a new canteen for the football club of the Robinson Tube workers. Now the important thing about this is that the present canteen is unsatisfactory. You see how the club secretary says that it makes them feel ashamed to entertain visiting teams. What are we going to put on top of that? This is marked Dark Bod, which means top of column, two decks, two lines each, at most twelve and a half letters a line in the upper deck, sixteen in the lower. Remember, M's and W's count as one and a half letters, I's and spaces as a half."

Jamey sat with his problem for a full half hour. Eventually he took his work to Mr. Droppings, feeling very proud of himself.

CANTEEN FOR
TUBE WORKERS
POOR CONDITIONS
TO BE IMPROVED

"That's not bad for a start," said Mr. Droppings. "The trouble is that no one is interested in whether the Tube workers get a new canteen or not, I mean, are they? Nobody's going to read a news item if they think it is going to be about that. And this piece is going on the front page, as it is local news. I'll show you what I'm sending down to the printers."

SPORTSMEN IN
HUT OF SHAME
TUBEMEN REVOLT
AT ENTERTAINMENT

"Now that doesn't give away what the story is about, and it makes people want to know."

Soon Jamey began to feel the thrill of working at the nerve center.

"Copy down," shouted Mr. Droppings in a high, piping voice. An enormous gorilla of a man came and took the football story, which had been cut up into little pieces and pasted on clean paper, with many indecipherable scribbles in red Biro. He wore denim trousers held up by a piece of binder twine and scowled horribly at Jamey.

"Don't worry about him," said Mr. Droppings. "So long as you don't paste your copy on horizontally, he can't do anything to you."

"Who did 'mutilated body of girl on railway line'?" demanded a man who sat alone, in awful majesty, at the end of the room.

"Droppings did," everyone shouted.

227

"Cut her down by two thirds and put a black inslip in the middle of her. You don't mention she was unclothed."

"I was thinking of the parents."

"Well, say partially clothed, then."

"Here's a piece for you to do. This is national news, so we will have it on an inside page. Make it a fourteen-point Light Cloister."

"Fourteen-point Light Cloister?" said Jamey. He was prepared to make it anything reasonable.

"Two decks, two lines each, upper deck nine or under, lower deck eleven or under."

Jamey took the story. Mr. Ephrun Williams, the eighty-five-year-old Labour M.P. for Llanwtyth, had been found dead in bed above the constituency headquarters with an unfinished plate of food in front of him. Acute food poisoning was suspected. Mr. Williams's death made vacant the seat he had occupied for thirty-five years, with a majority of 36,000 at the last election. Figures then had been: Mr. Ephrun Williams, Lab. 37,216. Major S. K. Le P. Brown-Pigg, Cons. 1,008. Mr. G. Price, Welsh Nationalist, 982. Mr. L. Pryce, Ind. Welsh Nationalist, 42. In his early days in Parliament, Mr. Williams had been something of a firebrand on the subject of ventilation systems in mines, and it was on his initiative that the regulations controlling this had been amended in 1932. Since then, they had been revised many times but Mr. Williams's intervention had been an important stepping stone toward understanding and improvement of this problem. He was also most interested in football, and was patron of the Llanwtyth Lads Football Union from 1934 until the outbreak of war in 1939, when it was disbanded. In a statement, Mr. Selltyd Jones, the party agent and treasurer, said that Mr. Williams would be much missed in Llanwtyth. He had had roast duck for lunch, and had seemed perfectly healthy at the time.

Jamey wondered how he could make this story appealing. There seemed to be no love interest, no implications of vice possible. If only there was a woman in the story. He played with

228

various permutations of "Soccer-playing Labour M.P. found in bed with duck," but could not fit so many pieces of information into a 14-point Light Cloister. If some of it was left out, it seemed too bald:

M.P. FOUND
IN BED

DUCK WAS
WITH HIM

Like that, it might have been the beginning of a nursery rhyme, instead of crisp reporting with sinister undertones.

M.P. FOUND
WITH DUCK

BOTH WERE
DEAD

Even that did not look very professional. In any case, he was not using up all his letters. If only he could suggest that the death mystery of Labour M.P. in bed with duck could probably be explained by the fact that it was the eighty-five-year-old M.P.'s indulgence in duck which led to death in bed, but he decided that it was beyond human ingenuity. It was a pity that he could not bring in the duck somehow. Jamey felt it was absolutely disgusting that a man who was supposed to represent the workers should be gorging himself in private on roast duck. Eventually he wrote:

LABOUR M.P.
POISONED

AGENT MAKES
STATEMENT

"Good heavens, you can't say that," cried Mr. Droppings, wringing his hands in agitation. "You'll have us in the most dreadful trouble."

229

"Why not?" said Jamey.

"In the first place you can't just say people have been poisoned. You must add 'Court told,' or 'it is alleged.' A quick way of doing it is to put it in inverted commas.

LABOUR M.P.
'POISONED'

"There. The next point is you can't say anyone makes a statement unless they've been cleared, and the agent has not been cleared yet. You are hinting that he may have poisoned the M.P."

"Well so he may, for all we know."

"Exactly. It is because it may be true that it is so dangerous to hint at anything. As soon as we hear he has been cleared, you can hint anything you like. Now the final and most important point of all is that this is a death." Mr. Droppings spoke solemnly, but there was a cutting rebuke in his tone. "And in newspapers, you've got to be respectful about deaths."

Jamey lowered his head. "Sorry," he said.

"That's all right. But just remember: Things which are all right in private conversation, and sometimes not even there, are never all right in newspapers."

"Sorry," said Jamey.

"That's all right," said Mr. Droppings. "Now I'll show what to put on this story:

DEATH OF
LABOUR M.P.

MR WILLIAMS'
ACHIEVEMENT

"Yes, of course," said Jamey. "I don't know why I didn't think of that."

"It is easy to be wise afterward. What may seem simple to you has taken me fifteen years' training. You have to be in the frame of mind to produce the essence of a long report in a few words, without distorting it or leaving anything out. It is more than a knack. It is an art."

"Gosh, sorry," said Jamey.

"That is all right," said Mr. Droppings, unbending. "Now I'll give you something you perhaps *can* do."

It was a short report that Councillor Mrs. Gerald Acne had been appointed chairman of the Streets Committee of the Town and Country Planning Committee of the Aldershot Council.

"It is a ten-point Plain, which means single deck, single line, up to seventeen letters. What are we going to put on it?" He was prompting Jamey to say the obvious, but Jamey could not for the life of him think what it was. How did one give such a bald narrative the elements of human interest? It had a woman in it, which helped, but where did one go from there? He had an idea.

"How about 'WOMAN OF STREETS'?"

Mr. Droppings winced, then chuckled lecherously.

"Excellent, but it would cost the paper about a million pounds in libel actions. Almost anything else would have done. Either 'MRS. GERALD ACNE,' which always makes people read it, because they think it is an apology for a libel, or, alternatively, 'STREETS COMMITTEE,' which tells people they needn't read it, as it is just filling up space on the page. You'll get to know all the tricks when you've been here as long as I have." Mr. Droppings gave a chuckle.

Jamey could think of no worthier aim. Fifteen years would indeed be well spent if at the end of them he knew all the tricks, how to describe Mrs. Gerald Acne's appointment in a single-line heading, how to be respectful about deaths while still giving the relevant facts. Fifteen years ago, Jamey was dressed in smocks and had to use the gardener's lavatory because he was not to be trusted in the grownups' one. During the war, it was difficult to clothe him, and Mrs. Sligger had bought numerous enormous dolls, and clothed him with their clothes, thereby

231

economizing in clothing coupons. No doubt Jamey had learned many useful things in the fifteen years since he and Philip had been banned from Farnham British Legion tea parties for children because they had a bad influence on the other children, but now he was a grownup himself, and fifteen years was no more than a description of time. Perhaps he would be married and have children. Far more important, he would be learning the tricks of subeditorship, so that at the end of that time he would emerge as rounded, skilled and experienced as Mr. Droppings himself. Perhaps, if he stayed long enough, he would become as famous as the legendary Mr. Tooley, of whom it was said that the *Aldershot Beam* had never been the same since his death. As Jamey sat with Mr. Droppings, distilling the human interest from each story that arrived on the desk, a terrible suspicion began to form in his mind, that perhaps he and Mr. Droppings were the authors of this splendid modern world, where love was free, and outdated taboos had been rejected. Perhaps the teen-agers of Guildford, and of the whole world, were just as moral as they had ever been, perhaps nobody actually ever did anything, and the whole business was an elaborate fabric of invention, such stuff as the dreams of subeditors are made of. Perhaps Jamey's case was not particular, everybody else was a liar too, and in fact no girl was ever violated until marriage, except such people as Deirdre Black, who invariably paid the price. Perhaps the whole stupendous fiction was sustained by people's desire to read what interested them. Who, having read the "Hut of Shame" story, would not have thought at the end that he had read the account of some sex orgy? The mind forgot what bored it, and nobody could possibly remember about the new canteen for footballers.

It was a ghastly moment, but Jamey's self-confidence came back when the chief subeditor called excitedly:

"Kill that concert notice. Who did the Courts story, 'Girl says I slept with fourteen Technical College students'?"

"Blakeston," everyone shouted.

"Blakeston," said the chief sub proudly, "we've got a picture.

Blow the story up to twenty-four C.B. across three columns on page one."

Philip Fringe rapped the table in front of him and rustled his papers. Only one other person had turned up at the Inner Cell meeting, which would give them both the opportunity to pass many resolutions which had been depleted or amended in the past. But even as Fringe and Whale voted unanimously for war against South Africa, the breaking-off of diplomatic relations with all European countries, the abolition of the sterling area, the nationalization of all motor cars, the sacking of Mrs. Price-Williams's secretary, the death penalty for crimes of racial intolerance or landlord profiteering, and the enforcement by law of free love among consenting adults, there was a certain hollowness about the victory.

Attendance had fallen drastically in the Trinity term, since Sligger had been sent down. As the gentle breezes of spring had carried them into an early summer, Angela Hammock had started walking out with a biology student from Merton. They were sometimes to be seen walking hand in hand round the gardens of St. Rachel's, and spent much time by the lake at the bottom of it, from which her friend brought back tadpoles in a jam jar, and later young frogs. He told her he had sound prospects of a job at one of the greater laboratories if he worked hard and did not allow himself to be distracted. Angela was thrilled by the idea that her John might get a job at one of the greater laboratories.

Bill English had taken an unaccountable interest in bird watching, and bicycled off every afternoon with a party of friends to indulge it. When asked about the Inner Cell, he always said he had an essay to write. It was true they were all taking Schools that term, but they had agreed at an early stage that the work of the Inner Cell took precedence over everything. When English and Hammock returned, they would regret their lapses. The Cell was now committed in every kind of direction. But Fringe wished they would return soon.

233

"We have had a useful meeting, friend," said Fringe. Another resolution which had been passed was that at meetings members should preserve strict anonymity, in case there was a spy from Special Branch, or the proctors, or Mrs. Price-Williams's secretary in their midst. It was a good idea, but lost some of its force when only two people were present.

"True enough, friend," said Whale. "Now, if you don't mind, I've got an essay to write." With a nod he left the meeting, and bicycled to Boar's Hill, where there was a dark-haired secretary called Jean, who lived in lodgings, and whom he loved passionately.

Mrs. Sligger did not read of the death of Mr. Ephrun Williams, the Member for Llanwtyth, in the newspapers. She very seldom read the newspapers, and when she did she saw different things in them than other people did. Something she had read in a newspaper many years before—it was on the subject of a trade agreement with Russia—had stuck in her mind, and that was what she decided newspapers were about. The news, as far as she was concerned in international affairs, was that we were no longer enemies of the Russians, and should keep the Americans at arm's length as it was they, not the Russians, who had designs on our Empire. So long as we had the Empire—and we still had it, although we had changed its name in order to make the natives feel more at home—we were the greatest country on earth, and anybody who said anything to the contrary was a fool and a coward. That was part of the reason why it was Mrs. Sligger's duty to lead her country to sensible solutions. The other countries would notice what had happened and would try to copy it in due course. But her first concern was quite rightly for her own countrymen.

When Jamey told her that there would be a by-election soon, she merely said, "Not until I've made my preparations." She never attached much weight to what Jamey said, and would certainly not take his word on such an important matter where she, if anyone, might be expected to know. Soon after, the nomination papers arrived, and Mrs. Sligger decided to keep it a secret.

Not being very good at keeping secrets, she told Lofty Parker that same afternoon, and Philip in the evening.

Philip said, "We must go down to Llanwtyth and start arranging for the campaign."

"Of course, I'd thought of that. I am going to take Anthony down tomorrow afternoon. I've appointed him my agent and treasurer."

"I shouldn't make him treasurer," said Philip doubtfully. "Wouldn't you like me to come down, too? I could look after the money."

"That's just like you. I'm trying to give this young chap a new start in life, show him that he is trusted and responsible. You would want me to keep him on a chain for all his life, I suppose, with a placard round his neck saying 'Convicted Thief.' We must try and forget the past, let bygones be bygones. There would be nothing for you to do in Llanwtyth except get in everybody's way. And if you think I'd trust you with the Liberal Party funds after the way you behaved with your father's checks, you must be mad." Mrs. Sligger spoke as if the Liberal Party funds were on a par with the foreign exchange reserves of the Bank of England. In fact, they amounted to four pounds ten shillings, and it was not sure who held them.

"You can't go down to Llanwtyth with Lofty alone," said Philip.

"And why not? Just what are you suggesting, young man? There's something quite perverted and rotten about you, I sometimes think, Philip. Just because your own standards are debased, you see evil everywhere. If I were to blow my nose in my handkerchief, you would see it as a sex symbol. Well, I'm a grown-up woman, you know, and can make up my own mind for myself, without having any of your priggish, middle-class, Victorian sermons to help me."

Philip had only the vaguest suspicions of what were Lofty's intentions, and would never have dreamed that his mother could be party to them. His mind up to now had always avoided putting into words what he thought. Now that the idea was forced upon him, he was utterly disgusted. Lofty was practically his own age, and people of his own age were surely able to see his mother as she was, an embarrassment to be suffered with whatever degree of patience one could muster. That this nervous, opinionated, feather-brained creature could even see herself as a woman struck him as a hideous perversion of nature. Philip's mind revolted from the implications of what she suggested. Far from thinking that if she blew her nose she would be drawing attention to her sex, Philip was quite unable to accept that his mother had ever had anything to do with sex. As for Lofty, Philip could scarcely bring himself to believe that anybody could be so wicked. It was worse than pederasty, which Philip was prepared to admit might be quite fun, worse than bestiality, which was purely comic, worse even than homosexual conduct between consenting adults in private, which was as revolting as anything he could think of. Anyone who was prepared to degrade his manhood to the extent of misbehaving with his mother was worthy of nothing but contempt. Philip decided to write to Brother Richard, at Cleeve, about the matter.

Mr. Sligger did not seem in the least surprised that his wife wished to go to Llanwtyth. He had read of Mr. Williams's death in his *Times*.

"You want to take young Crippen with you?" he asked. It was nothing to do with him, but he would not have thought the young man, to whom he had taken rather a fancy, would be much help to the Liberal cause.

"Don't you want to see Anthony put on a proper footing? He will be the greatest help to me. I can't see anything wrong with taking him." Something defensive in her tone put Mr. Sligger on his mettle.

"It's nothing to do with me if you want to take Crippen with you if you think it's safe. Take Al Capone, too."

236

"Philip wanted to come. If you like, I'll take him." Mrs. Sligger spoke as if to a small child who was frightened of the dark, and she was offering to leave the light on in the passage. If she had been less guilty, she would realize that her husband was thinking of something quite different.

Now Mr. Sligger saw an opening for his genius. "I don't know what you want to take Philip for. The young man doesn't want to go. He's quite happy here. Philip needs a rest after being shaken about in prison for so long. He wants to settle down. I can't see any point in taking him to see a lot of old women in Wales."

"All right, Philip will stay at home."

Mr. Sligger sat back in his chair with a happy smile. He had asserted himself in the only way he knew, and the result was a complete victory. He had prevented something from being done.

"It's all right," said Mrs. Sligger. "The old bag doesn't suspect anything."

"What is there to suspect?" said Lofty with studied innocence. Mrs. Sligger sighed. She had always dreamed that it would be like this.

Lofty was sprawled in the armchair of his bedroom, reading *The Times*. Mrs. Sligger went and sat on his knee, an incongruous sight, if there had been a third person to witness it. She, thin-faced and knobbly, turning fifty, in a cotton housecoat, he sallow and diabolically handsome, turning twenty-five, in his shirtsleeves.

"This is love," said Mrs. Sligger. "I am so looking forward to our weekend in Llanwtyth." She pronounced the name as anybody else might speak of Verona, Brugge or Ávila. "Do you know what I am going to let you do to me?" She could not, even in the throes of such exquisite anticipation, get out of her governessy approach to young men.

Lofty said he thought he had a good idea. He wished Mrs. Sligger would shift her weight, as he was most uncomfortable.

It would be unwise to mention it at this stage, as their relationship was not yet on a proper footing.

"I have no patience with those fools who say we are doing wrong. Love is everything, everything else nothing, don't you agree, Anthony?"

Lofty said he thought he knew what she meant. She shifted her bottom, causing him excruciating pain.

Mrs. Sligger had prepared several speeches for the occasion. Instead, she reverted to the script of a film she had once seen in Aldershot.

"What are we going to do about us, Anthony?" she said. Before he could answer she went on, "Love is a cruel master, and we must obey him. Oh Anthony, isn't it a terrible, wonderful thing how much we two are in love?"

"That's right," said Lofty.

Chapter 17

"Mr. Droppings is all right, but there's a filthy messenger who refuses to take my copy down because he says I put too much paste on it, and he might get his hands sticky. I think that sort of person stinks, don't you?"

"Is he a—?"

"Oh yes, he's completely working class."

"Steady on then, old boy."

Jamey felt there was some constraint in his friend these days. Guy seemed less frank about himself, and rather to feel that it was none of Jamey's business to inquire too closely into what had happened after he left Oxford. Now that Jamey recognized an old Oxford attitude he felt irritated.

"It's no good thinking people are wonderful just because

they're workers, you know. I see them the whole time, and a very large number of them are absolute hell." Of course some were all right. Jackie, the compositor, who always pinched Jamey's bottom and said "When are we going to get you a girl?" was completely charming. Some of the others were quite intelligent, although Mr. Combs, the blanket press operator, was one of the sourest, most spiteful people Jamey had ever met. Among the messengers and cleaners there were many whom in charity one could only describe as backward.

"You are quite wrong," said Guy primly. "Daddy employs a great many workers—over seventy thousand, as a matter of fact— and he tells me they are quite charming. I think he should know slightly better than you."

Jamey felt one of his rare surges of genuine egalitarian indignation. He did not feel sufficiently sure of himself to indulge it to the full, sitting in a deep armchair in Lord Robinson's drawing room, but he allowed himself a sarcastic laugh.

"Well, they're not such fun to work with," he said.

"It depends on whether you've got the common touch, I suppose," said Peter Garlick, Guy's new friend, who was also staying the weekend in Virginia Water. "As a matter of fact, I am quite lucky in that. We always seem to get on very well together."

"Exactly," said Guy. "It depends a lot on the sort of background you come from. They don't like people talking down to them who are really no better than they are themselves. Personally, I always treat them as equals."

Jamey thought, Just you try treating Mr. Combs, the insane blanket press operator, as an equal. Tomorrow, he would be back at work among them, tolerated with a friendly disdain by some, loathed by others who would do everything in their power to make him look incompetent or overbearing or young.

"Personally," said Garlick, "I would prefer to find myself among a lot of ordinary, decent working people over a glass of beer than at some frightful, middle-class cocktail party, drinking watered-down Martinis."

"So would I," said Guy.

239

Oh, would you, thought Jamey; you pair of ugly, jumped-up babies. Mrs. Sligger always put water in the drinks at her cocktail parties, and although Jamey held no brief for her, he was prepared to admit that it was quite sensible, as otherwise everybody got drunk. The Sliggers were one of the oldest Christian families in the country, and although Mrs. Sligger was not, as it were, of their *milieu*, he was prepared to bet she came from just as good a family as Garlick or Frazer-Robinson.

"How many glasses of beer have you drunk with the working classes?" he said.

"Oh several. Whenever one goes into a pub. I always try and get into conversation, to see what chaps are thinking."

"So do I," said Guy.

"What are they thinking?" Jamey felt his sarcasm was wearing thin.

"It's often quite interesting, actually. Far more interesting than listening to a lot of ill-informed idiots shouting their heads off about what they think they've read in the *Daily Cenotaph*."

"I don't know what makes you think we have the *Cenotaph*," said Jamey. "As a matter of fact we have the *Times*. People at work are only different because they've got it all from the *Mirror*."

"Not at all," said Garlick. "Working people are quite capable of forming their own judgments. In many ways they are more intelligent than us, because they're much less hidebound by outdated notions of class."

"Exactly," said Guy. Jamey thought of the naked hatred in the eyes of the subeditors' messenger, and agreed that Garlick was probably right. At least the workers were much less ambiguous in their loyalties. He felt the subject needed changing, but obviously it was not to be.

"In fact I think as soon as the government of this country is out of the hands of a small clique and more into that of the workers it will be happier for everyone."

"That's right," said Guy, searching in the cigarette box beside the sofa for one of the brands of cigarettes he favored.

"If you could see some of the people where I work, you wouldn't want to entrust the government of a dog's home to them." Jamey wished he had not mentioned dogs. The word had a fascist tinge.

"Of course, you think they're all dogs," said Garlick in a superior way, "because you're not sufficiently sure of your own position. No doubt you want to keep them all in kennels. But the workers must run the government, because they do the work."

"I don't see that that follows."

"What are you then, a Nazi?"

"I suppose I'm Labour, actually." It was the only thing one could be, on the *Aldershot Beam*. Although it was a stanchly Conservative newspaper, nobody would dare try and introduce anybody except a fully paid-up member of the Labour Party. Jamey felt that he probably was Labour, too, insofar as he was anti the right of jumped-up guttersnipes like Garlick to tell him the Sliggers put water in their cocktails.

But Jamey had succeeded in shocking his audience.

"In that case, I'm sorry," said Garlick, with a glance at Frazer-Robinson.

"We didn't know," said Guy. "You see, I am President of the Oxford Young Conservatives next term, and Peter is going to be Secretary. I am sorry we were being so political." He gave his charming laugh, reserved for parties at which he did not know the person he was talking to very well. A terrible constraint fell on the company. Garlick flicked some ash into an onyx container in an odious way he had which suggested there was a conspiracy between himself and Guy, from which Sligger was excluded. It was like the secret societies he and Philip used to form to exclude Barbara Arckwright, when they were all children and the world was a less complicated place.

"How are the girls?" said Jamey, famous for tact.

"The girls?" said Guy, as if he were not sure such a class of people existed.

"Are you getting in much practice at Oxford these days?" said Sligger, with a dirty leer.

241

"Practice?" said Garlick, more aggressive in his puzzlement. "I'm afraid I don't know what you mean."

The only girl staying for the weekend was Rosemary Potinue, very respectable and rather nice. She was some sort of relation to the chaplain at Oxford, and was unlikely to give them much chance to practice. Nobody knew where she was, but one assumed she had gone to her room for the afternoon as respectable, pretty girls are liable to do.

"Do you mean to say you have given up the hunt?" said Jamey, getting cross. He and Guy had started a private competition as to which would successfully go to bed with a member of the opposite sex first. It was tacitly agreed that the competition would not be affected by lies they felt bound to tell in company, but that as far as their race was concerned, absolute truth was the rule.

"Hunt? What hunt?" Garlick started to say in his stupid, irritating maner, but Guy overruled him.

"Things go on much the same," he said. Jamey took it to mean he had not got anywhere. If so, it was the first recognition of their former intimacy he had received throughout the visit.

"Sally Pratt-Bingham has come on," said Garlick. "Goyle did that. One must say a few things in his credit."

"How is Goyle?" Jamey had last seen him as a semiconscious figure having the Anne Etherington Memorial Picture removed from his head.

"He's all right," said Guy cautiously. "We bought him another picture to make up for the one we accidentally broke."

"Is it called the Anne Etherington Memorial Picture?"

"No, people had rather lost enthusiasm for that. We presented it to him in celebration of his becoming a father. It is called the Robin Black Birthday Picture."

"How's Deirdre?"

"I don't really know. I expect she's all right."

Poor Anne Etherington. Did nobody remember her?

. . .

Mrs. Sligger and Lofty returned to Farnham from their week-end, in a disgruntled mood. Things had not gone at all as planned. On the first night in Llanwtyth, Lofty had been disgustingly drunk, and had burst into her bedroom bellowing, "Lights out. No more talking," and many other coarse phrases which he had no doubt picked up in prison. Mrs. Sligger tried to calm him down, but when the noise got too loud she had to send for the hall porter who showed Lofty back to his room. After that there could be no question of anything happening, as too many people had heard the uproar on the first night and drawn their own conclusions. Lofty had been most understanding and quite penitent, consoling himself by getting drunk three nights running in the public bar of the Station Hotel. Mrs. Sligger only comforted herself that it had been the public bar, and none of her Liberal supporters were likely to hear of it. Lofty's companions had been railway employees, all of whom were certain to be Labour and had never even heard of the Liberal revival. Lofty said he had done a lot of good work among them—"Getting to know the people," he called it—and Mrs. Sligger thought he was probably right. She was still very much in love, she told herself, but it was not going to be as easy as she supposed. Farnham was no good, with Philip hanging around the place—even her husband might suspect something after a time—and Llanwtyth was too prim. She wished she had been given a more progressive constituency—somewhere like Coventry—where it might have been thought a point in her favor.

Philip received them with obvious distaste. "Jamey is not back from Virginia Water yet, and Father is working in his study," he said, before strolling off, with calculated insolence, to pick his teeth in his bedroom.

"There's no need to tell me that, young man," Mrs. Sligger shouted after him, "I can use my eyes."

She turned back to smile at Lofty. Whatever had or had not happened between them, there was now the understanding that they were lovers.

243

"Page fourteen is now fifteen minutes late," said Mr. Combs to the chief printer.

"We're waiting for a substitute Bod on the Red Cross story that bust."

"I have now been waiting for fifteen minutes for that page to come off the stone."

"We can't do anything until we've got that Dark Bod, Mr. Combs."

"Would it be too much to ask that the Dark Bod be forthcoming, Mr. Catchaway?" Combs spoke with studied insolence to the chief printer. He was a workshop man, and owed fealty to the floor manager. The printers, compositors, and linotype operators, being a more intelligent class of people, tended to look down on the men in the workshop. All were paid as much as junior ministers in the Government, but there were sharp differences on the intellectual level.

"Mr. Sligger is attending to the matter, Mr. Combs. I suggest that if you stand by your press, or whatever you call it, you might be in a better position when the page comes through."

"Mr. Sligger," shouted Combs triumphantly. "Now we've got to the root of the matter. Thank you very much, Mr. Catchaway, thank you very much indeed." Mr. Combs had known perfectly well what was keeping the page. He now addressed the company. "Do you hear that, everybody. The *reason* why all of us is kept up tonight, losing not only our beauty sleep but also the cherished company of our loved ones, whatever applies, is because Mr. Sligger is among us, occupying as he does a position of the greatest importance over us, as befits his birth and breeding and superior education."

"Wrap up, Codger," someone shouted.

"Don't mind him,' said Jackie, the woman's page compositor, "I expect his wife has just had a miscarriage. She is always having them."

Jamey stood over a damp galley proof with a Biro that was not working, and he pretended not to hear. The president of the local Red Cross, Mrs. Alice Fotheringay-Potts, had been presented with a silver-plated table lighter on her retirement after eight years' fruitful association with that body. Her retirement was not news, as that had been announced previously, but the manner of her doing so was thought worthy of notice. Jamey had to fit all this into two lines of not more than twelve letters each. His first attempt:

MRS FOTHERINGAY
POTTS DEPARTS

had bust on both lines, and the linotype operator had not even tried to set it. His second:

LIGHTER FOR
MRS POTTS

had been returned by the revise editor as libelous. We were not allowed to make jokes about people's names, he said. Now that he was on the stone, his heading would not have to pass the revise editor, the chief sub, the night editor, the style-and-good-taste man or anyone else, but for the life of him Jamey could not think of any combination of words, whether relevant or not, which fitted into the framework of a Dark Bod. He tried to set about it logically. Since "Mrs. Fotheringay" did not fit into a single line, and "Fotheringay-Potts" did not begin to fit into a line, and since "Mrs. Potts" was ruled out, one had either to call her by her surname alone, which would be insulting, and hint that she was a prostitute, or leave her name out of it altogether. The other important elements of the story were "Silver-plated table lighter," "Red Cross," "President," "Retiring," "Presentation." There seemed to be absolutely no combination which made sense in twelve letters or less. Clearly it was insoluble. One needed more to go on. What about "Eight years"?

LIGHTER FOR
EIGHT YEARS

"I shouldn't put that," said Jackie. "It looks as if she's been on a slimming diet in prison."

"Don't help him," screamed Mr. Combs. "None of us is allowed to help him. We aren't *heducated* like he is." Jamey pretended not to listen and bent still further over his galley proof. Concentrating so hard on pretending not to listen, he was unable to give much attention to the business of Mrs. Fotheringay-Potts's table lighter.

"It is most right and suitable that all of us poor people should be kept up for as long as possible, waiting on Mr. Sligger's pleasure. Of course it is. We are nothing but artisans, greasy mechanics, and shit."

"Speak for yourself, Codger," someone said.

Sleepy Sammy, who was compositor on the city page, suddenly woke up to the fact that something was happening.

"Here, what's happening?" he said.

Everybody laughed, and from the benches at the far end of the shop, where the sports page was made up by a surly, unhappy group of Welshmen, there came the beginnings of a song:

"Why are we waiting?"

"Why are we waiting?"

"Why are we waiting?"

Soon all the benches had taken it up, and Sleepy Sammy was banging the stone with the tin mug from which he drank his tea. Another compositor struck the metal lampshades with a thirty-six-inch twelve-point rule. Soon the place was ringing like a blacksmith's shop as more and more people took up the refrain.

Jamey stared at the list of important elements with absolutely nothing in his head. Then, in a rush, things started to come. The unmentionable prostitute Fotheringay-Potts was out, everything else was in.

EIGHT YEARS
FOR PRESIDENT

PRESIDENT IS
PRESENTED

LIGHTER IS
SILVER PLATED

"Why are we waiting?" sang everybody. Although many of them normally spoke in perfectly ordinary voices, it was a recognized convention that they spoke in B.B.C. cockney when they wished to be taken humorously.

"Whoy are we whiting?"

"Whoy are we whiting?"

Jamey did not understand. If the silver-plated president had never been presented to the Red Cross before, how on earth had she ever become their president? Few bodies would even take a secretary, let alone a president it had never met. Jamey simply did not understand.

"He's crying," said Jackie.

"Look. Oh, my poor little darling, he's crying," said Mr. Combs, carried away by the success of it all. It was quite true. Jamey was crying. Mr. Combs went up to Jamey and started to hug him, with a fixed grin to show it was all in jest. Jamey tried to push him away.

"It's a fight is it then? I have displeased his mighty Lordship. Come on, hit me then. Hit me." Combs danced around in front of Jamey. Absolute hush had fallen, and about forty men gathered round them to watch. "Hit me then. Show us all how strong you are, how our class isn't even fit to be wiped off the feet of you young gentlemen. Or aren't we going to demean ourselves? There's no need to be frightened. I won't hit you back. Let's just see you hit me."

Jamey paused. From the purely military angle, Combs presented no threat. He was small and weedy and unarmed. On the

247

other hand, there was a large crowd of uncertain sympathy. If only Combs would touch him again, he would be justified in hitting him.

"I shouldn't pay any attention to him, sir," said Mr. Catchaway, who had come up behind. "There'd be no end of trouble." Jamey looked at him gratefully, recognizing him at once as a decent fellow of the old type. Thank heavens there were still some decent people left in the world.

"The night editor's coming, and he'll fix the Dark Bod. I should hop it."

"For all his grand class, his Lordship's scared to hit me. Go on. I dare you," said Mr. Combs, resuming his dance.

"I'm not scared to hit you," said Jamey. "I don't particularly want to."

"His Lordship does not particularly want to hit me. Fancy! I am too unclean and pitiful an example of human misery for his Lordship to be pleased to strike me. He has *compassion*." Mr. Combs picked up a page-proof, and carried it daintily in one hand like a handkerchief. Sligger supposed he was imitating a homosexual, and was quite interested, because he did not know there were homosexuals among the lower classes. Certainly, Pratt-Bingham had not behaved like that in the days when he was off the rails before he settled down.

The night editor and the works manager arrived simultaneously.

"What's happening down here? You should all have been in bed half an hour ago."

"All right, scram," said Mr. Catchaway to Jamey, giving him a shove in the back. Sligger decided that perhaps Catchaway was not such a decent old-fashioned type as he had supposed.

The night editor glanced perfunctorily at the Red Cross story, produced a giant red Biro and scribbled on the top of the sheet:

PRESENTATION
BY RED CROSS

248

In two minutes it was set, in thirty seconds it was in the page. One minute later it was on Mr. Combs's blanket press machine, four minutes after that it was cast, and in another twelve minutes it was rushing round the rotary drum, printing 750 copies a minute.

Jamey drove his motor scooter home to Farnham in a despondent mood. A motionless couple stood by the side of the road, locked in an embrace. Soon, thought Jamey, they would get round to deep petting. He was too busy for that sort of thing nowadays, but he took a detached interest in other people's antics. He should have said to Mr. Combs, "Of course I'd hit you, if I didn't think you'd fall down dead." He wished he hadn't cried. Next time he would wipe the floor with any wretched, ignorant mechanic who got in his way. If only other people would realize that he did not hold it against them that they were humbly born. All he wanted was to be accepted as one of them. He suddenly thought of a perfectly good heading for that Red Cross story:

PRESIDENT
RETIRES

It was two o'clock in the morning by the time he got to Farnham Green. The light was on in Lofty Parker's bedroom. No doubt he had gone to sleep with it like that. Jamey was the only person in the house who did any work, the only person who grappled with problems of importance, like how to describe Mrs. Fotheringay-Potts in twelve letters; except for his mother, of course, but even after fifteen years on the *Aldershot Beam*, Jamey could not hope to be one half as grown-up as she. As he went to sleep, he wondered if he would get the sack for keeping the paper up half an hour. It was their own fault if he did, he decided.

"The trouble with Jamey is he hasn't really settled down in life yet. He's not completely mature, if you know what I mean."

Garlick blew some smoke out of his cigarette holder and began taking it to pieces. "You simply can't talk about the working classes as he does. People have got to realize that nowadays they are absolutely right, and what we must do is find out what they're thinking and agree with it, sometimes expressing it better than they could themselves, perhaps."

"Exactly," said Guy. "I don't think there is any such thing as the working classes, really. I mean Daddy is working class, if you come to think of it. He has to work for all that money. The great thing is to treat everyone as equals, whether they're the butler, the cook or the gardener's boy. Then all these class things simply would not exist."

"I always treat servants as equals," said Garlick. "I don't know what Jamey's got against them. I think perhaps it's because he's not used to having them around. But it seems so obvious—it doesn't hurt me, and they like it."

"I thought he was very nice, and I don't know what you've got against him. I didn't see him being rude to the servants, and Mr. Gregory certainly seemed to like him very much," said Rosemary Potinue.

"Of course Jamey's *nice*, Rosemary, nobody's denying that. We're just thankful we haven't got him at Oxford to embarrass the Conservatives. He stands for everything which people say the Conservatives stand for, and of course we don't nowadays. As for Gregory, he's a complete imbecile, and his judgments are not worth much."

"I am interested to hear you say that," said Garlick. "I don't much care for Gregory either. I dare say he's a homosexual."

"I don't think that's it," said Guy. Their butler had eight children by his wife and, it was rumored, another by an unmarried mother who came to cook. "It's just that he's a complete fool, and would never be any good if he had another job."

"Well, I don't care what you say," said Rosemary, "I thought Jamey was charming. He asked me to stay with him for the Farnham Regatta, and I think I shall."

"Please yourself," said Garlick with a superior smile. "It

might be quite exciting. He's very eccentric, our Jamey, dashing off in the middle of a weekend saying he had to be at work by five o'clock on Sunday evening. Anybody would think his work was important."

"I hear you had a bit of trouble last night on the stone." Mr. Droppings grinned wolfishly into his cup of cold, brown tea.

"Yes, I'm afraid I kept the paper up half an hour. Do you think there'll be any trouble?"

"It's hard to say," said Mr. Droppings, still grinning, "but I expect that as it was your first time by yourself, they will take a lenient view. Was it Mr. Combs's fault?"

"Yes. He started them all singing."

"Mr. Combs is an absolute nuisance. He kept the paper up three times last week. I shouldn't be too worried if I was you."

"Why can't they sack him then?"

Mr. Droppings spilled some tea in his agitation. "Sh," he whispered. "For heaven's sake don't say things like that. Somebody might hear you." He moved his chair away to dissociate himself from anything Jamey had said or might be going to say, and stared at the papers on his desk in a preoccupied way.

Jamey looked round to see if anyone had heard him. His eye caught that of the subroom messenger, who read the guilt in Jamey's expression and lumbered over. Jamey shrank, but the man had not heard him. He merely picked up Jamey's papers and swept them to the floor. Mr. Droppings chuckled.

"I was waiting for that to happen," he said. "I nearly told you, but I thought you would guess by the way I couldn't stop smiling. The chair you are sitting in belongs to the stand-in home copytaster, and he is quite right to turn you out of it. Nobody has any business to be sitting in that chair but the stand-in home copytaster, and he hasn't arrived yet."

"Sorry," said Jamey, collecting his papers from the floor.

"That's all right," said Mr. Droppings kindly. "I couldn't help laughing, though. But you mustn't worry about that sort of thing. You'll learn in time. It took me fifteen years to get

251

where I am. Now, nobody can catch me out, not even Mr. Combs in the workshop, or the chief sub himself."

DEAR JAMEY,

I was delighted to get your letter and hear that you were settling down on the *Beam*. After giving the matter some thought, I decided you would be happier there than in Crewe. News reaches me that you have already done some sterling work among labor relations, and nearly brought the whole paper out on strike one evening. Keep it up. I should have mentioned to you that Mr. Combs, the machine operator, is one of us, so next time you need not be afraid to hit him. There is no knowing what good that might not do, as all the other provincials would have to come out, too. I have told Combs you are a friend—he did not know that before, of course—and he may be getting in touch with you to arrange something.

If you can come up to London in the near future, we must get together and I shall tell you who are our friends on the *Beam*. As a matter of fact, we are very strong there at the moment. Also, I shall introduce you to the working cell which we have on the *Cenotaph*, and which I always hold up as a model to the other papers. The *Reverser*, needless to say, is hopelessly split between the revisionists and the old-type traditionalists. It might be of use to you to meet the *Cenotaph* people, so I have arranged for you to have the day off on July 20th, and we shall meet at the Topalino Restaurant in Greek Street for lunch at 1:15. Please do not be late, as the meeting starts at 2:30.

I do not need to ask you not to mention to anyone about our second encounter while you were in London last. I know you are a sensible person, but it might do incalculable harm if it got around that we saw each other in Curzon Street. I hoped to see you afterward, but you had left. You must realize, too, that if I thought you were not to be trusted, I should have to take steps.

Looking forward to our lunch at the Topalino,

Yours ever,
CHRISTIAN

P.S. I should be grateful if you would burn this letter, having read it, as one does not like to have too many letters lying around.

Jamey was not at all pleased with the idea of working in alliance with Mr. Combs. He rather imagined that he had outgrown the Creepy Crawley stage. Things that seemed important at Oxford, when he was with Fringe and Bill English and poor, misunderstood Anne Etherington, did not seem to loom quite so large now. No doubt it was a good thing to foster industrial discontent, so that by suffering the workers might eventually come face to face with truth and set themselves on the narrow path which led to the noble austerities of pure socialism, but Jamey fancied they could perfectly well discover the path without his help.

He liked having Creepy Crawley as a pen-friend, so that by balancing his reports against those to Rapey Rawley, Creepy's brother at Cleeve, Jamey could feel that his loyalties were fluid, and the essential Sligger was still a mysterious entity known only to himself, but he was certainly not prepared to put himself to great inconvenience for either. If Rapey had asked him to stand in a pulpit to testify to the immorality in the Farnham area, Jamey would very properly have refused. Creepy seemed to be expecting him to do it. Nevertheless, he was offered a free lunch, and afterward a chance to meet some very important journalists who might be a great help to Jamey in his career, so he decided to accept the invitation, without committing himself to any cooperation with the detestable Mr. Combs.

Mrs. Sligger was very busy these days with the by-election.

"I have a lot of forms to fill in after lunch, so I shall want Anthony to help me," she said.

"Right you are," said Lofty.

Mr. Sligger looked concerned. "Don't you think poor Crippen needs a rest?" he said. "I shouldn't like to spend my whole time poring over a lot of rubbish about female emancipation." Mr. Sligger had very old-fashioned ideas on what the Liberal revival was about.

"You must allow me to do things in my own way, Aidan," said Mrs. Sligger cuttingly. "Since I can expect absolutely no help from you, you must not complain if other people want to help me."

"I'm not complaining, only saying that if I was a healthy young man"—remote possibility—"I would not want to spend my time cooped up with an elderly housewife discussing her plans for world government."

"You seem to forget, Aidan, that not *everybody* happens to be like you. Anthony enjoys working with me, and even if he didn't he would realize that the work was too important to allow personal antagonisms to come into it."

"That's right, the work's too important," said Lofty.

Mr. Sligger gave him a sympathetic look.

"We have a lot of work to do first," said Mrs. Sligger. "Fun and games afterward. Now here is a form from the League of Empire Loyalists, which they send out to all candidates in elections. Do I believe that a Briton's first duty is toward the maintenance of his Empire? Yes I do. Do I agree that we should get out of GATT? I am not sure about that one. What do you think, Anthony?"

"Of course we should," said Lofty. "It stands to reason."

"Well, I'd better leave that one blank, just in case." Neither of them had any idea what GATT stood for, but it sounded vaguely unpleasant.

"Do I wish to see all power in the ruthless hands of American monopoly capitalism? I should say not. I have never liked the Americans, with their idiotic manners. We're all quite American enough already, without all this nonsense about monopoly capitalism. Am I in favor of the indiscriminate frittering away of our Empire? Certainly not. What silly questions these people ask. Am I prepared to stand by and see the Communists prevail in every corner of the world? No, of course not, although what these silly people don't realize is that the Russians are our friends nowadays. It is the Americans we need to watch out for. Still, they seem to be quite anti-American, too. Quite a sensible lot of people, really. Am I prepared to see Britain ruled by a lot

254

of foreigners in the Common Market, and am I prepared to accept the religious implications of our signing the Treaty of Rome? Sh, we must be tactful about that sort of thing in this house. Just put a very small 'No,' so that nobody will guess. We've outgrown any religious implications in this country, although to see the old bag going to church every Sunday you wouldn't guess it. In any case, the Church of England agrees with everything I say."

Later, when she was sitting on Lofty's knee in the uncomfortable way she had, Mrs. Sligger said:

"You are absolutely sure you love me, aren't you, Anthony? It isn't just physical attraction, is it? I know I'm sure, but I know young men are sometimes different. I hope you don't mind my asking."

"That's all right," said Lofty. "It's not just physical attraction."

Mrs. Sligger sighed. "I knew it wasn't," she said.

Chapter 18

Jamey had always been particularly good at knocking down coconuts with wooden balls. Rosemary was full of admiration. By the time he had won twenty coconuts, he ran out of money, and she produced sixpence from her purse for another three throws. He knocked down another coconut.

"Really, Jamey, I don't know how you do it."

"It's just a knack. You have a try."

"I don't think I could."

"Go on then."

Rosemary produced another sixpence and did some pathetic, girlish things with her arms.

"That's no good at all," said Jamey masterfully. "Let me show you."

Rosemary had only half a crown left, so Jamey bought five goes. He hoped she was enjoying herself, as he threw the balls with devastating effect to win another six coconuts.

"You're marvelous," said Rosemary, although her attention seemed to be wandering a little. "I shall never be as good as you."

"It's just a knack," said Jamey modestly.

"What are we going to do with all these coconuts?"

"Give them back to the man, I suppose." It was one of those moments when one could afford to be generous.

"It seems rather a waste."

Rosemary still had a ten-shilling note, so they decided to try their luck at the Tombola. There was such a crowd round it that they had to push their way through, and Jamey put his arm round Rosemary's waist to help her. She seemed to like it, so when they came out he kept it there. She gave a delightful, unaffected laugh. There could be no question, but Rosemary Potinue was a good sport, as well as sweet and pretty and quite bright. It did not occur to Jamey to think that he had set himself on the road to deep petting and seduction. It was just rather a pleasant way of walking around with a girl.

They met Philip trying to hit some playing cards with darts. He always fancied he had a skill with darts, but it was more a matter of choice than any talent he had been born with.

"Mummy's looking for you," he said, without turning round. When he had thrown his last dart and spent twenty-five shillings to secure a packet of Woodbines he turned round and said, "Hullo, hullo, hullo," in a suggestive voice. "Some of us are quick workers round here."

Jamey removed his arm guiltily, but Rosemary gave one of

her laughs. "There was a bit of a crowd at the Tombola," she said.

"I should say there was," said Philip. "There's Mummy talking to a fat woman by the Home Produce. I don't know what she wants. But for heaven's sake don't bring that awful Parker back here." Philip had taken one of his unaccountable dislikes to Lofty. Jamey liked him; and Rosemary, who had arrived the day before, said she thought he was quite amusing.

"Jamey," said Mrs. Sligger, "I want you to meet Mrs. Fotheringay-Potts. She used to be president of the Red Cross round here, and tells me they are looking for a new secretary. We wondered if you knew anybody, with your knowledge of local affairs."

"Well, there's always Mummy," said Sligger.

His mother looked very pleased. "I don't think I'm the sort of person they're looking for at all."

"Oh yes you are, Mrs. Sligger," said Rosemary earnestly and with such obvious sincerity that even Mrs. Fotheringay-Potts looked touched. "You would be wonderful."

"Well, we must think about it," said Mrs. Fotheringay-Potts. "I don't think I've met your boy before."

"Jamey works on the *Aldershot Beam*," said Mrs. Sligger proudly.

Mrs. Fotheringay-Potts stiffened. "I am sorry. I did not know. In that case, I have nothing more to say."

"That's all right," said Jamey.

"I have no comment to make on anything whatsoever. Now, if you'll excuse me, I am rather busy."

"But he's not on duty now," said Rosemary pleadingly to her bottom. "Please, Mrs. Fotheringay, don't think we're spying on you."

"That's all right, my dear. I didn't know he was not on duty. One gets so tired, being badgered by the press night and day." Jamey wondered why the press was so interested in Mrs. Fotheringay-Potts. It was a form of persecution mania he had en-

257

countered often in his dealings with the public. A local vicar who had written to the editor asking for assistance to raise money for the installation of a heating system in his church had told Jamey that he had absolutely no comment to make to the press, that if they wanted to print anything they must find it out for themselves, and could expect no help from him.

"Was it about the retirement presentation?" said Jamey.

"That's exactly what it was about. It is a complete scandal, and I'm only sorry one of them never got hold of the complete story. I wasn't going to tell then, of course, but as you are off duty and this is strictly off the record, you may as well know it. What I wanted was a cocktail shaker and ice bucket from Fortnum's. Then that wretched Miss Barnstaple stands up and says that although she's broad-minded enough not to be shocked, there were many people in the district who would not like to think of the Red Cross condoning the habit of drinking, which led to so many broken homes and accidents on the road every year. She knew that I could be trusted to use the gift in a moderate and sensible way, as when, for instance, there had been an accident on the road and whenever else alcohol is prescribed for medicinal purposes, but she thought it would set a dangerous precedent, particularly for the junior members of the organization. That's what comes from letting Nonconformists into the committee."

"Poor Mrs. Fotheringay, how perfectly ridiculous," said Rosemary.

"What did you think of the lighter?" said Jamey. He was on the first scoop since he had joined the *Beam*, and it was still his first week in the newsroom.

"The most ridiculous thing I have ever seen. Neither I nor my husband smoke, and even if we did we don't want something the size of an elephant taking up the whole living room to light our cigarettes with. And it uses more petrol than a Rolls Royce."

Rosemary said in a sweet, encouraging voice, "Do you think there was any malice in the choice?"

258

"Of course there was. They wanted to see the Red Cross in the hands of a lot of teetotal, vegetarian spinsters. Mind you, this is quite off the record," she added, as Jamey began to take down the details with a pencil he had borrowed from Rosemary.

"How perfectly frightful for you, Mrs. Fotheringay. Had you had any trouble before?"

"Trouble? I have been absolutely up to my eyes in it ever since we let that terrible Barnstaple woman on the committee, with her crony, Miss Drisscoll. My term of office should have lasted ten years, but I had to resign after eight because they made things so unpleasant."

"Ten years," said Jamey, copying it down in longhand. "So unpleasant."

"Did they actually *do* anything?" said Rosemary.

"There was practically nothing they did not do," said Mrs. Fotheringay-Potts with quiet dignity. It was evident that the interview was at an end. "You mustn't say anything, or I shall be in no end of trouble."

"That's all right," said Jamey. As they went away, Mrs. Sligger was saying, "Now, that's one thing I cannot understand. Bigotry in any form is always to be avoided, but I should think they would have discovered how the occasional drink, taken in moderation, can be perfectly delicious."

When they had left, Jamey did not dare put his arm round her again, so he said, "Let's go and look at the Tombola."

"Do let's," said Rosemary with a friendly eagerness which could not have been motivated only by her interest in who won a pot of honey, a child's bicycle or an electric alarm clock. The press around the Tombola was greater than ever, and soon Jamey felt himself struggling to keep his feet. They came out a few minutes later, his arm safely around her waist. They laughed conspiratorially. There was no knowing where this would end, Jamey thought, but for the moment he was too excited by it all to ponder. In any case, there was little hope of anything serious happening, as he had to be off the next day to lunch with Creepy Crawley in London. It was a miserable obligation, but now that Jamey had left the subeditors and entered his second stage of training in the newsroom, he felt that his career was, after all, quite important. Twelve pounds a week was his present wage, and by next summer it would be the union minimum of eighteen pounds a week. After his second year he could hope to get twelve hundred a year or more. Rosemary Potinue was no more than a pleasant intermission, but Jamey felt sad at the prospect of her departure the next day, probably the last he would ever see of her. The Potinues, he had discovered, were as old a Christian family as the Sliggers, but rather richer.

"It was an awfully good story you got for me from Mrs. Fotheringay-Potts. My first scoop."

"But you aren't going to print it, are you?" said Rosemary in dismay.

"Of course I'll use it. Isn't that what you want?"

"I did want it to begin with, but then she told us she would get into awful trouble."

"That was just a manner of speaking. She wanted us to use it."

"I thought she did, but we can't be sure. Oh Jamey, please don't say anything that may get her into trouble."

Jamey was not in the least concerned about getting Mrs. Fotheringay-Potts into trouble, and felt that his first loyalty should be to his newspaper. On reflection, however, he decided that Rosemary's peace of mind was the more important, and tore up his notes. She laughed, and did not mind when he gave her a little squeeze.

Later they watched Mrs. Fotheringay give away the prizes for some minor event. A photographer was there from the *Beam*, who recognized Jamey and winked at him before concentrating on the speaker. Sligger pitied the poor person who was going to have to sub the story. He would discover, try as he would, that Mrs. Fotheringay-Potts was simply not headline material, but one only learned in life through hard experience. He gave Rosemary another squeeze, and she laughed and said, "Your mother is looking at us rather disapprovingly. I think we had better pay attention to the speeches."

Jamey left Waterloo Station reeling with happiness and self-satisfaction. He had kissed Rosemary Potinue; not amorously, it is true, nor with any hint of passion or desire, but just a peck on the cheek as if it was the most natural thing for two grown-ups to do when they bid each other goodbye having traveled up to London together. And Rosemary had definitely looked pleased, as if it was a suitable and correct thing to have done. He rather fancied she had got just the same degree of pleasurable excitement as he had from the gesture. It was a great relief to be with a girl who was not either vastly older and more experienced, like Phyllis the Tickle, or hopelessly inexperienced and unapproachable like Barbara Arckwright, who had rather disappeared from the Farnham scene since Lofty had become Mrs. Sligger's Parliamentary agent.

He skipped along the platform to catch the underground which would take him, after many changes, to Piccadilly Circus, and burst into song: "Take a pair of sparkling eyes." Not looking where he was going, he fell into the arms of a porter from some remote underdeveloped nation.

"You got yourself a girl?" said the porter.

"Yes," said Jamey.

"So have I. We must shake hands on it." As the two stood shaking hands vigorously and giggling a little, Jamey felt a touch on his shoulder. It was Philip Fringe, looking more ghoulish than ever in a Bedford Grammar School blazer that did not fit (Fringe, of course, had been at Winchester), an open cricket shirt and a pair of light khaki trousers which shone when the light caught them.

"Hullo, Jamey, I didn't expect to see you here."

The porter did not like to be interrupted. "Has he got a girl?"

Jamey said, "I don't know. Have you, Philip?"

261

Fringe stuck his nose in the air. "Really, Jamey, I can see you have changed a lot."

"I don't think he has," said Sligger.

"Neither do I," said the porter. "Poor man. What a miserable life!"

As Jamey walked away with Fringe, he reflected on what a lot of simple wisdom there was to be found among the unsophisticated, childlike peoples of the underdeveloped world.

"What a charming porter that was," he said. "How much nicer than the English. I can't stand the English working classes, but when those Africans are nice, they are the salt of the earth."

Fringe sniffed. "I'm glad you say when they're nice. Most of us are nice when we're nice, you know. Still, they have their uses."

Jamey pitied him for not being in love. He put his arm on his shoulder and said, "Never mind, Fringy. The world'll straighten itself out in time."

Fringe struggled loose and said, "I am afraid I can't spend any more time gossiping, as I have a most important luncheon engagement. With Christian, as a matter of fact."

"So have I," said Jamey. "Creepy Crawley never told me he'd asked you. We may as well travel together."

"Very well," said Fringe, but he did not seem pleased that Jamey was still received in the Inner Councils. On the way there, he said, "In that case I suppose you know about this afternoon's plan."

"I am not sure I do. I think we are going to a meeting of the *Cenotaph* Inner Cell."

"I mean what the interdepartmental action group plan for this afternoon."

"I am afraid I don't. What is it?"

"If you do not know, it would obviously be out of order for me to tell you," said Fringe, extremely happy to have asserted himself again.

$\cdot$ $\cdot$ $\cdot$

At lunch Jamey said, "What is it the action group have in mind for this afternoon?"

Fringe said, "I thought I'd better not tell him, without definite instructions."

Creepy Crawley said, "It is going to be a magnificent gesture. I wish we could follow it up, so that the effect will not be wasted. But the action group are always impatient. I sometimes despair of ever managing to put over a coordinated plan. Of course, I don't know the full details yet. Philip is my liaison officer with the group."

Jamey felt that the matter was now closed, and tucked into his carefully chosen spaghetti with a touch of resentment. He did not like to be kept out of things.

"Tell me about Rosemary Potinue," said Creepy Crawley. There was nothing the man did not know.

"She's all right. A bit of a Christian young lady, if you know what I mean."

"I was afraid she might be. You must come and meet a young friend of mine called Phyllis Plimsoll. She is a most amusing little creature."

Jamey said he had already met Phyllis the Tickle, and did not wish to reopen the acquaintance at the moment. Creepy looked thoughtful.

"I know your Rosemary's uncle, the chaplain, very well of course. They are an interesting family, the Potinues. Stinking rich, most of them. One runs an agency for Christian university graduates, another for unmarried mothers, whether Christian or not, and then there's the interior decorator, who lives in Pont Street."

"I know," said Jamey. "He did my rooms at Oxford."

"Of course," said Creepy. "I expect that's how you met Rosemary. I have never met her, and very much look forward to the opportunity."

"She is very busy these days, actually."

"Did she ever tell you about her great-great-uncle—no, her

263

first cousin three times removed—Geoffrey Potinue, who pulled down the whole of Potinue except the chapel and went to live in the vault? Then he decided that wasn't big enough, so he hired Pugin to rebuild the whole of Potinue as a replica of Amiens Cathedral. Quite uninhabitable now, of course, but they manage."

Jamey said he had not yet heard that story. Everything was fitting into some pattern in Creepy's mind, and Jamey was glad that he had not corrected the impression of having met Miss Potinue through her interior-decorating uncle. There was no fighting the awful power of Creepy Crawley, but one could sometimes practice a gentle obstruction.

"You must tell your mother the story. I know she'd love it, although, of course, I have only met her once."

Jamey reflected that it would be extremely hard to find a person less likely to be interested by the story of Miss Potinue's first cousin three times removed, and once again rejoiced to think of Creepy Crawley barking up the wrong tree.

Fringe ground his teeth and thought about the plan.

The Inner Cell of the *Cenotaph* was not nearly such a homely affair as its Oxford counterpart. A man who had been pointed out to Jamey as the junior editor was in the chair. Two leader writers, the ballet critic, the health and Far Eastern correspondents, the deputy editor of the book page and Home Hints for Women were all there, as well as a sprinkling of home reporters and a few men whose rough manner suggested they came from the electricity and maintenance staff.

"Where is Poetry Corner and McGluskey from the newsroom?"

"McGluskey has been sent to cover this afternoon's event. Nobody's seen Poetry Corner for two days. He must be drunk, but they say he hasn't looked into Mooney's or El Vino's this week. His secretary says she thinks he may be ill."

"So long as his copy's in by Friday evening, nobody can complain," said the junior editor. "As you all know, we have been having some difficulty with our brothers on the *Reverser* side, who seem so anxious to purge their own ranks of any revisionism that they have no time for helping the movement. At long last, we have a coordinated plan. Starting from next week, we are going to press for military aid to Southern Rhodesia against her African neighbors, and they are going to press for aid against Southern Rhodesia for her African neighbors. Between the two of us, something must happen. We're urging the bosses to stand firm at Coventry, and on the Clyde. They're urging the workers to press their claims and not give an inch. Again, there is an example of how we can work together. After this afternoon's incident, we are going to press for the severest penalties against the perpetrators of this outrage, and the *Reverser* are going to demand that the Government resign. We catch them either way, but if we can get a few of them with really stiff sentences—say thirty years—it might have a better effect in the long run. When everybody protests at the savagery, we can call them all traitors, and the movement will get a lot of supporters that way."

"How do you know they are going to be caught?" said Fringe. Everybody looked embarrassed.

"I think we can leave that to the proper quarters?" said the junior editor, looking at Creepy Crawley. Creepy Crawley nodded.

"Good. Now remember this is a purely ban-the-bomb exercise. We don't come into the picture this time at all. When we've got the people in, then we can choose which are suitable for Inner Cell activity. What's the time now?"

"Two minutes to go," said Fringe, looking at his watch.

"I'll see what's happening," said Creepy Crawley. He went to the telephone. "Whitehall 4832. Damn, it's too early. I'm getting through."

"Buckin'ham Palace," said a voice.

"May I speak to Sir Rodney Reach, please. . . . Hullo, Rodney?" There was a loud click, then a whining noise in the receiver.

265

"They've done it. Exactly on time. Good work, Fringe."

People started getting up.

"Do you mean they've blown up the Palace?" said Jamey in great alarm.

"Only the Whitehall telephone exchange this time," said one of the leader writers with a light laugh. "If they've killed anyone, we'll be able to press for the death sentence. That should put the cat among the pigeons. The public may put up with any number of political prisoners, but even in England they'll scarcely put up with a political execution."

Creepy Crawley came up to them ten minutes later, as they were standing in the lift.

"I am afraid the matter has got a little out of hand. Two telephonists have been seriously injured, one of them very seriously. Now, we've got all the names here, have we, Philip? These are the ones who actually took part, these the ones who supplied the explosives and detonators?"

Fringe nodded, looking lost and a little sick. Creepy Crawley had suddenly become very grown-up.

"And they're all staying now at the house in Swiss Cottage?" Fringe nodded. "Good. We should have picked them all up within the hour. Goodbye, then, both of you. You have been very helpful, and if the nature of our work was different, I would put you in for a commendation."

"What do you think he is going to do?" said Sligger.

"I don't know. I'm washing my hands of the whole bloody thing."

Jamey felt much the same. If his future as a journalist depended on the movement, he was going to become something different. Whatever it might have been—and he still had only the vaguest idea—it was now discredited, and best forgotten as soon as possible.

Chapter 19

The sixty-third house in Bute Terrace, Llanwtyth, was exactly
the same as the other sixty-two. The door was opened by a small,
hard-boned man with a cunning, stupid face, who put his boot
on a jamb to prevent a horde of enemies rushing over the thresh-
old.

"I wonder if you could possibly tell me whether or not you
propose to vote Liberal," said Jamey, with a sweet smile.

"What if I tell you wrong?" said the man suspiciously.

"It doesn't matter. We can't do anything against you," said
Jamey.

"What's the point in asking, then?"

"We would just like to know what you think about the Liberals, and whether you really know what they stand for."

"And what if I say I do?"

"Then it's perfectly all right, and you needn't read any of our
pamphlets."

"Well, perhaps I'm going to say I don't know a thing about
them."

"Then we can tell you."

"I am not saying I don't know it already, mind."

Lofty took over. "The Liberals believe in freedom for everybody—no political prisoners either here or in Africa, and freedom for intellectuals behind the Iron Curtain, too. We believe
that education is a basic human right, and we propose to tackle
the class system in England which is shackling us to the nineteenth century and we propose to tackle it until it is beaten."

"Who said anything about class?" said the household of No. 63. "I didn't."

"Exactly," said Lofty. "We believe that you're just as good as any high and mighty lord in his Rolls-Royce, and you deserve the same amount of pay.

"That's right. Like bloody hell I'll get it too."

"Of course you will. The Liberals believe in higher wages for all the working classes, particularly miners."

"I'm in the Post Office. The miners get e-bloody-nough as it is."

"And Post Office workers. Where's the money going to come from? The bosses and the rich capitalist exploiters who never did any good for the working class."

"You mean you're going to let the bosses and the capitalists go on as they are?"

"Not at all. We're going to tax them out of existence."

"How are you going to tax them when they don't exist, then?"

"Practically out of existence."

"So you are going to let the bosses and capitalists go on as they are."

"Not at all. There aren't going to be bosses and workers any more, just workers, only the proper workers will get much more money than the people who wear the white collars."

"I expect you mean Post Office workers by that remark."

"No I don't. Post Office workers are an exception to the rule. They work properly."

"What we really wanted to know is whether you might like to vote Liberal," said Jamey.

"Why do you ask me, then?"

"Because we thought you might know."

"What would you say if I was to ask you what it was worth to have the answer to that question?"

"We just thought you might like to tell us whether you'll be joining in the great Liberal revival, or whether you don't mind being left behind."

268

"If it isn't worth anything to you to have the answer, it can't be worth anything to me to give it to you, can it?"

Jamey was exasperated. The man only represented one vote, and he was guarding it like a gold casket. "I am very sorry to have troubled you, then, Mr. . . ."

"Evans. Perhaps I'll think about whether to vote Liberal or not, and perhaps I won't. You might like my card to take away with you."

It was not a card, but a printed list of Labour Party officials. Victualing officer of the Labour Party in Llanwtyth was Mr. Florence Evans, of 63 Bute Terrace.

"I'm sorry, bach, we're all Labour in this house," said the tall, uncomfortable woman in No. 64.

"All?" said Jamey.

"That's right. Our Marilyn is Labour like the rest of us, aren't you, Marilyn?"

A fat, discontented girl in a tight sweater, reading a comic in front of the fire, said, "Can't you leave us alone for a minute, Mum? I'm busy."

"There you are," said the woman. "We're all Labour here."

"Can I talk to your daughter, then, please," said Jamey, who thought he sniffed a Liberal vote. Their appeal was chiefly to the young people, after all.

"I should say most certainly well that you cannot," said the woman. "She's in quite enough trouble as it is." The door shut uncompromisingly in his face.

"It seems a waste of time, really," said Jamey. "They're none of them going to vote for us, and even if they were, they wouldn't tell us."

"I thought that old woman in Number Twelve was hopeful," said Lofty.

"She didn't understand a word you were saying. I am afraid she may have been a bit soft in the head."

"Her vote's just as valuable as Einstein's."

It might well have been, but on the great day the old lady concerned, setting out from No. 12 with the firm intention of registering her vote, wandered in error to the municipal ladies' lavatory outside Llanwtyth Town Hall, and while there forgot the purpose of her journey. It was one of those unfortunate chances which make politics such a risky business.

"What we need," declared Mrs. Sligger in the British Legion Hall, "is to march forward, not backward. Those of us who want to march backward have not the best interests of themselves at heart. The Liberals are the only party which can take us forward, because they are the only classless party. If we are to face up to the challenges of the twentieth century, we must face up to them resolutely, not always glancing behind our shoulders or staring at our feet. Liberals stand for Progress, Prosperity and Practical Ideas for the Future. If you believe in any of these things you should vote Liberal, and even if you don't, because we have got to have them nowadays whether we like them or not, and it is no use fighting for lost causes. Britain is not a lost cause. Britain is the greatest country on earth, and under a Liberal Government soon will be again. We'll tackle the Americans squarely, and if necessary we'll fight them. Then we'll show them that not only have we the best Health Service, but also the biggest Empire of Sovereign Independent Peoples the world has ever known. Here are some figures. In the Commonwealth, there are seven hundred million people. In America, two hundred million; which is the mightier?

"Furthermore, we will revolutionize education so that everybody will receive exactly the same education, whether working class or not, whether possessed of so-called brains or not. Brains are not the monopoly of the so-called rich, and neither should money be.

"We do not believe in nationalization, except of land and housing, because it is outdated. We do believe that wealth should belong to the workers who help to make it. This I believe, and I believe to be correct."

270

"Hurrah, hurrah," cried Lofty, Philip and Jamey, clapping their hands.

December is a cruel month for elections. Christmas was not a feast which had reached the cold climate of Llanwtyth. The only sign that anything was amiss was to be seen in the Co-op, where a few colored pieces of paper had been hung from the solitary light bulb. It was only five days to Christmas when the party of Liberal campaigners sat round a cheerless electric fire in the Station Hotel, waiting for a telephone call from the Town Hall which would tell them that the counting was finished and an announcement about to be made.

"I think we've won," said Lofty. "I don't see who else could have, with three Labour candidates competing against each other."

"At any rate, we will have beaten the Conservatives to second place," said Mrs. Sligger. But she too was convinced that they had won, and was already making plans. "Among other things, we will have to improve the quality of Britain's railway hotels. This one is a crying disgrace. And I think I shall abolish advertising in public places."

"And alter England's sex laws," said Lofty.

"Of course I shall. I intended to do that, anyway. Sex must be made an attractive thing, not something to be ashamed of, if done properly."

"You'll have to be made prime minister first," said Philip, who was being very obstructive these days. This remark was considered in very bad taste.

"Time, gentlemen, please," said the barman to a few stragglers in the bar.

"It's getting very late," said Mrs. Sligger. "They should have finished counting by now."

"Perhaps there's been a recount," said Jamey, and everybody looked nervous.

"You can't call time on Election Night," said Mrs. Sligger to

271

the barman. "I will grant you an extension." She clearly felt that she was already the prime minister.

"You can't do that," said the barman. "But as you're staying here, you can pay for the drinks."

"All right," said Mrs. Sligger.

A crowd of very cheerful workers came in, oblivious to the time, and started ordering drinks.

"I knew we wouldn't have no difficulty. It's always the same when it comes to the results, whatever they say before."

"Do you mean the results are announced?" demanded Mrs. Sligger.

"That's right."

"But they were going to telephone me from the Town Hall."

"That'll be old Flo at the Post Office. He's working late, to-night."

"So the results are known," said Mrs. Sligger with a broad grin. "Well, here I am. I hope you'll all have some drinks on me this evening."

"All right."

"What were the actual figures?" said Jamey as casually as he could.

"I've got them here," said someone.

"Mr. Harley Griffiths, Lab., 14,970. Mr. Samuel Hill, Ind. Lab. 9,627. Mr. G. Price, Welsh Nat., 1,306. Major S. K. Le P. Brown-Pigg, Cons., 847."

"But you haven't got them all," said Jamey.

"There were some others. Do you remember about the others, Bill?"

"The Communist didn't do too well. About two hundred, I think. Then Taffy Pryce, who was Socialist Welsh Independent Nationalist this time, got a few votes, but they always come from his family."

"But the Liberals," said Jamey desperately. "How many did they get?"

"The man's obviously a fool," said Mrs. Sligger.

It transpired that the Liberal candidate had been omitted in error from the results. She had secured a hundred and twelve votes.

"They've faked the results," said Mrs. Sligger. "I'm going to demand a recount and an inquiry."

"I shouldn't do that," said Lofty. "After all, what we've done is to split the anti-Liberal vote. Nobody has gained except the Liberals, and a hundred per cent gain is not too bad. I think we should be proud of what we have achieved. It shows that the Liberal revival is gathering momentum at an unprecedented rate."

"You are quite right. I shall telegraph the leader in London and tell him the good news."

Philip sprawled in an uncomfortable armchair of the Railway Hotel lounge. The barman had gone to bed.

"It doesn't look like being a very jolly Christmas at home. I hope you have a good time in London."

Jamey was going to stay with the Potinues.

"Well, you'll have Lofty to keep you happy. I don't think Mummy minded too much about not winning the election. She did very well, all things considered."

"Why don't you go up and see her to make sure she's all right?" said Philip carelessly.

"Why should I? She's probably in bed."

"You are her favorite. She may be in a state." Jamey had always been everybody's favorite. Next year, when he was twenty-one, he would come into some money left him by a grandmother. Philip had not been mentioned in the will. It was not a lot—about £12,000—but a great deal more than Philip would have for a very long time.

"Well, I'm not going to."

But when Jamey was going to bed, he heard voices coming from his mother's room, and assuming she was still up he went in. Mrs. Sligger was in her dressing gown, sitting on Lofty's knee. She got up when Jamey came in.

273

"Will you learn not to come barging into ladies' bedrooms, Jamey? Get out."

When he had left without a word, she turned to Lofty and said, "Now I suppose we have shocked him. Oh well, he's got to grow up some day."

Jamey was still dazed from shock three days later when Rosemary met him on Grantham Station and they drove hand in hand in the back of the car to Mansby while the chauffeur watched them in his driving mirror and made fatuous conversation about the weather. The only action that Jamey had taken was to write a short, strongly worded letter to Brother Richard at Cleeve describing what he had seen in his mother's bedroom in the Station Hotel at Llanwtyth. But for once he felt he had not done enough. The names of Mrs. Sligger and Lofty Parker should have been pinned outside every village hall in Surrey. They should have been burned together on Farnham Green, as a terrible example to all the neighbors—the Arckwrights and Mrs. Fotheringay-Potts—to be faithful in marriage. Whatever his mother said or did now, she was hopelessly discredited, and Jamey would believe and do the opposite. If being grown-up meant committing something that came very close to adultery in sordid hotel bedrooms, Jamey was happier in his present state. He squeezed Rosemary's hand and said:

"What sort of weather have you been having up here?"

"Not too bad, really, all things considered," she replied, with a happy, conspiratorial little smile.

Brother Richard was his only support, now, the only man who would be as disgusted as he was by Mrs. Sligger's behavior. Of course, if one did not have any firm moral standards, there would be no excuse for finding it disgusting. Jamey thanked heaven for Brother Richard. It was really his father's fault, for contracting a mixed marriage, which Brother Richard would point out, and he would be quite right. Mixed marriages were really no good, any more than was marriage beneath one's station. He looked at Rosemary thoughtfully.

"We've had nothing but rain for a week now," he said.

The chauffeur was glad he had raised that point, and took it up with animation. Even if Mrs. Sligger's behavior was not so morally reprehensible, it was esthetically and genetically intolerable. They had arrived.

Mansby was not a distinguished house. It was built in 1910 by a fairly modest coal owner, who moved into a more spacious home after the war. The Potinues had bought it on their marriage, so as to be near Potinue, but the head of the family was so strange nowadays that they seldom visited him. There were no servants—the chauffeur who drove them with immense aplomb came from the local garage. But it was homely and warm, with every comfort which money could provide without servants.

After lunch on Christmas Day, Jamey sat drinking port with Mr. Potinue, Father Potinue from Oxford, and Master Edward Potinue, who was home from school at Stockton.

"I used to know Aidan Sligger, slightly, during the war," said Mr. Potinue, "and your grandfather, of course, was a great friend of my father. He used to come to Potinue for the shooting when we had shooting there, and I remember he once gave me two pounds as a tip. I never forgot that."

Jamey beamed and took another sip of port. He felt as if he had tipped the young Potinue himself. The Sliggers had always been generous. How nice it was to be accepted here, in an old-fashioned home with stuffed foxes' and stags' heads for decoration, far from the world of Peter Garlick with his electric cocktail mixers and dark glasses. Garlick would not have thought Mansby was smart. He would probably have produced his new transistor wireless during lunch, and he certainly would not have known about staying behind after the ladies had gone.

"I never saw as much of you as I would have liked at Oxford," said Father Potinue. "But, of course, there are so many people, one scarcely ever gets to know them until their second or third year. Guy Frazer-Robinson, of course, is a great friend, and I think he's quite an exceptionally nice boy. His background must be rather difficult, but I think he's found his feet awfully well in—you know—our sort of world."

"Who's he?" said Mr. Potinue. "Frazer-Robinson? Never heard of them."

Jamey beamed, although he had a feeling that Mr. Potinue must be one of the very few people in England who had never heard of them.

"Very rich industrialist—you know the sort of background. But they have settled down very well."

"I've got nothing against rich industrialists," said Mr. Potinue with a short laugh. But Jamey had an intoxicating glimpse of all these rich industrialists trying to muscle in on the small, gilded world of Potinues and Sliggers. Then when one thought of all the Garlicks trying to muscle in on the world of the rich industrialists, and all the wretched, gray people with names like Green-Beaumont and Berry-Williams trying to muscle in on the world of the Garlicks, one realized how particularly splendid one was.

"Now we must help the ladies with the washing-up," said Mr. Potinue. The men got to their feet and walked amiably but a little unsteadily to the pantry.

"Hullo, Jamey," said Rosemary. "You look flushed. I do declare you've got a bit tipsy."

"Now then, you leave him alone. There's nothing wrong with young Sligger," said Mr. Potinue gruffly, handing round the drying-up cloths. Jamey tried to hide his embarrassment at the general affection for himself by engaging Father Potinue in conversation, as the man least susceptible to his charms.

"I'll be seeing Guy at the New Year," he said, with greater seriousness and confidentiality than the information perhaps warranted. "We're all going down to Cleeve."

"How very noble of you," said Rosemary, who had been listening. "We just go to church at Potinue, and have to listen to a sermon by Uncle Angus on moving with the times."

Father Potinue had the grace to blush. "One has to say something on these occasions, and it's only once a year we have to celebrate the New Year," he said. "Where do I put this colander?"

"On the shelf with the frying pan," said Mrs. Potinue.

"At Oxford I have to tell them to move with the times every week. It's supposed to go down well with the modern student."

"Bloody lot of rubbish," said Mr. Potinue, "the modern student."

Jamey felt he was beginning to get things in perspective. He caught Rosemary's eye, and they smiled at each other, as Jamey dried a coffee pot and she a wine glass. It was only afterward that he realized they had been smiling at Mr. Potinue. In any case, they were both right, and Brother Richard was right, and so was everybody else except Mrs. Sligger and Creepy Crawley and Philip Fringe and Phyllis the Tickle and the miserable Peter Garlick.

"Shall we go for a walk after lunch?" said Rosemary, looking at Jamey.

"What a good idea," said Father Potinue.

"They didn't ask you," said Mr. Potinue.

"Yes, let's," said Jamey.

Brother Angelus knocked timidly on Brother Richard's door.

"I've found some more," he said, putting a few scrumpled pieces of silver paper on the desk.

"Aspro again?"

Brother Angelus nodded.

"In his waste paper basket?"

"No, beside his bed."

"Good."

Brother Angelus was dismissed. Rapey Rawley sat with his head in his hands. He might have been praying. There was no time to lose, as the Abbot's illness must be reaching a climax. Rapey only wished he felt better himself these days. The old trouble, too much water in his skin, was recurring. He was wearing himself out, but it was in a good cause. The abbacy secured, and Brother Richard Rawley would be content to die. There had been more comings and goings from his little room in the past few weeks than anybody could remember before. Every one of the brethren had been sounded, in the most tactful way, and notes taken and filed. None of them knew the purpose of the interviews, which were mercifully less frank than usual, but in each case Brother Richard had gauged as close as he could what might be the man's intentions in the event of an unnamed disaster striking the community.

On Christmas Day, Rapey did not mar the celebrations with his unctuous geniality, but sat aloof, watching and waiting.

"It really looks as if old Rapey has gone off his rocker at last," said Brother Augustine, a lifelong enemy.

"He sent for me one day, and I couldn't make out a word of sense," said Brother Theodosius. "He seemed to be very worried about something that was going to happen. Perhaps it is the bursar's new arrangement about washing that is disturbing him."

"It was bound to come."

"Liverpool?"

"I shouldn't be surprised."

There was never anything different about Christmas in Farnham Green. Perhaps Philip was more morose than usual, Mrs. Sligger more boisterous. Mr. Sligger was too bored to talk to his family, and spoke only to Lofty Parker, who told them about Christmas in prison, when some men had drunk the bottles of vanilla essence supplied for the Christmas cake, and one of them had nearly died. They ate a turkey which Mrs. Sligger unwrapped with the greatest care, and drank some of the port laid down for Philip's birth, but never given to him. Then Mrs. Sligger and Lofty washed up, singing carols as they did so, and Philip read an old copy of one of his mother's women's magazines in his bedroom. It was a gruesome day. Philip and his father had gone to church the evening before, accompanied by Lofty, who had shocked Mrs. Sligger by saying in a sentimental voice that everybody should go to church at Christmas. Afterward, he confided to her that he had only been buttering up the old bag, which made her very happy.

"I expect you were very pleased, Aidan, to see Anthony going to church like a good little Christian," she said, with a meaningful glance at Lofty.

"Lofty a Christian. That's a new one on me," said Philip unsubtly.

"I don't care how young Crippen manages," said Mr. Sligger. "He can go and join a monastery if he wants, but I don't think it'll help him much. He's got an uphill struggle."

The only thing which distinguished this Christmas from any other was the excitement which took place after dinner. Even this did not last long, and events settled into the memories of those concerned like a stone thrown into a pond, leaving no ripple on the surface.

Half an hour after everybody had gone to bed, Mrs. Sligger left her solitary bedroom to ask Lofty, as she later explained, if he had an aspirin. She hinted that she was suffering from a periodical ailment, one which need not worry them. Both Philip and his father knew that she was most unlikely to be suffering on that account, but neither mentioned it, in Philip's case because he suspected the real source of suffering was removed, in Mr. Sligger's because he had long since given up worrying about his wife's ailments.

In fact Mrs. Sligger, full of the Christmas spirit, had decided that this was the night she and her chosen one were to consummate their love.

Lofty's bedroom was empty, his suitcase gone. A search round the house revealed that an expensive bottle of hair oil belonging to Philip was also missing, as were the residue of the Liberal Party funds in Llanwtyth (£8.15.od.), Mrs. Sligger's tape measure which was able to give the disemboweled weight of any living creature and Jamey's 12-bore shotgun.

Everybody agreed that was the least important, as Jamey had more or less outgrown it, and could easily buy himself another one when he came of age in February if he wanted one. The tape measure was another matter altogether, and Mrs. Sligger was terribly put out by its loss. So gravely did it affect her, that she took to her bed for two days. But when she got up again, she seemed quite cheerful and never mentioned the tape measure. She had had a love affair, that was the great thing, and now she could face old age in tranquillity with Mrs. Arckwright and her new friend, Mrs. Fotheringay-Potts.

The New Year at Cleeve was traditionally celebrated by an invasion of old boys in a spirit which was a judicious mixture of reverence and debauchery. Between services at the abbey church, Old Alexandrians of many generations gathered in the village pub, whose landlord pretended to recognize them from their schooldays.

Jamey and Guy ordered their half-glasses of beer in the traditional manner.

"They say Rapey Rawley's unwell."

"I wondered why he's not around. Normally he's very busy with the old boys at this time. I hope it's nothing serious."

"I don't much mind if it is."

"Neither do I, really. Still, one does not want him to die." One did not want anyone to die.

"Sorry to interrupt," said a red-faced man who had been sitting alone at the bar, "but did I hear you say Richard Rawley was ill?"

"Yes," said Guy, a trifle coldly.

"Too bad. I used to send him letters and things. Sorry to interrupt."

"That's all right," said Jamey kindly.

"My name's Gangradden. I was here 1920-23. Bit before your time, I expect."

Guy agreed that it was a bit before their time, wondering why he had only stayed for three years.

"Then I joined the army. Became a Brigadier, actually," said the stranger helpfully.

"You must be Brigadier Gangradden," said Jamey. He explained how he had gone to Curzon Street to see him on the recommendation of the Potinue Agency.

"They've closed all that joint down," said the Brigadier gloomily. "Pity, it was a pleasant enough posting. Now I'm seconded to the Egg Marketing Board, as they're reorganizing the whole of the old department after that telephone exchange blew up. Shame you didn't join us in the old days. What do you do now?"

Jamey said he was a journalist. The Brigadier brightened.

"We're looking for a journalist on the Egg Marketing Board, believe it or not. Something about brightening the image of the egg, and all that rot. Would you join us? It's only fifteen hundred a year, but you get eggs and things free."

Jamey said he would like to join them.

"Good, then, that's settled. You'll have to pass the Selection Board or whatever they call it, but that's no difficulty as we've got old Jock Kiltooley in charge of it now, you know."

"Have you?" said Jamey, wondering who Jock Kiltooley was.

"Yes. I always say there's no harm in having Alexandrians around. It's the only way we can keep the other blighters down. Not that he'd allow that to influence his judgment, of course."

"Of course not."

When the Brigadier had gone, Guy said, "This is quite like old times."

"Yes, isn't it?" said Jamey. "What is Garlick doing these days?"

"He's gone into films or advertising or modern music or something. He keeps asking himself to stay, and I can't tell him to go away."

"I think he's rather a bore, actually," said Jamey, greatly daring.

"If you knew what I'd suffered, you wouldn't just think he was rather a bore."

281

Later, Guy said, "You weren't serious about being a Socialist, were you?"

"Of course not. I can't stand people who ask."

"Poor Jamey. I hope you didn't suffer too much from that ghastly Garlick. I think he's beginning to understand now that he's not wanted. When will you come and stay with us again?"

"I might some time, but I'm going to stay with the Potinues next week."

"She's a good girl, Rosemary. You know I'm beginning to think of Sally Pratt-Bingham seriously. Garlick can't stand her, as she always calls him Peter Onion."

"Aren't we a bit young?"

"There doesn't seem much doing for a bachelor these days." Guy spoke as if he had been a bachelor at many other stages of history.

"I expect you're right," said Jamey, and they both shook their wise old heads over their glasses.

The gray light of early morning was just beginning to bring some inkling of the misery outside into Brother Richard's cell when the watcher by his bed noticed the sudden spasms which interrupted his breathing. Without a word, the watcher left.

Brother Richard lay on his back and wondered why they were being so slow to arrange his coronation. Abbot Rawley of Cleeve would be wearing a massive topaz ring, and his vestments would be of gold. Even abbots, he supposed, had to go to bed, but he seemed to have mislaid his ring. As he searched under the pillow and on all his fingers he broke into a sweat, and lay back exhausted. One by one the brethren, awakened from their sleep, began to file into his cell. Brother Richard gazed at them blankly. He had heard that there was immorality in Farnham, which was not to be tolerated.

> "In an abundance of corn, wine and oil
> Have they multiplied,"

sang the monks. Brother Richard thought it was quite right that they should be singing round his bed. Nobody had thought to sing round his bed while he was a humble monk. There was a great deal of immorality in the world, but he flattered himself that he had most of it in his files.

> "From the arrow flying in daytime
> From the danger walking abroad in the dark
> From aggression and from the noonday devil,"

sang the monks.

Brother Richard still could not find the ring. He slapped his sides and wrung his hands, until the sweat stood out on his brow and his breath came in gasps.

> "A thousand shall fall at thy side,
> And ten thousand at thy right hand
> But it shall not approach thee."

Everything was in his files. There was nothing which could not be found there. They were the key to all wisdom and goodness.

> "He shall give his angels charge over thee
> To keep thee in all thy ways."

Suddenly, Brother Richard knew he was going to die. It came to him as no surprise. His time was over and he had not found the ring, but it did not matter. Brother Richard had been an exceedingly foolish person, but probably not a wicked one. He lay still for a moment.

> "They shall bear thee in their hands
> Lest perchance thou strike thy foot against a stone."

They told Jamey at breakfast. He said he was sorry to hear that Brother Richard had passed away, but he secretly thought he could manage without him now. Brother Angelus O'Reefe was in tears over his coffee, and even Brigadier Gangradden looked thoughtful and pulled at his mustache. Above them, the great bell of Cleeve Abbey boomed out over the fields, and some jackdaws, always dislodged by the noise, flew round the tower waiting for it to stop before they could resume their previous occupations.

Labécède-Lauragais, June 1963

7931   Wau
Waugh.

   Path of dalliance.